the Sweetheart horse

Ocala Horse Girls

Book 2

Natalie Keller Reinert

This book is a work of fiction. Names, characters, businesses, places, events, locales, and incidents are either the products of the author's imagination or used in a fictitious manner. Any resemblance to actual persons, living or dead, or actual events is purely coincidental.

Copyright © 2022 Natalie Keller Reinert
All rights reserved.
ISBN: 978-1-956575-49-1

Cover Photo: callipso_art/depositphotos

Cover Design & Interior Design: Natalie Keller Reinert

No portion of this book may be reproduced in any form without written permission from the publisher or author, except as permitted by U.S. copyright law.

Books by Natalie Keller Reinert

The Florida Equestrian Collection

Ocala Horse Girls
The Project Horse
The Sweetheart Horse
The Regift Horse

Briar Hill Farm
Foaling Season
Friends With Horses
Outside Rein

The Eventing Series
Grabbing Mane: A Duet Series
Show Barn Blues: A Duet Series
Alex & Alexander: A Horse Racing Saga
Sea Horse Ranch: A Beach Read Series
The Hidden Horses of New York: A Novel

Catoctin Creek
Sunset at Catoctin Creek
Snowfall at Catoctin Creek
Springtime at Catoctin Creek
Christmas at Catoctin Creek

Chapter One

TIME IS RUNNING out.

If I don't get it together, I'm going to be out of a job before the night is over. And I *need* this job.

"Get it together, Kayla," I mutter. "Come on, this isn't rocket science. You're just looking for a stupid little noseband...*gah!*"

I stick my pricked finger in my mouth for a second—no, less than that, because it tastes medicinal. I forgot about the liniment bath I mixed up right before I gave my boss a leg-up and sent her off to the warm-up ring. Have you ever slurped on a blend of witch hazel, rubbing alcohol, and assorted herbal tinctures which supposedly ease a show horse's aching muscles and tendons? I can't say I recommend it.

But there's no time to get a drink and wash this disgusting flavor out of my mouth. Every moment counts in show jumping—literally, in a jump-off between tied competitors, we can often measure the difference between winning and losing by mere fractions of a second. That's why Melody sent me back here to find a noseband that cranks tighter. She got to the warm-up ring, saw the quality galloping around out there, and I swear her eyes got ten times bigger. She looked back at me and gestured until I was right at her boot, cupping a hand to my ear so I could hear her frantic whispers.

The long and the short of it? Melody's first Grand Prix is probably a leap into the deep end of the pool when she's barely swimming the dog paddle. Hence: she's making a desperate bid for extra control over her horse, with a tougher noseband, which I need to find *immediately* and get back to the arena, or I can look for new work on Monday.

I bend back over the tack trunk, scrabbling madly through the heaped saddle pads and bandages inside, while the loudspeaker at the end of the barn aisle coughs its way through a countdown, ominously creeping towards my eventual termination of employment. Every two minutes, the announcer calls a rider just one more digit closer to my rider's number. When there are six riders still to go—no, five—I give up, panting, and lean against the front of the lacquered wooden trunk.

"I'm never going to find her stupid crank noseband," I whimper, and I'm instantly embarrassed by the sound of my own voice. Melody isn't the only equestrian employing grooms in Ocala, the horse capital of the world. I'll find another job.

Probably.

Quickly enough to save some money before my current live-in farm-sitting job ends?

Probably not.

Ugh. Living out of my Cadillac would be one thing—those old-ass cars have plenty of room for a girl my size to stretch out in—but where exactly is my horse supposed to go? I suppose if I leave the trunk popped open and keep hay back there for him, Crabby will stay close by my makeshift campsite.

I imagine myself living in a lonely corner of the Ocala National Forest with just my big bay gelding for a companion. At first it's a cute idea: the sky is blue, birds are chirping, and there are no demands on me from unreasonable horsewomen who shouldn't be showing at this level. I've always been very happy in the woods, after all. Back in Virginia, I was in a high school foraging club, and we'd go out into the state parks around the Blue Ridge Mountains and pretend we were hedge witches plucking plants and herbs for our potions. I could probably learn to live off the land in Florida, too.

Then, in my daydream, the clouds close in, thunder rumbles, and I remember Florida is the lightning capital of the northern hemisphere. Maybe I shouldn't have parked under these tall trees...

I blink away the imaginary storm and scold myself, "Come on, Kayla, you don't have time to waste. Real world here, girl. Real. World."

My mom used to say that to me, still does, in fact, and it really helps me snap back into the present when my daydreams get a little too wild.

I have been known to possess an overactive imagination.

Okay, time to focus. I can *do* this. I just have to lift out these saddle pads...and these gallop boots...and, oh, this entire bag of bridle pieces...

"Crud, crud, crud," I mutter. "So much *stuff*."

I'm making a mess, piling the contents of Melody's huge tack trunk on the spotless barn aisle behind me. If anyone saw me, they'd think I was a thief searching for something valuable, like a diamond-encrusted needle in a haystack. Luckily, everyone is home in their pajamas, or sitting in the stands for the Grand Prix, or warming up for their turn under the bright lights.

"And thank goodness, because I do *not* need a spectator for this —"

A clatter of horseshoes scares the absolute bejesus out of me. I leap up automatically, all of my equestrian instincts kicking in to keep me from being trampled by a loose horse. Because if there's a horse out here now, it must have gotten out of a stall and is running around the place scared, and a scared horse can be a dangerous horse—

In the half-light cast by the dimmed overhead lamps, I see a horse rear back in terror—because of me, the horrifying leaping specter in the darkness—and realize not only is it not just a loose horse from another barn, it is a saddled, bridled, and *ridden* horse. And the horse's rider is moving fast to stay in the saddle while the animal plunges and backs away, tail swishing and head high.

"Dammit!" the rider shouts, voice half-strangled with shock but still noticeably baritone.

A male rider, then.

And he's *pissed*.

At me.

I stand still and give the horse a moment to understand I'm a human. "Sorry," I whisper. "Very sorry about that."

"Be *careful*, why don't you," the rider bites out, a taut British accent in a disapproving tone, but his horse at least appreciates my voice, because now it knows I'm a human. The horse stops scrambling to escape and blows a loud snort at me, as if to ask why I had to go and scare them like that. Through this recalculation, the rider sits carefully in the center of the horse, hands wide and low on the reins. A sympathetic position.

At least the horse gets a little sympathy. The rider's expression is anything but forgiving.

Hey! I don't deserve this. I was minding my business when he turned up.

"I *am* careful," I defend myself. "It was an accident. I didn't expect anyone to ride through the barn in the middle of the night." It's only nine o'clock, but it feels much later to me, since I've been working since six a.m., trying to balance my farm-sitting gig with this new grooming job. I had to take care of six retired show horses before hustling over here to muck out, polish tack, and bathe and braid Otto.

The rider is slowly circling his horse to get its attention back, his hands still moving gently on the reins. Impressive, honestly, that he can stay mad at me while maintaining such a gentle feel on his horse's mouth. He's clearly a very kind rider. I wish he was this nice to grooms.

He snaps at me again. "Some of us are trying to get to the ring without grooms popping up like jack-in-the-boxes."

"Jacks-in-the-boxes," I mutter, unable to stop myself.

"What's that?" He cocks his head, as if he had trouble hearing me. Beneath the brim of his elegant, expensive riding helmet, I see a firm chin and a strong nose, a thin line of a mouth that's turned down at me. His eyes flash under the dim lights.

Handsome, sure, but I've got his measure. What we have here is just another rich boy. And he should have enough expensive private schooling to get his grammar straight.

"*Jacks*-in-the-*boxes*," I repeat, louder. For the jerks in the back. "And you're not supposed to be riding in the barns." I hitch my head towards the doorway a few feet away, where I know there's a red-lettered sign which reads NO RIDING IN THE BARN in what is definitely a snippy tone.

He splutters in response, which is exactly what I expected of him, and I turn back to the tack trunk I've left in a state of total disarray. The loudspeaker ticks on and Prissy, the Australian woman who does the announcements during the big show classes, lets everyone know, and me in particular, that Rider 278 is on deck.

Melody O'Leno is Rider 279.

That's it...I'm officially out of time.

There's no way I can find this missing noseband, get it to the warm-up ring and transferred onto Otto, Melody's beautiful and excitable Oldenburg gelding. Even without the time it would take to get to the arenas, Otto is seventeen-point-three hands high of sheer attitude and mischief. Wrestling a new noseband onto his ginormous head while he flings himself around like a ballet dancer wearing metal shoes could never be just a two-minute endeavor.

"Dammit, Kayla," I whisper to myself, surveying the messy tack trunks. "Why didn't you just stick with racehorses?"

Meanwhile, the man on horseback loses interest in shouting at me and rides off, heading for the arenas himself. So, he was just using the barn as a shortcut—pretty arrogant and rude of him, actually, since we aren't supposed to even *walk* through stables where we don't have horses stalled, let alone ride through them. But I've met plenty of people like him over the past week. Five days grooming for Melody O'Leno at Legends Equestrian Center's summer hunter/jumper circuit, and I already have a fresh distaste for the entire human race.

But that's all over now. Melody will tell me this trial period didn't work out, I'll be out of a job, and I can figure out something else. I pile saddle pads back into place and close the top of the tack trunk. Something stops it from latching properly. And then I see the problem, hanging out of the back of the trunk, wedged under the hinged lid. Just another leather strap in a sea of leather straps.

"You *stinker!*" I snap up the noseband and stand up so quickly my knees crack—a sound they probably shouldn't be making in a woman only in her mid-twenties, but whatever. I squeeze the padded leather and wonder if there's any reason to even *try* to get this thing to the ring.

From the direction of the Grand Prix arena, a sound breathes over the barns: a loud, collective sigh.

Oh, I know that sigh.

Someone just fell off.

Look, I feel bad for the rider, but this is a gift. As long as whoever took a tumble isn't back in the saddle right away, I've got a shot to get to the warm-up, wrangle this noseband onto Otto's Roman nose, and get Melody into the arena for her round on time...keeping my job, keeping my meager savings intact, keeping my chance at finding a rental somewhere nearby from descending to a complete and total no-go.

"Thank you, and I'm sorry," I breathe. A prayer to the horse gods, to the whims of luck, and to keeping a roof over my head and my horse's head.

Okay, time to run for the arena.

Horses and riders block the gate to the warm-up arena, so I have to slip through the fence before I can look around for Melody and Otto. The dazzling bright lights are too much at first after spending the past twenty minutes rummaging around a half-lit barn, and for a few precious, wasted seconds, all I can see are dozens of identical bay horses, ridden by identical riders in dark coats and hats.

After a few desperate blinks, their horses' differences pop out to me: socks and stockings, stars and blazes, shades of earth tones ranging from beach sand to darkest ebony. A rainbow of horses.

The riders all stay pretty much the same in my eyes, but that's okay. I can identify my horse.

Otto is one of the dark bays, with starbursts of dapples shining on his hindquarters. He has two white front socks and a simple white star and stripe beneath his plaited forelock. He's the kind of horse who gets extra zeroes in his price tag just for being so gorgeous. On Monday, when I started working with him, I was almost afraid to touch him. *You break, you buy.* But I'd have to win the lottery to afford to buy a horse like this. And not just the regular lottery. The freaking Powerball, if no one had won it for a solid three months.

Just as I locate him, Melody spots me and turns Otto's head sharply with her left hand, hauling the horse's head to the side like his reins are bicycle handlebars. That's why she needs the new noseband. Her rough hands have deadened Otto's mouth. I've noticed the way he runs through her commands and picks his own spots before fences, but of course, that won't work for Melody tonight. She wants his attention on her, and she doesn't care how she gets it. The monthly open Grand Prix classes offer ten thousand dollar pots, with five grand to the winner.

Even rich girls like to win big checks.

"Get it on him!" Melody hisses, leaning down from the saddle.

"Who fell out there?" I ask, reaching for Otto's bridle with tingling fingers. I can do this. Surely, if I can find the noseband at the last moment, fate is in control and doesn't want me to be homeless. Thanks, fate.

"It was Lucky Ocean," Melody says in an off-hand way. The name could be the horse or the rider; either way, I don't recognize it. A Grand Prix night on the summer circuit isn't exactly where Olympians meet. The big-name riders will continue to shun Florida's sticky summers in favor of cooler show circuits in New England. That's what climbers like Melody like so much about Ocala's summer shows; they actually have a chance at some prize money. She twists in the saddle, eyeing the LED screen over the Grand Prix arena. "Hurry up! She's finishing the course and then I'm—"

"Rider 279, on deck," the loudspeaker interrupts.

I didn't come all this way to fail at the last moment, but it looks like luck is deserting me now. Otto does *not* want this noseband switched out, and he's taller than me. Much, much taller; at only five-foot-five, I might as well try to bridle a reluctant giraffe. "Come on, you monster," I grumble, and Otto lifts it even higher.

This can't end this way. Visions of my horse and I cast out on the roadside, left to find shelter as best we can, are dancing in my brain. They're absurd, of course; Max and Stephen will never actually kick me out if I can't find a job and housing when they come home at last from Wellington. But I've already committed to the idea of taking care of myself, not begging a nice, wealthy couple to do it for me. I'm done hoping someone with a black Amex card will step up and start paying my bills, and I have to stop accepting my parents' generous back-up. I'm getting a little too old for this kind of support. Not that they'd buy me a horse and a five-thousand-dollar saddle if I asked for them, but I've never had to go hungry if things are short one month.

I'm thankful for their help, but lately I've realized I can't call myself independent if my parents are still happy to send me a check to cover groceries. And proving I can handle my own life has become increasingly important to me. My friends are moving up and moving on. I am not.

Losing this job isn't helping matters.

If only I could have kept riding at Posey and Adam's place! I was good at riding the young horses around the paddocks and the training track. But yearlings grow up and become tough two-year-olds, and I quickly realized fit racehorses were not in my comfort zone. My friend Evie is still galloping there every morning, and it's giving her the sinewy arms of a jockey. Those horses can *pull*.

I told Posey I'd be back in fall to start the new crop of eager, anxious-to-please babies. I'm just not jockey material, I guess.

Or maybe I'm never going to be more than an in-between trainer. Someone who can ride green-but-not-too-green horses, start them on their promising careers, and then move back to square one with a new horse.

It's that or just being at this incredibly fancy show-ground, surrounded by talented riders with more experience than me, is bringing me down.

Both, probably.

Suddenly, the strap I've been struggling with shoves through the eyelet in Otto's brow-band and I'm almost there. "Come on," I whisper, tugging the strap down with one hand, pushing the buckle into place with the other. "Stand still, Otto—"

The loudspeaker hums with an impending announcement.

"A round of applause for Lucky Ocean," the Australian suggests in her pleasant way, and the audience complies as the embattled rider makes her way back to the warm-up ring with dirt on her jacket. "Up next we have number 279, Melody O'Leno, on Otto Pilot. Rider 280, you're on deck."

"Let us *go!*" Melody hisses, yanking the reins as if I was planning to hold the two of them back. Otto flings up his head in protest, and since his skull is the size of an aircraft carrier, he knocks me over. I hit the ground with a thud.

My friendly boss doesn't stop to see if I'm okay, or even to check the buckle on the bridle. She just kicks Otto into a trot and heads for the arena gate.

For a moment, I consider my position. On my ass in the expensive footing of a world-class equestrian facility, with something that feels unpleasantly like muck on my hands. Even on my worst morning at the Thoroughbred training farm, I didn't get shoved to the ground by my boss. An obnoxious little inner voice chirps in my psyche: *If this is making it on my own, I'm not sure it's worth it.*

This inner voice has been plaguing me all week, while Melody's been bossing me around and her so-called friends around the showgrounds have been ignoring me or, worse, talking down to me like I'm some random find from the Greyhound station, not an experienced horsewoman fully capable of managing top-tier horses. I wouldn't like to say I've led a privileged life, but generally, I've worked for people who are nice to me. That run of good luck seems to be over.

Maybe I should just go back to hunting for a rich husband. Would it really be so bad?

When I brought this up over a visit home in March, my mom said yes, Kayla. Marrying a man for his money would be a bad idea. I don't know why I even told her I'd been trying. I tried to back things up, explain to her I was really trying to marry a man for his *horses*, but that didn't help.

"When are you going to realize life isn't a Disney movie, Kayla?" she'd asked, her huge brown eyes filled with concern. And then I'd felt bad for making my mom worry about me. She'd been depressed enough when I'd decided Virginia wasn't big enough to contain my equestrian goals and took off for Max and Stephen's job offer in Ocala. I've always been close to both of my parents.

"I figured that out when squirrels refused to clean my house," I'd joked. "I left all the windows and doors open for a whole freaking week, and all I got was one lazy raccoon who wouldn't give me back the TV remote."

And that was the end of the marriage conversation.

Anyway, I'd got myself invited to several rich-horsemen-charity functions over the winter, when all the big racehorse owners were in Florida, and it had become pretty apparent I would not find a Prince Charming, or even a Prince Tolerable, amongst the moneyed men of Ocala. Most of them were already married. And over age sixty.

So, I went back to Plan B, which is taking care of myself. It's a work in progress.

I'm looking for a way to get up that doesn't involve plunging my hands into more muddy, mucky arena footing when a familiar voice cuts through the amused murmur of nearby riders.

"Get yourself dumped, did you? I didn't even know you were riding tonight."

Oh, you have *got* to be kidding me!

I look around for the source of that derisive voice, even though I know exactly who it is without finding him. He's halted his horse a few strides away, and I can't help but notice the horse looks much more comfortable with me on the ground this time. That's good, that's progress. If nothing else goes right tonight, at least I have gotten this horse more comfortable with humans on the ground.

Nothing's changed about *him*, though. Same thin-lipped frown. Same imperious voice, clipped consonants, and a hint of good old-fashioned British disdain, as a sort of cherry on top of his whole sulky sundae.

I give him a narrow-eyed glare, but keep my tone sweet and solicitous as I inquire, "If I stand up suddenly, will *you* end up on the ground, too?"

He flashes an unexpected grin at me. It's really remarkable the way the smile lights up his face, even if it's not exactly warm-hearted. While the brim of his helmet still shadows his eyes, I can see more of his features now than I could back in the dimly lit stabling area.

He's not...*unattractive*, let's say.

When he's smiling, anyway.

But his grin fades into something more familiarly malicious as he reins his horse away. "I think you'd better dust yourself off and start looking for a new job," he advises me, glancing over his shoulder to make sure I catch every word. "Because if I'm not mistaken, your horse's bridle is coming apart in the ring."

I turn around, scrambling to my feet, his handsome face forgotten —just in time to hear that soft, collective sigh.

Chapter Two

"I'm telling you, it could have been worse."

I put down my sandwich so that I can fully concentrate on glaring at Posey. My stony expression is wasted on her, though; she's tapping a barn cat on the nose and making googly eyes at him. The barn cat blinks slowly, like she has him hypnotized, and flicks his white-tipped tail. He mews and pokes her hand with one soft paw. Posey laughs and shakes back her short mane of dark curls. She has been annoyingly carefree and light-hearted this spring. It's not that I want Posey Malone to be miserable. Please don't get me wrong. But when one member of your friend group is in a blissful honeymoon stage of a relationship and the rest of you are single, the Snow White act can get old.

"It could not have been worse," I growl, snatching the bag of chips Posey abandoned in favor of the gray and white barn cat. With no job to keep me busy today, I came over to Malone-Salazar Farm to skive lunch off my friends. Adam Salazar is still buying his girlfriend sandwiches from a local deli called Hoppers, part of some cutesy little bargain they made before they started dating, and if I text them early enough, I can get in on the lunch order.

I used to ride here, and my best friend Evie is still galloping here every morning, up at five o'clock to feed her own horse so that she can come and get on racehorses for a few hours. What can I say? Evie is obviously tougher and stronger than me. It hardly seems fair, since she's like a tiny pixie-elf even when she's standing next to me, and I'm no giant. But when she gets on the older racehorses, they respect her. I rode one three-year-old back from Gulfstream Park for a break and thought I was going to die. No brakes at all on that thing! I saw only two outcomes in my future: either the horse would rip my arms from their sockets or we would never stop circling that track. Posey rescued me, galloping alongside us and slowing my horse down, to my acute embarrassment, and *that* was when I realized my Thoroughbred training center employment would be seasonal, not year-round.

Evie watches me attack the bag of chips with amusement in her eyes. "You going to eat your way through your disappointment or look for a new job?"

"Obviously I'm going to look for a new job, Evie, but it's going to be in reining or cattle ranching or something else where no one knows me, because everyone at the equestrian center knows I screwed up Melody's bridle. The entire Ocala hunter/jumper business will have my picture next to their tack room door with DO NOT HIRE written on it."

"Imagine getting your picture up in every fancy barn in Ocala," Evie mused, absently braiding her long chestnut ponytail. "That's kind of impressive."

"Just the fame I was going for," I agree. "I was hoping to become notorious within a year of arriving, and look at me go."

"Take me with you," Evie suggests. "We could be this year's biggest story. Evie Ballenger and Kayla Moore, the notorious horse girls of Ocala's jumper world. Just sabotaging awful riders all over town."

"I won't deny she deserved to fall off," I admit. "You should have seen the state of her clothes. God bless the dry cleaner who gets that riding jacket, because the arena clay was just *ground* into it."

"Tragic," Evie murmurs, smiling to herself.

I like that about Evie. She has a vindictive side.

Posey finally stops harassing the barn cat and snatches the bag of chips away from me. I shrug at her. "Sadness makes me hungry."

"You're not sad," she informs me. "You're enjoying this."

"I'm enjoying being a month away from homelessness?"

"Oh, you know they won't let you go homeless. Max and Stephen adore you. And anyway, Ocala is one big job fair. You just have to know who to ask." Posey clearly believes she has a handle on the situation, and I figure she's right. Maybe she ran away from Ocala and spent years in New York City, floundering as a freelance writer, but since she came back, she's proven she was born for this work. She manages this farm along with Adam and thrives on the stress, the endless workload, and the strange politics of the horse industry. When she started riding here over the winter, Evie and I were the old hats showing her around, but now I feel like the baby of the group.

I don't love it.

"You need to find something that leads you in the right direction," Posey says now, reaching across the table to scoop a handful of chips from the bag I've swiped. "You like jumping. Stick with jumping. Don't go bouncing around to whatever farm will have you. Absolutely no reining or ranching."

"I just need something to get a deposit together on my own rental," I remind her. "It doesn't have to be my life's work."

"At some point, whatever you're doing becomes your life's work," Posey points out. "Because you're going to wake up and realize you've spent an awful lot of your life doing it."

This is deep, and we all take a minute to consider it.

I mean, seriously, what is my life's work? Is it just scraping together a living as a journeyman horsewoman, bouncing from one job to the next? Riding my one personal horse and hoping to show him once in a while, when money permits?

That isn't exactly what I had in mind for my life. I left my safe, simple job riding safe, simple sales horses back in my hometown because Ocala is where everything happens—at least, that's what that blogs told me—and I thought I would reach my destiny here. I am supposed to be training my own prospect and client horses by now, doing jumper shows and eventing with an eye towards becoming an upper-level rider and trainer. That was the plan. So, how do I get there from here?

Here being an accidental professional farm-sitter, whose extended stay on a beautiful private equestrian center in Ocala is about to come to its long dreaded conclusion. Max and Stephen, my bosses (and let's face it, my benefactors) are finally coming home from an extended winter at their Wellington estate down in south Florida. They'll come back with a professional barn manager, a groom, and no need for me to care for their retired show horses.

We love our little tropical paradise, Max wrote to me in his typically eloquent email style, *but south Florida in summer is like the surface of the sun, and even the beach is too hot for us just now. I'm not sure we'll stay longer than January through March in the future.*

It was a little hint: even if I find something to tide me over through the summer and fall, I shouldn't expect to take over Casa Max y Stephen for six months again once the Winter Equestrian Festival rolls back into West Palm Beach. This long stay was a one-time deal.

They're going to be back in a few weeks, right before Memorial Day weekend. And I'm going to be so freaking embarrassed if I have to beg them to let me stay. But I just don't know what comes next. If Posey's right, and whatever I am doing with my life is, in fact, my life's work, does that mean I should look for another farm-sitting job?

Maybe the horse show thing is just a pie in the sky.

What does that even mean?

Posey tidies up lunch, evidently ready to get back to her own life's work. Evie is flicking through her phone, already over considering anything so deep. She holds it up after a moment. "Look at this!" she says. "Shots of the winner of the Grand Prix last night. Someone named Basil Han. This guy's cute! Kayla, do you know him?"

She sticks the phone under my nose and I'm confronted with a hi-res image of the handsome jerk who knocked me down last night. He's taking the last fence of the course in beautiful fashion, bent over his big horse's neck with the precise form of a classically educated rider. There's no trace of a smirk on his face in this pic; just a determined set to his jaw and those thin lips, an expression of complete concentration in his dark eyes.

I find I have absolutely no words.

Posey leans over and takes the phone. Her eyebrows go up. "Whoa, he's a looker."

"A looker?" Evie laughs. "You've been talking about horses too much. This guy is a Grade A, one hundred percent certified lean, smokin' hot—"

"Alright, alright," I interrupt, not willing to give my warm-up arena nemesis *that* much credit. Sure, fine, he's good-looking, but so are a lot of people! I mean, yes, not everyone has such a determined set to their strong jaw, or such a fierce, competitive expression in their deep-set eyes, or such muscular thighs beneath their white breeches, but, I mean, on the whole, is he gorgeous? Devastatingly so?

Yes, yes he is.

I push the phone away. "He's not as hot in person."

"So you *did* meet him?" Posey sits back down, interested now. "Did you make a move? Are you planning one? He looks like he has money and plenty of it."

"I'm not chasing after his money," I inform them. "That is the old Kayla. The new Kayla is completely focused on horses."

"And what is the new Kayla going to do for money?" Evie asks brightly.

Posey taps out a tune on the table. "Well, she *could* ask her friends for work..."

"I don't want to ride your racehorses," I tell her, shrugging. "It's just not for me."

"But if you can't sort anything else out—"

"I'll figure it out," I say. "I always do."

No point in sharing that I often figure it out by calling my parents and asking for help.

That's the old Kayla, too.

So, I get busy trying to figure it out. Back at the beautiful farm where I've been living since last October, I set up my laptop on the marble kitchen bar, make myself a vanilla latte with Stephen's gleaming espresso machine, and settle down to flick through job listings.

"Today, I will find my next job," I announce. My words echo in the bright, empty kitchen and somehow sound smaller than I expected.

Never mind; it's just my brain playing tricks on me. I check all the usual places: Facebook, Yard and Groom, Equistaff, even the local sell-your-stuff websites. But mere confidence isn't enough to make a job appear for me. I'm in an odd in-between place as a rider; experienced enough to train a straightforward horse but not well-versed in upper-level work. I'm capable of riding a young racehorse, but if someone handed me a three-year-old warmblood and told me to get it started for a show career, I wouldn't be sure where to start. I need a particular kind of job. Riding green-broke horses and getting them started over fences would be ideal. And in winter, or even autumn, that might not be hard to find.

But summer is the slow season in Florida, and most of the work listed online isn't for riders like myself. There are a lot of farm maintenance jobs, with duties like mowing fields and fixing fence. Things I can do now and then in a pinch, but not repetitively, for fifty hours a week, through a sweltering Florida summer.

I search for an hour and find no new leads. Sighing, I look over my laptop screen and through the French doors lining the back of the house. Through the sparkling-clean glass, I can see the afternoon sunlight glaring down on the pastures, the shining metal roof of the barn, and the covered arena.

My charges, a little herd of retired show horses, are in the largest pasture, snoozing under the branches of a live oak tree. Lazy white cotton-ball clouds drift above its thick green crown, slipping through an azure afternoon sky. The weather has been dry, but since the calendar flipped to May, each morning is a little more humid than the last, hinting at a stormy wet season just around the corner. The outdoor riding arena will get wet and sloppy, and riding in the shade of the covered arena won't just be a luxury, it will be a necessity. Max and Stephen both compete in dressage at a high level—Max, more than Stephen—and they don't take time off for weather delays. Their competition schedule keeps them training year-round. It's the lifestyle I want for myself some day...except that I'm probably fooling myself by thinking I can have it, since they made their money in the outside world and spend it on their horses, and I would like to skip the first part.

I mean, I already *have* skipped the first part, really. There's no going back to school and getting a corporate job in my future. That ship has sailed. All that's left now is to find a way to exist in the horse world without living eternally broke.

"Easy-peasy," I whisper, closing the tabs on my browser one by one.

No work, no work, no work. Without really meaning to, I open Facebook again and just scroll for a while. Friends' horses, friends' ribbons, friends' farms...

Basil Han.

I stop flicking through the endless memes and pictures, as arrested by his haughty gaze on my laptop screen as I was in person last night.

I hadn't known his name until Evie brought it up at lunch, but there's no one else like him in Ocala, I'm sure of that. Basil Han is a slim greyhound of a man, with a sharp chin and a hint of cheekbones above a tautly posed smile. His black hair falls just over his ears and the collar of his shirt, covered with a green ball-cap that matches his tech riding shirt. Both pieces have the same logo and words embroidered on them: a golden jumping horse and *Han Worldwide*.

That's his stable name? He sounds like an anonymous corporation.

An anonymous corporation whose stretchy shirt clings to his abdomen and settles in a fold just above his leather belt, a fold which is so tantalizing I can barely take my eyes off it. Just to flick a finger beneath it and lift, see what muscles are waiting underneath...

"Nope," I announce. "Nope, Kayla. Real world, girl."

In the real world, we do not fall for guys just because they look good in riding clothes. And win Grand Prix classes. And hold the lead-rope of their gorgeous jumpers with the same gentle sympathy as they do the reins. Seriously, how soft are this guy's hands? His horse's mouth must be like cotton candy—one little touch and the whole thing melts into nothingness.

Okay, okay. This has to stop. Which of my friends is the mutual sharing his pics onto my feed? Ah, Leigh Nilsson, a striking half-Swedish beauty on the jumper circuit. Make sense. She's probably dating him. Good for her. They'll make a beautiful global power couple at all the Longines World Cup competitions. A pair of models with bloodlines as impeccable as their horses' are, how delightful for the rest of us schlubs.

A rumble of thunder disturbs my thoughts, and as I blink my way out of my Basilleigh fantasy, warnings pop up on my phone screen. Lightning, lightning, lightning!

"Coming, horses!" I snap the laptop closed and run for the door, tugging on my boots without bothering to find socks. Max and Stephen do not want the horses out in lightning; if I'm home when a storm threatens, they have to come inside.

Run, run, run. I hate this part, scampering along the fence-line (but not *too* close to the fence-line, in case the woven wire is struck somewhere on property and electricity zings through the entire network of fences, electrocuting me and whatever horse I'm leading), trying to get the horses' attention without letting them feed off my anxiety. If they run around and evading capture, I get soaked at best and zapped at worst. And lightning strikes happen. Every few months, a new story makes the feed store gossip rounds. Evie discovers these horrifying tidbits and brings them back to lay them at my feet like a cat presenting a dead lizard.

Did you hear about the guy who got struck by lightning while riding? He was six feet from the jump standard when it got hit!

Did you hear about the horses hit by lightning last week? One was touching the gate when it got hit. Fried the whole herd!

There are always people who will say to take those stories with a grain of salt, but have you *seen* Florida lightning? Blue, pulsing, fat as a telephone pole? I've been close enough to a lightning bolt to hear its frying-pan sizzle and watch the glowing electrons dissolve back into thin air and believe me, I do *not* want to test the conductibility of my rubber-soled riding boots.

I capture Lucas, Bubsy, and Rocky first; the three old gentlemen are happy enough to leave the security of their shade tree and follow me back to the gate. My gelding, Crabby Appleton, comes along behind them, while the two mares who go out with them remain rooted in place. I keep turning around and calling to them, but they're stubborn. They're going to make me go back out and get them. And the geldings are slow; age and the warm sun have soaked into their joints and made them drag at the end of their lead-ropes.

"Come on, boys," I urge, breaking into a jog as the temperature drops and a thick wedge of dark cloud hides the sun, its edges lined with ragged white fleece. "Let's trot a minute. Come on, please!"

I'm dragging them through the gate when the first raindrops hit.

Rain isn't the problem, horse-people will tell you. Horses can stay out in the rain. You can ride in the rain. But my dad's a pilot and he says that in a building storm, rain causes lightning. While I am hazy on the science (something about friction and ions I think), I believe him. A little lightning can become a lot of lightning when heavy rain starts falling, so I always run a little faster when the rain beats me to the barn. By the time I have the geldings in their stalls, the roof is roaring with the downpour, and the mares are standing by the gate like it was their idea to come inside the whole time. I curse them as lightning rips through the air and the ground shakes with thunder, but I have to run through the monsoon to get them in.

I always hate the moment when I have to touch a gate during a storm—one lightning strike along the miles of fence and I'm toast—and sure enough there's a crackle and a bang far too close, right as I unlatch the chain. I jump backwards in shock, and the mares plunge through the open gate, heading for the barn at a full gallop. I'm left in the rain to chase after them before they get into mischief in the aisle.

"Brats," I mutter, brushing water from my eyes. It's really raining now, tropical rain, huge cold drops that almost hurt when they hit your skin. Another lightning bolt lights up the gray world, and I bolt back to the barn.

The mares are already tearing at the hay bales I have out waiting for tonight's feeding; I drag each horse away one by one and put them into their stalls. They bang their doors irritably and glower at me from behind bars.

The rain stops.

The sun comes out.

All of that drama, for five minutes of rain.

"Of course it's done raining," I announce to the soggy sunshine. "And I bet *Basil Han* just went back into his barn and waited it out like a normal person."

I'm surveying the mess the sudden rain has made of my tidy barn —rivulets of mud, a broken hay-bale scattered across the aisle, wet leaves in the entrance—when I hear the roar of a truck engine.

I stand in the barn entrance and stare up the driveway in shock. They shouldn't be here—I have another three weeks—but there's no mistaking that black Peterbilt truck or the gleaming trailer behind it.

Max and Stephen are home.

Chapter Three

THERE'S HARDLY ANY time to ask questions; when your horse bosses come home with a loaded rig, you hop to it and get those horses unloaded. At least, that's the way I was brought up. Horses first, personal problems later...if ever.

But I definitely have questions when I see *who* is waiting to get off the trailer: not Max and Stephen's small stable of prized dressage horses. Nope, I find that Ice Cream Daddy, Classica KP, Daring Virtue, and the others have all been left in Wellington. Instead, the vibrating black trailer holds just one horse: a tall, golden chestnut mare with regal bearing and a look in her noble eyes which promises a personality somewhere between sensitive and volcanic.

I feel my own eyes widen as I stand in the trailer's side door. The mare arches her neck and leans around the trailer's central column to get a better look at me. She appears to be as astonished as I am.

"Perfection, isn't she?" Max's satisfied tone breaks through my horse-induced hypnosis. He comes up the ramp beside me, light-footed in soft European driving shoes. Max dresses like a Formula 1 driver on holiday in the Italian Riviera, which always makes for some interesting glances when he climbs out of the Peterbilt's huge, gleaming cab at truck stops. "We bought her from Sylvia Britton."

"Sylvia—" I run through my mental list of big-name trainers, downsize a little, and finally find her. "But she's a hunter trainer, right? This horse is—"

"Bound to be a wicked jumper," Max confirms. "She's got a huge future. I had a feeling about her and just had to have her. Not a lot of work on her yet, but I bet in a year's time everyone knows her name."

"That's—amazing," I falter, trying not to imagine where I might be next year. Any scenario short of living here on this gorgeous farm is sort of heartbreaking, and it's hard to listen to people make exciting plans when you know you're not part of them. For a second, I consider pleading with Max to just let me live in a corner of the tack room. This wouldn't be the hardship one might suppose. It's plenty big enough for me to bunk down on the couch. There's a galley kitchen along one wall, a full bathroom, and it's air-conditioned. Like everything else here at Bent Oak Farm, it's perfect.

The mare stretches out one exquisite leg, a dark hoof with a tiny white spot above the heel extending in a quivering handshake, then drops it and paws mightily through the shavings on the floor. I spring into action, as if her movement has broken some kind of sad, nostalgic spell, and start to slip a stud chain over her nose.

But Max shakes his head. "No chain," he says, moving forward to help me unlatch the chest bar holding her back. "She's got manners. A real classy girl."

No chain is fine with me. There's a plain leather lead hanging nearby; I snatch that and clip it to her halter, then unsnap the trailer tie. Max drops the chest bar and the mare pops forward eagerly.

Possibly, manners is too strong a word. She drags me down the ramp, and for several dozen feet down the barn drive, before I get her to circle and slow down. I consider a stud chain to be a friendly reminder that there is a human attached to the lead, but she is not my horse. And Max is right about class; when I manage to get her attention and bring her back to a halt, she doesn't argue with me. She just looks around with her ears pricked and her eyes wide, a slight tremor in her shoulders the only giveaway that she's a bundle of sparking nerves beneath that rich golden coat.

"Let's get her inside," Stephen fusses, approaching with a bottle of kombucha in one hand and an iPhone in the other. He's texting furiously, one-handed and without looking. Stephen doesn't use autocorrect and he doesn't worry about typos, so his texts are the stuff of legend. "I don't want her to freak out. Max? Which stall do you want her in?"

He asks this as if he is leading her in, not me, which is a reminder that Stephen has always sort of regarded me as a ghost, a halfway-there groom who might actually be an extension of Stephen's own, perpetually busy body which he simply hasn't caught up with yet.

"Kayla will know where to put her," Max replies comfortably.

I smile at this vote of confidence and lead the mare into the barn. She shies at the air curtain blowing down over the entrance and for one heart-stopping second I fear she's going to rear up—a chilling challenge for me to contend with, when she's already capable of lifting her head about four feet higher than the top of mine. But she powers through the scary wind with a deep breath that reminds me of myself when I've run into a roadblock in life, as if she realizes, like I often do, that the only way out is through.

She's happy inside the familiar confines of a box stall, sniffing with pleasure at the water buckets as I turn on their spigots to fill them, as if to say, *This, I understand.*

"Feather," Max says delightedly, watching her through the stall bars. "Look at you, Feather! Pretty girl!"

"That's her name? It's cute."

"Lucky Feather," he amends. "You know, like the one in *Dumbo?*"

I shrug. "I've never actually seen *Dumbo.*"

"Oh, thank God. It's too sad for words. I don't know what parents were thinking back in the forties. Well, I do, actually—they were thinking anything was better than Nazis, right? But anyway, it's Lucky Feather, and there's *such* a proliferation of horses named Lucky right now! Talk about the nineteen-forties! So, Feather it is."

"It's cute." I turn off the water and glance around the stall. Plenty of shavings, but she needs hay to munch on. "She can eat O&A?" I ask, thinking that she'd better be okay with it, because we're still working through the last of our winter supply of orchard and alfalfa blend, shipped to Florida from more temperate climes.

"She *loves* it," Max confirms, as if we're discussing favorite ice cream flavors. "She will tear you limb from limb for a flake."

"Great."

I'm splitting open a new bale when Stephen appears in the hay storage stall, glancing around the stacked bales with narrowed eyes. I know he's counting, to see how much I've used, if I'm staying on budget. I'm not insulted by his scrutiny. Hay prices have tripled since last year. I know, because I've been keeping a weather eye on things while I face having to buy my own supplies again...and the news has not been in my favor. The way things are going, once I finally have enough money put aside for rent, I'll have to spend it all on hay instead.

"You've done alright," he says finally, nodding at me. "You run a tight ship, Kayla."

I'm so astonished at his compliment that I can't find any words to reply.

Okay, so we have a new jumper for a pair of riders who concentrate on dressage, Stephen telling me I'm good at running the farm, and they're home three weeks early? What exactly is going on here?

"We'll be out of your hair by Friday," Max promises. "Just need to get Feather's training settled and then we'll head back to Welly to finish closing up shop down there."

"Do you need help with that?" I don't know why I asked; it's too far for me to go down and help pack up the barn and still take care of the horses here.

"We have help," Stephen says, in a tone which suggests *help* might be a strong word. He pours a glass of water from the pitcher in the fridge, looks at it critically, then takes a lemon from the crisper and starts slicing it up with slow, deliberate chops of a gleaming knife I've always been too afraid to remove from the block. I bought that lemon for a pasta recipe I saw online and haven't had the energy to try yet. But it's in Stephen's fridge, and now it's going into the water pitcher; fragrant sunbursts of yellow.

It's weird having them in the house, shifting little details of everyday life from my preferences to theirs, and I suspect they must feel the same way about me...at least, Stephen probably does. Max, as usual, seems oblivious to the creature comforts surrounding him. It's as if he knows whatever he needs will always be at his elbow, so he simply doesn't think about where they come from or who provides them.

"Our barn girl down there is fine for helping out," Max adds. "The working student chips in a little too. But Kayla, you're the tops in our book! It's nice to see the place so tidy and taken care of. We appreciate your hard work so much."

Flatter me, I think. *Lie to me. But just don't kick me out.* Aloud, I say, "It's my pleasure."

They both like that in their own way. Stephen raises his glass to me with a humorous little smile, while Max looks utterly charmed.

"The pleasure is *ours*," Max gushes. He pushes his glasses up on his nose. They're new, chunky with clear resin rims. He looks like someone's favorite uncle. Mine, maybe. If I told Max he's the gay uncle I never had, would he keep me around?

I have to change the subject in my own head, or I'm going to blurt out something desperate and pathetic.

"So, what is your plan for Feather?" I ask, trying to keep my tone casual.

Max smiles with delight. "Oh, she just spoke to me."

Stephen shakes his head gently, looking down at his phone. "You know Max and his psychic moments," he says drily.

I nod as if I do, although they're news to me.

"And poor Stephen knows I can't just let them go, can I?" Max laughs. "I did, Kayla. I had one of my psychic moments. I *communed* with Feather. And she said, *Take me home, Max.* So, I did."

"After writing a substantial check," Stephen murmurs. "I believe my net worth has dropped considerably."

"Your *Stephen* worth rose one hundred points!" Max assures him, giving his husband a cuddle that makes them both laugh. "You know to trust my instincts, anyway."

"Indeed, I have no choice."

"So, anyway," Max continues, turning back to me. "Had to have her, jumped at the chance, et cetera. And we wanted to get her into training right away."

"She's competing at..." I assume she must be at least in the low jumpers.

"Nothing," Max says, and grins at my shocked expression. "Yup! Total prospect. I'm a sucker. She's five years old. *Very* green-broke."

Very green-broke at five years old? After my winter of training eighteen-month-olds under saddle, the idea of barely starting a five-year-old seems outlandish. Even trainers who would never start a horse as young as the racehorse people do wouldn't wait much longer than the third birthday. Horses have their own opinions at age five. And a pretty serious sense of self-worth. And they know how strong they are, too. I remember Feather hauling me down the trailer ramp and feel a distinct sense of unease. She's an awful lot of horse for someone to train.

Stephen is texting rapidly with just his thumb. He says, "Max assumes her perfect trainer will appear and create a superstar."

"It's not about the money," Max elaborates, waving his hands. "It's about *her*. About finding the right person for her. I already know who it is."

"Wait, you didn't buy her for yourself? Is she a flip, then? Are you going to resell her?"

Stephen sighs.

Max ignores him, mood unaffected by his husband's dour attitude. He's used to it. "I'm going to partner her up with the person who will make her a star. The universe spoke to me, Kayla."

"But who is going to—" I stop myself, realizing with a strange surge of energy that *I'd* like to train this mare. I blink at Max. A crazy idea enters my head. Too good to be true, but I can't help but stammer, "I mean, have you—were you considering—"

"We have someone in mind, yes," Max says, and his eyes twinkle at me so mischievously that I feel a rising sense of disbelief. He means *me*. He's going to have *me* stay on and train this mare.

Could that possibly be it?

No, of course not.

Real world here, girl. Real. World.

My mom is right, even when she's a thousand miles away. Thanks, Mom.

"You know it's you," Stephen sighs, putting away his phone. "So you can stop beating around the bush."

Blood rushes to my head, roaring in my ears, and I have to clutch the marble countertop to stay upright. "Me? But—yes, I mean—only, where—"

Ugh, will the words just *come out* the way they are *supposed to*?

Max seems to get it. He steals a lemon slice from Stephen's water and pops it into his own glass before explaining, "We will not be here this summer, after all."

"Wait, *what?*"

"It's the craziest thing...we never expected it..."

"We're going on a world cruise," Stephen interjects in his dry way, as if he can't imagine a worse idea. "Six months. Six continents. Although I believe they ought to wedge in Antarctica for the amount of money we're paying."

"Antarctica isn't on my list," Max says cheerfully. "The other six continents are. And Stephen promised me if the opportunity ever came up..."

"And now it has, and I am living up to my promise." Stephen looks broodingly out the French doors. The evening sunlight is golden on the live oaks lining the pastures, and I get the impression he would much rather spend the summer here, watching the clouds march across the Florida sky. But in the next moment, he brightens and says, "Anyway, what could be more glamorous than a cruise around the world? The food is supposed to be outstanding on this line. I am looking forward to that."

"You look so good in a dinner jacket," Max tells him. "Let's buy you more."

"In Italy," Stephen assures him. "I've been waiting for a good opportunity to visit my tailor."

And they begin to talk about Italian suits, evidently forgetting I'm in the room, with my entire life—or, at least, the next six months of my life—hanging in the balance. Men are so aggravating.

"Guys?" I interrupt. "What's the plan?"

"Oh, we need you to stay," Max says without ceremony. "And I was thinking, hoping, you'd take on Feather as a project during that time?"

There's only one answer to this question. Fleetingly, I think of Feather's age, her lack of training, her arrogant posture. She's going to be tough to train. Possibly out of my league, a horse for a more experienced trainer. I acknowledge all of this, and then I reply, "Yes, that would be great."

Max claps his hands. "Yes! Stephen, I told you. She sees it, too. She knows Feather is the horse for her."

Stephen lifts his eyebrows. "Kayla, please understand when I say this isn't meant as an insult to you, but...Max, did you really think she'd say *no?*"

"You never know," Max says defensively. "Kayla, honey, I'm sure this is a literal match made in heaven. I brought home that mare just *knowing* the two of you would go together. So you'll stay right here until we're back in November, and we'll see how the two of you are doing. If it's working out, what do you think? Would she be a good payment for taking care of all the extra horses you'll have around the place for the rest of the year?"

Suddenly, everything Max has been chattering about comes into high-definition. He bought the horse to give to me. Work for him another six months (which is a gift in and of itself) and train the horse and—the horse is mine.

I have to sit down before my legs give out. The possibilities racing through my brain are too thrilling to be real, surely. But with the prospect of staying here through winter—because they'll go back to Wellington in January, anyway, so there would be no point in kicking me out in November when I'll be needed again so soon—now I can concentrate on training Feather, getting Crabby to some shows, and by the time the winter circuit rolls into Ocala, maybe I'll have enough of a name for myself that I can bring in a few horses in training. Really get started on my career.

My life's work could be just around the corner.

Max is thoughtfully running his finger down his phone. "Hmm."

"What is it?" Stephen glances at him curiously.

"Basil's new job fell through," Max murmurs.

My breath catches in my chest. *Basil?* Oh, surely not the same one. There must be more than one Basil in the horse show community.

"Oh, that's good," Stephen says unexpectedly. "Dumb luck for us."

"Stephen!" Max chides, chuckling. "You're the worst."

"What? He's a good worker, an expert rider. Keep him here while we're gone. Saves us hiring a new rider for the upper-level horses, and he'll be company for Kayla."

I don't need company. I've been very happy here alone, thanks!

"What's, um, up?" I ask, barely able to keep my voice casual.

Max shrugs. "I've had Basil Han riding for me over the past few months, and he thought he had a new position for the summer, but according to this text...looks like he's a free agent again. I didn't really want to lose him, so it's kind of lucky." He glances at me. "If you don't mind a house-mate."

Chapter Four

OF COURSE I mind having a house-mate. No one *wants* an extra person in their space, and if I do need someone to come over, Evie practically lived here with me half the winter, and I had Posey staying for a while (with Max's permission, totally above-board). It's a big house, after all. But those are people *I* chose to share my personal space with. Not a random show jumper from Wellington with a Swedish supermodel girlfriend and a real attitude problem with grooms.

It crosses my mind to tell Max just how rude Basil was to me at Legends Equestrian Center, but he obviously loves the guy and I have a feeling it will make me sound petty, somehow. Like I'm selfishly trying to keep him off the farm and out of my sweet gig of running the place while they're gone for *another* six months.

I try to take a deep breath and focus on the very real positives of the situation.

Max and Stephen are going to be gone through the summer and autumn.

Then they'll go back to Wellington for winter.

I have a place for myself and my horse to live for nearly a full year to come. Queen of my domain!

And, in payment for taking care of six more horses while they're gone, they're handing me a new horse, too. A new horse to train and possibly even show. Plus, I'll have some breathing room to really work on Crabby and get our jumping career together. This is the chance I've been dreaming of, to take that next leap forward and go from average, occasional rider to professional rider and trainer.

Stephen and Max are already making plans to head back to Wellington—"Too many horses there to leave for more than a day," Max informs me, as if they have a sprawling ranch and not a six-horse mini-farm with a part-time manager and full-time groom—but I can't wait to tell Evie and Posey my latest life update, so I pull on a pair of riding breeches and head out to the barn.

My horse is grazing in the field with the retirees, but he comes in willingly enough when I offer him a carrot. I pull a bridle over his ears and lead him out to the covered arena. Crabby Appleton isn't exactly the most chipper of horses in the barn, but he's amazing for long, bareback rides with one finger on the reins and the other nine texting on my phone.

The group chat with Posey and Evie has been quiet all day, probably because I was already complaining about my life with the two of them at lunch and now they are texting each other privately about what a whiner I can be. That's fine. That's what phone privileges are all about. I type *Guess what, not moving after all! The farm is home for another year!* and then watch Crabby's swinging ears as I wait for the satisfying replies to pile in.

Posey is first. *Amazing news!!!* She throws in some clapping hands and a couple of balloon emojis.

Evie takes a little longer. *Congrats! But what are the boys doing?*

I tap back a quick explainer on the cruise. The girls respond with general astonishment and more congratulations. It's all very gratifying, as if *I* have actually done something worthy of praise, and I'm feeling like maybe I did. I have been such a good farm-sitter that Max and Stephen feel comfortable leaving their horses and property in my hands for another six months, while they travel around the world, *on a boat* no less, and isn't that something to be proud of? Maybe I *am* doing my life's work.

I lift my head and look around the sunny farm, stretching in every direction from beneath the shadow of the covered arena. You know what? This could be it! Everything makes sense now!

Maybe I *am* just a really amazing property and farm manager, and I didn't even realize it. Maybe I am the most dependable and reliable and trustworthy woman in the entire horse industry, and I have stumbled into a career of living on other people's gorgeous farms, sleeping in their comfortable beds, cooking on their gourmet ranges —as soon as I learn to cook properly—

Crabby's walk slows, and he lifts his head, turning at movement inside the barn. My gaze follows the direction of his pricked ears, and I see motion through the barred windows. Someone walking—two-legged, thank goodness, not a loose horse. But also, odd. There's a person in the barn aisle where no person should be.

"Who is that, Mr. Crabs?" I ask gently, and Crabby flips his ears back and forth, telling me he doesn't know, but he's pretty sure I should check it out.

This is the only part of farm-sitting I don't love...the whole "just a girl alone on a farm" part. It's not as scary in Ocala as some other, less horsey places. There are a lot of women running large farms alone here. But even if female-only farms are typical here, I still find plenty of moments when all this open space and that long, quiet barn aisle, lined with empty stalls and storage rooms, can feel like the perfect place for unsavory types to lie in wait for me.

Sure, Max and Stephen are here right now, but they're back at the house, a quarter-mile away and shielded from a perfect view of the outbuildings by a gorgeous line of fine old live oak trees.

Plenty of opportunities to get murdered still exist, even when the men are in residence.

But there's no getting around it; literally, because Crabby is the kind of horse that charges towards things he finds out of place. Once I caught him stomping on a plastic grocery bag that had every other horse in the pasture ready to climb a tree. He hates anything that disrupts the status quo, and he simply doesn't have the normal equine gene that should tell him to run away from danger.

I guess he's directly descended from cavalry horses or something. And now he's convinced that we must go to battle against the stranger in the barn. He heads back to the barn at a snappy walk, his head held high. When the intruder appears in the doorway facing the arena, Crabby goes even faster. The enemy is in his sights.

Whoever is hanging out in the barn clearly sees us coming, but doesn't duck out of sight, which I suppose means he's not going to murder us. Not that I really thought we were in danger, of course, but my heart is beating a little faster than necessary.

Then, I see who it is.

My heart practically leaps into my throat. I start to rein back, surprised and dismayed, but Crabby gets annoyed and yanks back at me with his giant head, then sidesteps so quickly I slip right off his back and hit the mulch horse-path with a graceless thud.

"Oof," I mutter, pushing myself up with my hands. When I look for my horse, he's gone, already marching to war. The guy in the barn steps forward to catch his reins. A groan of disbelief comes out of me like the sound a bench makes when you sit down on it too hard.

Basil *freaking* Han.

He holds Crabby's reins lightly, with the same gentle fingers I noticed last night, and again online this afternoon. He's actually in the same clothes, so it's like he has stepped right out of my laptop and into my personal space with his overpowering good looks and cool charisma. The tan breeches still cling to his muscled legs, the hunter green tech shirt still clings to his muscled everything, and he's still covering his dark hair with the green ball cap sporting a jumping horse and the arrogant, capitalized letters of his business name. Han Worldwide. I *hate* that name. Worldwide what? Petrochemicals? Airplane parts? It's so generic. For a moment, I fixate on everything I dislike about Basil Han, distilled into that one stupid embroidered name.

But there's one subtle difference between the photographed Basil Han of this afternoon and the one standing before me right now. In the picture, I hadn't been able to see his eyes beneath the brim of his hat. Now he looks from my horse to me, and for the first time, I see his dark eyes in the golden light of the evening sunshine. For a moment, all my complaints dry up.

Hazel eyes the color of fine English leather gaze down at me from beneath a fine fan of black lashes. Eyes crinkled at the edges as his lips turn up in a smile. Eyes that make my chest feel suddenly heavy and light all at once, as if I've been inflated with a helium balloon. Eyes that make my stomach flutter with the weight of a thousand butterflies.

Eyes which do not recognize me from the last time I was on the ground looking up at him, just last night.

"Are you alright?" he asks, and the clipped British consonants of the last night are softer, his accent a suggestion instead of a command, as if he's only very English when he's upset about something. "It didn't look like a terrible fall, but…" And he trails off as I take his hand, ignoring a little rush of excitement when our fingers meet. It's only chivalry, I remind myself. It's only a man being polite. Understandable, how that might come as a shock.

"Fine," I breathe almost soundlessly, then I clear my throat and repeat, "I'm fine," in a more robust tone. Where did my voice go just now? It's no time to get all feminine and lose my edge. This guy is a

The Sweetheart Horse

favorite of Max and Stephen's...which makes him a threat to my job, as far as I'm concerned. "What are you doing out here by yourself?"

I manage to make it sound like he's definitely up to no good.

Basil's smile fades at my tone, and he stuffs Crabby's reins back into my hands. "I'm having a look at the facilities," he informs me. "Max and Stephen said you'd be out here feeding and you'd be happy to show me around."

Feeding? I glance at my watch. Oh, yeah, it's about that time. I rarely stand on ceremony about hard and fast feeding times with the retirees, and as the days have been heating up, I've been pushing back their dinner times later and later. But there's no doubt that in Max and Stephen's world, the horses eat at five thirty on the dot.

It's five forty-six.

"I was just about to feed dinner," I inform him, thinking quickly. "I moved dinner to six so they're not eating grain at the hottest part of the day. It's better for their digestion."

"That's a good idea," Basil agrees smoothly. "I like to feed my horses four times a day to keep their digestion rolling smoothly. You can't be too careful."

Four times a day! He must love being glued to the barn. I walk Crabby back to his stall and Basil falls into step beside me, the heels of his Blundstone boots clicking on the concrete aisle. "How many horses do you have?" I ask.

"Just one right now," he says, slightly defensive.

"Oh, me too," I tell him, knowing that won't make him feel any better about running a one-horse stable. "Crabby here. I've had him since I was fourteen."

Basil looks my horse up and down. "He's very cute," he says, pronouncing the word *cute* as if it's from a language foreign to him.

I'm not sure it's the right word. Crabby Appleton is seventeen hands of big bone and bulky muscle. My childhood trainer admitted he was a Dutch Warmblood because his paperwork said so, but suggested he might be, in her words, from the wrong side of the fence. For years I repeated that, laughing about it because I thought it meant he was some kind of horse gangster from the bad part of town, until another trainer told me she'd meant he wasn't a purebred Dutch Warmblood at all, but that some other stallion had jumped the fence and gotten his dam in foal. I found this deeply insulting to my monstrous Dutch horse and dropped the joke immediately.

So in short, Crabby is more beastly than cute.

And that's just fine. But I don't appreciate anyone else dropping the word *cute* with such misgiving. He's mine to make fun of, and mine alone.

I take off his bridle in the aisle and Crabby files into his stall without assistance. He picks up his feed tub from its place in the corner and hurls it at me without missing a step.

"Whoa," Basil says, impressed. "He's got quite an arm."

"His father pitched in the majors," I reply, scooping up the feed tub. I slide the stall door closed and turn around, facing Basil. "We won our regional Children's Jumper championship in my last junior year," I inform him. "And he's evented up to Training Level. So he's odd-looking, but he's talented, okay?"

"I don't doubt it," Basil agrees pleasantly, and I have to wonder if I imagined the way he said *cute*. Maybe he didn't say it any kind of way, and I'm just being sensitive. "Want to show me where the feed is and what your routine looks like?"

Okay, I'm not being sensitive when I say *this* is ringing all sorts of alarm bells. "Why do you need to know any of that?" I demand.

Basil looks startled at my tone. "Because I'm running the farm starting in June. Of course."

"Running the—" I stare at him, speechless. Dark brown eyes like fine English leather, my foot. Devious empty eyes like a demon in human's clothing, more like. "I run this farm. Just fine. Why would that change with you staying here? Nothing has to change, there will just be a few more horses here and—"

Oh.

I hear it now. A few more horses. All of whom are in training, and they didn't mention what was going to happen with those horses. Of course they aren't going to turn out six top-level dressage horses for six months, and even if I'm capable of beginning Feather's career as a jumper, I don't have the dressage chops to keep up with Max and Stephen's herd of dancing horses.

"From the chat I just had with them," Basil says, "I'll be taking over the place while I'm training their horses. And you'll be working for me. I wish they'd said something to you, but I suppose it was all just decided in the last hour or so."

"Maybe you're mistaken," I retort, even though of course he isn't. It's just that the triumph of my afternoon has crumbled so quickly, I barely know which way to turn, let alone what to say to the person who is taking my winnings away.

"I'm certain I'm not." The British accent is coming back. "I assure you, they were quite clear on the matter—"

"No," I say, my back going up at his clipped tone.

"Pardon?"

"*No*, I'm not going to work for you! In fact, I'm going back inside right now and I'm going to—"

"Is everything okay?"

It's Max, and judging by his sympathetic expression, he has heard everything.

Well, maybe I was shouting just a little. But I have my reasons. Twenty minutes ago, I was pondering how I was so good at my job, maybe I'd found my life's work. And now I face the possibility that I don't even have my old job anymore, just a shell of it.

I'm being granted the right to stay here and work for someone else, which doesn't feel like the same thing as being queen of my domain or finding my life's work, at all.

"Max," I say helplessly, and find there's no question to follow up with. I want to say a lot of things, like *Why?* and *Him, seriously?* but none of this is really professional, and if there's one thing I want Max to see me as right now, it's a professional.

A person who can handle the farm with six more horses to care for.

Max's smile is strained. "Maybe we should go inside and talk."

"After we feed, perhaps? The horses will expect their dinner on time." Basil's solicitous, smug, smarmy, horses-first routine just about sends me through the roof. Ten minutes won't kill anyone, and ten minutes is all I need to explain to Max that he's making a big mistake, I can manage on my own—

"After you feed," Max agrees, looking fondly at Basil like he's the favorite child. "Meet us in the kitchen, okay?"

Chapter Five

THERE IS A cheese board laid out on the marble counter, and a bottle of sparkling wine sitting open, bubbles lazily fizzing their way to freedom. Stephen is sitting in an armchair in the sprawling living space alongside the kitchen, looking out over the farm through the unshaded windows lining the back of the house, sipping from a vintage coupe glass. He glances up at me as I slip off my paddock boots at the back door.

"Where is Basil?" he asks.

Basil stomped away from me after I told him he couldn't help me feed. I don't know where he is now. I shrug, then regret the gesture. It makes me look like a pouting teenager. "He might have gone to make a call?" I suggest, straightening my shoulders. "He seems to be on his phone a lot. Really busy, I guess."

Stephen's smirk tells me he knows what a cheap attempt at putting someone down looks like. "I know you don't want him here."

I don't know what to say to that. Deny it? Go all in on the reasons why Basil isn't needed here? I'm still trying to decide which direction to take when Max sweeps into the kitchen and scoops up the cheese plate, shoving it under my nose.

"Have some of the brie, it's your favorite one," he urges me. "Try it with these dried cherries. It's divine, really."

Max loves to force food on the people he cares about. I feel a slight measure of relief as I take a cracker and dab brie on it, then top it all with a dried cherry. "Mmm," I assure him around a mouthful. "Mah favorite."

"I know," Max says, smiling delightedly. "French, you know." And he pours me a flute of sparkling wine.

I settle onto a barstool and admire the bubbles in my glass. How many people have bosses who push wine and French cheese on them? I'm so lucky.

I'm not going to let Basil take this away from me.

Speak of the devil, here he is now, dark eyes flashing as he takes in the cozy little scene: Max and I at the bar with our champagne flutes, Stephen rocking nearby with his charming little coupe glass, the cheese and the crackers and the dried fruit. There is a gentle classical track playing from unseen speakers. I try to use the house well while they're gone, but the truly genteel aspects of living here don't show up to their fullest until Max and Stephen are home and putting it all to work at once. But I know what this looks like to Basil: a beautiful example of the good life, and it could be his for the taking if he just bumps me out of the way.

Well, I'm fighting him for it.

"I know the two of you have a lot of questions," Max begins. "It turns out that things aren't as simple as offering you both a job."

"We have budgets," Stephen puts in, his voice dry. "And Max does not pay much attention to them."

"It's true." Max titters a little and Stephen just drains his coupe glass.

I shift uncomfortably on my stool and look away from them. I love these guys, but most of our relationship has been via phone calls or texts. That has meant I've never had to see any of their personal problems come to light. Maybe Max is a spender and Stephen is a saver, and that's just their cute little back-and-forth, but it's a friction

The Sweetheart Horse

that's new to me and I don't know how to process it.

This is why barn help should just stay in the barn when the owners are at home.

Max clears his throat and starts over. "I want both of you to be here, but it means certain cuts in plans. Kayla, you are owed a raise for adding seven horses to the mix, let alone going from a temp worker to a year-round one. And Basil, I need you riding our Wellington six so we don't lose too much ground with this crazy vacation." Max gives another titter while Basil and I share an uneasy glance. I wasn't counting on a raise, but losing out on one doesn't make me happy. Basil is probably steeling himself for making less money than he counted on. His dark eyes hold mine for a moment, and in their depths I imagine I see nervousness, trepidation. He's worried that he's about to lose something. The job? Or something more?

Doesn't Max see that by keeping the two of us here, he's going to make us both unhappy? Why can't he just send his horses to Basil's place and leave me alone? Assuming Basil has a place, which I definitely did, right up until I saw the alarmed look in his eyes.

Maybe Basil is the next thing to homeless, too.

The idea is startling. He presents as rich, but maybe this job is the only thing he's got going on. Just like me.

I don't like the thought of Basil being anything like me, so I shove it out of my head. Mr. Han Worldwide is likely doing just fine.

"Luckily, I think I have something that works for both of you," Max continues, unaware of the commentary running through my head. "Stephen and I have talked it over, and it's the best way to make things work for everyone. Basil? I'm going to keep you at your previous hourly wage."

Basil's eyes widen momentarily, but his mouth tightens—so he was definitely expecting more. "Right," he says.

"But I know I'm expecting more of you…with this job, you won't be able to do much else," Max continues. "So I'm giving you the ride on Ice Cream Daddy this winter. You're riding him more than me this year, so you can compete with him."

We both jump. Physically startled out of our sitting positions. "You're giving him the ride on Twistie?" I gasp, just as Basil replies softly, "Thank you."

Max looks at me with amusement. "Now, don't be jealous, darling. We got you a nice present, too. What about Feather?"

Stephen coughs. "Be serious, Max."

"Of course." Max's smile doesn't fade. He looks at me dead in the eye, and as I meet his amused gaze, I wonder how he could possibly match what he's giving Basil. Ice Cream Daddy, affectionately known as Twistie Treat around the barn, is a superbly talented Holsteiner gelding with big ribbons in both dressage and jumping. If Basil is trying to further his reputation in the show-ring, in either discipline, Twistie Treat will be a big help.

But Feather is a good bonus, too. After all, Basil won't own Twistie. He won't make any money should Max decide to sell the horse. Whereas Feather…

Max sees the decision in my face and looks satisfied. "I know she doesn't know much, but if you were to train her up and get some show miles on her, I'm sure you could sell her for a profit…or you could keep her. It's up to you."

"It's a lot easier to make a profit when someone else bought the horse," Stephen puts in.

It's not about the money, of course. It's about the chance to use Feather to build my career. So I know I have no argument here; even with Basil coming on board, I'm staying.

"Well?" Max swirls his wine. "Are you in? I know this is a change from what you're used to, so I just want to be absolutely certain. Can we count on you to stick around while Stephen and I suffer through this ridiculous trip? We really do need you to manage the farm with your usual aplomb, darling."

"Of *course* you can count on me," I tell him. And I flick my gaze to Basil's dark, English-leather eyes before adding, "I'll take care of this place like it's my own. Nothing will change."

The cicadas are singing their night-song when I go back out to the barn for night-check. Max and Stephen are still up in the house and it's throwing me off, having them around with their laughter and sarcasm, wine on the countertop and sonatas on the speakers I never use. When my phone chimes with the alarm at ten, I'm grateful for the excuse to head out to look at the horses, who will at least be predictably quiet and happy for their goodnight carrots.

Most of the little herd is outside for the night, but I've left in two mares, Ginny and Dot, to keep Feather company. They whinny hopefully when I come into the dimly lit barn. I know the mares want to go back outside, and when I see the state of their stalls, I wish I could give them what they want. But Feather is watching me through the bars with bright eyes and pricked ears, and I know she'd panic if I left her in this strange barn alone. So I pitch everyone more hay, resigned to the fact that I'll be doing some serious stall-stripping tomorrow morning, and give them some carrots to make up for my cruel refusal to let them go out with the boys.

"You'll go out tomorrow night," I tell Feather as she nibbles at a bite of carrot, her lips soft on my palm. "I just need you to get used to the sounds and smells of the place in daylight before I let you wander around in the dark, okay?"

She jumps backwards as I say it, as if she's seen a ghost. My heart is beating a little faster when I turn around, and it doesn't slow down when I see I'm not alone.

"Basil," I say. "What the hell, man? I thought you went home."

He shrugs his slim shoulders. I wish I could see his face, read his expression, but at night I only turn on half the overhead lights, and he's still wearing that damn ball-cap. The shadow from the brim falls across his eyes and nose, and I get only the barest impression of his taut lips. He looks around us, offering me a glimpse of his firm-jawed profile, before saying, "Night-check is my favorite time in a barn."

"Mine too," I admit. "Although I usually keep everyone out at night. No reason for them to stay inside. Your barn must be full all the time, right? Expensive jumpers who don't get much turnout, I'm guessing." I'm not a fan of keeping horses in, although my practical side knows why high-dollar horses aren't afforded much freedom.

"I don't have a barn," Basil says, and he steps closer...so that I can see he's amused. By my assumption that he has a barn? Or that he keeps his horses under lock and key? "Now he'll be coming here, obviously, but right now I have my horse at Mary Jo Winter's place. You know her?"

I've heard of her, of course. Mary Jo Winter has a bronze medal in show jumping and regularly finds herself on Nations Cup teams. "I don't know her," I admit. "Not quite that special, I guess."

Then I realize he's said *horse,* singular.

Only one? That's surprising. I'd expect someone like him, with money and connections and a bland business name stitched on his shirts, to have a string of prospects and competitive horses.

"Knowing someone like Mary Jo isn't about being special," Basil says, and for a moment I almost like him. "Just connected with the right people." His mouth twists into an odd sort of smile.

"I guess Max and Stephen are my 'in' to the right people," I say, "but only if they stick around long enough to make some introductions."

"Well, with your luck, you don't need the introductions," he replies, his tone noticeably cooler.

"Excuse me?" I feel like laughing at him, but I don't like the way the temperature has dropped. "What luck? I haven't had a lucky day in my life."

Basil turns towards Feather, still lurking just behind the stall bars in hopes of more treats. "May I introduce you to luck?" he asks, sarcasm dripping from every word. "They *gave* you this horse. Because they felt bad for you."

"They're giving her to me as pay," I remind him. "For six *months* of work. She's basically twenty grand in the salary they owe me, the way I see it. Because I'm good at what I do, and they don't want to lose me—rightfully so."

Basil's laugh is harsh. "If that's the way you want to see yourself, barn-sitter."

"Excuse me? I'm a caretaker. A farm manager. A trusted professional farm—"

"A barn-sitter," Basil repeats, making the title sound pathetic. "And you're getting a horse of a lifetime for sleeping in their house and making sure their horses' water buckets are full. I saw your excuse for 'work' tonight—everyone gets a scoop of grain and turned out for the night. Are you kidding me? This place runs itself. You don't *do* anything."

I stare at him for a moment, too shocked to reply. As he looks away, evading my gaze, a hot rage simmers in my bloodstream. Who exactly does he think he is, talking to me this way? We've *barely* even met, and he's just going to stand there and judge me? Say I don't do any work, after observing me in less than an hour on this farm? What a freaking joke! "I work my *ass* off around here," I hiss. "And I do a full-time job for less than a part-time salary. There's a reason they trust me here—"

"Trust you? Then why am I going to be living here, too? I almost didn't agree, you know. I don't want to try training horses while the farm is being managed by a glorified working student—"

"Are you *kidding* me?" I retort, my raised voice echoing through the empty stalls around us. "A working student? You don't even know what goes on here, you have no idea what I do! You just show up, wah-wah I don't have a job, and boom, you get a free ride off Max and Stephen? You're taking advantage of them—"

"Like you are?" Basil counters. "Tell me how you're different from me? We're both here working for minimum wage and a free ride. At least they had to offer me a Grand Prix horse for the winter circuit. You should probably hold out for something better than a green-broke mare next time."

I'm too flustered by this abrupt change of direction to find an immediate answer, and in the ensuing silence, Basil shakes his head and paces a few steps up and down the aisle. I can't understand why *he's* so angry about his gig—we're both getting good deals here. And I'm well aware that even if I don't want him around, he's a better choice to ride the show horses than I would be. He must know he's better off with me here, taking care of the chores and horse care than trying to do it all himself. So what, exactly, is his problem?

Then, I remember the way he spoke to me at the horse show—not that he knows it was me on the ground, spooking his horse—and I think I know.

"You think you're better than I am," I say. "You think you're better than everyone else, don't you?"

Basil looks at me. "That's not it," he says, shaking his head.

"Of course it is! You're so obvious about it. You and your super-special Grand Prix career," I tell him. "You think you're so great because you've been on better horses than me, don't you? But I could do it, too, if I had access to the right horses. Let me guess: you have family money, a family farm."

Something strange flits across Basil's expression and vanishes before I can get a read on it. "And what if I do?" he asks, challenging me.

"Then you haven't done anything to gain my respect," I retort. "Earn it, why don't you?"

"I don't need your respect," Basil informs me coldly. "I just need the horses fed by seven a.m., and the aisle swept and clean so I can get started first thing. Oh, and if you haven't been dragging the arena daily, time to start. I don't think Stephen and Max would appreciate my riding their horses on anything less than perfect footing."

And before I can reply, Basil Han is turning on his heel, leaving me alone in the dark barn.

Well, almost alone. I dig another carrot from my pocket and slip it through Feather's stall bars. The mare takes the treat with eager lips, and I feel a sense of warmth and well-being that crowds out all the irritation Basil has caused.

He got the rides, but I got the horse.

And if he's mad about it, then that's a victory, too.

Chapter Six

THE ONLY THING that I haven't fixed yet is the problem of a second job. Farm-sitting is about to become more work with the addition of six horses—well, seven, when you count Basil's incoming horse. But since my raise is literally just more work, in the form of a horse to care for and train, I still need a paycheck if I'm going to save any money for showing this winter.

Posey, proving herself to be the best friend in the world, gives me her afternoon job riding at Amanda Wakefield's barn. Amanda runs a private training enterprise out of her gorgeous family farm, a farm she lives at all alone, schooling off-track Thoroughbreds for their new careers. It's a good job, and Posey just hands it to me, like it's an old saddle making its way from one rider to the next, rescuing friends in their hours of need.

I'm a little skeptical of the offer. "Amanda won't notice if one day I'm riding her horses instead of you?"

"I'll tell her first. She knows I'm over-extended right now. Don't worry, she'll love you. And you can ride in the morning, which is better for her, anyway. She was nice to let me make my own schedule when I started working with Adam again, but I know she'd like someone to ride with her every morning." Posey rubs her forehead and laughs. "I kind of can't believe I've been working two jobs for this long. I'm exhausted. Amanda's just not the kind of person you can abandon easily."

"Well, you're way too nice," I assure her. "Like, ridiculously way too nice. This is a great job!" And it is, too—a cut above the kind of training gigs I've held in the past. Amanda's off-track Thoroughbreds are all classy as hell and they get a few months of let-down before she starts training them as hunters. That means they aren't super-fit speed demons, like the adult racehorses I swore off riding earlier this year. "Seriously, if you change your mind, I'll understand."

"I'm way too tired," Posey laughs. "Adam has me going nonstop at the farm. I shouldn't even be here, but I told him I needed a half-day off or I was going to lose my mind." She splashes some water over her chest and half-chuckles, half-sighs. Beside her, Evie grins and shakes her head.

We're in the Jacuzzi tub having an afternoon soak while a gray, misty day swirls outside the steamed-up windows of the solarium. With just a few days before the Wellington horses arrive and Basil officially moves in, I wanted to get the girls over for one last hot tub party…just in case Basil is such a pain that these little get-togethers become a thing of the past. Evie and Posey are my best friends; no way I will subject them to my bitter new house-mate against their will. We'll just have to find somewhere else to hang out.

Maybe we can kick Adam out of the big house at Malone-Salazar Farm and hang out there. Posey's barn apartment is nice, but Adam's house is almost as gorgeous as this one.

No hot tub, though.

"I think Adam's wiped out, too," Evie says. "You guys should go on a vacation."

Posey just laughs, like Evie has lost her mind.

"I was wondering why you didn't bring him over today," I admit. "He's always right behind you. When you got out of the truck alone, I was worried you guys were in a fight."

"Not a fight, just needed a half-hour away from him." Posey rolls her eyes. "You know how it is. We work together, we fight together, we do everything together. Running a farm with your boyfriend is *not* easy. And then people ask why I don't live up in the house with him! They have no idea. My apartment keeps me sane. For now."

"Please, I'm about to live in the same house as this Basil guy and I'm not even into him," I sigh. "Pretty sure my easy life is over. We're going to be fighting like cats and dogs."

"I don't know," Posey muses. "Have you considered he could be the answer to your prayers?"

"Excuse me?"

"You used to be on the prowl for a rich husband, remember?" Evie reminds me, with her usual tact.

I give her a little splash. "That's really mean of you."

"Oh, come on! I fully support you. It's not easy getting anywhere in this business without family money. If you can marry some, go for it." Evie shrugs her slim shoulders. "Posey's not ashamed of going for the big money, right, Pose?"

"I am ashamed, actually," Posey sighs, but Evie just laughs at her. We both know she'd be with Adam whether there was a pot of money at the end of the rainbow or not.

But Evie's right, too. Family money is how most of these horse-people do it. Amanda lives in palatial splendor in her absent parents' house; so does Adam Salazar. Our friend Alex Whitehall married into family money and has a huge Thoroughbred farm to show for it, while her best friend, Jules Thornton-Morrison, has always been broke and struggled for years to find her own farm. For me, growing up somewhere in between those two extremes, the initial prospect of making it in the horse business without a bulging bank account was really daunting.

So, yes, I did spend a little too much time over the winter trolling for a wealthy horseman to put a ring on my finger. Luckily, it really didn't go beyond some sparkly dresses and heavy makeup at galas mostly attended by senior citizens. And watching Posey fall in love with Adam, right in front of me, was the wake-up call I needed.

After all, I'd come to Ocala to make it on my own.

It just became so apparent, so quickly, that making it on one's own isn't actually the norm.

"Good news is, I don't need a rich husband anymore," I remind them—and myself. "I get a new horse *and* keep a place for us to live with this contract extension. All I need is a part-time job to make up for the tiny stipend they pay me...and since Posey doesn't have any baby racehorses for me to ride..."

"Not until September," Posey laughs. "Unless you want to do sales prep on yearlings? I don't have any need for help, but plenty of barns do. I could hook you up."

"Groom yearlings all summer and get my head kicked off?" I shake my head, dismissing the idea. "Come on, fam. Surely we can do better than that."

"Well, then stick with Amanda. She'll take care of you."

"I will," I promise. I would *love* to have someone like Amanda Wakefield take care of me. She's the most generous person alive, according to Posey. Maybe I should think about marrying *her*.

Evie is still considering Basil as the future Mr. Moore. "But seriously, Kay, you might want to give this guy a shot. Maybe he's not that bad. Is he rich? I assume he has money."

"He has to," I sigh, remembering the way Basil dresses. "He has that generic golf-slash-sailing-slash-polo fashion sense. Expensive tech shirts, breeches, boat shoes. If he's not rich, he's dressing that way on purpose and I can't even imagine what kind of sick, twisted mind would do that."

"Oh, like frat-boy chic," Posey nods. "They'd eat him for breakfast in Queens."

Posey lived in New York City for the better part of a decade before she moved back to Ocala. She swears she's happier here, that she's found her place in the world and horse girls should just accept being horse girls instead of trying to change everything about themselves, but every so often I feel jealous of her experience in the outside world. While I was going to college in a small Virginia town and pretty much living with the same kind of people I'd gone to primary and high school with, she'd been in the big, scary city. On her own. Sometimes I wonder: should I have gone to New York instead of Ocala?

Would that have given me the challenge I'm craving, yet afraid of?

Probably, New York City would have eaten *me* for breakfast, and I'd have gone crawling home to Mommy and Daddy, anyway.

And anyway, maybe Posey had discovered she couldn't deny her inner horse girl by moving to the big city, but she'd also missed out on years of riding. Since she doesn't have big horse show dreams, that didn't really set her back. But I do, so I don't have the time to lose. I want to be further along than I am right now, not lagging years behind.

Posey and Evie are debating whether men should wear collared shirts casually. "In the saddle, yes," Evie says. "But if the shirt is not paired with breeches, I don't want to see a collar."

"I think that's fair," Posey agrees.

"He was wearing breeches," I remind them. "But I wouldn't put it past him to wear a collared polo with, like, khakis."

"Unless he's going on a job interview, absolutely not," Evie decrees.

"So we can agree, he's not husband material," I say.

"If we're judging him by his clothes, I guess not," Posey replies, rolling her eyes. "But either way, you're going to be living with him? He's going to be here, right?"

"Yes, right here. In this very house. I don't know what it's going to be like with a guy here, but I'm guessing...awful? Awkward, for sure. The absolute best-case scenario is awkward."

"Very awkward," Evie nods. "No more running around the house naked."

I start to protest that I don't do that now, but remember just a week or two ago I went to get a drink of water at three a.m. without bothering to get dressed. Absent-minded moments like that are going to have to stop.

"For real though, don't even give him half a chance to interfere with the way you do things," Posey advises, her expression turning serious. "Just shut him down every time he complains. Tell him you're in charge of running the place and he's welcome to live literally anywhere else. Why doesn't this place have a barn apartment? You could've made sure he lived out there instead."

"I know, right?" I've spent several happy hours over the past few nights just staring at the ceiling and imagining Basil living in the barn. The tack room could work as a studio apartment if a person wasn't too particular. Unfortunately, I think Basil is probably *very* particular. "But no luck there. He's going to be staying in the Hunt Room."

"The one with all the fox-hunting decor? But isn't that Evie's room?"

"It *is* my room," Evie mutters darkly.

I grimace. "Not officially, though. Basil looked at the rooms and decided he wanted it, so there wasn't anything I could say. The important thing is that it's upstairs, away from me." I've been living in the maid's quarters on the first floor since I first started here. Small bedroom, en suite bath with a nice tub, close to the kitchen. I like it; the bedrooms upstairs are mostly too large to feel cozy when I'm living here on my own. Also, climbing a staircase when there is a perfectly good bedroom suite on the first floor seemed a bit foolish.

"And what about the horse?" Posey asks. "Have you started riding her yet?"

I shake my head. "Not yet. Just been doing a little ground work with her."

That's too fancy a term for the truth. I've had Feather out of her stall and paddock a few times to groom and bathe. But I haven't done much with her besides put her in the cross-ties and clean her up. It's been...an adventure.

Every time I start working with her, she does something which makes me wonder if she has any basic training at all. Like the time she pulled back on the cross-ties in the wash-rack and nearly flipped herself over fighting the ties. Or the first time I picked up one of her hind hooves and she panicked so hard she almost fell on me. I couldn't even touch her with a hard plastic sweat scraper or she'd hit the ceiling.

And then there's the little problem of keeping her in a paddock. It turns out Feather really is a born jumper, just as Max believed when he had his psychic moment with her.

She demonstrates this knack for jumping every night now.

By jumping out of her paddock.

I'm not sure what to do about it, but every morning I've come down to the barn to find Feather standing in the aisle. She flicks her ears forward and whinnies to me, ready to eat her breakfast.

It's crazy. The paddock fences are four feet high, at least. Is *this* what Max was talking about when he said she'd be an amazing jumper? Did he see her leap over a fence at her farm down in Wellington?

Of course not. He would have mentioned it; these things are sort of important for a farm manager to know.

I know I should tell someone—Posey, Evie, even Max or Stephen

—but something is stopping me. A fear, I suppose, that Feather will turn out to be a mistake. Maybe Max will come back to the barn, look her over, and decide he's returning her to Sylvia's barn. "Don't worry, dear, we'll find you another horse," he'll say, but he's going on a six-month vacation and I'll have to wait until he comes home.

I can't risk it. I *need* Feather to work out. I can't explain why she matters so much to me.

She just does. Horses are like that, sometimes.

"Well, you ought to get busy with her," Posey suggests, pulling a seltzer out of the cooler next to the Jacuzzi. She cracks it open and sighs. "Summer's coming and you won't want to ride *anything* you're not getting paid to get on."

"I think that ship has sailed," I reply. "May in Florida counts as summer."

"Hell, April counts as summer. At least, the second half." Posey grins at me. "I'm not moving back to New York, though. You want to head back to Virginia?"

"Land of ice storms?" I shake my head. "No thanks."

It's not really the ice that's keeping me in Florida—that's why we have indoor arenas—but Posey and Evie don't need to know all my personal drama relating to my parents and their adoring, constant support. Trust me, I know it doesn't seem like a real problem. I'm aware. That's why I keep it to myself.

Posey's phone pings suddenly, and her eyebrows go up as she reads the message. Then she hops out of the Jacuzzi, splashing water across the terra-cotta tiles. "Time to get back to the ranch," she announces, grabbing a towel. "We've got a drop-off from Kentucky coming in and the trailer's almost here."

Evie looks disapproving. "More horses from Kentucky? Don't you guys have enough?"

Posey shakes her head ruefully. "You'd think so, wouldn't you?

Someone needs to tell Adam. He won't listen to me."

"Boo-hoo," I say. "My boyfriend won't stop buying me horses."

Posey flicks her towel at me. "Just wait and see what your life is like with twice as many horses and the job with Amanda," she says. "Then we'll see what tune you whistle."

Too many horses, I think, watching her go. Isn't that the dream?

Evie opens another hard seltzer and says, "That girl has it all, and she doesn't even know it."

"I think she does know, though. She's just tired."

"We're all tired." Evie takes a meditative sip. "This is a tiring life, even when it's fun."

Can't deny that. I nod, sinking down into the bubbling water. I'm tempted to close my eyes, just to rest them a bit, when Evie laughs and says, "A boy in the house, hah! What's your mom going to say, Kayla?"

I don't think she'll love it, to be honest.

But my mom gets me. I owe her so much. More than I can ever repay her for, although she'd tell me that's just what parents do. They support their children.

To *this* extent? That I feel like I have to put actual miles between us just to prove I can make it on my own? Maybe not. But it's hard to be mad at her about it.

My mom never doubted my future as a professional horsewoman. She never doubted my commitment to horses, never questioned it, never tried to convince me to do something more stable (if you'll pardon the pun). She even led the way with my father, a professional pilot who already knew a thing or two about unlikely career paths, but who was deeply uncertain what to do with a daughter who only talked about, read about, or wrote stories about horses. She brought him around, they helped me with riding lessons and rides to under-the-table working student jobs, and they kept my bedroom open after I moved out...just in case I needed to come home for a little while.

And I did, several times. There aren't many secure jobs in this profession. Even with good bosses who cared about me, I was let go from positions, more than once, with no savings and nowhere to go but home.

Mom encouraged me not to worry too much about the ups and downs of riding horses for a living. "You love horses, right?" she would ask me, every time I came home broke and depressed from another unexpected dead end.

"Of course I do," I'd reply.

"Then just let it happen how it wants to happen, baby," she'd tell me. "Until you can honestly say you'd be happy doing anything else, keep searching for the right path. You have my blessing on this."

My mom is right. She is wise. My dad isn't quite as wise—he still wishes I'd go to vet school or law school—*any* kind of graduate program would make him happy—but he knows my mom and I are in on this game together and nothing he says is going to change our minds.

Mom loves horses, too, that's the thing. She loved horses like crazy but when she was a girl, loving something out of your reach wasn't enough. You had to have a way in, and short of joining the circus, my mom wasn't going to get out of her gritty Baltimore neighborhood and onto a horse. There just wasn't an opportunity.

She got an education and found a career and met my dad, and they moved to the suburbs of northern Virginia, and when I turned out to be as horsey as she'd been, she took me to riding lessons every Saturday. Then to ride my leased pony every day after school. And things progressed from there.

Not as quickly as I would have liked, of course. Despite all the books I read which assured me wealthy, lonely widows were dying to bestow middle-class kids with perfect show ponies, or that there were ample riding academies where I could work for the right to ride a dangerous but misunderstood future champion, my riding career remained very lower-level until my sophomore year of high school.

That was the year I met Dana.

She was another boarder my age at a big eventing barn full of teenagers. I was leasing an aged Quarter Horse gelding named Sparky who had lost most of his spark; Dana owned a dark brown Thoroughbred named Rocket who lived life in a perpetual state of panic. Dana let me ride him once, while she rode Sparky. That one-time ride became a regular swap. It turned out we each had the other person's ideal horse.

And Rocket became that dangerous but misunderstood future champion I'd dreamed of, bouncing through the local jumper shows with the kind of exuberance that makes onlookers gasp (not for good reasons), bringing me lots of small blue ribbons to decorate my bedroom with. More importantly, Rocket got me riding jobs. High school kids are under a lot of pressure to perform, and I was surrounded by other teens who needed time off to study for the SATs, perform in the school musical, volunteer at the children's hospital, and generally pad their college applications in whatever way possible. Since I didn't have any lofty secondary education aspirations, riding their horses became my after-school job. A *lot* better than wiping up frozen yogurt spills at Sixteen Handles.

Long story short, my mom supported me every step of the way. She made my father stop arguing with me when I spent my savings to buy Crabby Appleton. She pulled some strings at work to help me get a scholarship to the local college so I could acquire a business degree, which would supposedly help me run my own farm someday. And she helped me pack my grandmother's old Cadillac and load

Crabby onto the trailer to Florida when I decided my future was in Ocala.

Someday, I'm going to buy my mother a horse of her own. As a way of saying thanks for all the sacrifices and the pep talks and the nights she sat up figuring out finances so I could keep riding.

I might never be rich like Max and Stephen, or like Adam Salazar, or even like I bet Basil is. But I'm going to be successful, and I'll mark that success when my mom is sitting on her own horse at last.

Somehow, I'll make it happen.

Chapter Seven

How ever I reach my dream of finding personal success and buying my mother her very own horse, it *won't* be with Basil Han's help.

If I didn't already know it, this is pretty apparent on the afternoon he moves in, bringing just a couple duffel bags of horse stuff and a small rolling suitcase with him. I assumed he'd have a lot more luggage, so when he walks through the front door unannounced, I poke my head out the front door and am surprised to see a small sedan sitting in the circular driveway with the trunk closed and no obvious bags or boxes stuffed in the backseat.

"You don't have anything else?" I ask, closing the door again—the afternoon is roasting hot and humidity is already fogging up the glass window next to the front door.

"Isn't this enough?" he retorts, swinging his rolling bag around as he faces me. He's still in his uniform of breeches, tech shirt, and boat shoes. With the Han Worldwide hat sat on top of his head, he looks like a robot who wears the same clothes every day. A horse-boy bot. "Did you expect me to show up with a steamer trunk?"

"Okay, first off, *what?*" I shake my head at his stupid comment. "Are we in *Newsies?* Second, is this the vibe? We just fight constantly for no reason?"

"If you're going to ask stupid questions—"

"I asked because I was offering to *help* you!" I can't believe he's going to start off our summer this way. Obviously, I don't want him here, but I'm not looking for six months of enmity, either. I take a breath and steady my voice. "There's no reason to be so pissy about it. We both have to live here, apparently, so maybe we could pretend to like each other."

Basil's jaw tightens. For a moment, we stand and stare at each other. I feel like we're two cats trying to decide who should strike first. Then he shrugs and looks away, gaze sweeping around the two-story foyer. "I don't have a lot of stuff. I like to travel light."

"Oh. Well, I can help you carry something upstairs if you want." One of the duffels is sliding off his arm, hanging precariously from one elbow. "Here, give me that bag."

Basil lets me take the straps off his arm. "Thank you," he says stiffly. "That actually goes to the barn. You can leave it here—"

"I'll take it to the barn," I offer. "I have to get out and muck stalls, anyway."

"The stalls aren't done? Why didn't you do that this morning?"

I bristle all over again. "I worked this morning at my *job*." I've started going to Amanda's at eight o'clock. The gig is six mornings a week, five hours a day. With Amanda's grooms taking care of tacking up and cooling out the horses, it's enough time to ride five horses and hustle back home for lunch and a rest before I handle the barn chores here, ride Crabby, and work with Feather.

With the Wellington horses installed in the barn, my day is now twelve hours long, but it's fine. That's what it will take to make it from farm-sitter to celebrated trainer.

"Oh," he says. "I didn't realize you had a job."

"Well, I do. You should like my hours, by the way. I'll have your horses ready for you by seven the way you so politely requested, and then I'll be out of your hair until the afternoon."

He nods and looks up the staircase. "That's fine," he says absently, as if he's already lost interest in me. "So, just leave that bag in the tack room if you're going out there."

Still fuming about his attitude, I haul his duffel bag out to the barn and leave it on the tack room bench. I look around the space speculatively. He *could* live out here if I annoyed him enough. It's a nice tack room, and I keep it clean, so it always smells pleasantly of saddles and saddle soap.

Basil could do a lot worse than moving a cot out here and taking it for his own personal studio space.

Outside the tack room, the barn aisle is a few degrees warmer and smells of hay, with an undercurrent of manure that's not usually present. Adding the Wellington horses to the barn has doubled my workload, and I haven't quite figured out the new schedule yet. No wonder the guys felt so guilty about all this extra work that they felt they had to give me a horse to make up for it.

My mom couldn't believe it when I told her they were paying me with a horse. "See?" she laughed, when I told her the crazy news. "I told you someday you'd find a way to have lots of horses. And your dad was right, too."

"He was?"

"Yep, he told you that you'd never make any money! Look at you now; you're not even getting paid in cash!"

We laughed about that, and I left her to tell my dad about the horse deal.

I didn't want to hear him groan and moan about what a rip-off it was. Ordinarily, I'd defend my new horse to the death. But Feather is proving to be extremely problematic.

The jumping out of the paddock thing is just worrisome—what if she gets off the farm? But she's still such a wild child when I try to groom her. Half the time I'm afraid to walk her out to the ring to do some groundwork. I've done some remedial lessons on moving away from pressure, using my hand to imitate where my leg will be when I ride her. She's fine when she pays attention to me...but often, her ears and eyes are looking away from me, out of the arena, across the fields.

If I had to defend my decision to trade all this work for Feather right now, I'd be hard pressed to come up with a strong argument in her favor. "I like her, and she's very athletic, and I know she can jump because I can't keep her in a paddock," are not the best points to convince a doubting father that his little girl hasn't been jerked around by some wealthy cheapskates.

It takes me a few hours to get the barn back under control, but by five o'clock I'm happy with the state of things. I'm also pretty sure there won't be any storms this evening. The sky is clear, the sun is harsh, the heat is miserable. Might as well get everyone fed and turned out, I figure.

By the time I get to Feather, the other horses are outside. She has been pacing her stall, annoyed that I make her wait until last. "I'm sorry, baby," I tell her. "But since you're my horse, I feel like I have to do the others first. You get it, right?"

Feather kicks her stall door. I take that for a no.

"Okay, well, let's get you outside." I slip into her stall and slide on her halter. She shoves her head at me while I struggle to get the crown buckled. "I ought to just open your stall door and let you go," I grumble. "Since you'll end up out here in the morning, anyway."

She certainly doesn't seem any happier once I have her turned out in her own paddock. She looks at me, then over the fence and into the distance. Towards the herd of retirees, all ambling along towards their favorite shade tree.

"I know, baby," I say. "But I'm not ready for you to go out with other horses yet."

I've been agonizing about turning Feather out in company all week. On the one hand, she will probably stop jumping out of her paddock if she has a friend. But which of the retirees would make a good pal for her? Or should she just go out with all of them? The herd hasn't changed in over a year, and they all know their places. Putting Feather out there will shatter the status quo. The mares are tough, and I'm afraid she'll find herself getting beaten up every night. Whereas the geldings are sweet, and I'm afraid she'll beat one of *them* up. Like she's the new inmate on the cell block and she has to make the weakest horse out there her bitch or risk being everyone's bitch.

God, horses are a pain sometimes.

Feather gives me a long, measuring look, then switches her attention back to the herd. She whinnies plaintively, as if to tell me what she's missing, and suddenly breaks into a trot along the fence-line, her head turned towards the distant horses.

"Please don't run the fence-line," I call. "It's too hot for this. Whoa, baby, slow down—whoa—" Now she's cantering, her whinny carrying over the fields, and the horses in the pasture are looking our way, concerned.

Ugh, this is not what I want. I'm just about to turn back to the barn for a handful of carrots, thinking I can catch her and calm her down with some snacks, when Feather jumps out of the paddock.

She has a neat, handy jump which helps her clear the high boards as well as the electric wire running along the top. In fact, it's such a pretty, athletic maneuver that for a moment I just stand there in surprise, marveling at what a clean jumper she is. And she's *mine*. Lucky me, if I can get that kind of jump in the arena!

I'm watching her galloping across the field, her ears fixed on the astonished herd of retirees, when I hear a low voice behind me mutter, "Damn, that was a good jump."

I can't help my smirk as I turn around and ask Basil, "Jealous much?"

His mouth flattens into a straight line for a moment. Then he shakes his head. "Of a horse you can't keep in? Hardly. That's a liability I don't have time for."

"She's just going through an insecure period," I inform him. "Because she's not used to the farm."

"Oh, an insecure period, is it?" He nods his head, indicating I should turn back around. "Then the local welcoming committee should boost her right up."

I whirl, confused. Then I see what he's getting at, and my heart sinks. One of the horses has trotted away from the herd to meet Feather, and even at this distance I can see her flattened ears and determined strut. "Dot, you mean old bitch," I whisper.

And then I take off running, desperate to stop her.

Chapter Eight

OBVIOUSLY, I CAN'T catch up with Feather on my two spindly legs. But I have to do *something*. I can't just let Feather clash with Dot, the high-headed mare who is galloping up to meet her. Dot is the queen of the farm, a twenty-year-old matriarch who rules the pasture with an iron fist. For the first few months I was here, she actually had to be turned out alone, but over the winter, she started to mellow out. Stephen said eventually everyone feels their age. Even the toughest mare imaginable, which is what Dot is.

She joined the rest of the herd reluctantly, then became their leader. The geldings and other mares follow her every move without question. If Dot says it's time to go to the water trough for a drink, everyone picks up and heads to the trough. If Dot says it's time to stand by the gate and holler for their next meal, that's what happens. And if Dot says someone is on her shit list, then the rest of the herd agrees that the other horse is up to no good and deserves whatever is coming to them.

If Dot wants to put on her angry eyes and shove one of her herdmates around, that's one thing. But the way she's racing at Feather right now, determined to let the new mare know she can't sit with them, looks downright dangerous. Someone is going to get hurt, and I can't afford for it to be either of them.

So, I'm running.

"*No, no, no, no, no, no.*" I'm gasping the word over and over. It's all I can think to do, as if mewling like this is going to make it to my new horse's ears and convince her to turn around and jump back out of the pasture. She doesn't know she's in danger, the big dummy. She's a happy-go-lucky baby horse who thinks everyone is a potential chum, everyone is just waiting to be her friend. Well, life isn't like that, Feather!

The mares meet, not with a collision like a car crash, but with a screeching halt, flying turf, and loud snorts. I stop dead and wait for something to happen. I'm still a good fifty feet away, and there's nothing I can do now.

A short distance from the scene of the future crime, the other horses start forward, ears pricked, waiting for Dot's assessment of the situation. If she says they hate Feather, they hate her. If she says Feather is fine, they'll accept that, too. But what are the chances Dot lets in my goofy youngster? Mares are so judgmental.

Dot's ears flick forward, then sweep back as Feather leans in to touch her, nose to nose. The old matriarch looks more like a snake than a horse. The mares breathe each other in quickly, then Dot jerks back, squeals and paws the ground. Feather takes a quick step back in response, her eyes going round as she realizes that not everyone on earth is destined to be her playmate.

Dot shakes her head, whirls around, and kicks out. Feather squeals and backs away. She looks at me and I swear she seems to ask me why this other horse is being so mean to her.

Then the roar of an engine startles everyone. Dot's eyes flick past Feather, and her ears come forward. The mare's entire expression changes, from outrage to greedy hope, and she whinnies. Behind her, the rest of the herd starts forward, eyes bright with anticipation.

I turn around and see what has everyone so delighted. The sight shocks me: it's Basil, driving through the pasture on the old four-wheel-drive Gator.

The Gator doesn't see much use these days; it mostly just sits in its parking spot in the machine shed, along with the ancient tractor and the low bulk of Stephen's antique Jaguar, draped in a custom dust-cover. Very rarely, I take it out to move hay or retrieve the feed delivery if the truck leaves our usual pallet of grain by the house instead of the barn (no one can ever explain why this happens). But life here is rarely strenuous enough to need what's essentially an off-road golf cart.

Maybe if I used it more, I would have thought to grab it for this job instead of just running across the field like a crazy person, but who knows? I clearly haven't been thinking straight throughout this entire situation.

Fortunately, Basil has.

He drives right up to Feather and Dot, throws the Gator into park, and leans back, reaching into the cargo bed. With a couple quick tosses and pretty decent aim, there's a pile of green alfalfa behind Dot and she's spinning around eagerly to get a mouthful, Feather forgotten. The other horses spot the hay and nicker, their strides coming more quickly. Basil pitches some more hay out, making enough piles for everyone. Then he turns to Feather, who is watching the scene unfold with wide eyes.

He hands her a bite of hay and, while she's chewing it eagerly, slips her halter over her head.

And just like that, the drama is over.

I feel my wooden legs start to regain life and stiffly jog over to the Gator. Basil hands over Feather's lead-rope. "Your horse, madam," he jokes, grinning.

Jokes? Grinning? Who is this guy? He just saved the day for me, and now he's being *nice* about it? Maybe Basil was body-snatched last night. If so, that's fine. I like the alien version of him much more than the original.

Feather shoulders past me and puts her entire head into the back of the Gator to get at the rest of the alfalfa. "Ow, stop it!" I complain, and just like that, Basil's smile drops.

"Your horse is rude," he informs me. "You really want to teach her some manners before you even *think* about riding her."

"I know." It pains me to admit it, but she *is* extremely rude. "She doesn't seem to have a lot of training on her."

"No." Basil looks her over for a minute, then asks, "Are you up for the job?"

"Of training her? Of course I am."

"You've done it before?"

"I spent all last winter starting Thoroughbreds for the track," I inform him. "I have some experience with young horses."

"Ah," Basil says.

"What's that supposed to mean?"

"I'm just not sure it's the same thing, that's all." Basil puts his hands in his pockets. "She's five years old and she's done very little. That can be quite a big challenge, is all I'm saying."

I'm fully aware that starting long yearlings is nothing like getting on a fully grown warmblood mare with her own opinions and plenty of muscle to back them up, but Basil doesn't get to see my uncertainty. It's not for him. So I say, "I think I can handle it," in a lofty tone.

"I hope you can," Basil replies, sounding sincere, which truly just makes things worse.

I'm trying to think of a reply, something succinct and snappy yet which expresses how much I dislike him, while still acknowledging he just did me a serious favor by distracting the alpha mare and catching my horse, when a rumble of thunder shakes the ground beneath my feet. It's startling enough that everyone, horses included, stops what they're doing and looks around for the source.

A dark cloud over the trees lining the east side of the field does everything but wave and call out good evening.

"Where did *that* come from?" I sigh, annoyed. "Now I have to bring these idiots back inside."

"Well, I'd better put this away," Basil announces, and he guns the Gator motor, zipping off before I can ask him to stop and let me hop on the back.

This would have been the perfect opportunity to teach Feather to pony off a cart, I think grimly, turning my mare away from the other horses. She tugs at the lead, wanting to go back and share their alfalfa.

"I'll give you some in the barn," I tell her, tugging back. "After I've come back out here in the damn lightning to drag these guys off that hay."

The rain sweeps in just as I get Feather into the barn, along with a few bolts of lightning that are close and bright enough to stop me from even thinking about going to get the other horses in. Great, I think, putting Feather in her stall. Now I'm putting my horse inside and leaving the farm horses outside in a thunderstorm. Can't wait for Basil to tell Max and Stephen about *that*. I have no doubt he's going to act as an informant for all the things I do that he doesn't approve of, although maybe they won't be so easy to contact when they're sailing across the Atlantic. I imagine Basil wearing headphones, bent over an old-time radio and tapping out his tattle-tale messages.

The storm takes up residence above the farm, crashing and banging and pouring down rain, so I'm trapped in the barn for the time being. I wander into the tack room and find Basil there, arranging his things. His empty duffel bags are open on the floor, and there are two new saddles on the wall racks, each one shrouded with a green dust cover. *Han Worldwide* is embroidered on the sides.

The constant splashing of Basil's stupid business name across his tack and clothes annoys me. It just sounds so crass and industrial. Why couldn't he at least call it *Han Show Stables* or *Han Sport Horses,* something that fits our business? Something traditional and dignified?

If I ever have my own business—*when* I have my own business, I mean—I'm going to give it a traditional, elegant name. This is an elegant sport, after all. When you overlook the dirty parts, which is most of it, admittedly. Something pretty, like Azalea Sport Horses or even Kayla Moore Equestrian. Something *horsey.*

Not a name which could just as easily be referring to selling house paint or importing tractor tires.

Basil is fussing with a bridle he's just hung up, re-wrapping the leather in its tidy figure-eight, but he turns around when I clear my throat. "Yes?" he asks impatiently, as if I'm distracting him from very important business.

"Just wanted to thank you," I say, shrugging. "For bringing the hay out and getting Dot's attention off Feather."

"Oh, of course. Just saw you were in a tight patch and did what I could."

It *would* have been nothing, had this favor come from a normal person. But coming from Basil? I consider it downright angelic. I can't actually say that, though. The last thing I want to do is praise him for being borderline nice to me. A thanks is all he deserves. So I just shrug again and turn to leave him to his unpacking. I can kill some time cleaning up the feed room, I guess.

It can't rain *forever,* I think.

His voice stops me at the door. "It was a good jump," he calls. "Too bad it came out of the paddock. She's one of those, I guess."

"One of those incredibly talented jumpers?" I suggest, pausing to give him an arch look. "One of those amazing natural athletes?"

Basil laughs. "One of those horses you can't keep in," he says, giving in. "That's a hard trick to break them of, you know."

"She just needs a job. Once she has something to occupy her brain —"

"So you're going to start riding her."

"Of course I am."

"When? Tonight?"

"Friday." I feel my fists clenching at my sides. "I'll ride her Friday night, after I'm done at Amanda's. Why? Do you want to watch?"

"I do, actually, but only to make sure you aren't killed. I don't want to be left taking care of all these horses alone."

Well, there it is. I knew there had to be an insult waiting for me, after that 'I did what I could' aww shucks routine. The only question is why I stood here and begged for it, when I could have left well enough alone. Could have left *Basil* alone. But no. Something about him keeps me coming back for more abuse.

Stupid of me. I turn away now, determined not to get into another fight with him.

Whether I like it or not, he's here now, and I have to learn to live with him. Constant arguments aren't the answer.

But I can't resist calling over my shoulder as I leave. "You're going to be very disappointed, Basil."

"In your riding?" he asks. "Impossible."

And he means that as an insult, too. Jerk.

I stand in the barn aisle for a moment, listening to the dissipating rain tap gently on the roof, and then I know what would make me feel better. I walk out to the pasture gate, ignoring the rolling thunder as it moves on across horse country, battering other farms and ruining other people's quiet evenings, and call Crabby.

***

The Sweetheart Horse

Riding Crabby is like meeting up with an old friend. The sort of friend who always thinks you look great, congratulates you on tiny achievements, and makes you feel like a million bucks.

I probably shouldn't have named him Crabby, but when I first bought him, he was a bit of a grouch and didn't really do anything to indicate what a great pal he'd turn into.

Crabby could be a better athlete; he's part of the reason I haven't made it very far with my horse show dreams. But would I trade my buddy for the most athletic horse in the world? Of course not. And I appreciate that Crabby is always available for a chill ride when I need one. He isn't going to test me, or decide he's suddenly afraid of every jump in the arena. He's just steady, friendly, adorable Crabby.

There is a lot to be said for a horse like him.

After we've done an easy warm-up, I point Crabby towards a jump and he bounces over it eagerly.

"That's my good boy," I tell him, letting him canter away from the jump and towards the top of the arena. I sit back in the saddle, aware my elbows are out and my knees are loose, but not too worried about it. I haven't taken Crabby to a show since we moved to Florida last year, and he doesn't seem to miss competition.

Now that I have Feather, the pressure is totally off Crabby to do anything in the show-ring. She can be my show horse—whether she wants to event, jump, or stick to dressage will be entirely up to her. I like the idea of letting horses pick their careers. Amanda is the same way. She says to put a solid walk, trot, canter, and halt on every horse we retrain from racing. Once we've done that, we can tell their natural way of going and what gets their engine going. Do they carry themselves uphill and round, perfect for dressage? Do they love hopping over small jumps? Are they bold and brave out of the arena, or do they hug the fence and look for a buddy? It all matters. Amanda is teaching me to be more observant of my horses' body language and behavior, lessons I know will benefit me for the rest of my career.

Crabby's body language always suggests he is happy with whatever. Jump? Sure. Canter around aimlessly? Absolutely. Looking for the next jump? Yeah, we can do that. I let him take a flier over the small square oxer near the gate, barely moving out of the saddle as he soars over the fence with a flat back. It's an unconventional way to take a fence, but Crabby's never been an ordinary horse.

"Silly boy," I laugh, clapping him on the neck as he turns of his own accord at the top of the ring and keeps on cantering, his strides coming faster and faster. We're really whizzing around the arena now. I leave my reins loose and give him his head so he can do whatever he wants. Crabby takes it into his head to jump a cross-rail, and I move with him. If he's happy, I'm happy. It's as simple as that.

I hope it can be this way with Feather.

As Crabby slows to a trot, then a walk, my mind stalls on the subject of Feather. I've been putting off riding her, but Basil has me backed into a corner. Ugh, Basil. He was rude. I shouldn't let his words get under my skin, I *know* that, but they do, because whatever else Basil is, he's a horseman. He knows what he's doing in the saddle, and it makes me nervous when he suggests I might not have the chops to start Feather.

Because I think he might be right.

And I don't need anyone negative in my space, hammering home these insecure feelings. I can do it if I believe in myself, right? But it's hard to believe in yourself if there's someone judging you from the sidelines, waiting for you to fail.

Crabby stops by the arena gate, his sign that he's ready to go in, and I jump down from the saddle to open it for him. I glance up the barn aisle as we walk inside, but the tack room light is out and there's no sign of my new house-mate. Basil must be up at the house, probably getting ready for his first big day of riding tomorrow...or maybe he's just lounging in one of Max and Stephen's designer chairs, sending a bunch of tweets about the stupid girl he has to room with for the next six months.

I pause to straighten a crooked halter, letting Crabby walk on up the aisle without me. He stops outside the tack room and pushes the door open with his nose.

"Don't go in there!" I warn him. Crabby loves to go into the tack room. He'd stay in there all the time if I let him. He looks back at me, then his gaze returns to the tack room door...and he jumps back, snorting.

Basil appears in the doorway.

Good grief, Crabs, I get it! He freaked me out, too. What the hell is he doing hanging out in a dark tack room?

"What is this?" Basil demands, gesturing at the snorting horse in the barn aisle.

I slip my hand onto Crabby's reins. "My horse," I retort. "You have a problem with this one, too?"

"I don't have a problem with *any* of them. I have a problem with horses wandering around loose, though. You seem to have a hard time with this."

"This horse doesn't need to be glued to my side," I inform him, and I let go of the reins again. Crabby looks around the barn aisle and then back at me with wide, innocent eyes. "Go to your house," I tell my horse. "Go on, go to your house."

Crabby flutters his nostrils in reply, then walks down the aisle and turns through his open stall door.

I throw Basil a triumphant look. "See?"

Basil just shakes his head, unimpressed. "Try that with Feather, and you'll be chasing her down the highway!"

"Not now that I know she brakes for alfalfa," I remind him. "I wasn't thinking clearly earlier today, or I'd have gotten her a treat before I tried to catch her. Luckily, she's a good girl who thinks with her stomach, so she'll be easy to train." As I say it, I realize it's so obvious—if I teach Feather to stay close to my side around the barn, she'll be much more amiable when I'm on her back. I need to go down to the feed store and get a bag of alfalfa pellets to use for cues and rewards.

Finally, a plan! I feel so much better, I actually smile at Basil.

He looks alarmed, like my happiness means nothing good for him.

Like maybe he hopes I'll fail with Feather.

But why would he want me to screw up with a horse? What good does that do him?

Chapter Nine

I'M GROWING TO love my job at Amanda's farm. Not just because it's a break from the prospect of running into Basil every time I leave my bedroom, although that's certainly a perk. But because Amanda is a kind, compassionate rider and human. Two things that are pretty lacking in the professional horse world.

The last horse of the morning almost comes as a disappointment. I mean, it's noon, and the sun is murderously hot, so it's clearly time to finish up. But I enjoy this ride. Amanda saves her favorite horse for last. He's a gorgeous hunter prospect named Stuffy McGoo. She can't really explain why he's called that, and I can't really explain why the name suits him so well when he's a fairly regal hunter, but it just works. I usually save a wild-maned Thoroughbred named Torrance for my last ride. She's a lovely ride: interested in her work and light on her feet.

Amanda says that Posey named the Thoroughbred filly for a rider neither of us have ever heard of.

"Torrance White? Torrance Watkins? Something like that," Amanda explains, wrinkling her forehead while she tries to remember. "She said the filly is really well-bred and has the potential to jump anything we point her at, so it was somehow a good name for her?"

"Wait." I'm thinking furiously. "Torrance Watkins sounds familiar, now that you mention it."

"Hang on, I'll text her," Amanda decides, pulling out her phone. I circle the filly around Stuffy McGoo, who snoozes on a loose rein, until Amanda gets a response. "Oh, Posey says she won gold at the L.A. Olympics, and we should be ashamed of ourselves for not knowing more about great female riders."

I squint at her, thinking. "Okay, but when did L.A. ever have the Olympics?"

Amanda bursts into laughter. "I'll ask her!" A pause. Amanda tilts her head. "Now she says if we still had VCRs she'd bring over all her old Olympic equestrian video tapes and make us watch them."

"Ask her what a VCR is."

Amanda nearly falls off Stuffy McGoo, she's laughing so hard.

These are the kinds of conversations that pepper our mornings together, making the workload feel easy and the atmosphere light. It's the opposite of life back at Max and Stephen's, where Basil is constantly glowering in the background like someone ran over his favorite saddle.

I can't understand what has him so frustrated with life. He keeps to himself, but he's never far away when we're both in the house, sulking in the living room or mincing around the kitchen, making very basic meals. I'm no chef, but something about his constant grilled cheese or microwaved noodles gets on my nerves. So instead of making myself my usual standbys, a big salad with deli chicken for protein, or a pot of pasta with chopped vegetables and goat cheese, I've started cooking actual meals, even going so far as to use the large and intimidating propane grill in the outdoor kitchen.

The first time I grilled a piece of chicken, it turned out delicious. I ate it with great satisfaction at the dining room table, while Basil slouched at my usual spot along the bar in the kitchen, slurping noodles.

Feeling adventurous with my initial success, and slightly aggrieved by Basil's hangdog expression as I carried my empty plate past him, I resolved to make something for the both of us. A lucky find at the grocery store resulted in a medium rare steak which looked and smelled fantastic. I offered Basil a portion with undisguised glee. It was all I could do not to wave it under his nose. A steak! The first one I'd ever made! He had no idea how lucky he was.

Basil looked at that steak like I'd grilled up an old shoe and plated it for him. "I don't think so, thanks," he said, and then he went and fixed a bowl of noodles, while I sat at the kitchen bar eating steak and a baked potato.

I mean, if that isn't an unnecessary escalation of hostilities, I don't know what is. And no, he's *not* against eating red meat. I've seen hamburger wrappers in his car.

Not that I glance into his car when I'm walking out to my truck in the morning.

Amanda thinks Basil is going through something big. Possibly he is planning to come out to his friends and family, she suggests, or he is recovering from an addiction. To Amanda, everyone has a reason for being withholding or unkind. She doesn't seem to agree with me that some people, *most* people even, are just constructed that way. They're just awful people.

"Everything has a reason," she says gently. "We may not like it, or understand it, but that's just the way it is."

I think Amanda is a little too empathetic to be trusted with advice about humans, but her empathy comes in handy with horses. She's good with her rides, helpful with mine, and has a lot of suggestions for my work with Feather, as well. I'm grateful for her interest, because Basil seems allergic to offering advice, despite his apparent need to see me get Feather going under saddle. After the stormy night when he gets me to say I'll ride her by the end of the week, he avoids me—even going so far as to leave the barn if he's still down there when I come in to do my afternoon chores and work with my horses.

I suppose I should be grateful he leaves me alone. It would be distracting having him leaning on the rail while I work with Feather on the ground. All I need is Basil hanging out nearby while I fumble through our groundwork sessions, laughing about how stupid my slow mare is.

His attitude has me revising my initial opinion of him as a kind rider. I know I must be wrong, though, because if he wasn't a good horseman, Max and Stephen wouldn't have trusted their stable to him. And that just makes Basil one big conundrum to me. It's impossible to reconcile what he's shown me of his personality with my idea of a sympathetic rider—especially when I spend my mornings with Amanda, who seems to be made of kindness and butterfly wings.

And who thinks Basil is defensive because he is hiding some secret struggle.

So when Amanda pockets her phone and asks me how things are going with Basil, I just shrug and lie. "It's fine."

"Really?" Her eyes glint with curiosity. "You aren't fighting constantly anymore?"

"I mean..." I have to think about it. "We don't see much of each other."

"Why is that?"

"Our schedules clash," I say. "I'm here in the morning, he's riding the horses there. Then he's inside or off the farm in the afternoon, and I'm taking care of the barn and my two horses." My two horses. It sounds so cool, even if one is an aging lazy-bones and one is a hot-headed tantrum on hooves.

"You never see each other in the house? What about the evening?"

Amanda walks Stuffy McGoo in a leisurely circle around us. She's enjoying this conversation more than I am. "Come on, it's been nearly two weeks. Surely you guys are getting to know each other."

I let Torrance turn after Stuffy McGoo. The filly nips at his neck and the gelding just nods his head, like it's no more than he expected. "Amanda," I say, "you're implying something here. What do you want me to say? We're no longer fighting, and we've started planning our big wedding?"

Amanda's toothpaste-commercial smile twinkles at me. "I just wouldn't be mad if someone as hot as Basil Han moved into one of my guest rooms, that's all I'm saying." She shrugs. "Even if he's more interested in my horse than me."

"Who, in *Feather?*" I snort with laughter. "Please. He hates Feather."

"Okay, but maybe he doesn't?" Amanda suggests. "Maybe he's mad that you got her. You said he only owns one horse, right? He would probably love a prospect to sell. Getting a ride for the winter is great, but he's not planning on being an FEI dressage rider, so...is it really what he needs?"

"What are you saying?" I ask, bringing Torrance to a halt. The filly wags her head impatiently. "You think he's mad at me because of Feather?"

Amanda shrugs eloquently. "I think you should ask him what he thinks of her," she replies. "Get a straight answer. And if he admits he wants her, then you guys can work that out. Call a cease-fire. Wouldn't that be nice?"

I don't answer her.

"Come on," Amanda prompts. "Don't tell me you want to fight with him forever. You live in the same house. Your horses are in the same barn. This has to be hard on you. On *both* of you."

I think about the dinner I cooked him. She's right. It's not fun having your nice deeds thrown back in your face. But more than that, I'm tired of Basil sighing into his soup every night. He obviously doesn't know how to cook anything else. At the very least, he needs to let me fix him some food. It's no trouble, for heaven's sake. I can just as easily make dinner for two as for one.

But first, he needs to be honest with me about Feather.

"Fine," I agree. "I'm going to make him 'fess up. He needs to be perfectly clear on whose horse Feather is."

Amanda shakes her head, but she's smiling. "Try to be kind," she suggests.

Kindness is really the last thing on my mind as I drive back to Bent Oak Farm.

I just want Basil to drop the act. And I think Amanda's right: I think Basil is sulking because he thinks I got the better offer from Max. He probably sees getting a young prospect in exchange for six months of work as a real sweetheart deal, while all he gets is riding lessons and the opportunity to show a horse this winter—which, as Amanda pointed out, is not in his chosen discipline. Basil will be a much more effective trainer with all this dressage work, and he knows it, but that can't really compare to the more immediate satisfaction—and compensation—of training and selling a horse in the jumper ring.

After all, Max said he believes she'll be an amazing jumper. And Basil did say she had quite a nice jump when he saw her leap out of the paddock and into the retiree pasture...

It's convincing stuff, and by the time I get back to the farm, I'm ready to find out for sure. Not because I want things with Basil to be more settled and comfortable, as Amanda suggested—the opposite, in fact. I want to call him out, and make sure he has absolutely no illusions about who gets Feather when our six months are up. He's not going to somehow win a shot with her if I don't manage to have her winning blue ribbons by the time Max and Stephen come home.

Basil is lounging in the living room, freshly showered and sipping lemonade with an actual lemon wedge in it, like some kind of rich person. Which I suppose is what he is. Luxurious Mr. Han Worldwide, with his Grand Prix jumper and his elegant posture in that expensive chair of Stephen's. He's ditched the preppy clothes this afternoon in favor of a cornflower-blue cotton shirt and a pair of loose linen shorts, which all seem to accentuate his long limbs and sleek muscles.

I find I have to pause for a moment to regain the head of steam which powered me into the house.

He looks up at me with a languid expression. "What's up, Kayla? Have a nice day riding the off-tracks?"

I hate it when he calls retired racehorses the off-tracks. It sounds like he's making fun of them. His remark gives me the fresh edge of annoyance I need, overpowering my momentary hesitation. "I did, actually," I snap. "They're nice horses. Maybe not as nice as your big fancy warmbloods, but I like them."

Basil's eyebrows come together. I feel a grim satisfaction. I've annoyed him. Good, he was looking too comfortable.

"Seems uncalled for," Basil remarks. "I was just asking a question to be polite."

"*So* polite," I sigh, leaning over the kitchen counter as if I'm swooning. "*Such* a liar." I stand up straight. "I know why you don't like me, Basil."

"What?" Basil leans forward, staring at me. "Where is this coming from?"

"You want Feather. It's so obvious." I clench my fists by my side. "You keep putting her down around me when she's an amazing prospect. You barely speak to me. You're mad at me for getting her when you wanted her."

Basil's eyes narrow and for just a moment, I think I have him. Then he looks away, shaking his head. The amused little smile on his face makes me want to scream. "I don't want your mare," he says. "Why would I want a half-broke prospect when I have Jock?"

Ah, Jock, also known as Highland Fling, the beautiful horse I spooked that night at Legends Equestrian Center. How long ago was that now? Three weeks? It feels like forever. So much has changed. Hard to believe I thought my life was complicated then, and that if I just got to stay at Bent Oak Farm, everything would be fine.

Well, here I am, but things feel even more complex. And it's all because of Basil. His little barbs, his constant insults, the way he darts back to the house when I come down to the barn in the afternoon, the way he refused to eat dinner with me.

"Kayla," he says. "Listen to me. You're more than welcome to Feather. Don't you think I have enough to do? I'm riding seven horses a day. The same number as you, actually. Do *you* want another horse to train after you've gotten through all of them?"

I shake my head. He's right. Seven horses and no groom to handle tacking up and cooling out? That's a full-time job.

"Trust me on this," Basil says softly. "My life is hectic enough without adding Feather to the mix. Anyway, why would I want to take her from you? You were so excited about her. What kind of person do you think I am?"

Suddenly, I feel foolish.

Not just because I've accused Basil of being jealous of my half-broke mare, but because I've spent so much time thinking about him. Obsessing over him, actually. Watching for him, letting him hurt my feelings, cooking up conspiracy theories about him. Basil wonders what kind of person I think he is...but he probably doesn't want to know the answer.

I slide down into a chair opposite him and rub my face as if I can wipe away all my uncharitable thoughts. "I'm sorry I came at you like that," I say after a moment. "I'm just tired, I guess. And we *haven't* been getting along, have we? Am I imagining that?"

Basil looks as though he thinks there's a lot more wrong with me than exhaustion. But his dark brown eyes seem to twinkle as he says, "No, you're not imagining that. But I guess we can both do better. Want a glass of lemonade?"

He has never offered me anything before. "Sure," I reply, startled.

Basil takes glasses from the freezer and pours us both healthy measures from a pitcher. He tops it with a lemon wedge, then glances at me and asks, "Mint?"

I nod, speechless, as he plucks leaves from a plant on the counter. Wait, where did that come from? Basil's buying potted plants now?

"This is very fancy," I tell him, accepting the frosty glass. "Maybe the fanciest lemonade I've ever had."

"You should get out more," he advises me, sitting back in Stephen's favorite chair. The angular lines of the arms and headrest seem to match his coltish limbs. "Or just be nicer to yourself. It's the little things, y'know?"

"Little things like mint in lemonade," I say. "And what is it in your ramen noodles? I know you're not just using the salt packet."

"Oh, my mother would kill me if I used that nasty little packet," Basil laughs. "No, there are broth bases you can buy at the store...I'll show you next time. You can use it, too. I have plenty."

"Thank you...but...why didn't you eat the steak I grilled for you?"

"I was just in a really terrible mood," he admits. "My mother called."

I wait, but he doesn't say anything else. Maybe he has *that* kind of mother. Nagging him about his future or complaining about the neighbors. "Okay," I say finally. "I know how moms can be."

He looks at the floor. "Oh, she's not like that," he mutters.

Well, good grief, what did I say wrong now? "I didn't mean to say your mom is awful," I say. "I'm just saying I know how moms can be. You know, like, always pushing you and stuff."

Basil presses his lips together. Then he looks up at me, his dark eyes uncertain. As if he has something to confess, but he's not sure how I'll take it.

Suddenly, I'm nervous.

Then he says, "I have anxiety."

Oh. I blink a few times. Anxiety is normal. Everyone has anxiety. I think. Maybe it's just the people I know. "And it's triggered by... beef?" I ask, just to get a laugh.

Basil chuckles. It's gratifying. Maybe more than it should be. He says, "No, just sort of general anxiety, you know? And it's bad in the evening, I get to missing my mom—my *family*," he tries to correct himself, the words running over each other, as if he's afraid of what I'll think of a mama's boy who misses his mother when he leaves home, as if anything could be more endearing. "She always eats soup for dinner. My mother, I mean. Broth and noodles. I just feel better when I do, too. So when I talked to her, I couldn't really do anything afterwards until I'd had some soup."

I stare at him in dismay. Not because he admitted to having anxiety, of course. But because now he's *likable*. And worse than that, he's relatable.

Thanks a lot, Amanda. Now I don't want to fight with Basil anymore. I want to be his friend. I imagine us being chummy roommates, making popcorn, and having movie nights. And because I don't know if he is going to feel the same way, I can sense my own anxiety rising. What if he goes back to insulting me, making fun of my horse, and avoiding me? My feelings were better off when they didn't know they could be hurt.

He doesn't look like he wants to fight, though. He looks cornered, as if he's afraid of what I'll do next.

So I decide to be relatable, too. "I miss my mom a lot," I tell him. "She's back in Virginia. We've always been so close, but I don't talk to her now the way I used to. And that sucks."

Basil nods, relief on his face. I don't know if it's because he thought I'd laugh at him for missing his mother, or that it simply feels good to admit he misses her. He asks, "Do you miss her cooking, too?"

I do have to laugh at that. "Oh, no. My mom is a terrible cook. We're very big on takeout and delivery in my family. When I manage to cook something really well, I feel *farther* from my mom, not closer!"

Basil cracks a smile at that, and the skin around his eyes crinkles so delightfully that I feel a hot little rush of sensation run over my skin. It's enough to make me clench my toes and press my hands tightly together, waiting for the tingling to subside.

It takes a moment. I feel like as long as Basil is sharing this delighted smile with me, I'll be riveted to this spot, watching him with a feeling that is suspiciously like, that is verging upon, which is almost...

...like I might have a tiny crush on Basil Han.

Chapter Ten

RIGHT BEFORE MAX and Stephen left for the port, Max promised me he'd have Feather's former owner send up all her records. "Very thorough woman," he'd assured me. "Keeps training logs on all the horses she breeds. I'm sure you'll know just where to start with her once you've gone over her paperwork."

So when a brown envelope is stuffed into the farm mailbox along with the usual assortment of mailers and horse supply catalogs, I feel a stir of excitement that's much easier to explain that the thrill I felt with Basil the day before.

After all, I don't know anything about Feather. Breeding, background, reason for existing on this earth: everything about Feather is a mystery. It's great when Max has a psychic moment with a horse, but that's not exactly how most of us work in the equestrian world. There's usually a little more deliberation and fact-finding that goes into the purchase of a horse.

So I rip open the envelope while my car is still running, air conditioner blowing cold air at my face and fluttering the pages as I pull them free. I thumb quickly through the thin printer sheets, hoping for a heavier stock that will be her registration, praying for something European and Olde World like Jock, like the rest of the Wellington horses.

Nope, nothing here.

Okay, that's fine. Maybe her registration is digital or something. I flick through the dozen or so pages with a little more care this time, glancing at each page. There are five handwritten pages of notes, with dates heading each paragraph, so that'll be the training diary. I'll have to read those closely. Then there are three pages of health records, going all the way back to—I raise my eyebrows—the day she was foaled. Four years and two months ago.

Feather's only four! But they thought she was five. Well, that's interesting. Good, bad, I'm not sure, so I'm just labeling it as interesting for now. I look at the vet notes with an appraising eye, checking for surgeries or anything else worrisome.

Nothing but vaccinations, worming, and…reiki?

Yes, there's a lot of reiki on here.

Like, six sessions a year of reiki.

I don't even know what reiki *is*, but Feather is apparently very experienced with it. Far more so than she is with any veterinary work. I see vaccinations, but nothing else. I mean, if she doesn't ever get hurt, yay? But also, I hope she isn't on a reiki-only health plan.

And next I find, dated from last summer, a talk with an animal communicator.

An animal communicator? That's, um, unconventional.

But fine, I know a few highly respected trainers who swear by their horse psychics, and if it works, great. What did Feather tell this medium of hers? I squint at the handwriting's squashed-together letters and choke back a disbelieving laugh.

"Feather prefers to make her own choices about work and expects to be respected."

Well, gosh, Feather, wouldn't we all like to make our own choices and be respected? I'm pretty sure it doesn't take a degree in animal psychic communication to figure *that* out.

I chalk up the mind-reading to a charlatan and move on.

The last page is not, as I was hoping, a print-out of a registration from some obscure European breed agency. By now I've accepted that I won't find anything labeling Feather as an Elite Hanoverian or a registered KWPN (I can never remember what those letters stand for). But I can learn to live with a registered Austrian Goatherder Horse or a Welsh Village Trotter or something along those lines, as long as she has *some* bloodline to boast about.

Instead, what I find is a printed certificate with an image of a cartoonish Pegasus above some frilly lettering informing me that Lucky Feather, chestnut mare, is a certified Celestial Being with all the rights and privileges granted to such beings on this earthly plane. It's signed by Sylvia Britton, Celestial Being Master Communicator Level III.

I put down the paper and gaze blindly through the windshield, shock taking all the wind out of me.

She's not a registered Hanoverian or anything else recognizable. She's nothing.

No, this is worse than nothing. It's much worse. It's bizarre.

What on earth did Max fall for? Celestial beings and animal communicators and reiki in place of veterinary records—and he paid money for this horse? And then paid *me* for six months of hard work with her?

Take it easy, I tell myself. She's a lovely horse. This doesn't change any of that. Breeding and registrations don't mean she isn't an athletic horse with a ton of potential.

I know that, deep down. I *know* that.

But all of this psychic woo-woo isn't doing me any good, especially when there's a barn full of blue-bloods just beyond this house. I should have been more discerning; I should have made Max disclose this stuff before I accepted her as half a year's pay. I should have told him to go find me a horse with actual breeding and potential.

God. And you know what's worse? Basil is going to laugh his head off when he sees this stuff.

Literally, just yesterday, I was accusing him of wanting my horse for himself. And now he's going to find out she's a mutt straight out of the New Age section of the bookstore.

There's no way he won't make fun of me for this. And the worst part is, I can't even blame him for it. This situation is ridiculous, and I'm ridiculous for falling for it.

A few fat raindrops splash on the windshield. The prospect of getting stuck in the car during a thunderstorm gets me to switch off the car and go into the house. I toss the mail on the console table just inside the front door, adding to a dangerously listing stack of mailers and catalogs. I know I'll have to go through it and throw stuff away before the pile reaches the ceiling, but I'm not up to it quite yet. Also, I'm secretly hoping the housekeeper will do it for me.

The envelope of Feather's history stays at my side until I reach my bedroom, where I intend to find a very good hiding place for it. I survey my messy little room, contemplating my options. Under my mattress, or in my closet, stuffed underneath the heels I wore to the Christmas ball so many months ago?

But before I can get the envelope stashed, Basil shows up, bearing yet another glass of mint lemonade—he's really into that stuff, but I admit however he's making it is working, because it's delicious. I accept the glass with a grateful smile. We got along yesterday, and we're getting along today, too, I guess.

This is nice.

He's wearing a quizzical expression. "What's that?" he asks, nodding at my shameful mail.

"Nothing, nosy," I retort, and then instantly feel ashamed. "It's Feather's health records," I admit, in a more subdued tone. "I'm just filing them away."

"Oh, anything good in there? It's a pretty fat envelope."

"Nothing," I lie. "Very boring. Spring shots, fall shots."

"Ah well," he says. "Did you hear that?"

Basil walks into the hall before I can answer him. I hear the front door opening, and then he says, "Hello, Posey!"

I drop the envelope and dart into the hallway. Posey is coming inside, smiling curiously at Basil. "Hi there," she says cheerfully. "How's it going, Basil?"

"Pretty good," he replies. He looks at me, smiles, and says, "Posey's here."

"That was odd," Posey says as I hustle her into my bedroom and shut the door. "What happened to grouchy Basil?"

"I exorcised him," I tell her, and explain about our conversation yesterday. "So now I guess we're friends? It's weird."

"Do you think his whole hangup was that he has anxiety? Maybe it's really pronounced, and he's embarrassed about it."

"Could be," I say, just as Posey's eyes fall on the envelope.

She picks it up and brandishes it at me. "News?"

"Nothing exciting."

Posey glances at the return address. "Sylvia Britton! Would you believe I was at her barn earlier this year? She had a Thoroughbred broodmare I was interested in."

Honestly, the horse world is so small sometimes I think we all just exist in a Petri dish. "You're kidding. That's where Feather came from."

"Oh, wow." Posey puts down the envelope as if it might explode. "Did you tell me that before?"

"No...why?"

"Only, Sylvia's a bit strange," Posey says. "I'm surprised I didn't tell you about it before. Oh, you were in Virginia visiting your parents, that's why."

"Tell me," I say, sitting down on the bed. My knees are suddenly weak. "Tell me everything."

"Well, her farm is really nice," Posey begins. "Horses are fat and shiny. Kids wear their helmets. Tack is clean."

"Get to the weird part."

Posey winces. "She was wearing about fifteen crystals in leather thongs around her neck and she had a groom perform a cleansing ritual with a smudge of sage around the horse I was there to see."

"Oh, gosh." It's worse than I thought. "Sage, huh? That stuff stinks."

"Then she anointed the horse's head with essential oils."

"Gosh." I can't think of anything else to day. "I mean...gosh."

Posey nods. "She rode the horse for me first, even though I thought I made it clear I was interested in her as a broodmare. Super good breeding, not sure why she wasn't already in a program. Anyway, Sylvia made sure the horse's head was pointed to the north at the mounting block, because that's the horse's cardinal direction, and if I didn't make sure to align the horse to the north, I'd have a lame horse on my hands."

I have no more words. Not even gosh.

"The horse was nice," she reflects. "And very sound. I got her bred on the first jump, and she's out in our field this minute."

"Did you have her head pointing north when you bred her?"

Posey laughs. "You know, now that you mention it, I think she *was* facing north. Do you think that's why she got in foal so easily?"

I rub my face. "Did she say anything about Celestial Beings?" I ask finally.

Posey shakes her head. "No, but they sound awesome."

I shake out the paperwork and hand it over to Posey, ready to be laughed out of existence. She flips through the pages, her eyes growing wider with every turn of paper. When she gets to the Celestial Being registration, she gives me a sympathetic look. "Oh, Kayla."

"I know."

"I'm running this place for six months and getting paid with a Celestial Being," I say, not sure if I should laugh or cry. "I thought she was worth twenty grand, at least! I thought I was actually getting a really sweet deal."

Posey pulls me close for a comforting hug. "There's no such thing as a free lunch in Hollywood or a sweet deal in horses," she reminds me, chin bouncing on my shoulder. "But she's still nice. And she's certified celestial, which you don't see every day. So that's something."

I pull away. "I'm not ready to joke about it."

"Sorry," Posey says. "Want to go grab some lunch? That's why I stopped by, actually. I was just driving past and thought, hey, wonder if Kayla wants to get some food."

"Definitely," I agree. "Can we go somewhere with pie? I think I need pie."

The pie cheers me up so much that I almost forget about the Celestial Being paperwork. I have three slices, one of Key Lime, one of French Silk, and one of apple. Posey eats a Caesar salad and watches me, clearly impressed by my follow-through. Then she suggests I take home a slice of pie for Basil. And since he was being so nice earlier, I decide to bring home an entire pie.

"We can split it for dessert," I explain.

"You're eating dessert together now?"

"I know," I say. "I didn't expect it, either. But it's surprisingly nice not fighting with him constantly."

Posey drops me off at home and drives off without coming inside, saying Adam will be waiting at the farm with another ten-mile long list of work for her. She says this with a smile on her face, which makes me think being overworked with Adam is better than being well-rested alone.

Basil is in the kitchen, looking at his phone and sipping tea. "Hello, roomie," he says in a surprisingly warm tone. "Nice lunch out?"

"Yes," I reply, and put the takeout box in front of him. "I brought you some."

He opens the box and does a double take. "Is this a key lime pie?"

"You like this kind, right?"

"Of course I do. Mind if I have some right now?"

"Be my guest."

"Did you want some?"

"Oh, no," I laugh. "That's what I had for lunch."

"You had...pie? For lunch?"

"Duh, it's delicious and full of vitamin C."

Basil is laughing now. He gets down a plate and serves himself a slice of pie, and once he's sat down with it, he asks, "So Feather's records...anything interesting in there? Any surprises?"

I look at him sharply. "What do you know?"

"A little," he says. "I've actually been to Sylvia's barn."

"You have, too? Has everyone been there but me?"

"Well, she sells nice horses, and she's not far away from the farm in Wellington."

"Oh, right." I guess if Max was going to look at horses there, it makes sense that Basil would have gone along, too. "Was it Feather?"

"Hmm?"

"Did you go see Feather? With Max?"

"Oh." He forks up a piece of pie, contemplates it. "No. Different time."

"And the sage and the oils..." I prompt.

"Yes," he agrees. "In full effect."

"I guess Max likes that kind of thing," I say, considering my drama-prone boss. "The rituals and the spirituality. It probably makes him feel special, like he's doing something unique. I guess he is. It's not like Sylvia is in a cult or something."

Basil coughs and puts down his fork.

I gaze at him suspiciously. "Basil?"

"Hmm?" He wipes his mouth with a napkin. "What?"

"She's not in a cult, is she?"

"Who, Sylvia?" Basil laughs. "Well, how would I know that? You can't exactly just ask someone if they're in a cult. It's considered rude. Also, there's always the risk they'll say yes and then try to convert you."

"Good point," I agree, although I still think there was something a bit odd about the timing of that cough. I put my chin on my fist, brooding over the possibilities, until Basil finishes his pie.

"That was amazing," he says. "Now, how about we go work with Feather?"

"What?" I stare at him, and the idea of cults goes right out of my head.

"You want to ride that Celestial Being of yours, right?"

"Celestial—you knew?" I want to hug him. I want to smack him. I can't decide which would make me feel better. "All this time, did you know?"

"I'm afraid so," Basil admits. His smile twinkles from his lips to his chocolate-brown eyes, and I have a hard time feeling mad at him. "But look at it this way: she's a rare breed, and that's pretty exciting, right? Not your every day warmblood. *Everyone* has something shiny and European. But when everyone's special, no one's special, isn't that the saying?"

"It's from a Pixar movie," I snort. "But yeah, it's true. I guess."

"Well, I owe you for this pie," he says. "So, let's go ride her."

Chapter Eleven

"Well, first off, you can't look so scared."

I turn to glower at Basil's light-hearted criticism, but he just gives me a smile in return. This smile which is new to me, but which he keeps turning on for me like a lightbulb in a dark room.

It's almost enough to make me forget the task at hand.

But not quite enough.

"I'm not scared," I grumble.

Yeah, that's a lie. I am scared. Feather is tacked up and waiting for me to mount, and suddenly I've got the coldest pair of feet in history. I might as well be standing on an iceberg. I can't ride this mare. She's an untrained chestnut mare who stands seventeen hands high and is probably athletic enough to buck me straight to the moon. Getting on Feather sounds like the worst idea of the year. The century. The millennium. I could go on.

With hopeless longing for a simpler way, I remember the long yearlings I rode over the winter at Posey and Adam's farm. They were so small, so sweet and trusting. With a few exceptions, those babies would no more think of bucking me off than they'd consider skipping their breakfast. Posey always said in the Thoroughbred business, they started their horses before the horses knew they could form opinions. That was the secret, she said, to easy saddle-breaking. Always grinning, but she had a real point.

The Sweetheart Horse

Why isn't Feather eighteen months old and full of gentle curiosity about the human who wanted to climb on her back? Because the look four-year-old Feather is giving me right now is more astonished than curious or trusting. She cranes her neck around to look at me and lips at the saddle flap.

"I thought you said you'd started horses before," Basil says, his tone growing suspicious. "You *have*, haven't you? Because that bit's important."

"I have," I say, but my voice is anything but convincing. I step backwards off the mounting block, completely out of courage.

Feather plunges forward, and Basil has little choice but to let her circle around us. Her energy is impatient and confused. My Celestial Being is perturbed by my lack of action. And my assistant is annoyed by my lack of gumption. I can tell by his expression, which is defaulting back to his grouchy face. So I try to explain myself.

"I've started young horses, but they were—*younger.* And smaller. And, oh, I don't know, it was in a very controlled system where it didn't feel like there was a ton of room for things to go wrong. Whereas we're just standing in the middle of the covered arena."

I gesture at the vast open space around us. While it's fenced in on all four sides and the gate is closed, the covered arena is very large. Plenty of room for shenanigans.

"I heard they start racehorses in their stalls," Basil says. "Are you saying you want to get on her in the stall?"

"Oh, gosh, no. I'd hit my head on the beams. She's three feet taller than those little racehorses, that's the thing."

"She's a big girl, alright," Basil agrees, surveying my mare. Is it my imagination, or does he look the tiniest bit covetous?

No, we already worked this argument out, and I think he's made it clear he doesn't envy me. Especially when she shoves her nose down to the ground, sniffs the arena footing with an elaborate snort, and then begins pawing energetically. Dirt pelts my boots and half-chaps. Basil takes a step back to avoid getting caught by a hoof. "Knock that off," he growls, tugging on the reins. "Get back around to the block, you big monster."

"I don't think I can do this," I admit. "I just can't ride her."

For a moment, I feel profound relief...and then it's gone, and then I cringe, because I can't believe I said something so pathetic in front of Basil. *To* Basil. Where's my pride?

Swamped beneath a tsunami of nerves, that's where.

But Basil doesn't seem too surprised that I've lost my desire to ride my young horse. And instead of teasing me about it, he offers me some advice. "It's normal to feel anxious about getting on a horse for the first time," he says. "But listen to me for a moment. All you have to do is get on her back and sit quietly. I'm at her head. I'll keep her feet moving. You won't have a thing to worry about."

"And you'll keep her head up," I remind him. "Right?"

Head up, can't buck. The oldest truth in the world. Unless Feather really is remarkably athletic and can figure out how to turn into a bronco without getting her head between her knees.

"I'll keep her head up," Basil agrees. "But as long as her feet are moving forward, I think you'll find she won't want to buck. I mean, just look at that face." He gestures towards Feather, who has stopped pawing and is standing next to the mounting block like an old, experienced pony. She gazes at the two of us with the wide eyes of an ingenue. Basil asks, "Do you think she wants to put on a bucking bronco routine with you? Because I don't see it."

"Okay," I sigh, realizing there's no way around this now. All that's standing between me and my mare is nerves. That's simply not a good enough reason not to start her this afternoon, and I know it. I nod at Basil, putting on my steeliest expression to mask my inner terror. "Let's do it."

Basil gives me an understanding look. "It's going to be fine."

For some reason, I believe him.

I step back onto the mounting block, and as Basil brings Feather around, I give the saddle a good wiggle. She turns to look at me with an inquiring expression. For a moment she has the sweet, questioning look of a yearling, and I almost forget how frightened I am.

Almost.

"Alright," Basil tells the mare, jiggling her reins to hold her attention. "Stand up straight so your mum can climb on."

It's odd to hear Basil call me Feather's mother; that's the kind of talk I thought was reserved for girls and horses. At the riding school back home, my mother couldn't remember anyone's names but the horse's, so she called people by their horse's names—and she wasn't the only one. "Clyde's mom is having a birthday party, and she wants you to come," she might say, or in a conversation at a horse show, I'd hear her saying to another horse show mom, "look at Princess's mom! She really looks cute in those new boots." And of course Posey is Lucky's mom, to Evie and me.

Although, I've never called Amanda any horse's mom. Not sure why that is. Maybe because her horses are all for sale—

"Are you getting on, or does she have to circle again?" Basil demands, and I come back to the present. I do a quick check of my body, making sure everything is where it needs to be for this first ride.

Hat on head. Hands on saddle. Heart on sleeve.

In one quick movement, I slide my boot into the stirrup and swing up into the saddle.

I'm very good at mounting. Everyone says so. I glance at Basil and note his impressed expression.

The only one who isn't wowed by what a fantastic mount that was is Feather. She's too busy figuring out what on earth just happened. She stands still for a moment, body tense, ears flicked back at me. Then she adjusts herself, and the stiffness in her spine releases.

"She's been ridden before," I say, and Basil nods.

It's almost anti-climactic. For a few days, I was almost convinced no one had started Feather. That I might be the first person ever to sit on her back—a feat almost as awesome as it was frightening. Now I'm just the tiniest, most unreasonably bit disappointed.

"It was probably a while ago," Basil suggests. "And you don't know how much work was actually done on her."

As if he's reassuring me that she really is a blank slate.

"Well," I say, "I guess we find out now."

Basil is good at the tedious task of guiding her around the arena, keeping her to a sedate walk while I concentrate on moving with her unbalanced walk. Riding the Thoroughbred babies taught me that a young horse will often panic when they can't figure out how to move with a rider's weight changing their balance, so I try to keep my hips fluid and my lower back soft as she carefully considers each step. It's a constantly changing process, made even more complicated by her potential for sudden moves. If she spooks, which I really hope she doesn't, I have to be able to move with her without flying out of the saddle; if she bolts, which I *really really* hope she doesn't, I have to shift my center of gravity forward to stay with her or risk scaring her even more badly than whatever outside force set her off in the first place.

Minor stuff. Starting young horses is a blast, right? This is why I prefer the small ones.

After five minutes of walking around the arena, though, it becomes pretty evident this particular Celestial Being (no matter how hard I try, I can't stop thinking of her with that stupid name) is not in a hurry to spook or bolt. In fact, her primary interest turns out to be rubbing her head against Basil's shoulder. He grunts and gives her a gentle push as she goes in for another scratching session. "Your mare is itchy, madam," he says over his shoulder in an exaggerated butler voice. "May I suggest the tea tree oil shampoo in the wash-rack."

"Sorry about that," I giggle, unable to do anything to save him from Feather's determined itching. I have to sit still up here and he has to take all the abuse. It's a pretty pleasing turn of events. "I promise to give her a good scrubbing when we go in."

"Now's probably a good time," he suggests, and carefully reins Feather back to a halt. She shifts from side to side, pushing her head at him playfully. "Get off her before she forgets to behave."

"Well, you have been a huge help." I carefully hop down from the saddle. Feather side-steps to get a good look at me, as if she forgot what I looked like while I was on her back. I hold out my hand for her to sniff, wishing I'd remembered to put some treats in my pockets. "Do you have a lot of experience with green-broke horses?"

Basil rubs his hand along her neck. "I've done a few. Back in England. I was a working pupil at a farm with quite a lot of home-breds for a while."

"Oh? Whose farm?" Suddenly I'm keen to know what he's been up to out in the world, Mr. Han Worldwide and his mysterious background before he burst onto the Ocala scene with that Grand Prix win last month.

"The Hullworth brothers," Basil says, looking away from me as if he's embarrassed. "Patrick and Ian Hullworth."

"*Oh.*" I can't help my surprised reply. The Hullworth brothers are old-school English horsemen. Martin Hullworth, their father, was an Olympian in the 1960s. Ian went to the Olympics five times; Patrick twice. They were famous for what they weren't: the Hullworths weren't splashy, diamond-encrusted international show jumpers, but a pair of gruff Yorkshire farmers who kept their horses in old stone barns and were famously photographed riding a tractor to the village pub after a hard day's work.

I can imagine Basil Han working on those rocky Yorkshire dales with those two old billy goats about as well as I can imagine Feather working the cosmetics counter at Nordstrom.

"You must have learned a lot there," I venture, as Basil doesn't offer any further elaboration.

He thrusts Feather's reins at me and turns away, starting back to the barn. Over his shoulder, he says, "A lot," and with those two words, I'm left wondering if something awful happened to Basil at the Hullworth farm.

Chapter Twelve

SOMETHING AWFUL. I'M so dramatic.

I chuckle to myself as I run warm water into a bucket, adding a generous dollop of the tea tree oil shampoo, which Basil suggested. Feather sidesteps and looks at me; she's gotten better in the crossties, but I'd still think twice before leaving her alone in the washrack, even to run into the tack room and grab something. My Celestial Being is picking up manners, but it's going to be a slow slog at her age.

Something awful. Why would I think Basil is harboring some kind of deep, dark secret about his time in Yorkshire? It's far more likely he doesn't want to talk about his past with me because he still doesn't think we're friends. Not *real* friends, anyway. He's being nice because we have to live and work together, that's all. And that's fair. I get it. That's what I decided yesterday too, right? That it was getting too difficult to live with my enemy, and we'd be better off with the air clear between us?

And now it is, and I was right. It *is* better. Basil and I are on good terms with each other.

And I should be fine with that; I *was* fine with that, up until this afternoon. But then, Basil had to go and be helpful. And that changes things for me. I'm a sucker for a person who has gone out of his way to help me. Call me crazy, call me a softie, but I was raised to be kind. I was raised to be gracious. I was fortunate enough to be mentored and supported by giving and generous people. And so when I'm helped, I want to offer help in return.

There's not much I can do for Basil that I'm not already doing, and it's all technically in my job description anyway—mucking out, feeding, turnout, making sure no one gets zapped by lightning without that electricity going through me, first. But one thing I can do is listen. I'm a remarkably sympathetic listener. Some people have remarked that I'm the best listener they've ever poured out their hearts to, not to brag or anything. And enough people have discovered my sympathetic ear over the years that I've gained a bit of a sixth sense about secrets that want some space to breathe.

At least, I'd like to think I have.

"Stand still, miss," I tell Feather as she shifts in the wash-rack, craning her neck around to get a better look at what I'm up to. I hold up the sudsy wash bucket and let her sniff the bubbles. She snorts. "It's a nice soapy bath, for your itches," I say. She sticks out her pink tongue and touches the froth, then steps back, making a face.

"I didn't say soapy bath, *for food*," I laugh, and dip in the sponge, getting a big dollop of froth and slapping it onto her neck. Feather is alarmed at first, then gets into the feeling and leans into my hand as I scrub the shampoo into a foamy lather. "This will make your skin feel nice," I croon, getting into the spirit of things. She likes it when I talk to her. "You'll be comfy and cozy and oh-so-dozy..."

Basil walks by, his hands in his pockets, his face far away, and I suddenly forget how to rhyme words.

"Hey," Basil says, looking up from his laptop. He's sitting at the kitchen counter with a sandwich on a plate next to his elbow. "You want anything to eat?"

I'm so surprised by the offer, I don't even have an answer. I open the fridge door without thinking, on total autopilot; it's past two o'clock and I'm starving.

"Guess not," he says, watching me stand in the open door.

"Oh, my goodness, I opened the door without even knowing I was doing it." I close it again. "Sorry, I must need a nap."

Basil pushes the plate towards me.

Something clicks in my hazy brain. "Wait, did you make me a sandwich or something?"

"I had a big hoagie roll, so I made the whole thing. You're welcome to the other half, though. It was way too much."

I could easily eat an entire hoagie, but I elect not to share this information. Basil's whippet-slim, but I suppose it's less about dieting and self-control and more that he has unattainable, rich-person genetics—a fault of his which I simply have to learn to live with.

In the meantime, half a sandwich that I don't have to make sounds like a pretty good deal. I sit down, making sure there's an empty barstool between us for a buffer zone, and accept the plate he pushes down the counter to me. "Feather already seems less itchy," I say, looking for a good place to get started on the huge sandwich. "Thanks for the shampoo."

"No problem. Jock tends to get sweet itch in the summer, so I keep heavy-duty stuff on hand. He was happier up north."

I glance at him curiously. "Where did you have Jock before you came to Florida?"

"Vermont, until last spring. And upstate New York before that. He's from Pennsylvania, actually. A real northern horse, I suppose. Last summer was his first full one in Florida, and he had a big reaction to the bugs here. But it's been manageable."

"How long have you had him?" I want information now; I want to get to the heart of his weird demeanor when he mentioned the Hullworths. "Long time?"

"Just two years," Basil replies, his eyes on his laptop. "He was meant to be a sales investment, but he went so well for me, I was able to keep him."

"Do you usually have a lot of sales horses?"

He frowns, still looking at his screen. "I've had a few at a time, yes. But right now, obviously, I don't have any. I wouldn't sell Jock for anything." His voice grows fierce, as if I was suggesting that I could get a really good price for his horse.

"That's how I feel about Crabby," I say, ignoring his aggressive tone—I don't think it's meant for me. "But I've never actually had a sales horse. I've just ridden other people's. It must be really hard, putting all that time into a horse and then just selling them off. I guess you get used to them coming and going, though."

He glances at me, one eyebrow curving skeptically. "You think I just pat them goodbye and forget about them? Every single one is hard to let go."

"Well, I didn't mean—I just guess you have to learn to forget them, right?"

Basil closes the laptop and leans across the empty stool, closing the distance between us as if he really needs to make his point. "I don't forget *any* of the horses I've sold."

He sits back on his stool and puts his elbows on the counter, sighing.

I put down the sandwich, feeling like I've been unfairly attacked by its maker. "I didn't mean anything by it, Basil. I was just observing that it must be hard for them to leave after you ride them and get attached. That's pretty cool that you keep up with them, actually. I've never heard of anyone doing that. More trainers should have policies like that in place."

Basil chuckles. "You should tell my uncle that."

"Your uncle? Why?"

But he's done confiding in me. Basil stands up and scoops his laptop under one arm. "I need a nap," he announces. "Riding seven horses in this heat is taking it out of me. Keep it down, okay?"

And he marches out of the kitchen before I can protest that I *never* make the teensiest bit of noise.

Pretty weird, I think, turning my attention back to my sandwich. And pretty impressive, if what he said is true. It's nice to know that Basil has that kind of heart; that he cares about horses beyond their ability to bring in a dollar. Not what I would have expected of Mr. Han Worldwide, honestly.

But over the past week he's been giving me a lot of clues that he's not what I originally thought. Basil came across as another spoiled rich boy at first, but the guy is more than privilege and money and a slight, sexy British accent. He's got problems, he has regrets, he might even have a big heart. He certainly has a soft touch with horses. And if I'm being perfectly, painfully honest with myself...well, all of those things hit a sweet spot with me.

Crap. I better not start giving Basil any more credit, or I'm going to start thinking—like Posey suggested—that he could be the answer to my eternal cash-flow problems.

Basil had the right idea about a nap. Once I've finished that monster of a sandwich, I have no choice but to fall asleep myself—after a quick shower, naturally. There's nothing quite like sinking into my bed for an afternoon nap, clean and lotioned and cool, with the blinds closed against the blazing summer sun. And since it's only three o'clock, I don't even have to set an alarm. I'll wake up well before it's time to feed dinner at six, *and* all the horses are inside, so lightning isn't an issue, either.

Utter bliss.

I must have fallen asleep immediately, because when my eyes flip open to a dim and uncomfortably warm room, I feel like no time has passed at all. The worst kind of nap. "Ugh," I mutter, pushing myself up on my elbows. "Why is it so hot?"

Then I realize it's quiet as well. My overhead fan isn't spinning, and there's no comforting hum from the little one I keep by the bed.

I lean over and pick up my phone from the charger.

Low Battery Warning.

"Oh, come on..."

I glance at my laptop. No green light on the charger. I reach out to my bedside lamp and flick the switch. Nothing.

"Oh, for the love of God, Ocala, *why?*"

Our power goes out with no reason here. Not because of lightning—we never lose electricity during the most fierce of thunderstorms. Not because of downpours or wind. No, our power outages only come on sunny days when absolutely nothing is going on in the neighborhood. The hotter the afternoon, the better, it seems.

And now it's almost five, which means I'm probably going to be feeding horses without power this evening. That poses a problem. The well is electric, for one thing, so if any of the pasture troughs are low, I won't be able to fill them. The stall fans won't be on, so the horses will be sweaty and annoyed (rather like I am right now, actually). And worst of all—for me—when I come inside from feeding in the heat, there will be neither air conditioning nor the prospect of a shower to cool me down...and no way to make dinner. I'll have to drive to town and pick something up.

What a pain.

I hear a thudding on the staircase and then Basil's footsteps in the hall outside. "Kayla?" he calls. "Kayla, do you know why the power is out?"

I sigh and pull on my discarded shirt and shorts. "It's so random here," I say, opening my door. "You'll get used to it."

He turns in the kitchen doorway, looking disoriented. He must have just woken up, too. "It's so hot already," he says.

"Yeah, air conditioning doesn't exactly stay inside Florida houses," I sigh. "Especially with all those western-facing windows on the house. Maybe we'll get lucky and a storm cloud will block the sun before it hits ninety in here."

"Ninety *degrees*," Basil clarifies. "Indoors. Did you mean to say that?"

"Yeah. It can get bad, Basil. We really need an emergency generator." I rub my face; it's already getting sweaty in here. "Look, I'm gonna go out and feed early, okay? Just to get things out of the way. Everything in the kitchen is electric, so I'm going to have to head into town to find dinner. You can come, if you want."

I think about taking Basil to dinner with me and feel a little wobble of excitement in the vicinity of my stomach. Would he agree to go with me? Would we have a nice, friendly conversation over apps? Would he tell me all his secrets? I could tell him some of mine—provided he's interested in the story of the time I accidentally jumped a school horse over a six-foot jump when I wasn't even supposed to jump outside of riding lessons. Is that even a good story? I'm already second-guessing my conversation and he hasn't even agreed to come eat with me. I'm *sweating*. Why is this so complicated? Why isn't he answering me?

"You don't think the electric will come back on soon?" Basil's voice is at a higher pitch than usual. Maybe it's just the heat making us both crazy.

"The last time it randomly went out, it didn't come on until morning," I tell him, watching his face blanch. "Yeah, I know. Not ideal. It just hasn't happened to Max and Stephen yet, or we'd probably already have solar panels and a huge battery powering the house."

Basil mutters something about the power always staying on in Wellington and turns away, heading into the kitchen. He puts his hand on the fridge door, then stops, clearly remembering that opening the refrigerator is off-limits in a power outage. Especially in this kind of heat. "I'll come out and feed the horses with you," he decides. "Maybe there's a breeze out there."

Five minutes later, I can safely determine there is no breeze coming to save us. It's still and humid outside, with the sun hanging at its most glaring and hot angle of the afternoon. We walk out to the barn slowly, sunlight burning on our backs, and I try to think cold thoughts: frosty margaritas, waves crashing on a beach while snow falls from a gray sky overhead, penguins sliding down icebergs. The margaritas are at least attainable. Maybe a Mexican restaurant is in my future. Does Basil like tacos? Dumb question, everyone likes tacos.

The horses look grumpy and the barn is weirdly quiet with all the fans turned off. I have Basil unplug all the fans, just in case there's a power surge later, while I get the feed buckets ready. Then he helps me dole out dinner, the horses kicking their stall walls and rattling their water buckets impatiently all the while.

"It sounds like a high school marching band practice in here," Basil complains.

"The very first one," I suggest. "Before anyone knows what they're doing. I'm just thankful we don't have to ride anyone this evening," I add, as Basil brings back the last empty bucket. "Because, boy, they are in some serious moods."

"I don't blame them," Basil grumbles. "It's bloody horrible out here. *And* in the house. Maybe we should get a hotel room and put it on Max's credit card."

For some reason, the idea of getting a hotel room with Basil makes me blush and choke at the same time. I manage to turn it into something like a scoffing laugh. "You're joking, right?"

Basil squares his shoulders. "No, I'm not joking. Air conditioning's part of the deal. You wouldn't sign up to live in a house in Florida without it, would you?"

"Well, no, but the power goes out sometimes. That's just life."

Basil sniffs. "Well, it better not happen more often. I don't care for the heat." He looks around. "And I don't really like the idea of no electricity after dark, either."

I look at him for a moment, a thought so ludicrous it can't possibly be correct swirling in my brain. "It gets really dark out here," I say after a moment's consideration.

Basil's jaw tightens. "How dark?" he asks, with what seems like studied nonchalance.

"Oh my God, you're afraid of the dark." I cover my mouth, instantly sorry I said anything. It just burst out of me. "I didn't mean that. Sorry."

He gives me a narrow-eyed glare. "I'm not afraid of the dark! What a ridiculous thing to say! I just don't look forward to banging about the house while trying not to run down my phone battery."

"We have a bunch of flashlights," I assure him. "And hey, maybe there's a moon tonight." And I pull out my phone to check the moon phase while he splutters angrily about not caring if there's a moon in the sky tonight or ever.

But I mean, come on. No one complains this much about the dark unless they are a little, tiny, slightest bit afraid of it, right? He'll feel better if he knows there will be moonlight. I just know it.

"A waxing gibbous," I announce with satisfaction, once I find the info online. "Should be rising just after sunset. So that's good. We'll have some light out here."

"We won't *be* out here," Basil snaps. "We'll be in the house, melting. In the dark, which I am fine with."

"Listen, maybe it won't get to that," I say, changing tack. "The lights could come on at any minute. Let's just turn the horses out and go get some dinner."

"I'm not hungry now. I'm far too hot to eat anything."

"We'll go somewhere very cold and have drinks. Your appetite will come right back."

He can't help but be interested in cold and drinks, obviously. He peers at me, the peevishness leaving his face. "You have a place in mind?"

"The *perfect* place," I say. "I hope you like mariachi."

Basil looks completely bewildered. Hah! Finally, something I know more about.

Chapter Thirteen

EL BRONCO IS a classic Tex-Mex joint, with painted pottery suns smiling from the walls, striped blankets hanging from exposed ceiling beams, and a grinning mariachi band draped in velvet and silver walking from table to table. A local favorite, this restaurant gets so hopping it can be hard to grab a table in horse show season, but summer showing hasn't caught up with the winter circuit yet, so we're handed two massive menus and shown to a booth in the back without having to wait.

A server walks by with a sizzling platter of steak fajitas as we open our menus, and Basil looks after her appreciatively. "Well, that would certainly hit the spot," he says. "Do I do it? Do I get fajitas?"

"Dude, you do you. But I'm here for the margs and the cheese."

"The cheese?" He looks at me inquisitively, as if he expects me to recommend the cheese board, but before I can answer, there's a server standing before us with a notepad and an expectant expression.

"I'll get to the cheese," I promise. "Two margaritas, please?" I do not employ my high school Spanish at Mexican restaurants, unlike some people I know. Everyone in Ocala is at least a little bilingual, whether they realize it or not, but I figure a bad accent is the worst kind of patronizing. "On the rocks, with salt," I add.

"Two on the rocks, got it," the server mutters, and darts away.

"Okay, *now* tell me about the cheese. Is there a special cheese board?"

I have to smirk. Bless his English little heart. "No, but if you order one of these—" I tap the Combinations section of his menu, which has at least thirty different choices listed, "they will give you a plate that is basically three different entrees under a blanket of melted cheese, and then it's the world's best guessing game while you dig in and see what's in there. Enchiladas? Burritos? A chile relleno? You win, no matter what!"

Instead of looking excited, Basil looks slightly pained. "I don't know what any of those things are," he says.

"You don't know what—what enchiladas are?" I tilt my head at him. "How is that possible?"

"I mean, I've heard the word before, but—" He shifts uncomfortably and for a moment I think he might actually get up and leave. I remember his anxiety and realize that I'm pushing on a pressure point, putting him in an unfamiliar situation and then teasing him, however gently, about it.

"Hey," I say gently. "Look at me, Basil."

He flicks his dark eyes to mine, and I hold his gaze.

It's more stimulating than I expected.

For a moment we just gaze into one another's eyes, and I have the strangest feeling fluttering in my stomach and expanding in my chest, as if something important is happening, something I can never forget.

But of course that's just the hunger and the heat stroke talking. We're at a Mexican restaurant and a mariachi band is two booths away, singing at the tops of their lungs. Nothing life-changing is going to happen tonight unless there's a power surge and the house burns down while we're out.

And I'm pretty sure Max and Stephen have their grid proofed for that sort of thing.

"I mean," I begin falteringly, pulling my thoughts together with an effort. "What I meant to say was—have you never gotten Mexican food before? Because I can teach you about it. I'm an expert."

"There's just not that much of it in England," he says apologetically. "You know, Mexico is a *really* long way from the U.K., not a couple of hours away like it is here. We have other things, we have Indian, and we have Chinese, and we have a *lot* of Italian for some reason..."

"Well, today is your lucky day," I interrupt, ready to leap into action. "I can't believe you don't know about enchiladas, or—or—*any* of it! I'm ordering for you. No, even better, I'm ordering for both of us and we'll split some plates so you get to try all the good stuff."

I take his menu away from him so he's not tempted to go rogue and order on his own, and when the server returns with our sloshing goblets of margaritas, plus a basket of chips and a dish of salsa, I'm ready to give her a listing of what we need: "A combination twelve, a combination twenty-four, a combination thirty, a side of tamales, extra guacamole, and two extra plates."

She looks appreciatively at me as she writes it all down. "Coming right up. You must be hungry."

"Starving," I assure her.

"Seems like you just ordered a lot?" Basil suggests as the server departs, edging her way around the band, who are now just one booth away. "Like, half the restaurant?"

I wink at him. "Relax. It's all amazing for breakfast and lunch the next day, too. I could eat cold enchiladas all day, every day."

He picks up his heavy goblet and holds it up. "Well, a toast to my culinary education, I suppose. Or is it gastronomic?"

"I have no idea," I assure him, but I clink my glass to his, anyway. "A toast to your first big night of Tex-Mex, and a toast to the utility company. May they get our A/C back on soon."

"Hear, hear," Basil agrees, and we both take long, satisfying gulps of our margaritas. Basil smiles at his glass, then me, and I start to ask him if he's ever had a margarita before, but the mariachi band finally arrives at our table before I can say anything else, and for the next five minutes, all hope of conversation is lost.

When my order arrives, the sheer amount of food momentarily stuns Basil, especially since most of it is covered, as promised, under a thick blanket of pale melted cheese. I dish out a sampler plate for each of us, add a hefty dollop of guacamole, and push his portion to him with a smile. "Left to right. You ready?" I say, pointing. "Taco, that's easy. Eat that first before it gets soggy. Then bean burrito, chile relleno, chalupa, verde chicken enchilada, roja beef enchilada, cheese enchilada, and this is rice and refried beans. I didn't have room for the tamale, but here, we can split this plate." And I push the plate of tamales to the center of the table.

"Good God, woman." Basil surveys the selection of entrees with wide eyes.

I snort. I'm having a really good time shocking him with all this food. I should have ordered more, just to freak him out. Like I told him before, it's all good as leftovers, so none of it will go to waste.

Assuming the fridge is on when we get home.

"Relax, you don't have to finish it," I remind him. "Take a bite of everything and then rank it for me, worst to best."

"Seriously? Should I have a ballot sheet?"

"You can use your phone," I suggest. "Make a list."

He shakes his head at me, smiling like he's just taken my measure for the first time. "You're insane."

"Maybe." I take a bite of taco and smile serenely at him while I chew. "Eat the taco first," I remind him around a mouthful. "They're the only things that won't keep."

Still shaking his head, Basil picks up the taco—dropping half the interior, of course, because he's not careful to keep it horizontal—and takes a bite. I wait for the expression of heavenly happiness to spread over his face, as he realizes that tacos are the gods' own food, ambrosia in a corn tortilla. He chews, and after a moment, he nods to himself. It feels like triumph.

I know I'm watching him a little too carefully. It's just a taco, for heaven's sake. But I love tacos, and I want to know, for some reason, that Basil does too. I want to share this little hunk of delicious joy with him. That's all it is. Basil has turned out okay. Friendly, even. I'm starting to think our first meeting was just bad luck. Maybe we're going to get along just fine from here on out. That would be great. That would be amazing. That would be—

Slow down, Kayla. Real world, girl.

My mother's voice intrudes as if she's sitting in the booth next to me, watching me work myself into a frenzy over Basil. She's always so good at keeping me on track. When I hear her voice from a thousand miles away, I know it's a warning from my subconscious: don't get too excited about something that probably will never happen.

But that's not what this is.

I'm not getting, um, *ideas* about Basil. I am curious about him, I am interested in him, I am hoping we can become actual friends. That doesn't mean I'm hoping things will go any farther than that.

I have had a few moments where I've been overwhelmingly attracted to him, but that doesn't mean I want to rip off his clothes and go to town on him.

He's just a good-looking guy. A handsome guy. Okay, a sexy guy who looks amazing in a pair of breeches. But that doesn't mean I'm sitting here fantasizing about what his abs would feel like under my fingertips.

Okay, Kayla, I'm leaving now.

Yeah, Mom, I really don't blame you there.

Let's just drill this down to what it is. He's being helpful about Feather. That's all that's going on here. He's been helpful and understanding about Feather, and I am paying him back with a good dinner. Plus dropping some serious knowledge about tacos that this boy was desperately in need of. Look at him, chomping through that taco! He's going to crunch through his own fingers if he doesn't slow down. I know I've done well. Debt repaid.

Until the next time he helps me, I guess.

"Good stuff?" I ask sweetly as the last of the taco vanishes.

Basil widens his eyes at me as he swallows. "Fantastic," he says finally. "And that crumbly white cheese on top, what is it?"

"No idea, but it's my idea of heaven."

He gamely sets to on the rest of the plate, making appreciative noises and jotting down notes, to my intense amusement—and satisfaction. There's something very pleasing about introducing someone to your favorite food and finding they're instant fans of it, too. And more than that, I just feel pleased Basil likes something I knew about and he didn't.

He stops for a little break after a round of everything, and slides his phone around so I can see the scores. "Bean burrito six out of ten, green enchilada nine out of ten, interesting." I look up at him. "Are you not a bean man, Basil?"

"They're very salty." He lifts his empty glass and the server pounces, pouring him a fresh drink from a pitcher she's been wandering the floor with. "Oops. Now you'll have to drive us home."

I cover my glass with my hand to make sure she doesn't top off my drink, too. "Back to the dark, scary house," I laugh. "Getting drunk so the monsters won't get you?"

"I'm trusting you to keep the monsters away," Basil says.

"I can do that. I'm really scary."

"I know. I remember when you scared Jock."

I look at him. "You remember what?" I ask carefully.

"You were the one in the barn that night at the equestrian center." Basil picks up his fork again, but his eyes are on mine. Dark as a horse's eye, yet lit from within, catching the light from the votive candle on the table, and somehow sparkling at me with amusement. "You were digging through Melody O'Leno's tack trunks. What were you trying to find?"

"A noseband," I confess. "She was demanding a different noseband before the class and I couldn't find it. It was stuck in the lid of one of the trunks."

"You told me it was 'jacks-in-the-box,' not jack-in-the-boxes."

"And? What about it?"

"You're wrong," Basil says lightly. He picks up a chip and dips it into the salsa. "I looked it up. And it's 'jack-in-the-boxes'. That's the plural. I was right."

I consider him for a moment. He eats the chip, takes another. His smile is supremely smug. "I can't believe you looked it up," I say eventually. "How long after I said that to you did it take before you were googling it?"

"Just today, actually," Basil admits. "When you were riding Feather, I suddenly realized where I knew you from. It had been bothering me for weeks. I knew you were sort of familiar, but I just couldn't place you. Melody's groom, though. That makes sense. I've known Melody since I got to Florida last year, so if you were around her barn, I'd have seen you."

I don't really know what to say to that. Figuring out who I was had been bothering him for weeks, really?

I'd had no idea he'd given me that much thought.

And I don't love the image he has of me now. Working for his colleague in the Grand Prix ring, Melody. Someone who fetches and carries, who mucks out and fills water buckets. While he's a rider. The important one, the one in the saddle, jumping the sticks and bringing home the prize money to pay my meager salary.

I don't mind being Max and Stephen's farm-sitter in front of him; there's pride and prestige in being a farm manager.

But I hate for Basil to think of me as a groom.

Basil is digging back into his enchiladas, apparently unaware that he's upset the balance I thought we'd achieved. What does it matter? Even if I know about good food, I'm still just a groom to him. Beneath his notice, to the point where it took him three solid weeks to remember where he'd seen me before.

I can't fully explain my disappointment, but it's real.

Suddenly, I'm not hungry anymore. The server comes back, notices I'm not eating, and slips away to the kitchen for some takeaway containers. Basil, meanwhile, cleans his plate and eats the tamales as well. *Someone* likes Mexican food, I think sourly as I stack my half of the burrito and enchiladas into one of the boxes. I suppose now he'll tell all his friends that he discovered it on his own. Or maybe he'll be generous and say his *groom* turned him onto it.

Basil doesn't notice I've gone quiet, or that I quit eating. He picks up his phone and updates his food rankings, moving the tamales up to spot number one, and shows it to me with a grin. I nod and smile, secretly thinking that he has very good taste. Tamales really are sensational, though I'm not sure they're better than tacos.

And then, in the ultimate boss-move, Basil picks up the check before I can reach for it. I watch him drop a credit card onto the tray and bite my lip. Dinner was *my* idea. He should at least offer to split, not take the check without even asking, like he's taking the help out for a little treat after a hard day's work. I'm stewing silently as the server takes the bill away to run the credit card at the register. All I want to do is take my leftovers, get in the car, and get home to find a cold house and a hot shower waiting for me. No conversation, no smiles, no heart-pounding moments when our eyes meet and I have the strange and shivering sensation that something momentous is happening.

Just air conditioning and soap. That's all I want.

Really. I promise. Nothing else. I close my eyes and wish for electricity.

"Kayla? Hey, what are you doing here?"

I open them with a start.

Posey and Adam are standing by the table, and Posey is looking between Basil and me with a delighted expression.

I try to send her a telepathic message: *No, this isn't happening. Not what you think. Stop smiling like that!*

But Basil steps in and says the wrong thing, as one would expect. "Kayla here took me out for a night at her favorite restaurant," he announces with gusto. "I'm honored *and* stuffed, as you can see."

Posey flashes me a delighted look before she holds out her hand to Basil. I notice she's clean and showered; the electricity is still humming away at Malone-Salazar Farm, of course. "It's very nice to see the two of you out together," she declares.

Is she purposely reading way too much into this dinner?

"The power's out," I tell her. "And Basil is new to Mexican food."

"Is that right?" She looks him over speculatively. "Letting Kayla show you the ropes?"

"That's exactly it," he replies, with a droll little smile. "She's the boss!"

I realize Basil is just the tiniest bit drunk. How many margaritas did the server pour him? Maybe I couldn't have afforded the check, anyway. My budget doesn't extend to more than one. He confirms my suspicion when he continues, "I've heard *you* are the berry best of bosses, Pose."

Berry?

Posey's smile grows rather fixed as she realizes what she's dealing with here. Before they can get into an endlessly spiraling conversation, I take Basil by the hand, intent on dragging him to the door.

Basil looks at me, then down at my hand. Suddenly, his fingers tighten around mine. He has strong hands from riding tough horses, and the pressure is startling.

Almost painful, but in a stimulating way.

For a moment, my head spins.

Then I get control of myself. Because that's what I do. I find my way back to the real world. The only world that matters. With a quick twist of my fingers, I free them from Basil's grasp. They seem to burn with remembered sensation, and I press my fingernails into the tabletop, gouging the weathered wood.

"Gotta head home," I say to Posey and Adam. "This one needs his bed." I grimace over at Basil, who is regarding our unclasped hands with a brooding expression. He's already entering the introspective stage of drunkenness. Something tells me he's a very annoying drinker.

"I see," Posey says, guardedly amused. "Will you guys be alright?"

"I've got it under control," I assure her. "Have a nice dinner! Goodnight!" I can't scramble out of there fast enough; I nearly forget my purse. Adam hands it to me with a gracious smile, while Posey tucks a hand into the crook of his free arm, her curious gaze following me right out the door.

Basil trails me out of the restaurant, taking my hand again as we step outside into the humid night. Lightning is flickering in the distance, illuminating a giant cloud criss-crossed by the black grid of power lines. It reminds me of our predicament at home. "All the gods

The Sweetheart Horse

I can think of, from Athena to Zeus, please let the power be on," I pray aloud. "Basil, come on. Let's get out of here."

But Basil's forward momentum has run down, and he's standing in the center of the parking lot with a faraway expression on his face. Experiencing a vision? Muttering an oath to the gods about never allowing Basil near tequila again, as a sort of addendum to my first prayer, I wave my hands in his face. "Basil! Hello! You're going to get run over by a redneck in a two-ton truck if you stand here."

He shakes his head gently and then his dark eyes fasten on mine. They're wide and surprisingly lucid, as if he's just stepped out of his intoxication and rejoined us in the land of the sober. "You're a remarkable girl," he says to me.

"What? Come on, come get in the car." It's not easy shaking off his words; who pays a compliment like that? Drunk men, that's who. In the real world, do they say things like *remarkable*? No, never. I tug on his arm; I'm not about to grab his hand again. His bicep is firm beneath my grip, and I bite my lip for a moment before I get hold of myself. "Basil, come on."

He lets me guide him to my Cadillac and obediently slips into the passenger seat when I open the creaking door for him. I slam it shut, and he looks up at me through the glass.

I look back at him, allowing myself to get lost in those deep brown eyes.

Just this once.

A remarkable girl.

Such a weird thing to say. Such a nice, weird thing to say.

"Let's get you home," I say, more to myself than to Basil, and I head around to the driver's side, keys in hand. I'm not giving him an opportunity to accidentally lock me out of the car.

At least one of the gods heard my prayer, because the lights at the front gate are blazing against the torpid Ocala night, and the motley assortment of lamps we left on in the house this afternoon shine through the windows as I pull the car up in the driveway.

"Power's on," I sing, but Basil is asleep with his head against the window, and he doesn't stir.

I decide to leave him in the car while I go check the horses. If he wakes up, he can get himself inside. Or he can come out to the barn and join me. Whatever. It's a free country.

I force myself to walk away without looking back. *A remarkable girl.* Can those words stop ringing in my ears, please? They don't mean anything, but they've definitely got a hold on me.

The horses are close to the barn, which makes me guess the lights just came on a little while ago, and they wandered up to see if any humans were out there working. Humans who might be good for some treats or extra hay if they played their horsey cards right. Well, I'm a sucker. I throw a bale of hay into a wheelbarrow and push it out to meet them at the fence-line. There's some scuffling as I scatter the hay into little piles along the fence, but then everyone settles down to eat their dessert hay as fast as they can before someone else can take it. The horses in the individual paddocks rejoice in their lack of competition, eating more leisurely.

I lean against the fence and watch them, happy to be out here in the muggy night with horses and nothing else. There are a few mosquitoes whining around my ears, but the worst of them are gone until sunrise, so it's not like a bloodbath hanging around out here. And the low rumbles of thunder from that storm to the east are oddly soothing, the grumblings of a god going about his own affairs.

Although perhaps not for long. That god is creeping nearer, too. Lightning snakes across the sky, criss-crossing through a mountain range of clouds, and the whole world is lit in glaring white for one shocking split-second.

When everything goes dark again (except for the lights from the barn and the house, thank goodness) I suck in a breath and count slowly until the thunder grinds across the land.

Ten miles? Give or take? I should probably head inside. I turn away from the horses—and see Basil walking towards me. He has a bottle in his hand, and for a moment I'm afraid he's hit the beer in the back of the fridge, which neither of us ever bother with. Then he holds out a bottle to me. It's a VitaminWater.

"Thanks." I unscrew the cap and take a drink, thirstier than I realized after all that cheese. All that cheese! "Oh, man. I left all those leftovers in the car."

"I took them in." Basil looks over the horses before his eyes land on mine again. I can see the barn lights reflected in them, pinpricks of gold in the darkness. "I'm sorry if I said anything foolish at dinner."

"Foolish?" *A remarkable girl.* He doesn't even remember it properly. "No, you're fine. Thanks, though."

"I think I was a little drunk," Basil continues. "I lost count of times that girl refilled my glass."

"They like to do that there. I should have warned you."

"Well, I didn't have to drink it, either." He shrugs and smiles. "As long as I didn't embarrass you in front of your friends. Or strangers, for that matter."

Did he embarrass me in front of Posey and Adam? I'd have to think about that. And if I thought about it, I'd have to think about all of it: the moment his fingers tightened around mine, the way he stopped in the parking lot and looked at me with those dark, fathomless eyes, and told me I was remarkable. What did that mean?

"No," I say, pushing the evening to the back of my brain as best I can. It didn't mean anything, and it's better to forget about it. "You didn't embarrass me. It's fine."

He nods and his gaze drifts back to the horses, lingering on each one in turn. He stops at Feather, pulling happily at hay next to her new best friend Dot. "Let's work on your mare again tomorrow, yeah? She went really well today."

I open my mouth to reply, but lightning flashes through the sky again and my words escape as a little gasp of surprise. The thunder that shakes the ground beneath our feet is far closer than ten miles this time, and we both set off for the barn with a mutual decision which doesn't need any words. By the time the wheelbarrow is put away and the lights are out, the wind is picking up, cool and rain-scented. We hustle back to the house together.

When I stumble over uneven ground, he reaches for my hand to help me stay upright, and then lets go immediately.

And that's just *fine*.

Chapter Fourteen

How does a person sleep after a night like that? You don't, that's the answer. Anyone who tells you otherwise is a liar.

He called me a remarkable girl. He took my hand.

The words float through my head, over and over.

Look, I'm not a romantic person. I mean—I am, yes. I fantasize about fairy tale endings all the time. But not with relationships. I don't sit and think about my perfect partner, the man or woman who can fulfill all my needs. Real world, remember? My parents have a great relationship, but my mom has always made it clear that being in a set of two isn't the only key to happiness.

Maybe that was a mistake, though.

I roll over in bed and stare up at the ceiling. The storm passed before midnight; now moonlight spills through the blinds and leaves a criss-cross pattern, wavering in the spinning fan overhead. Why do some thoughts only come into your head in the gloom of night? Why are they so pressing in the darkness, and so pointless in the daylight?

The truth is, I'm embarrassed about the way I behaved over the past winter. The dressing up. The tinkling laughter. Bending over to make sure a man twice my age heard my vapid joke. I went to those cocktail parties and charity galas to support Posey in her return to Ocala and horse racing society...but I also went because I was tired.

Tired of feeling behind the curve, tired of watching other people succeed, tired of seeing project horses turn into show-ring powerhouses while I couldn't scrape together enough money or time to make a big horse for myself. Tired of thinking I could do it for myself, on my own, when it would be so much easier to convince someone else to buy these things for me.

I know, I know, I know! It's embarrassing. But I just want a big horse, so much. I just want a chance to compete. I'm here in Ocala, where the upper levels of every horse sport are fully engaged in every season, and I'm just bouncing around on Crabby in the evenings. It's been almost a year; I thought I'd be closer to competition by now.

The fairy-tale ending I see for myself, the one that dances around behind my closed eyelids when I can't fall asleep—it's never been about the big wedding, the fantastic engagement, the perfect mate. I've been searching for Mr. Right for years, but it's been about Mr. Right *Horse*. The one who can jump like a jack-rabbit, dance like a debutante, and has a will to win.

Not like Crabby, bless him, my sweet boy—I would never give up Crabby, not for anything, but he's not the horse I hoped he'd be.

Maybe it takes a certain kind of mindset to think that if I didn't get that big horse before I turned twenty-seven, I never would, but I've had that in my head for the past few years and twenty-seven is creeping closer and closer and…I just want a *chance*.

But it was fine. I got over it. I stopped batting my eyelashes at unsuitable men with big farms. It was just a little winter depression, that was all. Of course I can manage on my own two feet, and look—now I've got Feather. If she isn't a chance, I don't know what is. Of course she's half-crazy and less than half-broke and has no breeding to speak of—that's where the fairy tale stories come from! On the horse front, I would say, things are looking up.

Maybe that's the problem now.

My brain has been freed up to consider other things.

Like soft-spoken men in beige breeches who take my hand and call me a remarkable girl.

Why did he do that? Why did he say that?

Why can't I just put it out of my head and fall asleep?

"Are you ready to ride Feather?"

Basil is sitting at the kitchen bar, still wearing breeches and boots from his morning riding.

I'm still wearing mine, too, but that's because I've just walked into the house after working at Amanda's farm all morning. He usually finishes at least an hour before I do and is showered and clean by the time I get home.

So, he's been sitting around in riding clothes all his time, waiting for me to come home. I run a hand over my face, fleetingly thinking, *I'm too tired for this.* I didn't fall asleep until the wee hours of the morning. It wasn't long before my alarm was trilling and I had to stumble out to bring in the horses, feed breakfast, and start another long day.

The idea of riding Feather is not appealing. But of course, my idiotic brain won't let me turn down time spent with Basil.

Not after last night.

He's looking at me expectantly, as if he thinks I'll just head straight for the back door and walk out to the barn. "Well? What do you think?"

"Right this second?" I ask warily, opening the fridge door and pulling out the water pitcher. "Can I eat something first?"

"It's hot out, though. I'm not sure you want to eat something and then ride," he says fussily.

He's right about the heat. The late night storm left behind rain-cooled air this morning, but this reprieve was quickly swamped with humidity. Now the sun is blazing in the middle of the sky and the temperature is a sizzling ninety degrees, with no clouds in sight.

Look, I love the idea of training Feather with Basil's help, not least because it means I can admire Basil in his breeches, but even with that carrot dangling in front of me, I'm not eager to go back outside for a while. I gulp water, then ask, "Can't we wait until evening?"

"You won't want to ride this evening," Basil says. "Once the boots come off, they're off. We both know it."

It's true—at least, in summer it's true. I don't mind heading back out for an evening ride when the weather is pleasant, but it's melt-your-face-off season. The idea of doing anything beyond evening feeding is repugnant.

"Lunch," I plead. "I just rode five off-track Thoroughbreds and two of them think that heat and humidity are a recipe for mayhem. None of them had the good manners to just put their heads down and get their rides over with this morning. It sucked. Now I am hot and tired and hungry."

Basil looks disappointed in me. "You can't put in one more ride before lunch?"

"Why is it so important to you that I go out and ride right now?" I demand, growing frustrated. Basil's newfound interest in me might be more tiresome than his previous disdain. I might not turn him down as a riding coach, but I definitely don't want or need a life coach. I'll go outside again when I'm *ready*.

He shrugs. "I have to go and meet someone this afternoon, and I don't know when I'll be back."

"Someone?" My eyebrows go up as I face him across the kitchen bar. Basil never sees anyone. He has been here for nearly a month, and in that time I've seen no friends come over, have observed very little texting, and have heard him mention outside engagements exactly never. He hasn't even gone back to Legends Equestrian

Center for another Saturday night class. Basil seems to exist in a curious vacuum. Maybe that's why he touched my hand, I think in disgust. He's just desperate for human contact. I ask, "Is it a *secret* someone? Or can you tell me who it is?"

Basil glances down as if he doesn't want to meet my eyes. "Not a secret," he mutters, sounding exactly like someone who has a secret. "Just a family member in town. They want to have a coffee this afternoon. It's not a big deal, but it would probably make it hard for me to help you with Feather. That's why—"

"Fine, I get it, I get it. Let me eat a granola bar, and I'll go back out into the surface of the sun to ride my horse with you." I sit down for a moment, realizing how ungrateful I sound. "I really appreciate your help."

Basil gives me a tight smile. "I'm happy to do it," he says. "Anything for you and my favorite Celestial Being."

"Oh! That reminds me. Amanda is delighted that Feather has had regular reiki sessions and recommended her favorite practitioner to me so we can keep it up." I pause, hearing myself say *we* like it's an out-of-body experience. How apt. Basil doesn't seem to have noticed, but I'm embarrassed. "So that *I* can keep her reiki going," I amend quickly, "and make sure all of her vibrations are in order, so forth, so on, et cetera."

I hear myself babbling to cover up that illicit *we* and shut up. Granola bar, Kayla. Fill that mouth of yours with granola bar. The crumbs will keep you from saying anything else.

"Well, that's excellent news," Basil says absently, looking at his phone.

I guess he didn't hear a thing I said.

Or maybe he did, and he's ignoring it on purpose.

To make me feel better? Or because I've made him uncomfortable?

Good grief, it's hard having a housemate. This would all be a lot easier if Evie lived here. I need a buffer zone between Basil and me. Anything to keep our words and actions from feeling so ridiculously momentous when, for the most part, we're just stumbling through our days without any idea what we're really thinking.

That's me, anyway.

"Outside?" I suggest, crumpling my granola bar wrapper. "To melt for the sake of a horse?"

"Outside," Basil agrees.

He stands up and holds out his hand.

I shouldn't have made such a big deal about his outstretched hand. I know that. I should have just taken it and laughed and swung it back and forth a few times before dropping it at the door. I could have left things well enough alone and pretended there was nothing suggestive or overly friendly about it.

But instead of that, instead of being easy-going and friendly and *normal*, I drew back and then, to cover that up, I spun around like I'd forgotten something and my heel slipped on the tile floor and I went down like a boulder sliding off a mountaintop.

And now I'm on the floor with a pounding pain in my tailbone and a red blush over my face, while Basil looks down at me with clear concern written on his features.

I've definitely made this weirder than it needed to be.

He's reaching for me again, asking if I'm okay, and I'm really not, I'm in a decent amount of pain from hitting the floor and a horrific amount of emotional turmoil from whatever that just was—why did he reach for my hand? What did it *mean?*—but I let him help me up, anyway. His fingers are strong and cool on mine, and when he stands me upright and lets go, I want to hang on for dear life.

He surveys me with worry, his dark eyes finally coming to rest on mine. The concern in their depths is enough to send shockwaves through my spine, and I lean back against the kitchen bar just to feel something solid. He tilts his head as I step back and says, "That was a hard fall. Maybe riding's not such a good idea."

"No, I have to ride," I insist, even though a few minutes ago I didn't want to go near another horse all day. Equestrians have a built-in contrary mechanism which makes us demand to ride the moment we might be physically incapable of doing it. Healthy and hale? Give me the day off. Broken collarbone? I demand to be allowed to gallop a cross-country course immediately.

On the sliding scale of injuries to strenuous riding, a bruised tailbone seems to match up with riding a young horse around an arena for fifteen minutes. Nothing crazy. Just peaceful getting-to-know-you vibes. The perfect level of work for a broken butt.

So I push off from the bar and totter towards the back door, while Basil trails behind me muttering about cold compresses and aspirins. At least he doesn't try to take my hand again. Wouldn't want that.

Wouldn't want that at all.

Basil feeds the horses their lunch after his riding day is done, so everyone has mouthfuls of hay when we walk into the barn, but they're still excited to see humans return early. This might mean *more* food! There's a clamor of hopeful neighs and whinnies, horses pacing their stalls impatiently, expectant noses poking through the stall bars. Feather evidently knows I'm there for her, because she bangs on her stall door with a fore hoof, making a forbidden racket as the door swings on its sliders.

"Such a bad horse," Basil teases. "No manners at all."

"She's really awful," I agree wearily.

We stand in front of her stall and watch her grow more and more heated.

"This probably is a bad idea," I say eventually. "She's pretty worked up."

"Get her out and ride her," Basil says, and it's spoken casually, but I know it's a command.

No turning back now.

"Knock it off," I tell Feather, reaching for her halter. She rushes to the door, pressing her nose against the frame. I sigh and push the door back with my right hand, holding up my left hand to push her back. "Stop crowding—dammit—*ow!*"

Feather shoves past me, knocking me to the ground as she muscles the half-opened door back on its runners and gallops down the aisle. Her hooves are skidding on the pavers and she's whinnying shrilly, as if she's calling on every horse in the barn, or maybe her demon cohorts, to come and join her quest for freedom. Meanwhile, I'm left on my back on the barn aisle like a flipped-over turtle, trying not to howl at the pain in my bruised tailbone. Good lord. Do I need to eat more or something? Because apparently I need some padding between my coccyx and the outside world.

Basil makes a grab for her mane, like any good horseman might, but she spins around and heads in the other direction. She bounces her way down the aisle until she reaches the doorway and stops, presumably because she's just hit the wall of heat produced by the noontime sunlight and realized that freedom isn't free. It comes with a heavy price—in this case, sweltering temperatures.

She turns around and looks at us, considering her options.

"Feather, not again," I say, exasperated. "Please stop being a maniac."

"She's not a maniac," Basil reminds me. "She's a Celestial—"

"Not *now*, Basil," I snarl. For some reason, his crack just isn't funny right now. She's not a joke, she's my horse, and she's also my payment for half a year's work, and I'd really like for her to stop acting like a feral wild child. If Max wasn't sailing across the Atlantic having some kind of Gilded Age fantasy trip, I'd probably sit him down and ask him exactly what he was thinking when he bought this mare and then handed her to me. Is she supposed to be a punishment? A challenge? Or did he genuinely think she was a mature horse ready to take a competitive career?

Whatever he was thinking, I'm stuck with the result. And it's not what I wanted.

"I'll get some carrots," Basil says meekly, heading into the tack room. One snap of a carrot later, Feather is walking up the aisle to meet him, her nostrils flared wide as she seeks out her veggie quarry.

"It's not so bad," he says, once he has the halter over her head and she's crunching happily on a second carrot. "If she kept running away even with treats involved, *that* would be a problem."

"I know." I *do* know. He's right. But it doesn't change the heavy, disappointed feeling in my chest. Maybe I'm being a big baby; maybe I wanted something perfect right out of the box and that's an absurd wish for any horse-person, especially one who has just been handed a horse for free. But she's not for free, I remind myself spitefully. She's literally six months' pay for managing a full stable of horses. Her dollar value exists, and it's my sweat equity that's getting devalued here.

Well, she is what she is.

We get her tacked up with a minimum of fuss, although that's probably because Basil is holding her instead of the two of us wasting time trying to keep her settled in the cross-ties. Out in the arena, she tosses her head and looks back at the barn, then at me, as if to remind me that better things are waiting for her inside. Like shade, and her fan, and a nice pile of hay. It's the kind of look which makes me wonder why we do this all summer. But you can't let a four-year-old feral mare sway your opinion. She doesn't have your career's best interest in mind. According to the psychic's notes in her files, Feather only has her own interests in mind.

"On we go," I tell her firmly, and Basil arranges her carefully next to the mounting block.

I assumed she'd straighten out and behave like she did yesterday, but today is clearly a different story. Once I'm in the saddle, she's squirrelly and silly, pushing against Basil with her mouth gaping against the bit, flicking her tail and then spooking when the sound of the hair smacking my boot sounds scary. At least, that's what she'd like for me to think. But she forgets I spent all winter riding yearlings…well, to be fair, she has no idea. That's my little secret.

"I spent all winter riding yearlings," I say, just to get that out in the open.

Basil glances up at me. "I know about your racehorse job."

"I was telling Feather."

He rubs his hand along her neck and she repays him by slamming her head into his shoulder. Basil grunts. "I don't think she cares, as much as it pains me to say so."

He's right. Feather doesn't care about us today. Whatever cooperation we enjoyed yesterday, she seems to say, this was not meant to be an everyday occurrence. Did she say we could take her out of the field and turn her into a working horse? No, she did not. And she hasn't made up her mind to agree to this promotion at all.

"We better sweeten the deal," Basil says after an exhausting turn around the arena. "Can you wait here a moment? I'm going to go grab some treats. Make this into a game."

"Treats sound great, but I don't think I can promise to wait here," I say uncertainly. Feather shifts anxiously beneath me, already annoyed at having to stand still.

"Just turn her in some nice big circles, that'll occupy her birdbrain." And he runs off before I can tell him that I don't appreciate her name being used against her. She's not a birdbrain!

Feather shies sideways and then backs up several steps while I try desperately to get her to turn in a circle. Okay, maybe she's a birdbrain.

We're moving in an uncertain and wobbly circle, Feather's walk coming in fits and starts, when Basil comes back. He has a fanny-pack on.

I start laughing. I can't help it. A fanny-pack! I snort and wobble and Feather does the same thing, only horse-sized, and she spooks herself. She flies sideways, and I do a mirror image in the opposite direction.

When I pick myself up out of the dirt, Basil is busy feeding Feather a treat.

"Thanks," I tell him wryly, brushing sand off my breeches. "I hadn't fallen off anyone yet today. Feels refreshing, you know?"

"Look, I got her to stand still instead of running off for a change. Isn't that something?" And he gives her another treat, revealing that he has a fanny-pack full of the little green forage pellets I've been using to sweeten her groundwork.

"I think they make special containers for treat training," I say.

Basil raises his eyebrows. "What do you think, I'm made of money?"

I do think that, actually. I would be very disappointed to learn it's not true.

"Let's get you back on," Basil says. "And this time I'll give her lots of rewards so she knows this is something to look forward to."

His trick works: Feather is so interested in the fanny-pack full of treats that she barely notices me clambering back onto her back. And the same goes for the walk around the arena. We manage a round in either direction, plus some halts and turns, without any spooking or drama. I'm not sure she's really paying attention to me when a pied piper loaded with alfalfa pellets is leading the way, but that can come later. For today, it's enough to keep her happy to do a little work, not fighting us every step of the way.

"Did you learn this at the Hullworth farm?" I ask, as he feeds Feather a treat for being a good girl and halting without throwing a fit.

Basil doesn't look up, just shakes his head. "They weren't particularly treat-happy, the Hullworths," he says after a moment's pause.

Something in his voice has changed; he sounds stiff, reticent.

I know I should leave it, but now I'm curious. The Hullworths are the stuff of legend and a few conspiracy theories, made fantastic by their silence and isolation in the Yorkshire dales. So I persist, asking, "But you learned a lot about young horses there, right?"

He gives Feather another treat, although she's done nothing to deserve it, unless you count looking adorable. After a long moment, he replies, "I learned a lot, not all of it necessarily good."

"Oh. I, um—" Stuck my foot in it? Yeah, pretty much.

Basil glances up at me, his smile strained. "Sometimes you learn what *not* to do," he says. "And I suppose that's just as valuable."

"Harder lessons, though," I say.

He nods. "Let's do some more walking off your leg," he suggests, and I know the subject is closed.

Fair enough. I really should be focusing on my horse.

"It's going to be different every day," Basil reminds me as I dismount after fifteen minutes of our lead-line session. "Tomorrow she might be attentive and ready to learn without needing candy every five seconds. Or she might be a total drama queen. You've started young horses, so you know this."

"I do," I concede. "But I don't have to tell you that the difference between riding a long yearling and riding a four-year-old is pretty huge."

"I've never ridden a yearling, but I can guess."

"They're too surprised to say no at first," I joke, "and then they're too sweet and cooperative to fight very much. So yeah, there are good days and bad days but, here's the thing, you're only about four feet off the ground."

"I see the appeal." Basil hands me Feather's reins with a sideways smile. "Well, you've ridden your horse twice in two days. How do you feel?"

I look over my mare. She's beautiful, but she doesn't look like the gift from heaven that she resembled on the first day I saw her. Now I see her with more jaded, everyday eyes. Feather is a nice horse, not a goddess. And she's a feral heathen, besides. I'm less and less certain that Max's gut feelings about horses are infallible, too. All in all, I'm not sure how I feel.

"Tired, mostly," I answer.

Basil chuckles. "Spoken like a true horsewoman. Let's wash this mare down and then we can go have a nap. I have a couple hours until I have go out."

I glance at him, flustered, but Basil is already walking back to the barn. That *we*—he didn't hear it, I guess. An honest mistake, like when I said it earlier in the house. We can have a nap...in our bedrooms, on separate floors of the house.

Obviously.

Why would I get the idea that he meant anything different?

I follow Basil back to the barn, Feather tugging happily at the reins next to me. She's not tired and obviously in a hurry, but I can barely pay attention to her.

Not when Basil is right ahead of me, looking so professional and sculpted in his breeches that he could be a riding-wear model. I feel a sudden heat in my hand, a prickling in my fingers, as if he'd taken it in his grasp and given it a little squeeze.

Oh, dear gods, all of you, what is happening to my brain?
Clearly, the heat is getting to me.

Chapter Fifteen

"What do you think?" Evie shimmies out of the little dressing room at The Tack Trunk like she's Marilyn Monroe trying on the birthday dress. Of course, her clothes couldn't be more different from that famous naked-look gown, while somehow also being just as form-fitting. She's wearing a pair of high-waisted riding breeches which nearly swallow up her tiny frame, along with a show shirt made of some slinky white material. It's garnished on top with a hot pink paisley collar. She strikes a pose, stabbing the air with one sharp hip. "Well? Am I a dressage queen yet?"

"We'll have to pick up some red lipstick at Walgreens," I suggest, looking her over. "And some shiny earrings. But the white breeches are definitely working for you."

"They hold me upright," she laughs, plucking at the fat waistband. "I mean, these are almost a corset. Look—" She pulls up the show shirt. "They're at my *rib* cage!"

"Well, you wanted high-waisted."

"I know, but my god." Evie peers at herself in the mirror. "I'm ready for the Spanish Riding School now."

"We're fresh out of white deerskin saddles," the tack shop owner says, walking over with her hands behind her back and a schoolmarmish expression on her face. "You'll have to settle for something in a nice black finish. Made of cowhide."

"Oh, I have a saddle," Evie assures her. "Today's all about the fashion."

The owner's mouth twists into something like a smile. "Those breeches do the job for you. Showing at the Legends dressage series?"

"Yeah, and I'm really nervous about it." Evie fiddles with the button on the breeches' front. It's engraved with a horse head and the company name. I wonder how much that detail adds to the price tag. Twenty bucks? Fifty? I was brought up to be skeptical of fashion. She admits, "My first time doing straight dressage."

I bite back a joke about how Evie is very experienced at gay dressage, something Max would have guffawed at. I don't think the tack store woman would appreciate it. She's older and has a very conservative vibe. I suspect it pains her to sell a show shirt with a bright paisley collar, even if it will be hidden by a plain white stock tie in the dressage arena. "You'll do fine," I say instead, "and you'll totally look good doing it."

Evie gives me a grateful look.

"I'll take these breeches," she tells the woman, who nods us towards the drowsy teen at the cash register, then goes off to stare disapprovingly at a customer shopping the tall boots. Evie glances back at me, eyebrows raised. "I should've bought these online," she whispers. "I know we're supposed to keep local business alive, but do *all* of them deserve life?"

"Well, you needed to know how they'd fit. These European sizes are weird."

"True." Evie steps back into the dressing room and starts peeling the riding pants off, not bothering to close the curtain. The Tack Trunk is almost empty, anyway, and we're all women here. "I can't believe I'm doing a rated dressage show! Who even am I?"

"An excellent rider with a very demanding trainer who is going places in life?"

"That doesn't sound like me."

"It's you," I assure her. "And yes, I'm very jealous of you." Evie has cobbled together enough savings to rent her own little place *and* take regular riding lessons with an upper-level event rider, and now she can even afford to do a couple of rated dressage shows without breaking the bank too much. And these new breeches, which will only be worn in the shows, cost more than two hundred dollars.

This could be me, if I hadn't refused to get on full-size racehorses this summer. She's making bank at Posey's and making even more by going over to some other farms to breeze horses.

While I'm doing okay working with Amanda, there's no riding money like racehorse riding money.

Her exercise rider gig is also giving her a lean, muscled physique that completely suits her petite frame. She looks like an Italian greyhound, only not sad. When she slides off the show shirt and stands before me wearing just a sports bra, her upper arms nearly make my jaw drop. "Evie, you're *fit*."

She laughs and tugs on a t-shirt. "I know, right?"

I examine my own arms. They're fine, but nothing to write home about. "I'm jealous of you."

"Don't be. No one's beating down my door. I'm always hairy and sweaty and filthy, just like you." She sits down to slip her paddock boots back on. "And I don't live with a man, like some people."

"Oh, that's nothing to write home about, either."

She gives me a coy smile. "So you haven't done the dirty with Basil? I'm so disappointed! I thought having a boy roommate would be fun for you."

I open my mouth to tell her how wrong she is...but instead, I just drop my gaze to the scuffed brown carpet. "More like a daily adventure in confusion," I admit.

Evie makes a little peep of excitement. "Are you for real right now?

Tell me everything!"

"I swear nothing is going on," I insist. "It's just...it's weird."

"Weird how? Weird *how?*"

I consider denying everything. But this is Evie. My best friend. Just because I haven't seen much of her this summer doesn't mean we give up telling each other everything, right? And who else am I going to tell? Suddenly the secrets are crowding in my throat, jostling to be the first one out. I have no choice but to give in. "Okay." I lower my voice, because tack shop walls have ears. "Here's the thing. I think there's a slight, um, *attraction*. Between us, I mean."

"Between the two of you?" Evie squeaks with delight. "Mutual?"

"Shush! Come on!"

"Oh, we're talking about this." She gathers up her purchases. "But not where the grouchy tack shop woman can hear. We're ringing these up and then we're going down to the coffee place I saw and we're *talking* about this."

Ten minutes later we're sitting a few doors down from The Tack Trunk with iced coffees in front of us, and Evie is waiting for me to spill my guts.

Only, I don't know what to say.

"Start at the beginning," she commands, when I fail to start gabbing. "Tell me what parts of his anatomy turn you on the most. Then we can talk about what parts of *you* turn him on, and how to best showcase those for maximum attraction."

"Oh my God," I protest, but I already know the answer to my half of the question. "It's his ass and thighs," I confess, embarrassed to my very core. "Don't get me wrong, his face is great," —and his chest, and his arms, and his slim abdomen— "but when he turns and walks away from me, I can't stop staring."

"It's the breeches." Evie nods professionally, as if she is a sexual attraction investigator and this is all part of the job.

"Understandable. Go on."

"He has nice cheekbones," I falter. "And, um, nice hair?"

Nice isn't the word. Basil has beautiful black hair, glossy as a raven's wing. Ugh, did I just go there? Even mentally, I know it's not a good idea to start talking like I'm in a romance novel.

Glossy as a Percheron's rump. There. That's a lot less poetic. Stay there. Stay in reality.

Real world, Kayla.

I won't mention his graceful hands, or the way his touch has burned my skin. That's just...well, it's a little too much for coffee conversation, I guess. For me. Evie would probably disagree. She's mentally totting up the parts of Basil I've mentioned and is probably awarding points to each one.

"Nice face, nice hair, sexy ass, good legs." Evie sips her coffee, considering me. "Is it purely physical? What about personality? What's the chemistry like? How would you say you two are doing on compatibility ratings?"

"*Ratings?* He's not a computer program, Evie."

"Hostile," Evie murmurs. "Defensive."

Jeez, maybe she *is* some sort of private eye. "Why do you sound like you're dictating notes?"

Evie laughs. "Oh, I'm just fooling around. I'll stop. Tell me *more*, Kayla! What are you going to do about it?"

"I'm not going to do anything about it. This isn't anything. Just a silly crush because he's a hot guy in breeches and I'm around him all the time. Which is basically what you said would happen."

And he's good with my horse and he makes me feel like an accomplished rider and when he looks at me in a certain way, I feel like he sees me as something more than a coworker, and there's a piece of him that is sad and distant which I want to see and heal, and he called me *remarkable*...

I'm not sharing any of that, though. It's irrelevant. Better ignored until this whole thing blows over. Which, of course, it will. Every crush comes to a sad little ending, in my experience. My dating history is short and insignificant. Because horses always come first.

"Well, I think you guys would be cute together," Evie concludes. She picks up her coffee and sips through the straw with an elaborate gesture.

"Hardly," I mutter. "Also, no one else knows, and you can't tell anyone. Including Posey."

"Oh, but I want to tell Posey!"

"Absolutely no telling Posey!"

"Boo. Why not?"

"Because I think she suspects something," I explain lamely. "She saw us at the Mexican place the other night and she gave me this look like...like *uh-huh*."

"So I can't tell Posey you like Basil because she might think you like Basil?"

"Correct. Yes."

"That logic seems flawed."

"Just, please don't." I don't want to explain myself. But the truth is, I want this crush to have room to die without embarrassing me in the process.

"Fine." With the grace of a best friend, Evie drops it.

We both push at the ice in our coffees for a few moments. I look around at the scenery, desperate for anything to take my mind off this uncomfortable conversation, but we're sitting outside a strip mall cafe, so the view is pretty much limited to the cars and trucks in the parking lot.

Evie looks up at me again, and I sigh at her wistful expression.

"What?" she asks, defensive.

"I know you're thinking of something I don't want to do."

"I just think maybe you should go for it with Basil."

"Go for it? What do you mean?"

"Like...jump his bones."

"Evie, for God's sake—"

"No, listen to me. You're into him. He's your type. So why not—"

"How is he my type?" I interrupt. "When have I ever said to you, 'I wish I could meet a nice British Commonwealth guy with a promising Grand Prix career and a dark secret, that would be the dream?'"

Evie raises her eyebrows. "I mean, what about that *doesn't* sound like the dream?"

She has a point.

"Anyway," Evie continues. "By *type*, I just mean he's a rich horse guy. And you've made it pretty clear for, like, forever that you'd like to meet and marry a rich horse guy."

"Forever? We've only known each other for less than a year!"

"Okay, well with you, that feels like forever. And I mean that in a *nice* way. In a best friends forever type of way. So? What's wrong with him? He rides, he has money, he's our age, he looks good in breeches...what's the problem? Fall in love with him already, save us all the stress of waiting."

Her logic is sound. However embarrassed I am about this phase now, over the winter I *did* make it clear I wanted to meet and marry a rich horse guy. And Basil does seem to check all the boxes, while being an appropriate age for me. Plus, as she points out, I'm attracted to him. So, now that he's not behaving like a stuck-up prick all the time, I guess there's a possibility? Of something?

But we're barely even friends. We've just started being nice to each other. I shouldn't go pushing my luck by trying for something more.

"Just don't rule it out," Evie urges me. "Maybe you don't have to sneak into his bedroom tonight. But maybe tomorrow you'll feel differently."

"Well, maybe you're right," I say cautiously. "Let's not go crazy, though. It's probably nothing."

"You need a plan," Evie muses. "So when the moment is right, you can get right to it. Have you considered just showing up at his bedroom door in lingerie?"

"Evie!"

She nods ruefully. "I know, we don't know what he likes. Too lacy, you remind him of his grandma. Too much leather, he thinks you're only into horses for the strap goods."

"And the whips," I say, giving in to her ridiculous stream of consciousness.

"And the whips," she agrees. "Oh, I know! Just go for sexy horse girl."

"What, for the love of all that is holy, is sexy horse girl?" Why am I even asking this question? We dress in tight pants every single day. Isn't that sexy? Maybe Evie is thinking I should ride in daisy dukes and a crop-top. Talk about stirrup leather rubs, though. No guy is worth that kind of pain.

"You know." Evie gestures at herself, at the big paper bag from The Tack Trunk on the chair next to her. "Riding clothes, but like, *very* sexy. Breeches are hot, but what's the cut and color that makes you look hottest? Maybe the high ones, like these, could really do things for your waist. And then we find a top that's super form-fitting and hits you in all the right spots. I'm thinking a cute quarter-zip, unzipped obviously, with a super tight sports bra underneath—"

"Why super tight?" I interrupt. "Am I cutting off my breathing for this guy? It's not that serious."

"It's to push your boobs up really high. It's like in *Bridgerton*. You know, in the olden days, you just had to get a proposal before anyone else, so you had to go at them with your cleavage and then they lose all control and have to have you. It's the historical approach."

I glance doubtfully at my chest. I guess with some real shape and padding, I could accomplish cleavage. But it's probably not worth the pain. "I don't know. Are you thinking he's into that because of the accent? Because I think he's originally from Hong Kong, not England."

Evie laughs. "No, doofus. I'm thinking he's into that because he's a straight guy. Come on." She stands up and shoulders her bag. "We need to go to a different tack shop for this."

Evie's hard to resist when she has a plan, and I have nothing else going on anyway. So I let her drag me across Ocala on her sexy horse girl mission. I think she's crazy, but I could use some new riding clothes, anyway. I go through riding tights pretty fast when I'm riding six or seven horses every day.

We emerge victorious from the third and final tack shop into a late afternoon thunderstorm, the rain pouring from the heavens through golden sunlight, and we stand under the front overhang for a few moments, considering our chances of getting to Evie's Jeep without drowning in the heavy tropical rainfall. I could make a run for it, but I'm weighed down by a plastic bag containing two pairs of gorgeous, sporty breeches that Evie says squeeze me in all the right places, plus a couple of riding shirts with short cap sleeves and daringly low front zippers which will do nothing to prevent a sunburn, but, she swears, everything to attract Basil's lustful gaze.

"Not when I have a second-degree burn," I complained when she picked them out, but Evie brushed me off.

"Just don't wear them when you ride outside, and you'll be fine," she explained, and of course, she was right. They're not for working at Amanda's; they're for sashaying around the house and barn in the afternoon and evening, or getting on Feather in the covered arena, Basil's watchful eyes on me as I swing into the saddle to train my young horse under his tutelage.

"Oh, now I get it," I exclaim. "This is like a sexy professor and student movie."

Evie eyes me uncertainly, as if this is the strangest thing I've said today. "A what movie?"

"You know, like—um—" I can't think of any examples.

"You're thinking of porn," Evie says. "That's a porn."

"I swear I'm not watching porn. When would I have time for that?"

Evie just laughs.

I adjust the bag in my grip and consider the potential associations my brain is making here. Am I really going to try to seduce Basil Han?

I have no idea.

I guess I'm just going to see what happens.

"Of course you are," Evie says, and I realize I've said that thought aloud. "Plus, no one is saying you *have* to do anything. Just let it all flow naturally and have fun."

"You're becoming a real dating coach, you know that?"

Evie squints into the sunlight shining through the curtain of rain. "Always good to have a backup career," she says. "Hey, wait—is that Basil now?"

I resist the urge to jump behind a pillar and look in the direction she's pointing. A gleaming silver truck is crawling through the parking lot. For a moment I wonder why she'd suggest it's Basil; he drives a small sedan. And then I see the decal on the side.

Han Worldwide, with a jumping horse in gold.

"That's so weird," I say, just as the truck drives past us. In the driver's seat, there's a middle-aged man I've never seen before.

"Does Basil have a relative in Ocala?" Evie asks, watching the truck head out to the main road.

"No…oh wait," I remember. "Yesterday, he said he was having coffee with a relative…maybe that was him?"

"Interesting."

"It really is," I agree. "I've never seen that truck before. I wonder who that could be." The uncle, maybe? Basil mentioned an uncle when I was asking him about the horses he's sold in the past. "I think Basil might work for his uncle. But he hasn't been really clear on anything about his business."

"Hmm. Sounds like Basil has some secrets."

"Oh, that's for sure," I laugh wearily. So many secrets. More every day.

The truck turns north onto the road. Headed for my farm? We're in the middle of Ocala, so the driver could be going literally anywhere, even getting on the interstate and driving all the way to Detroit. But I can't help but wonder if there's going to be a surprise visitor in the house when I get back.

Chapter Sixteen

Sure enough, the truck is in front of the house when I get back. In my usual parking spot, as a matter of fact. How presumptuous. I park my old Cadillac close to the garage where Stephen's small collection of antique sports cars live in quiet dignity and haul my tack shop bags up to the front door.

I hear voices as soon as I get inside.

Not just conversation either, but raised voices, a phenomenon this house rarely experiences. The sound echoes around the cavernous foyer, stopping me cold on the braided doormat, a little too afraid to continue down the hall to my room. It sounds like someone in the kitchen is having a temper tantrum, and my bedroom door is too close to the kitchen for me to sneak in without being noticed.

Whoever this guy is, he doesn't sound like the kind of person I want to run into while he's having a bad day. What's he yelling about, anyway? I stand with my hand on the doorknob, ready to race back outside if I have to, but also prepared to stand here all afternoon and eavesdrop. It's not hard. The hallway funnels everything he says to the foyer, where the words spin around me, full of vitriol.

"You have a *duty* to the family to uphold and I don't see you acting on it!" He's really bellowing now. Something slaps against a marble countertop—I can't help flinching. If that was his hand, it must have stung. But it doesn't slow down his tirade. "You have been here almost a month and we've received nothing—no contact, no leads, no recommends to buy. How are we supposed to keep this business going when you, our rider, aren't doing your job? Riding other men's horses instead of finding fresh prospects for us? You said Ocala was a new market, you said it would change the game for us—"

"I am doing my best, what's best for all of us," Basil retorts, and I hear a ragged edge to his voice—like exhaustion tinged with sadness. The sound brings an unexpected heat to the back of my eyes. He says, "Uncle, this job is an *opportunity* for me. You're talking like it's a speed-bump, but I'll be a better, more connected rider at the end of it."

"I'm not interested in your *opportunities*," the man sneers—Basil's uncle? Is Han Worldwide really his business? Maybe Basil is an employee, too. If he is, he has a terrible boss. The uncle hisses, "I'm interested in *results*. We need fast turnarounds and you assured me you had the job well in hand. Now, you slow down. This isn't what we agreed on. You better think carefully about your next move, Basil. Or you're going to find the end of my patience."

He delivers this last line with the air of a final blow, and something tells me he's about to storm right up the hall and out the door, where he'll find me in the foyer listening. Well, that can't be allowed to happen. I dash for the stairs and skip up them as fast as I can, hoping I can get to the upper landing before I'm discovered.

But he's not finished yet. As I pause on the second-floor landing, his footsteps reach the foyer, then stop. "And another thing," he begins, his voice echoing in the space around my head. I scamper down the hallway, eager to put some distance between myself and Basil's family feud. I'm about to duck into a spare bedroom when he says, "About the mare from Sylvia's barn."

Basil's voice is wary as he says, "We were wrong about that horse."

I stop and whirl around, staring down the empty hallway as if I can see their fight one floor below me. My shopping is slipping through numb fingers, bags tumbling to the floor. Clothes spill out soundlessly. My sexy horse-girl wardrobe, to seduce the boy next door.

The one who has been lying to me all along.

"No," the uncle barks. "I talked to Sylvia again. She said you weren't there to stop them and there was nothing she could do about it. That horse was supposed to go to *us*. Where were you?"

"They didn't ask me to come."

"You said the working student goes everywhere with the master! You said you were their little fetch-and-carry servant, you'd be invited on every trip, every visit—"

"I was wrong, okay?" Basil's voice sounds oddly strangled, as if he's choking back a sob. I think of his anxiety; this can't be easy for him. *Don't forget to breathe,* I think, wishing my words would float through the floor and find their way into his brain.

Maybe it works, because he is a little steadier when he demands, "Uncle, how could I know for sure? They went without me, they bought her, it's done. Forget about it."

"It's not done," he insists. "I have a buyer for her now."

"He gave her to someone else," Basil replies. "That's it. She's not ours to sell."

"It's *not* done," the uncle repeats. "Sylvia and I had a deal—"

"I guess the deal fell apart, okay?" Basil is almost shouting now. I feel almost happy for him. *Keep fighting,* I think. "Not everything can follow your careful little plans, Uncle. There are more players in this game than just you and Sylvia. You have to account for *their* plans, too. Sometimes, someone else will win."

There is a pause. I can hear my breathing, a bird chirping outside, the soft sigh of the air conditioning coming to life. In the distance, a horse whinnies. I wonder if it's Feather. I have an irrational desire to race downstairs and barricade her stall, anything to keep this stranger from thinking he can just pluck her away from me and sell her again. I have no clue what is going on, but one thing seems clear: Basil's uncle is used to making his own rules.

The silence stretches between us: the two locked in their battle, and me, the third, unknown above them like a watching spirit.

Maybe I'm like a Celestial Being. The thought nearly makes me burst into hysterical laughter.

"We took you to England. We put you through school. We let you go to that farm in Yorkshire," the uncle says slowly, as if he's thinking aloud. "You were supposed to become a great rider. You've let us all down."

"I went a long way," Basil retorts. "As far as I could go with them."

"You could have gone farther."

"We were done."

I'm dying for him to keep going. I need to know what happened in Yorkshire like I need oxygen.

"We bought you the Highland horse," Basil's uncle continues, disappointing me. "We let you keep him, because he was supposed to make you a great rider...do you hear the pattern here, how quickly it forms?"

"We won a Grand Prix a month ago, and we'll win another one before the summer's over, if you just leave us alone—"

"I'll leave you alone," the uncle says. "If you fix this. Fix things *quickly,* or you'll be on your own. I want the client list completed. Get horses shipped out. And the mare—"

"The mare isn't for sale," Basil says.

Basil's uncle growls something unintelligible. I can't believe it. *Now* he stops shouting?

The front door opens and closes. I hear the big truck out front turn over, the engine roaring as he slams a foot on the gas pedal.

And then Basil's tread on the stairs.

Oh *no*. I look around wildly and see closed doors all around me. The upstairs is uninhabited, apart from Basil. I can choose any room at all, hide until he goes back downstairs, and never bring this up. Ever.

Except that I'm going to die of nervous curiosity if he doesn't explain just what the deal is with Sylvia, his family business, and Feather. Even the mysterious allusions to Yorkshire are fading in comparison to this apparent horse deal they were all working on. That Max blew up by buying Feather and giving her to me.

I should stay right here and get some answers. Ask him. No, not even ask—*demand* an explanation. Because it sure sounds like they're all operating, if not on the wrong side of the law, on the wrong side of ethical business. Not that this would be any shocker in the horse world, of course.

But it hurts, somehow—it hurts like a weight on my chest, to think Basil might be involved in anything underhanded. I just started to like this guy. I don't want to believe he's up to no good.

Even if he was, though, he told his uncle it was over. And if I'm totally willing to believe that Sylvia Britton is capable of running a scam with that shouty uncle of his, I'm just as happy to believe Basil is ready to run for the hills. I mean, he's *here* now. At Bent Oak Farm. With good horses to ride, easy access to the Ocala summer circuit, and a place to live. Max and Stephen are good bosses. Benevolent, even. Yes, they don't always pay the best in cash, but they certainly pay in perks. This house. This farm. Feather—although she has some caveats, she's still a very nice horse, out of my price-range for sure. Basil has his first ride with Max's trainer coming up soon, and that alone is worth hundreds. He doesn't need whatever scam his uncle had him hocking before.

And I have no doubt there's a scam lurking behind this shouting match. Come on. No one straight-faced registers their horse as a Celestial Being without fudging around on business deals; I've been in the horse game long enough to know that trouble follows the witchy types every single time. If a horse owner even *mentions* karma or their particular brand of do-right-by-all spirituality on their Facebook page, they've probably screwed over at least a dozen people over the years. It's a weird disconnect with reality they all seem to share. Maybe vibes are just insidious by nature, and if you listen to the universe too closely, it'll lead you down some dark paths. I don't know.

Either way, I have a decision to make right this instant—face Basil, or hide.

Oh, please, like that's a decision. *Hide,* that's the choice. And I'm almost out of time; Basil's nearing the top of the stairs. Without thinking, I open the closest door—Max and Stephen's bedroom, which surely must be off-limits even if they've never mentioned it—and plunge inside.

It's dark in here, even with the huge windows overlooking the fields and barn; they have heavy blackout curtains pulled tight, probably to keep the heat out. I know the housekeeper comes in here twice a week to dust and vacuum the carpets, but there's still a heaviness to the air in here, the slumber of a room which goes unused and whose inhabitants have gone away. I sit down on the bed and regret it when the military-straight duvet creases beneath me. I'm going to have to straighten up when I leave.

In the hall, Basil's footsteps march past the closed door. He sounds rigid, heavy. Like he's stomping away from the fight, an upset child. An angsty teenager. It's surprisingly easy to imagine Basil as a teenager; bonier than he is now, less muscle to pad those coltish limbs, his smooth black hair overgrown between cuts, falling over his dark brown eyes. And his life is such a natural series of events: falling in love with horses, patting his childhood pony, riding his first big course. Competing—where? Before he came to Florida, there was New England, and before that, Yorkshire. He must have started as a child in England; his uncle said something about that. The kind of man who gives a child a dream and then demands to be paid back in full.

I imagine Basil in Pony Club, his adolescent face serious as he studies a course at a rally. Someone—his mother, maybe, since he talks about her with such affection—standing nearby, holding the reins and waiting until he's completely satisfied he knows his way around the jumps.

He would have been good in Pony Club. Careful, comprehensive. Taking only the most calculated risks. Finding his way through skill and dedication, not a teenage sense of immortality. A sense of duty to the horse—that's what Basil has, something you don't see nearly often enough.

That guy just now—the uncle—must not have been around much when Basil was learning to be a horseman. Because he's clearly just a typical investor, trying to wring money out of living things as quickly as possible.

And the worst kind of boss for a sensitive, anxious person like Basil.

How does Basil stand working for him?

In the hall, Basil enters and leaves his bedroom, and walks into the bathroom. I hear water running in the bath.

Well, I guess he's not coming out to help feed the horses with me. I'd gotten used to his company out there over the past few nights. I check my phone; it's almost five o'clock. I better get out there and start chores. With a sigh, I push myself to my feet, then lean over the bed and start tugging the duvet straight.

But I tug it a little *too* hard, apparently, because I knock over a decorative pillow. It's a hard, fat sausage of a pillow, which tumbles off the bed and onto a bedside table.

Where it knocks down something hard and plastic—one of those wireless phone chargers, I think. It's dark and hard to tell. I reach for whatever it is and my foot catches on something else unseen. *Slippers?* I think, just before I completely lose my balance and tumble forward, taking out everything on the bedside table with my flailing hands.

"Good grief," I mutter, once things have stopped falling on me. A lamp, an antique alarm clock which emits a single desperate *brrrrring* as it hits my chest and rolls onto the floor, and a small statuette of a horse which, thank heavens, seems to have escaped without broken legs. "Clumsy Kayla strikes again."

I'm just starting to lift things back into place, wincing at the spot on my arm where the lamp smacked me, when I realize the water has turned off.

And the bathroom door is opening.

And Basil's footsteps are in the hall. Slowly, slowly, as if he is trying not to be heard.

Oh, no. He's heard me, and he's coming in here to check.

Emergency! Time to panic!

I consider trying to roll under the bed, although I'm really not sure what the plan is after that, but the door is already flung open, late afternoon sunlight flooding across the dark bedroom, and Basil stands in the doorway with a towel wrapped around his waist, water dripping down his chest, and a disbelieving expression on his face.

Which is a fair reaction, because I'm sitting on the floor next to our bosses' California king with a lamp by my side and a model horse in my hands.

We look at each other for a long moment, the seconds ticking by on the antique alarm clock.

Um...what's my move here?

Nonchalance, maybe. I can play this off. After all, I am the *official* farm-sitter here. He's just here to ride the horses. For all he knows, I'm actually supposed to be in this room every week, playing with the model horses so they don't get lonely.

"Hey," I say, brandishing the little horse like it's my excuse for being on the floor. "Sorry if I scared you. I, uh, came up here to check on something Max was asking about in his last email, and I fell over his slippers. Stuff fell. It was a whole thing." I shrug.

Sure, this is a gamble; I'm trusting Basil doesn't know Max well enough to try to find out what I was looking for. Or that Basil trusts me enough to not think I'm sneaking around the master bedroom without permission.

I mean, I wasn't sneaking. I was *hiding*.

Basil nods slowly. "What were you checking on for Max?"

Of course he wants to know. I'm such an idiot. He was Max's working student. What did his uncle call him? The fetch-and-carry boy? Something like that. It's mean, but kind of true. Working students are like their boss's shadows. Always there, always aware of far more than they let on. He probably knows Max better than I do. Almost certainly, in fact.

"Oh, just a paper. He—um—wanted to know it was put away safely." I look over the table. Why did I say paper? There aren't any papers anywhere in this room. Of course, they wouldn't have left out mail or documents. They're so *tidy*. God, I'm an idiot. "I don't see it though, so I guess he filed it before they left. I'll let him know."

Basil is still just standing there, staring at me with a blank expression. Finally, he asks, "Did you hear him?"

"What?" I adjust the lamp just so on the bedside table.

"Did you hear my uncle?"

"Your *uncle*? You have an uncle? Was he here? Gosh, Basil, you should have said—"

"Don't play dumb."

I close my mouth.

He sighs, and suddenly I'm very aware of his body. That makes one of us, anyway. It's like he doesn't realize he's standing there naked except for a towel, water beading on his chest and arms and calves while I'm just forced to watch. It's like he's somewhere else. He's not even worried about my fake paperwork story. His mind is on his own problems. I realize this as he says, the words coming slowly, "My uncle is an idiot. I hope you didn't hear anything that worried you. The stuff he said about the horse at Sylvia's..." He hesitates. "It...it wasn't Feather. There was a different mare."

He's lying.

I don't know how I can tell so quickly, but I know. Basil is lying to me. Basil is dripping wet beneath a white towel wrapped around his waist, and he's lying to me. Honestly, it's all a little much to take in. Why would he care enough to lie?

Why won't he go and put some clothes on? I can't cope with this kind of mystery while he's standing there all wet and...naked.

"It's fine," I say at last, and that's a lie, too. "You don't have to get into it with me. It's your business."

I need to know everything. I'm bursting with curiosity and I'm slowly cracking with hurt, but I'd never tell him either of those things. I don't want to see his expression take on that fearful expression; I don't want to see his anxiety take hold of him.

I realize this probably means I'm moving beyond crush status, that my interest in Basil is going far beyond healthy parameters for two people living together on a work assignment. But there's nothing I can do to stop it.

"Seriously," I say. "No questions."

And relief flits across Basil's stiff features. He nods slowly, and his shoulders sag—although the towel remains tautly in place, for better or for worse. "Thanks," he says, his voice husky. "Things are complicated."

I have to look away from him, for a myriad of reasons, so I take a speculative look around the room, as if I'm still searching for that lost document. "Well, I guess I'm done here," I say finally, thinking, Take the hint, Basil. It's getting hot in here. Figuratively and literally. Where is the air conditioning? Isn't it usually frigid in this house?

"Right," Basil says, and he glances at the surrounding doorway, as if he just realized he's standing there half-nude, blocking my escape. "Of course."

He starts to back into the hall, so I push myself to my feet, and then he says, "Oh, you missed something."

Basil slips past me, his towel brushing my leg, and stoops to pick up something small. He holds it up to the light. It's the little horse statuette. "Cute," he says. "Isn't it?"

"Very cute. I'm glad I didn't break it when I fell." I take the statuette and examine it. Everyone loves a good toy horse. I flip it over to see if there's a brand name etched on its little belly.

I gasp.

"What is it?" Basil leans over, his forehead nearly touching mine. I can't react to how close he is, how good he smells, how warm his body is, because I'm still staring at the words on the horse's belly, carved there in tiny italic script.

Celestial Being Level I.

"You have got to be kidding me," I say.

Basil chuckles. "Well. The Celestial Beings strike again, huh?"

"Basil," I whisper, in no mood to joke. "I think Max is in a cult."

Chapter Seventeen

"WE DON'T KNOW that this is a cult," Basil says, for the tenth time, at least.

"This is definitely a cult," I retort. Again. We've been going through this, back and forth, for the past fifteen minutes. I pull down a hay bale from the stack in the storage room and toss it into a waiting wheelbarrow in the barn aisle. "Throw me that knife, will you?"

Basil tosses me the knife—it's a box cutter, and the blade is fully retracted, I promise—and I slice open the sweet-smelling bale of timothy hay. At the same moment the flakes of hay burst apart, a gust of cool wind puffs through the barn aisle, sending hay chaff floating over my sweaty face and neck. It's itchy and annoying, but I'm used to this kind of discomfort. The important thing is that it's going to rain in a few minutes, so we need to get the horses fed and cozy because we can't turn them out while there's lightning flashing all around the farm, and also that Max and possibly Stephen are in Sylvia Britton's horse cult. Oh, and probably Basil's uncle, too.

I don't know what to do.

"There's nothing you can do," Basil points out when I voice my uncertainty again. He's been saying the same thing since we found the horse statuette in Max's bedroom, since he went into his room to put on clothes while I sat down on the bed and stared at the carved words *Celestial Being Level I*, since he heard the rumble of thunder and insisted we go out to get the horses fed even though he was cleaned up for the evening already and really shouldn't bother helping me. "There's absolutely nothing wrong going on here," he says. "It's not like they're sacrificing humans to the horse gods or something."

I glance at him over my payload of hay. "Yet."

Basil grins, and his expression is the lightest I've seen it this afternoon. Something in his smile just makes me feel better. As if we aren't living in an empty mansion owned by cultists who may or may not be at sea, who may actually be in hiding somewhere nearby, waiting for the right moment to pounce and sacrifice us to their horse gods. This is a thought I just had and I share it with Basil immediately, in case he agrees and decides we should climb into my Cadillac and hit the road.

"You're being dramatic," he says when I've finished explaining my latest fear. "Sylvia is not running a cult. Even with the Celestial Beings thing, it's just people enjoying a weird spirituality. How is worshipping horses any different from all the other religions on earth?"

"This is different," I insist. "Trust me. I feel it in my bones. This is a big old scammy cult out to get people's money. Haven't you ever listened to a podcast about cults, Basil? What are you doing with your life? Have you never had any leisure time?"

"Evidently I'm doing all the wrong things," he replies drily.

"Well, it all adds up," I inform him, on a roll now. It's all so clear! "Max couldn't give us raises, remember? Well, he sort of gave you one, since you were a working student before. But he couldn't give us what he *said* we deserved, so you got the riding lessons and the winter ride, and I got the horse. But the horse is from their cult! And the cult wants her back! It's a set-up, I'm telling you right now."

"A set-up for what? A ritual murder? Is that what you're getting at?"

"Maybe not a ritual murder," I concede. "That may be over the top. But maybe they just trade things, like, to keep their money on the inside. Maybe that's where Feather comes into it."

"Feather was for sale for real money," Basil says. "I can assure you of that."

I glare at him, suspicious all over again. "How do you know that? You said you weren't trying to buy Feather."

He holds up his hands. "I was at her barn, okay? I can tell you that all of Sylvia's horses have price-tags. She's an established breeder and trainer, Kayla. Whatever else she may be, Sylvia Britton is not a cult leader. She just really likes incense and essential oils. At worst, she's kind of a kook."

"That's what they always say," I mutter darkly. How can he not see the obvious connections here? And his own uncle, making threats about getting Feather back! "You're being way too easy-going about this. All the evidence points to horse cult."

Basil shrugs. "Look, even if it is, that's not our problem. If Max and Stephen want to start giving their savings to Sylvia or whoever's in charge of their little heavenly horse journey, that doesn't really affect *us*."

"Until they're turning the farm over to the cult and we're out of a place to live and horses to ride," I remind him.

"That's not going to happen."

"How do you know?"

He sighs and bends over the hay bale, scooping up an armful. "We'd better hurry or we're going to get soaked on the way back to the house."

"What's the rush?" I know I'm being belligerent at this point but, like, a cult! This is worth discussing.

"I have to get cleaned up again and changed," Basil says, not meeting my eye. "I have dinner plans."

For a stupid moment I think he has a date and my heart does a ridiculous sinking thing, dropping from my chest right down to the soles of my boots. Then I remember his uncle—gosh, I'm just witnessing more drama than one day can handle, folks—and my heart rearranges itself. But that's not really great, either, because his uncle is clearly a problem. "Don't go," I hear myself saying. "Stay home and have dinner with me. We'll order pizza."

"I can't get out of this dinner. But thank you for the offer. You should stay out here, let the horses eat, then hop on Feather for a little hack around the arena." Basil tosses his last flake of hay to a waiting horse and slides the stall door closed. "Can you handle turnout alone after it storms? I should really get going."

"Of course," I say, because until a few days ago I always handled turnout alone. "But you're crazy if you think I'm riding Feather alone."

Basil, already on his way out, pauses and looks back at me. "Why not? She's been good for you every day. You don't need me to take her on a walk. Just take a pocketful of treats and give her one every so often to let her know how fun and delicious riding can be."

I love the way he offers horses treats for every little thing. You'd never get that impression just talking to him, but Basil is a big old softie. Why did he come across as such a jerk when we first met? I'm going to have to ask him someday. I'll add it to the list. The Basil-Han-is-a-mystery list.

But we won't get to that tonight. He's already waving goodbye and running up the path to the house, his strides coming faster and faster as the approaching storm heaves its dark belly over the farm. The wind whips through the aisle, whistling in the eaves.

"Well, I'm alone with a cult horse," I muse aloud. "This evening has not gone the way I planned."

What did I plan? Maybe trotting out the sexy horse girl outfit for Basil's approval? Getting on Feather while he stood in the center of the ring and watched my cleavage nuzzle its way into view above my unzipped shirt? Taking my mare for a little trot and then going back to the house, ordering a pizza, and engaging him in sparkling conversation from across the kitchen bar while sultry jazz music from one of Max's music subscriptions played on the hidden speakers?

Well, something like that, yeah.

Feather pokes her nose against the stall bars, and I have to give her soft muzzle a little boop. She lips at my fingers. "You're a good girl," I tell her. "When you're not being a wild horse who doesn't respect fences or cross-ties. Should I get on you, even with Basil gone?"

It sounds tempting—at least it sounds better than going into the big house alone and thinking about what other culty things might be lurking in corners or even hidden in plain sight. I can't explain why the little horse gave me such a fright. Maybe it's just that I thought Max and Stephen were the best things that ever happened to me, and it hurts to see that they might be involved with something so sketchy. Even worse, that Feather is connected to the whole thing.

Like at first, I thought they were paying me an enormous compliment and giving me a real sweetheart deal by paying me with Feather, and yet ever since then, circumstances keep changing, diminishing her value again and again.

It makes me distrust our entire arrangement. It makes me wonder if they've lied to me about other things. If they've lied about where they are right now. Maybe a cruise around the world isn't Max's lifelong dream, the very top of his bucket list. Maybe they're doing something with their little cult, getting brainwashed into giving Sylvia all their money or, like I said to Basil, into murdering nice, unsuspecting horse girls who just want a shot at making it as a professional in their expensive world.

I wish with all my heart Basil hadn't left the farm tonight, because I'm getting myself worked up. "Take it easy," I tell myself. "Just relax, okay?" But for some reason, my brain doesn't listen to me. Seems ridiculous, doesn't it? I ought to be the one person who can order my own brain around, but it doesn't work like that. I wish for my mother's voice to enter my brain and remind me to stay in the real world, but she must be busy or something, even the version of her which just lives in my head, because she stays silent.

So, I take my brush box and my tack down to Feather's stall. I'm not trying to get into an argument with my mare tonight, not trying to do any real training, which means the cross-ties and wash-rack are off limits. I just want to saddle her up, take her to the covered ring, and go for a nice walk with lots of treats, the way Basil suggested. A ride will clear my head. When I'm back on the ground, everything will seem normal again.

I hope.

But Feather doesn't agree with my plans. She begins to fuss the moment I go into her stall, and things escalate even when I try to keep the grooming session low-key. She stomps her hooves while I curry-comb her, swats me with her tail as I run a soft body-brush over her back, and swings her hind legs menacingly when I try to pick her hooves. When I go out to get the saddle, I hear her slide her teeth up the wall and decide maybe it's best to not go back inside, after all.

Feather watches me through the stall bars with wide, innocent eyes.

"You're being crazy," I tell her.

She flicks her ears back and forth, managing to look completely adorable. *Who, me? Crazy? You got me wrong.*

"Ugh, you chestnut mares. Do you really want to live up to the stereotype, Feather?" I should call up Evie, who claims to love riding mares. Or Posey, or even Amanda. Anyone who has a little more mileage on youngsters than what I've managed to rack up. It's so frustrating to have spent a good fifteen years in the horse business and still feel over-horsed with a mare like Feather, but here I am, overwhelmed by her lack of training.

It's such a shame Basil isn't here. I've gotten used to his help, his soft touch with a horse.

"What would Basil say about your weird attitude right now?" I ask Feather. She runs her nose along the stall bars. "He'd say treats, is that it? Win you over with treats? Well, it's worth a try."

Basil thinks anything can be accomplished with a little treat. The other day I came into the barn earlier than usual and saw Jock actually reaching for the bridle while Basil just stood there holding it. The horse practically bridled himself! Did Basil teach him that trick with treats in hand? Probably...how on earth else would you do it?

I'd like that kind of magical relationship with Feather. If a fistful of alfalfa cubes is what it takes, well, they're cheap.

"One minute," I tell Feather, and I dash off to the tack room while she nickers hopefully after me. It's that little throaty voice of hers that spurs me to take *two* handfuls from the treat bag sitting open on the tack room counter. I shove them into the stretchy pockets on my riding tights, taking out my phone to make room. I leave it on the counter and pat my bulging pockets There. I'm a walking, talking, horse treat dispenser. "Let's do this thing," I mutter, heading back to my horse's stall.

She's very excited when I reappear; I guess she heard the crackling of the plastic bag and knew something tasty was on the way. I slide open her door again and she charges at me, nostrils rippling with a silent nicker.

"That's better," I say uncertainly; do I really want her throwing herself at the door every time it opens? But she's standing in front of me with her lip wiggling in excitement, so I dig out a treat and let her grab it.

Feather crunches with delight and shoves her nose into me, demanding more. I've just got my hand in my right pocket, tugging out a second treat, when she runs her nose down my left leg and her nostrils widen with delight.

Treats!

"No, no," I'm protesting, but Feather is already rubbing her upper lip over my bulging pocket, wiggling it back and forth with surprising force. I remember suddenly that horses can use their upper lip the same way elephants can use the tips of their trunks. They use it to pull food close to their *teeth*—

"Get off!" I shriek, shoving at Feather's head, but it's too late. She opens her mouth and takes a tremendous bite out of my riding tights.

The stretchy fabric shreds in her teeth instantly, no match for this kind of biting pressure. And as Feather yanks backwards, trying to escape my flailing arms, half my pant leg goes with her.

Fine, three-quarters of my pant leg. It's enough to feel naked.

The treats spill over the floor as my ruined tights sag to the shavings, and she dives in for the feast, crunching through everything I'd stockpiled for our ride in about three seconds. For a moment, I stand there and stare at her, too shocked to move; then I realize that all this exposed skin where she previously located delicious alfalfa cookies is not the best idea. I back out of the stall and slide the door shut.

Safely outside, I take stock. My left leg is naked, and there are pink marks on my skin where her teeth raked against my skin, but luckily, it's not more than a few scuffs off the top layer. It doesn't even hurt.

Still, I'm a little shaken up. I don't think I've ever been bit by a horse before. The potential for what *could* have happened is more rattling than the actual scrapes she's left behind.

Note to self: don't keep treats in pockets. Get a fanny-pack like Basil's. No wonder he doesn't stuff his breeches pockets with pellets. He stands to lose quite a lot if a horse goes in for a mouthful and misses the mark.

"Now, what am I going to do?" I ask Feather. She picks up her head and looks at me through the bars, still chewing enthusiastically. I've probably taught her human thighs taste delicious. Great. My man-eating mare. I lean on the stall door and sigh in exasperation. "I sweeten you up with treats and you take off my pants with your teeth. How is this productive?"

All I know is, our workout is cancelled. The storm is passing, so I might as well turn the horses out for the night. I'm obviously not going to ride in these destroyed tights, and I know if I go back to the house to change clothes, the Rule of Air Conditioning will come into effect and I won't be able to force myself back out into the humid night. Forget it. Everyone goes outside.

But first, let me just snag my shredded pant leg from Feather's stall before she does something stupid, like eat it.

I slide open her stall door and start inside, but somehow manage to catch my toe on her stall mat. I must be tired because I lose my balance and tumble to my knees. My hands smack the shavings just inches from where Feather is digging loose treats out of the bedding and her head flies up in surprise, her hard nasal bone catching me right between the eyes.

Stars explode in my vision; then there's only darkness. I feel myself crumpling to the floor; a tremendous pain squeezes everything in my forehead together and I gasp. I hear myself whimper.

Feather, of course, sees the open door and takes the opportunity to leave town.

There's nothing I can do to stop her; I'm crumpled up in a ball on the floor of her stall, my head throbbing, my vision blackened, my voice moaning. I hear her hooves scampering up the barn aisle; I hear her speed to a brisk trot and then a canter, against a chorus of excited whinnies from the horses she's left behind. Who knows where she's going? There's no way I can get up and go after her. Not until this pounding in my forehead stops.

What if it doesn't stop? What if I have massive internal bleeding and I'm going to die here on the floor? What if Basil comes in late tonight, wondering why the barn lights are still on, and finds me cold and stiff in Feather's stall? And what about Feather? Could she jump over the perimeter fence and gallop away? Is she on her way to Ocala right now? Is she getting hit by a car? A truck? How am I ever going to find her?

Suddenly I realize that while I've been listing one disaster after another, the pain in my head is slowly letting up. Still agonizing, but almost bearable. I cautiously open one eye, then the other.

I'm not dead.

Potentially not even dying.

That's a plus. Maybe things are looking up. And that could mean other circumstances will improve, too. For starters, maybe Feather didn't run away, and is grazing right outside the barn. I shift myself a little, thinking I'll get up and find her—but nope, my head says, it's not time to move yet. I close my eyes against the renewed thudding in my skull. Wait it out, Kayla. Just wait it out. I organize my arms and legs into an almost-comfortable position in the shavings, sliding one hand beneath my head.

And I wait.

I can't say how much time has passed when I hear the sound of a car engine in the distance.

The Sweetheart Horse

But when I open my eyes and flick my gaze around Feather's empty stall, I see that it's fully dark outside her window. The horses are quiet; they must have accepted no one is coming to turn them out. And there's no telling where Feather might be.

A car door slams far away. At the house. Basil is home. I shift slightly, adjusting my hand beneath my head. It's asleep, past the pins and needles stage and fully asleep. I wonder how long I've been out here, and if Basil will think I'm doing night-check, or if he'll come out looking for me. Eventually he will, right?

I really wish I hadn't left my phone on the tack room counter.

From outside the barn, I hear a horse snort in the distance. Feather? How far away is she? I need to get up. If I can't call Basil to come and save me, I will have to save myself.

I get as far up as grabbing the stall bars with my fingers before dizziness takes over, and the world goes dark again.

I awaken again to hands on my forehead, their touch cool and comforting, yet moving too quickly. "Slow down," I murmur, but those words aren't what I hear. Just a slurred combination of consonants and vowels which can't be reconstructed into words. The fingers slip to my throat and are still there.

I feel safe with that pressure against my neck. When it's gone, I want it back. I try to roll over, seeking out that hand.

Fingers flutter down my arm. "Hold still," Basil says.

Basil! What is he doing, running his hands over me while I sleep? I didn't know things were progressing in this direction, but sure, why not? Let's get married, let's train horses together, let's be a rich show jumping power couple. Solve all my problems, Basil. You stuck-up, handsome, infuriating, helpful prince, you.

"Are you awake?" Basil asks gently.

"Awake," I try to say, but I know it doesn't come out right. "Yes," I say instead, and getting out one simple syllable does the trick.

"Okay, stay that way," he says. "No more naps. I called an ambulance and I need to go find your horse. Are you okay here?"

I want him to stay. But find my horse? That sounds bad. Is my horse missing?

There's no way to ask with just one word.

"Kayla? Are you okay?"

"Yes," I sigh.

Horses come first.

When he's gone, I feel cold and a little—just a tiny bit—afraid. My head aches with a slow throb. I curl up on the shavings and try to remember what happened before this point. But all I can think about is Basil's hand as he sought my pulse, the pressure of my beating heart meeting the pressure of his searching fingers. It's the most real and the most imaginary thing in my world right now. And even when I hear the clatter of hoofbeats, and the approaching wail of an ambulance siren, I'm only listening for his voice to tell me everything is okay.

Chapter Eighteen

I'M ONLY IN the hospital overnight, but it's enough time for everyone I know to find out, panic, and send flowers.

"You have a lot of pollen in here," the nurse who has been keeping an eye on me says, looking at the florist deliveries covering every surface. "I might have to move the patient next door; she's sniffling like crazy."

"I'm sorry. I didn't expect this," I assure her weakly. I didn't. But I can't deny I like it. There are six different flower arrangements in my little hospital room, ranging from a chipper bouquet of daisies set in a plain vase (Posey's contribution, and the cutest) to an austere collection of lilies in a shiny copper-colored bucket (from my parents, along with a card which reads *Please be careful, we love you*). It's exactly what I'd expect them to say to me. Full support, with a healthy dollop of concern.

Amanda has sent rosebuds, Evie an African violet she knows full well I'll kill and cry over after it's dead. A few other friends have provided small bouquets as well. The floral delivery came all at once this morning, while I was picking at my flavorless hospital eggs and wishing someone would bring me a cold brew from Starbucks. I almost asked the delivery guy to do it but he had a whole cart of flowers to deliver waiting for him in the hallway, so I just watched him set up all the vases and then looked around in shock and no small amount of gratification.

But my roses lost a little bloom when I realized none of them came from Basil.

"Well, just tell whoever picks you up to bring a van," the nurse suggests. "Or there won't be room for you on the ride home."

"Thanks," I say, not revealing this opens up an entirely new line of questions. I don't know who is coming to get me. Did my friends make any plans? Who is listed as my emergency contact, and for that matter, who checked me into the hospital? Had I arrived alone, or had Basil followed after? No, he would have called someone. He would have broken into my phone somehow and called a friend. I mean, my password is just 272229. The numerical code for CRABBY. I would hope that's obvious.

That must be what happened. Basil would think this is a job for a girlfriend.

Not a house-mate.

I look at my flowers and sigh. I try to summon my mother's voice to remind me to stay in the real world, but she's oddly absent this morning. Maybe Feather knocked her helpful presence right out of my head. Because now, instead of retreating to the safety of reality, I'm able to keep floating through my own personal Fantasyland. One where Basil has sent me the biggest bouquet of all, and maybe a teddy bear—no, a big plush horse, bay with four white socks the way those toy horses always are, and he laughs at me and says, "This is a reminder to stay away from chestnut mares," and then he leans over, one hand gently cupping my chin, and he whispers, "I was so afraid for you, Kayla," and his lips come closer to mine, and my breath catches—

A white-coated doctor bursts into the room and starts prodding at my forehead, knocking my daydream to the floor, where it shrivels up and disappears. I submit to the doctor's hurried ministrations, listen to her instructions for how I must behave after I'm sent home, and ask for my phone so I can arrange a pick-up. The doctor assures me she'll find a nurse to retrieve my phone from wherever it's been stowed, and leaves me alone again.

"That's fine," I murmur to myself, shifting position. It's time to get out of this bed. "I'll call Evie and she can come get me after morning gallops. It's fine."

I spend the next half-hour trying not to think about Basil at all.

So when Basil pokes his head around the door and says, "Knock-knock," in a hopeful sort of way, my eyes nearly fall out of my head.

"Basil!" I exclaim, then wince and lower my voice. Too much exuberance is not good for concussions. "Basil," I repeat in a much more subdued tone, "what are you doing here?"

He comes into the room, head tilted curiously as he says, "I'm bringing you home, silly."

I blink at him a few times, trying to get my head around this development. He's not even in riding clothes, despite the morning hour. He's wearing slim-cut jeans which are all wrong for Florida in summer, and a short-sleeved, button-down shirt in a plaid cloth so smooth looking, I want to stroke it.

"I thought maybe Posey would come," I say eventually. "I don't have my phone yet. I'm not sure where it is."

He's eyeballing the masses of flowers around the room. "No, I checked you in, so I'm the one they called to come and get you. You're my responsibility."

What a wonderful thing to be called by the guy you're nursing a violent crush on, a responsibility. Everyone's favorite thing. I mutter, "Sorry about that."

"No, it's fine. I put down my phone number, fully expecting to get called." He lifts the copper bucket from my parents. "This is nice. How did everyone find out you were here so quickly?"

"You didn't tell anyone?"

"No, what did you think? I'd post that I'd brought you to the hospital on the Han Worldwide Facebook page?"

I've never looked at the Han Worldwide Facebook page. Why is that? Why are there completely obvious corners of the internet I haven't bothered to inspect while looking for answers to Basil Han and his strange unknown world?

Maybe, honestly, it's that I simply don't want to know.

I know this guy now, and I actually like him. But I'm guessing that, if his uncle is any indication, there's a lot about Basil *not* to like. Or at least, about his business and his family.

I'm much happier in the dark.

"You must have told someone," I suggest.

"I told Amanda and Posey, and Posey said she'd tell Evie," Basil explains. "I figured Amanda would want to know why you're not at work this morning. And Posey would be a good backup contact if I had any trouble getting here this morning."

"But how did you get their numbers?" I ask hopefully, thinking that if he did guess my phone password, that's a sign that he *really* gets me.

"I looked up their farm pages on Facebook," he says. "Their secretaries connected me."

"Oh, right. Thanks." Well, that's disappointing. But logical. And more respectful than breaking into my phone, I guess.

Basil is toying with a purple blossom on the African violet. He isn't even looking at me. I need to stop reading into everything he says or does. I say it to myself, in my own voice: *real world, Kayla*.

"Feather's fine, by the way," Basil says.

"Oh, my goodness." My horse flares into high definition in my mind. "I guess I just assumed—what happened?"

He lifts an eyebrow, shakes his head. "She jumped into the retiree pasture and was out grazing. Alone. She didn't even go out to join the rest of the horses."

"That's...weird." I remember something Basil said once about not liking horses who jump fences. *That's my own thing,* he'd said, or words to that effect. "At least she didn't go out to the road or something. Jumping into a field is a step in the right direction, you know?"

His smile is wry, humorless. "Kayla, listen...I have to tell you, if you have to reach that hard for a silver lining, maybe this situation should be a wake-up call."

Excuse me? Rude! I sit upright, shoving the stiff hospital linens away, and demand, "What is *that* supposed to mean?"

"I don't think she's a good horse for you," Basil says flatly. "And I think you should sell her."

My fingernails dig into the mattress. *"What?"*

"I think you should sell her." He runs his hand through his hair. It falls forward, brushing his forehead, covering his elegant eyebrows. He needs a haircut; when did that happen? How much time has passed since we first met? Weeks and weeks. We are old friends now. Old enemies. Basil shakes his head, looking away from me. "Sorry, let's not talk about it here. Let's just get back to the farm, okay? And I'll explain myself better."

"Fine." My tone is as bland as those eggs I couldn't finish. Obviously, no one wants to hang out in a hospital. But if Basil thinks this discussion will be easier at home, he is sadly mistaken. He's going to explain, in detail, why he thinks I should sell Feather. And I'll probably have to admit what actually happened last night, the whole treat debacle and—oh, yikes.

"Basil?"

"Hmm?" He's looking at the flowers again, probably wondering if he's supposed to carry them all out to the car. If he asks me, the answer is yes.

"Were—um—did you notice anything—weird?"

"Your breeches were ripped," he says, not turning around.

"Yeah. About that."

"She bit you. Right? I saw the torn off fabric in the stall."

"Sort of. I mean, yes, she bit my pocket and that took off the whole pant leg. But it wasn't—she didn't do it *randomly*."

"Horses shouldn't bite off people's clothes," Basil tells me firmly, as if he's teaching a preschool lesson. *A is for apple. B is for bite.* "Do you agree? Or am I off target here?"

"No, I agree, obviously, but—"

"You can't make excuses for a horse just because you like her."

I hate being interrupted. "She had a reason, if you'd just *listen*."

Basil folds his arms over his chest and gives me an impatient stare. The entire pose gets my back up, and it certainly doesn't predispose me to admit something embarrassing to him.

"Forget it," I grumble, and I push myself out of bed, ignoring his helping hand. I slip-slide over to the doorway in my silly hospital socks and poke my head into the corridor. A nurse at the nearby desk looks up and gives me an inquiring glance. "Can I get a cart for my flowers?" I ask.

If I was not looking forward to staying home alone with Basil all afternoon—and I wasn't, not particularly, since he has decided Feather is public enemy number one—it's not an issue. Posey and Evie both come over, armed with the entire contents of the candy aisle at the drug store. At least, the good stuff. Nothing without generous chocolate coatings or fillings. They spread the candy packages over the coffee table in the living room and make a big show of getting me comfortable on the couch before settling in for an afternoon of gossip and gruesome horse stories. A rainstorm rolls in and batters the windows, giving a naturally cozy feel to the occasion. Basil takes one look at the afternoon slumber party in the living room and disappears to parts unknown.

I try to push him out of my mind, focusing on my friends—who certainly have an impressive mental library of bad falls, nasty injuries, and disturbing veterinary emergencies.

"And *that's* what happened to Maryann Schwinn's mare's hooves," Posey concludes a particularly grisly piece of feed store gossip. "Let that be a warning to everyone."

"That was disgusting," Evie complains.

"Which part?" Posey asks interestedly. "The part where the abscess blew out the coronary band, or the part where the hoof wall separated—"

"No more," I blurt, unable to shove aside my own problems any longer. "Ugh, you guys. Listen. Basil wants me to sell Feather."

They stare at me in disbelief.

"You have a head injury," Evie says. "Please, let us tell the scary stories. It's our gift to you."

"No, he really said that. This morning when he picked me up at the hospital. He said I should just sell her. Why would he say that, you guys? He was helping me with her. We were actually bonding over her. I think we might be friends, then this, out of the blue."

"It's not exactly out of the blue," Evie points out. "Since she put you in the hospital."

"Yeah, maybe he's just really worried about you," Posey suggests, her eyes glittering at the idea. "Maybe he doesn't want his future wife dame-branaged by a horse kneeing her in the skull constantly."

"Constantly? It was one time. I really doubt it happens again." Whoever heard of getting a head-butt to the skull by a horse, anyway? I'd really done myself a stupid injury this time around. When Evie lets this slip at the feed store—and she will, I know Evie and her love of gossip—everyone is going to use it as a cautionary tale for years to come. I'll walk into some boarding stable full of tweens and a coach will be bellowing, "Chloe, what have I said about bending down in front of your horse? Didn't you hear about that girl who got kneed in the forehead?"

I wonder if they'll change the ending and make it so I died. It's a much more convincing moral when I'm a casualty of my own carelessness.

Except that Basil doesn't seem to think that was it. He blamed Feather. Why? He knows accidents happen with horses all the time.

Evie gets up and grabs another bag of popcorn from the kitchen counter. She tosses it onto my lap. "Here, eat something healthy."

"Cheese popcorn?" I open the bag, shrugging. "I guess it's healthier than M&Ms."

"Not the peanut ones," Evie says. "But I ate all those."

Posey looks at her in admiration. Evie can eat anything—anything!—and remains petite. Posey says that will end the day Evie turns twenty-eight, but that's two years away so Evie feels safe with her junk food eating habits. "Someday, Evie," she begins, but Evie throws a pillow at her and Posey takes the hint. She glances at the living room windows and says, "The rain's letting up. I'm going to run out to the barn and check hay and water, okay?"

"Okay," we echo, and Posey slips out the back door, stuffing her feet into a pair of my rubber boots along the way.

Evie gives me a gleeful grin. "Now, let's get serious without the boss here."

"Your boss," I remind her.

"Whatever. Tell me why it matters so much what he thinks."

"What?"

"What *Basil* thinks," Evie emphasizes. "About Feather. Why do you care?"

I tuck my chin into my chest. "He's a professional," I suggest.

"Come on, Kayla." Evie leans forward, her eyes sparkling with amusement. "Tell me the truth! Has this crush progressed beyond physical desire? Are you totally obsessed with him now? I mean, only yesterday we were buying you a sexy outfit to seduce him, and now you're absolutely mooning over him."

"I'm not mooning!" I cross my arms over my chest and fix Evie with a ferocious frown. If she were a dog, she'd cower. But she's Evie, so she just laughs.

"You're all, 'What would make *Basil* happy, what would *Basil* say?' about your own horse! The normal Kayla would not give a damn what he thinks. Admit it. You're not just into his skinny body. You want his arrogant little brain, too."

"Not when you put it like that," I say mulishly.

"Ah-*hah!*" Evie puts her fists in the air like she just won a marathon. "I *knew* it!"

"Calm down," I say witheringly. "I live in the same house with the guy. A crush was almost certain to happen."

"Look who is so clinical about it. This is all science, right?" Evie shakes her head, laughing to herself. "Into Basil Han. For more than meaningless sex. This isn't about pheromones and tight bods, Kayla. This is true love!"

There's no stopping her when she's in this mood, but Posey won't be out in the barn forever. Urgently, I say, "Listen to me, Evie. You can't tell Posey."

"*Still?* Are you still upset she saw you two canoodling at a restaurant?"

"We weren't canoodling." We weren't even touching—most of the time. But Posey saw it first. When she saw us together, even though Basil and I were sitting across from one another in the booth, a little light went on in her brain—I saw that spark of recognition, even if I didn't realize at the time what she was seeing.

She saw Basil and I as a couple. She saw the spark between us before I did.

Which is great, but here's the thing. No one wants to see their friends coupled up nice and snug as much as the *only* friend in the group with a steady partner. Posey will be all over the two of us, pushing us together with every sappy trick in the book.

And I just don't need that kind of pressure. Because Basil and I are nothing but maybe-friends.

And yeah, once when he was drunk he called me remarkable and squeezed my hand.

It was memorable. It felt like something might be starting.

But it's not a relationship. I need to stop running over all the times we've touched or spoken in soft voices or given each other what felt like meaningful looks, and accept that Basil doesn't see me that way. Or if he did, for half a second, it doesn't mean he's going to pursue it.

Evie, on the other hand, is still savoring my confession with delight. "You have wanted a rich, horsey guy to marry. And the minute you stop looking, one shows up! In your *very house*," Evie continues dramatically, as if she is the host of my own personal dating show. "A stranger who would quickly become so much more than a stranger, a friend who would quickly become more than a—"

"Stop," I snap, unable to take any more teasing. "I wouldn't have told you this if I'd known you were going to be a total dork about it."

Evie looks offended. She tosses back a few more M&Ms and throws the bag on the coffee table. "Fine," she says at last. "You're on your own. Good luck being in love with your roommate."

"I'm not in love with him," I hiss. "I have a crush on him. It's not the same thing. And anyway, I'm over it already. If he doesn't want me to have Feather, then he's not the guy for me."

"You're *that* into the horse that bashed you in the forehead, left

The Sweetheart Horse

you for dead, and jumped into a pasture to graze alone?" Evie shrugs. "I admit, Kayla, this would have me concerned. She sounds a little—um—anti-social, let's say."

"What did you want her to do, call the ambulance? She didn't mean to hit me in the forehead, and when she did, it scared her, so that's why she ran away."

"Are you sure?" Evie asks. "Are you sure she didn't rush the door and hit you in her hurry to get out of the stall?"

No, I'm not sure. Because she's been rushing the door for weeks, and we've been working on the problem, but it hasn't gone away. Shouldn't she have more respect for me by now? Ugh, is Feather getting worse instead of better?

"Kayla?" Evie's voice is soft. "Are you okay? Not having a little coma, are we?"

"No, I'm fine." I sigh and lean back into the cushions of the easy chair. It's the one Basil usually sits in, and I imagine I smell him on it: his spicy body-wash, his fresh antiperspirant. "I'm fine. I'm just disappointed. Feather might have knocked me over, for all I know. She's got a bad habit of rushing the door when I open it."

Evie makes a sympathetic grimace. "She needs a Come-to-Jesus," she says, using an old horseman's term for a serious attitude adjustment. "You gonna be the one to give it to her?"

I don't know. I don't know what to do about Feather. And the worry about her swamps whatever upset I was feeling about Basil. I mean, boys? Versus horses, they're just not that important.

Evie is telling me a story about a horse she used to know who was famous for jumping out of every stall he'd ever been put into when Posey comes back inside, sweat trickling down her forehead. She abandons my muddy boots at the back door and brushes frizzy hair from her face. "It's a million percent humidity out there," she grouses. "I think the rain is simply the air. It's not falling. It's just the *air.*"

"Thank you for haying," I say. "I hope Basil will do tonight's feeding."

"Me too," Posey sighs. She dampens a kitchen towel and starts mopping her face. "I have dinner with my mom and Adam tonight, or I'd stick around and help out. Where is Basil, anyway? I thought he didn't do anything but ride Max's horses."

"I don't know. He has family in town." I resist the urge to describe Basil's strange, unpleasant uncle to them. I don't know what's going on with the Han family business, but I don't want Evie spreading stories about them all over town. Although Evie might have some stories of her own. I pause, considering the potential ramifications, then throw caution to the wind and ask, "Evie, have you heard of Han Worldwide?"

Evie has been looking at her phone, but she puts it down and turns her head slowly, dramatically. *"Han* Worldwide, you say?"

"Why are you doing a villain voice?"

Posey sighs, the sound carrying from the kitchen.

It hits me: they know something.

Something bad. Or at the very least, something not great.

Something they have been keeping from me because they...think I like Basil? Because they like Basil? Because Basil is really a serial killer and I'm being used as bait by the FBI?

Okay, it can't be that last one. Just the painkillers talking.

"I know you aren't big on internet stalking," Evie begins.

"Uh-huh." I'm cringing already.

"But I am, obviously, and...well, I've been keeping up with Han Worldwide since you said he was moving in." Evie pops a handful of M&Ms. Because she's nervous about what she's about to tell me? I feel my fingers clenching the leather seat. If Han Worldwide turns out to be a front for drug smuggling or something, I am going to be so mad...

"Basil's company isn't a horse company," Evie says. "It's an import/export business, and they invest in all kinds of dumb stuff. Oil. Railroads. Mines. Bicycles. The horses are like a weird side business, and they've only been at it a couple of years."

My fingers relax. "Well, that's okay, isn't it? I mean, at least they aren't factory farming horses to go to meat packers or something like that..."

"No." Evie looks uncertain. "But when a big business is trading a few expensive horses on the side, that's usually not very good, either. Because they're used to real profits, not horse profits."

She's right, of course. Horse profits are largely imaginary, because horses cost so much to care for while they're in training. Whereas oil and bicycles can be stored and forgotten about. I assume.

This makes it seem really likely Han Worldwide is using show horses as a money laundering scheme. It ought to be a far-fetched idea, but if there's one thing I've learned in the horse business, it's that fraud and felonies are never far from the feed room.

"Okay, but who runs it?" I ask. "I know it isn't Basil. It's the uncle, right? The one who came to town yesterday."

"The CEO is someone named Edward Han." Evie shrugs. "Could that be the uncle?"

"Definitely," I say, and then the events of yesterday afternoon clarify in my muddled brain. "Oh! I heard them arguing yesterday. Basil hasn't been producing horses for them like he's supposed to be. And there's something else." I frown, trying to recall. Jeez, what an inconvenient time to get knocked out by a horse. I could really use all my brain cells intact right about now.

"You heard them *arguing?*" Evie leans forward, excited. "Wait! When were you going to share this information? Did you not think this was important?"

"A lot has happened in the past twenty-four hours," I remind her.

"Including a head injury."

"Oh, sure. Blame the head injury! Fill us in, fast."

I sketch out what I remember of Basil and his uncle's argument in the kitchen. It's all a bit hazy now; all of yesterday is, actually. The other girls look at each other, dissatisfied with what they've heard.

"I don't know," Posey says. "I mean, he *sounds* like a good guy in all of this."

"This could still work out," Evie agrees. "You can reform him."

But I'm not sure I agree.

There are just so many secrets around Basil. So many mysteries. And if my initial inclination was to avoid researching his past on my own, now I can see what my intuition was telling me. *Stay out of it, Kayla.*

I don't need the drama.

Basil Han is an excellent horseman, a decent friend in a crisis, and wears breeches like a male model. But he's also mixed up in weird, unexplained messes which include a horse cult and a borderline abusive relative-slash-boss. And that's just the beginning, I feel certain. He consistently shrinks away from answering questions about his past.

These are all very red flags.

No, I need to get over this Basil crush. And if Posey saw a spark of something between us?

Well, sorry, little spark. It's time to stamp you out, grind you beneath my heel, and forget you ever lit in the first place.

Real world, buddy.

Chapter Nineteen

But no one tells the little spark it's been extinguished.

When Basil comes home around five, the girls having left to take care of their own horses and lives, my heart gives a pathetic little leap of excitement. I've stuck carefully to the living room sofa all afternoon, heeding the discharge nurse's warning not to exert myself and Posey's insistence that I not fall down and hurt myself again without someone home to call 911. Except for a few trips to the bathroom and some detours to the fridge for more seltzer (thus ensuring a speedy return to the bathroom), I haven't moved in a good six hours, and I'm getting sick of looking at the same four walls.

Basil's inquiring face makes everything feel bright and new again. "How are you?" he asks, settling down next to me.

"Pretty good." I run my fingers over my forehead without really meaning to, and my own touch makes my heart flutter as I remember the way he ran his fingers up my throat last night, feeling for my pulse. Shouldn't be hot, but is hot. Noted and filed for future exploration, possibly with a board-certified therapist. I put on a bland expression and say, "I'm just bored, really. And I couldn't get Evie and Posey to stay to feed the horses, so—"

"So it's on me tonight." Basil sighs. Not angrily, not even in exasperation, but the sound still fills me with embarrassment. Feeding and turnout is my job and I'm pushing it onto him because my crazy horse knocked me down. Basil gets it, though. Horses come first. He shrugs and says, "That's fine. I just need a minute off my feet, and then I'll get changed and handle it."

That's when I notice Basil is in his riding clothes. Not just the schooling breeches and scuffed boots he wears around the farm, but *good* riding clothes: a pair of high-waisted beige breeches, tall field boots with the back zippers half-down, one of those Han Worldwide logo shirts in a fancy blue fabric. I furrow my brow at the get-up. "Where were you today?"

"Just trying some horses around town." He sounds weary. "Jumpers. Sales prospects. My uncle—" his voice trails off. "I just need some sales," he says finally.

"You'd keep them here? Along with Jock?" I wonder if he has permission to use stalls, or if he'll have to get hold of Max and Stephen to ask. I think they're in Portugal, or maybe it's Northern Africa by now.

"They wouldn't be here," Basil says. "I'd have a buyer for them right away."

"Well, you can't *know* that—"

"Trust me, when I get in a sales horse, it's on its way out the door." His voice takes on a steely edge, which reminds me of the night we met. "I only select horses which are right for the clients on my wait-list."

I didn't like him that night at the Grand Prix, and I don't like him right now. "Sounds pretty sus to me," I remark airily, picking up my phone and scrolling blindly, anxious to show him the conversation is boring, not worth my full attention.

"Well, you're not a professional," Basil huffs, and he gets up, leaving me alone before I can lash back at him with a snippy retort of my own.

Jerk, I think, and almost without meaning to, I open Google and type *Han Worldwide horses for sale.*

Nothing.

Han Worldwide show jumper.

A few links pop up, but none of them are sale ads. They're just mentions of Han Worldwide as the owner of various horses placing well in competitions. Highland Cross shows up most recently, reminding me of something else I overheard yesterday during the great Han battle. Something about his uncle buying Basil the Highland horse...*we let you keep him,* he said.

There's a sinister lining to those words. A threat, if I'm not mistaken. And I can't imagine how much it would hurt Basil if his uncle chose to sell Jock. That horse means the world to him—and to his career in the show-ring. I suppose that's what has Basil back out on the horse-hunting trail again. The fear of losing Jock.

What a horrible way to be treated by a person's own family! I can't imagine my parents or even my non-horsey extended family doing anything so terrible. Veiled threats, bribery, just to keep me in line with their business goals? No wonder Basil wanted to get the hell out of Wellington. He was probably just trying to put some distance between himself and that uncle.

I close my fruitless web search as Basil comes back into the room, now wearing gym shorts and a t-shirt. Somehow, he looks just as good in nondescript workout clothes as he did in fine riding apparel. I suppose that is the tyranny of a hardcore crush. One I really need to get over. "I'm going out to feed," he announces. "Don't fall off the couch while I'm gone."

"Don't worry," I say, waving my phone at him. "I'm just over here studying for my Celestial Beings Level I exam."

Basil's grim expression cracks into a grin. "Make sure you pay close attention to the chapter on what to do when the aliens show up," he says. "I'm going to rely on you to get us into that UFO safely, okay?"

"You can count on me, Bas," I reply lightly.

His grin shifts slightly, becomes something softer. "You've never called me Bas before."

"Oh, bad idea? It just popped out."

"No, it's fine," he says. "I'll be back in an hour."

I watch him leave, the door closing behind him with a soft click. *Bas.* The nickname is like a little caress, like our friendship just deepened once again, as if I'm gliding farther and farther into a crystal-blue spring, the rocky floor falling away beneath me. Pretty soon, I'll have left solid ground behind altogether, and then...

Real. World. Kayla. I shake my head, rub my face, like I can physically remove all traces of this crush from my body.

But I can't shake him off that easily.

"I found something." Evie sounds guarded, like she'd enjoy being excited, but she knows it's not appropriate.

"You found something about what?" I mumble. I just woke up.

"About Han Worldwide," she says urgently. "I thought about you and Basil, and I figured I owe you a better sleuthing job than the one I've been doing. So I really dug into things. Pulled out all the stops. And I found something surprising."

"They donate millions of dollars to charity?" I guess, hoping against all signs to the contrary.

"Kind of," Evie replies. "If you count sharing the same business address as the Church of Celestial Beings as a charity."

What.

The.

What.

"Do you know what this is?" Evie continues. "Celestial Beings? Sounds like a cult. They're based in West Palm Beach. Which I guess is a good place for a cult. A lot of money and crazy people. Maybe they're like Scientologists."

"They're horse-people," I blurt. "It's a horse-people cult."

Evie is quiet for a moment. She's so rarely quiet that the silence seems theatrical. Then she says, slowly, "Kayla, is there anything you haven't told me about Basil?"

"Maybe?" I hedge.

I don't know that Basil's really involved, after all. I mean, yes, his uncle is up to something with Sylvia, and she's definitely the source of all this Celestial Being nonsense, so the uncle must know about it, too...

The uncle might be involved, too. Another memory from yesterday's fight surges through my consciousness. *The mare from Sylvia's barn.* What did Basil's uncle say to him?

"That horse was supposed to go to us. Where were you?"

Evie's voice is soft. "Kayla? Are you okay?"

I'm not okay. It's all connected. *They* are all connected. Sylvia, Uncle Edward, the client list of buyers Basil is supposed to be buying for. Han Worldwide adding horses to their list of goods bought and sold.

Basil might not be in their cult, but he's still part of it.

My heart is pounding, and the thudding makes my head ache. I tip back onto my pillows and whisper, "Evie, I have so much to tell you."

Evie absorbs my wild tale without interruption, which really speaks for what a good friend she is as well as how insane this whole thing is. She has made it her business to collect the bizarre gossip of the horse world from every feed store counter in Ocala. But she's never heard of anything like this. She can't even think of anything to say as I unfurl the strange, sordid details I've absorbed since Edward Han came to visit Bent Oak Farm.

And why should she interject anything? Let me speak, the crowds will cry. I'm an original story, a Lifetime movie waiting to happen. *The Horse Cult That Ruined My Life,* based on true events. Or maybe they'll call it, *Not Without My Horse.* That's pretty catchy. It also implies I'm going to be involved in some serious anti-horse-napping measures, which, frankly, I don't feel physically or mentally up to. Hopefully Basil isn't actually planning to steal Feather if I refuse to sell her to him, once he finally gets up the nerve to ask.

Because that's where he's heading, right? His uncle is demanding Feather. So this is the ploy, as I see it:

First, he's kind and helps me with her, then he leaves me alone with her, knowing I'll probably get hurt, and finally he plants the seed in my brain that she's dangerous and the wrong fit for me. But *he* knows the perfect home for her, if I'm willing to sell to him...

Ugh, it's so obvious.

I wrap up my story with this anticipated schedule of events, and Evie sighs softly. "You agree with me, right?" I ask her. "About Feather?"

"It's so hard to tell," she says. "I mean, Basil obviously likes you. That could change things."

"He doesn't like me," I assure her. "That's part of the game."

"I don't know, Kayla. Maybe falling for you is the wild card for him. Maybe that's why he's in this fight with his uncle to start with."

"Oh, I suppose I make him want to be a better person," I joke.

"It could be—"

"No." I can't believe that. I can't go down this road. I've already decided to be over Basil. I will continue saying it to myself until it's true. "I'm over Basil."

This time, Evie snorts. But she lets it go. "So, um, what are you going to do about Max?"

I've thought about this, too. "Nothing. They're not here, so until they come home, I don't have to change anything."

"And when they come back? You were planning to stay through the winter, until they go back to Wellington. Does this change?"

It's my turn to sigh. "I don't know, Evie! I have five months to figure this out."

But she makes a good point, because I had months to figure out where I'd go last time they were coming home, and I didn't manage to do anything but get fired from a wannabe jumper's barn and fall into the dirt in front of Basil Han.

Evie sums up the situation neatly, saying, "So, you're just going to live in a cult member's house, with another possible cult member, or at least a cult lackey, and hope nothing culty happens."

I shrug, aware she can't see me through the phone, and say, "Yeah, that's about right."

It's not a *great* plan, but for right now? As usual, I don't have anywhere else to go.

Chapter Twenty

I HANG OUT in my bedroom until nearly ten o'clock. That's late for me. But I have so much to worry about, and no privacy to do it outside of my room. Basil will be in the kitchen or the living room, watching TV or looking at his phone, the spicy scent of his broth hanging in the air since I have been tucked up in my bed all day, unable to make a shared supper for the two of us.

In the past month, we've gone from enemies to friends, people whose daily lives have become subtly intertwined. I don't know how to end that. But I also know things can't stay the same.

I need a switch I can flip, which stops me from caring about Basil. And until I find it, I decide, I will stay right here in my room.

But of course I can't stay in here forever. I'm on medication, and it's past time to take the next pill. With food, the label warns me. Or else.

The prospect of a sick stomach on top of this headache is more than I can face, so I eventually psych myself up enough to emerge from my hiding place. And when I do open my door into the hallway, I find, to my surprise, that the kitchen and living room are both dark. The only light on is the little bulb above the water dispenser in the refrigerator door.

I look back and forth, as if my answer is in the shadowy foyer. I didn't hear Basil go upstairs, haven't heard him walking to the guest bathroom or heard the water running for his shower. And as I tick off these clues one by one, it occurs to me that I hadn't recognized how much time I spend listening to Basil's comings and goings, his schedule and patterns. I hear everything—well, not *everything*, thank goodness—but I've internalized the sounds of his presence in this house, the squeaks, the creaks, the water in the pipes.

It's astonishing, the little ways Basil has become part of my everyday life.

I pad across the cool tiles and peer through the windows lining the living room. To my surprise, I see the arena lights are on.

At almost ten o'clock at night? What's going on out there?

Maybe the aliens finally showed up.

I push aside the thought, which is really only half-jest, and slide my feet into my rubber boots; the ones that Posey borrowed earlier. No, I'm not supposed to be up and about, but I have to know what's going on. Anyway, it's just a few minutes' walk out to the barn, my path lit by small solar lamps, and I can sneak into the entryway leading out to the covered arena. I'm not going to exert myself. I just need to see what he's doing.

When I get out there, my heart skips a beat. And then it sinks. Even my poor beating heart is confused now. That can't be good.

Basil is riding Feather.

I don't know how to react. Part of me wonders if he's just getting a head-start on her training now that he has reached the phase of his plan where he convinces me to sell her. Another part suspects this has nothing to do with buying my bad mare and everything to do with the fact that she put me into the hospital. That this is personal, an inability to let her slide for another day.

Either way, I accept it.

Maybe I've reached my capacity for shock today.

Or maybe it's just that he's doing such a nice job, I have no desire to end the training session.

He's walking her in big, loose serpentines, with those soft hands of his carried low and his legs light against her sides. She's paying attention to him, her ears flipped back, but it's not until they're right up against the closest rail of the arena that I realize he is talking to her in the gentlest voice I think I've ever heard.

"You just need someplace to put all this energy, right, missus? You're a good girl, everyone knows it, I know it, we just need to make sure it shows, okay? Can't have you bumping and bopping and bucking and bouncing..."

I smile at his alliteration; it reminds me of the day I tried to hold her attention with a little rhyming sing-song. Something about Feather is so child-like, and not just because she's a young horse. She just has an air of unearthly youth; I think she will always be this way.

Maybe it was all the reiki sessions. Or the sage, although I can't imagine anyone benefiting from the acrid sent of burning sage.

The two of them round the curve and start down the long side of the arena, and his voice starts to fade. But before he's too far away to hear, I catch one last line.

"We have to have you ready for your mama Kayla to ride when she feels better, Miss Feather."

My heart melts into a puddle.

He's not trying to steal my horse for his uncle, or for some mystical woo-woo horse cult. Basil is trying to help me, the best way he can. By working on my horse for me while I'm laid up.

I'm still digesting this realization when Basil wheels Feather around in a long, gentle turn, and faces her directly up the walkway to the barn. His eyes widen as he sees me, and he starts to raise a hand in greeting. But Feather snorts as tries to gather his reins into one hand, dancing sideways, and he has to abandon the wave.

That's fine. I give him a little wave, anyway.

The Sweetheart Horse

Basil's smile is sideways as he rides Feather towards me; it's clear he's not sure how I'm going to react. Meanwhile, my mare sees me and her ears prick, her gait picking up some steam. I can almost imagine she's happy to see me.

"Hey," I say, as Basil slows Feather to a clumsy halt.

"Hey," Basil says. He tips up the brim of his helmet and looks at me carefully. Assessing my health, I think. I find it devastatingly romantic. This is what it is to be a horse-girl. Just looking for a guy to look after us when we're concussed and wandering the barn after hours. "I thought you went to bed," he says. "Is everything okay?"

"I was awake. Just resting. I saw the lights and came out to check on you." I walk up to the arena railing and lean over, putting my hand against Feather's neck; she's warm but not sweaty. She lips at my t-shirt sleeve and fastens me with that innocent gaze. I don't know who I'm more crazy about, or who is a less ideal candidate for my affection. At this point, what's another bad decision amongst friends? And we are friends. I'm sure of it now. Maybe I'm still willing for us to be more than friends. I tip my head at him, smiling. "Training my bad horse for me, Basil?"

He shrugs, slipping the reins into his right hand. He reaches down and gently places the back of his other hand against my forehead.

I take a deep breath at his touch, feeling a shiver run across my skin like a brisk breeze has suddenly gusted through the warm arena.

"No fever," he decides, taking his hand back and resting it on his thigh. My eyes follow the motion, as if I can will his fingers back to my skin. "I think you'll make a full recovery, Kayla Moore."

"It was just a concussion," I remind him.

"No such thing as *just* a concussion," Basil nags—and I don't even mind, because I'm grasping for any sign that he cares about me. "But I'm glad you're okay. I'm a little embarrassed, though. You weren't supposed to catch me giving Feather a schooling session. I'm sorry, I just didn't think she should go a few days without any riding after the way she's been behaving."

I should really really mind that he's riding my horse without my permission, but owing to the idiotic nature of women who get goosebumps when men touch them, I'm fine with it.

"Oh, I'm not mad. It's nice of you," I say. "I mean, I assume you know you're training my horse for free."

Basil laughs hard enough to startle Feather. She wobbles forward and to one side, pulling Basil out of my immediate space, and I'm just ridiculous enough to feel a little cold in the void left behind. He looks over his shoulder as the mare walks away, saying, "I think you should go and sit down, or better yet, go inside and rest in the air conditioning. I'll be in shortly. She's going quite well." He hesitates, then says, "I know I said you should sell her, but I was—well, I was worried. I don't really think she's too dangerous for you. I just think she needs some catching up."

That's all the reassurance I need. It was all in my head.

"I'll sit down," I tell him. "I want to watch you ride."

And for the next quarter of an hour, that's exactly what I do. I sit on a bench by the arena and quietly observe Basil school my feral mare, getting her to walk and trot nicely without flying into a panic or a temper tantrum every time her will is overruled by his, and his riding is so pleasant to watch that I don't think about anything else at all.

Certainly not the way I felt when he touched my face.

After he's given her a bath and turned her out—with the retirees, at my suggestion, since she has jumped into their field twice now—Basil turns his attention to me. He scoops one arm around my shoulders, surprising me.

"Let's get you back to the house," he says, giving me a squeeze I'm sure is more chummy than any big show of attraction. Of course, I'm just his house-mate who got myself hurt in the barn. He doesn't have any feelings for me, which would, say, encourage him to hold me a little closer than necessary.

Because, for a moment, it sure does feel like he clutching me tightly to his side.

But then he lets go, and we walk side by side up the dark pathway. I hold my arms stiffly at my side, making sure my hand won't swing and bump into his. Because if it does, I might accidentally clutch his fingers, and I don't like to think about the level of embarrassment that will result if he doesn't grab my hand right back.

Around us, the walkway's solar lights are slowly going out, dull glowworms fading into the moonless night. Far away, beyond the house, beyond Ocala, maybe even beyond the distant beaches, soundless lightning billows upwards into an enormous thunderhead. Silent streaks of yellow electricity race across the sky. I swear they should crackle as they pass, but the only things we hear are singing frogs, snorting horses, and our footsteps on the mulch path.

"Big storm out there," I say.

"Sure is."

I cringe to myself. We can't even make the weather seem interesting. Isn't there anything else I can say? Something that isn't about cults, or Feather, or unreasonable uncles?

"One time in Yorkshire I was caught in a huge storm," Basil says suddenly. "I didn't even know there could be lightning storms like that in England. I was up in a stone barn and the lightning was just everywhere. The electricity in the air made the hair on my arms stand up."

"I've heard of that! I always thought it was just something in books."

"Nope, it's very real…and very scary." Lightning dashes across the sky, spreading so many tentacles it surely *has* to make a sound, but darkness reclaims us and there's nothing. Not even a sizzle of electrons fading into the black. We stop walking and watch the dark sky, hoping for another display. "But of course," Basil continues, "for sheer quantity, Florida has the rest of the world beat."

"Have you been in a lot of other places?" I ask, watching where my feet go as the last solar light blinks into darkness. "England and here and…"

"I was born in Hong Kong," Basil says. "Moved to Los Angeles when I was very young, then England, then here in the States. I've traveled for riding and shows, but my mother and uncle live in West Palm Beach."

"Where does Florida rank for you?"

Amusement tinges his voice as he replies, "Florida is first right now, although sometimes, in the middle of the morning when I'm on my third horse and the sweat is pouring into my eyeballs, it falls to last. But then I come inside and rediscover air conditioning and decide it's not so bad." He pauses, then adds, "I have more friends here, too."

"Oh?" If he has friends, he's keeping them very quiet. I rarely hear him mention talking to anyone else. "That's nice, having a lot of friends."

"I wouldn't say a lot," Basil says. "But, it's like…the people I know here are like the storms in Yorkshire."

Confused, I turn to look at him; the nearby porch light shines on his face and gives away his affectionate smile.

"For sheer intensity," he says, "Yorkshire wins."

My mind races around his metaphor. He said there was only one storm in Yorkshire. But of course there must have been other ones. Weaker, boring storms he wouldn't bother to write home about, hardly lasting in his mind once they'd come and gone. Okay, but he

The Sweetheart Horse

doesn't mean that *I'm* the intense friend, the one who makes Florida his favorite place—

Basil is gazing at me with a sudden intensity of his own; his dark eyes sparking with chips of gold from the porch light. We're the same height, and I'm suddenly aware that it would be very easy to take the lead here. I can step forward, close the six inches or so between us, and press my lips against his.

For better or for worse, I'd know in about ten seconds whether this thing between us exists...or if it's just something in my own, painkiller-addled brain.

I'm still trying to get up the nerve to go for it when Basil leans forward and gently kisses me on the lips. His touch is light, as careful and respectful as his hands on a horse's reins. At once I feel I have a glimpse into this man's soul, a soft-hearted boy who only wants to love and be loved, and as his lips retreat from mine, all I can think of is gaining more of him. More of his heart, more of his lips, more of his *everything*.

"Oh," I murmur, shocked and delighted and horrified all at once as my body springs to life, all my past indecision no longer an issue. Every inch of me is ready to press up against Basil and just, I don't know, do embarrassingly intimate things to his body. Touch him. Stroke him. Shove him against a wall and push every inch of myself against him as I kiss him absolutely silly.

All that from one soft kiss, scarcely more than a brush of the lips. But if it was a question, I'm more than ready to answer.

My kiss isn't gentle, and it isn't a question. It's a demand. Basil seems to hesitate at first, but then his hands wrap around my face and hair, tugging me towards him, and the moan in my throat is echoed by a growl in his.

There's more to this gentleman than softness and sweetness.

All of my body is in on this kiss, but even first kisses need breathing room. We both release one another, slowly and regretfully, and as I tip my chin up to take a ragged breath of humid air, lightning rushes across the sky behind Basil's unruly hair, reaching impossibly across the farm and towards the distant horizon. There is the slightest suggestion of thunder, scarcely more than a vibration in the air.

Basil looks around us, blinking as if he's just remembered we're outside, in Florida, in July.

"We should go inside," he whispers, and there's a ragged edge to his voice, a huskiness I've never heard before.

Inside, I think. *Yes, excellent plan.* "Let's go inside," I agree, and I take his hand. It's a bold move, I know, but he kissed me. *He* kissed *me.*

He *kissed* me.

I think we've earned ourselves a little hand-holding.

He resists just a moment before his fingers relax in mine, and I wonder if the same argument went running through his mind.

Chapter Twenty-One

I WAKE UP early, beating both my alarm and the sun. It's not a race I enjoy winning, but once my eyes fly open and the events of last night come crowding into my consciousness, I knew there's no going back to sleep. That last precious hour between the sheets would be wasted tossing and turning, so I get up and pull on a loose t-shirt and a pair of boxer shorts. I'll sit quietly over coffee for once, instead of throwing it into a travel mug and racing out to bring in the horses, feed them breakfast, and sweep the aisle—yes, I still have the aisle pristine before seven a.m., as a more arrogant Basil of the past demanded.

I expect to be alone at five o'clock in the morning. But as soon as I open my bedroom door, the aroma hits me like a final boarding call at the airport. Coffee. He's already up, then.

Already up and sitting at the kitchen bar, blinking with heavy lids at a steaming mug in front of him. He looks like a sleepy bear. A skinny, athletic sleepy bear, who stayed up until midnight with me, before we realized we were falling asleep on my bed, sheets tumbling to the floor and pillows scattered. I told him he could stay, but he demurred, saying he'd rather not inflict his snoring on me.

I said I doubted he snored, but I was willing to find out.

He said he didn't know for sure either, but that I needed my sleep.

"Concussed people shouldn't sleep," I told him. "It's medical science."

"That has been debunked," Basil informed me, kissing me as he disentangled himself from the duvet. "I'm just supposed to make sure you wake up normally the next day."

He puts down his mug. "You survived the night."

"I could have died," I remark. "You should have stayed with me."

"I was going to come in and check on you if you weren't up by six." He smiles at me. "And here you are, a whole hour early."

Something inside me unfurls and stretches, and I feel my lips reciprocating in kind. So now we're smiling at each other across the wide expanse of the luxurious kitchen, and the air smells of coffee and cinnamon, and the sky outside the windows is the deep, glowing blue of earliest pre-dawn. *This is like a movie,* I think.

"I made coffee," Basil says eventually. "I know it's usually your job, but I think you'll find I'm fairly good at it."

"Let's see, shall we?" I shake myself free of our mutually appreciative gazing session and go to the coffeemaker, my mind working frantically. In the movies, romantic leads always have something interesting to say on the morning after. But I don't think sparkling conversation over a predawn coffee is a realistic expectation for my debut performance. For one thing, no one has written me any lines. I'm stuck ad-libbing here. "I used to get up at five every morning," I say eventually, filling my favorite unicorn mug. I must admit his coffee smells heavenly. "When I worked at Posey's place. I didn't like being up so early."

I don't mind it right now.

"Why *do* racehorse people start so terribly early in the morning?" Basil's voice is amused. He shifts to one side to make room for me at the bar, pushing a stool my way, sliding the sugar and creamer down so I can sweeten up this devil's brew. "It's uncivilized, riding horses before the sun comes up," he says. "At least let them wake up a little."

No, what's uncivilized is being expected to make conversation before I've fully woken up with the man I spent several heated hours with the night before. My gaze strays around the kitchen and the living room, and I can't help blushing a little as I see the upturned cushions on the long gray sofa.

We left the place in a bit of disarray on our way to my bedroom last night.

Just thinking about what we got up to sets my cheeks on fire and my heart thumping. The sudden rush of blood shoves against the sore spot in my forehead and I wince, ducking my head to let my hair hide my expression.

"Kayla?"

"Hmm?" I resist the urge to wave my hand at him to be quiet, at least until I have this pain under control.

"Are you okay?"

"I'm fine." It's already subsiding. I swipe my hair back and give him what I hope is a convincing smile. "Just, um, a little headache this morning..."

"Another day off your feet," Basil says authoritatively. "Maybe you should go back to bed."

"It's not that serious," I protest, not wanting to end our morning coffee session so soon, even though our conversation hasn't exactly flowed. I never realized before just how little I have to say right after I've gotten up, but this is a solid reason not to get involved with your house-mate.

Although it does make me wonder what marriage is like. Maybe by the time I reach that point, my future husband and I will have already reached an understanding about silence before breakfast. Honestly, I don't know how else we'd coexist.

Next to me, Basil is launching into some sort of dissertation on a news story he was reading on his phone. His words warble in and out of my brain without leaving any real impression. All I can think is that I enjoy his voice and his accent, but maybe not right now.

"I'm not good in the morning," I confess when he reaches a stopping point. "I'm barely conscious right now."

He snorts. "Are you saying I just told you that entire story for nothing?"

"That's exactly what I'm saying."

Basil laughs and rubs his hand across my back. His touch makes all of my nerves sing at once and I snap upright, but he doesn't notice anything strange. His fingernails crease the fabric of my t-shirt and find the line of my spine, slowly working their way up towards my neck. My skin is prickling all over, anticipating the moment his fingers touch that sensitive spot just below my hairline. When it comes, I take a deep breath, my coffee cup rattling against the marble counter.

Basil smiles, like he's gotten exactly what he wanted. "I'm going out to feed," he says, standing up. I miss his touch immediately. Something in his expression tells me he knows it. "You stay here and drink your coffee. No exertion allowed." He turns to walk away, then glances back over his shoulder. A wink, so devilish I can hardly believe it's happening, sends a flick of electricity through my veins. "Unless I'm with you," he adds.

Oh, all the gods! Did he just *say* that? Basil, the king of the double entendre: I never would have expected it. I watch him walk out the back door, waiting until it's shut before I let out the long, shuddering breath I've been holding. Things have progressed at quite a pace in the past six or seven hours. We kissed. Then we made it around a few bases. Now coffee, and a warning not to do anything physical unless *he's* involved.

A helpful voice pipes up in my brain: *He also pretended not to know his uncle is involved with the Church of Celestial Beings, or are*

The Sweetheart Horse

we not talking about that right now?

No, we aren't, brain. We are deliberately going to leave that until later. Right now, I'm going to sit on that couch over there amongst the overturned cushions and drink my coffee and just savor the memory of last night. And maybe, because I've been very good, I'll let myself imagine what might happen next.

Only good things, because it's my imagination and my right to be optimistic. Ridiculously optimistic.

Just for this morning, let me have my Fantasyland.

It ends up being very boring, sitting around the house all day alone, even if I do give myself full license to engage on some very daring flights of fancy regarding myself and Basil. Become an international power show jumping couple? Yeah, I'll take one of those, please. Travel around the world finding Olympic prospects together? Don't mind if we do.

I know it's all just for fun, killing time while I wait for my doctor-prescribed downtime to run out so I can get back to my actual business of feeding and riding horses (which doesn't sound like a real job to me, even now, after ten years of getting paid real money to do these things). But there's something comforting about these daydreams, too. Things haven't exactly been all roses in my mental space over the past few months. From having to quit riding at Malone-Salazar Farms, to getting fired by Melody O'Leno over her own inability to ride without a crank noseband, to realizing that what I seem really good at isn't riding but farm-sitting...I mean, there's not much glitz in realizing you're not a confident enough rider to handle racehorses, and there's really no glamor in being the one who stays home feeding and mucking stalls. And to top off that particular bummer sundae, of course, is Feather, the horse who isn't at all what was promised.

Basil is a nice departure from all of these disappointments. The way he has emerged from his grumpy shell to become a supportive, kind person; the soul-stirring pleasure I take in his touch and his kiss —well, you get the idea. I haven't had a boyfriend in a long, long time. I'm willing to give Basil a shot, even if Evie would say he just wants to induct me into his cult.

Probably they're only after rich people for their cult, anyway. I should be safe.

So when Basil comes in around one o'clock, smelling strongly of horses and the rubbing alcohol he uses in their rinse water on very hot days, I've already built up a substantial fantasy life in which we're a romantic couple. This may lead to my greeting him *way* too exuberantly. "Hi, Bas!" I announce, leaping up from the sofa.

He gives me a flustered look. "Should you be jumping up like that?"

"Oh, don't be such a mother hen," I say, annoyed. "I'm fine."

"You wouldn't be if you were outside." He pulls the water pitcher from the fridge and produces a lemon from the crisper. These men and their spa water. "It's brutal out there today," he says. "Is all of summer going to be like this? Just humidity and heat and bugs?"

"I'm not from here," I remind him. "I think it's like this unless there's a hurricane, then it's like this, only times ten."

"Sounds super." He drinks a glass of water with his head tipped back, his slender throat exposed. I want to run my teeth over his skin.

"I guess you're missing English summers now," I suggest, thinking of Yorkshire, wishing he'd tell me something else about his time there.

"I always miss the English summer," Basil admits, with the air of a weakness. "Especially the wet ones, the cold drippy ones where everyone complains there's no summer at all and they're getting rain in their Cornettos."

I have no idea what a Cornetto is—maybe some kind of corn chips we don't have here—but I nod appreciatively, anyway. No one would want damp corn chips. "We've had a few of those in Virginia, where I'm from. People always say 'it's not really summer,' like the season owes them something straight out of a magazine."

"Yes!" Basil pours another glass of water and drops in a few more lemon slices, as if he's afraid an acute case of scurvy is one step behind him. "When we should all know the season—the planet, I mean—owes us nothing. Literally nothing owes anyone anything, if you think about it. It's all a social construct."

I don't love where this conversation is going. It sounds suspiciously like the argument of a player who is trying to get out any potential repercussions after a night of supposedly shared passion. "So, you're saying that you don't owe me anything," I say flatly. "I don't remember saying that you do."

"Of course I don't owe you anything, and you don't owe me anything." Basil is nodding emphatically, like I've made a fantastic point. "Feather, for instance. I am riding her because she needs ridden and you're not up to it yet. Not because I want you to give me something in return."

"Because that would be really gross if you did," I point out. "Obviously."

"Obviously," Basil echoes, looking away. "I mean—er—"

"Bas," I say.

He looks back at me, his gaze all but pleading with me to fix this hole he's dug for himself.

I take pity on him. "I don't think this is the direction you meant to take our conversation."

"It really isn't," he admits. "I just—well—I didn't want you to feel like we had to somehow, you know, *get even*."

I shrug, ready to drop the whole thing. I can always lay awake all night wondering what he meant. There's no point in arguing about it now. "Trust me, I don't feel that way."

Basil smiles ruefully. "Lack of sleep is making me incoherent."

I bite back a racy comment about how he'd better rest up for tonight, and instead merely suggest a nap.

"I would love to take a nap, but I have to go check out some horses for sale across town at Legends," he says, looking morose.

"Oh." I don't know what I expected. Maybe that he'd stay here and we'd make out for a while, then sleep away the afternoon? Is that too much to ask?

"Do you want to come?"

"To look at horses with you? Yes, absolutely!" A little strong, but at this point, whatever.

We're going on a horse-shopping date!

Everyone knows that's the very best kind of date, right?

Chapter Twenty-Two

THERE'S A VERY real delight in walking around one of the premier show-grounds in the United States—possibly the world—alongside an up-and-coming show jumper. People around here know Basil as a strong contender, and they want to talk to him. Well, they want to be *seen* talking to him. They want a little of that reflected glow. In the horse world, who you know is just as important as how well you ride. Some would argue it's more important.

So now, the summer circuit wants a piece of Basil Han. As we cut through cool, air-conditioned barns on our way to the stabling where his horse tryout awaits, people are coming up to him with halters over their shoulders and Gatorade bottles in their hands and custom boots on their feet, looking around for horse show gossip reporters and bloggers who might snap their picture and publish a career-favorable mention of that moment when they were seen casually chit-chatting with Basil Han, winner of May's open Grand Prix and favored to win the July installment in a few days, as well.

The bit about winning the upcoming Grand Prix is news to me, information which I glean second-hand while hovering at his shoulder and trying to look like a supportive, nonchalant girlfriend might appear. Rather than what I actually am, a surprised woman who has recently made the confusing upgrade from house-mate to romantic companion and isn't really sure of either her status or what her new bedroom partner is even talking about. On the inside, I'm wondering when he was going to mention his plans to me. I thought he was concentrating on Jock's flatwork this summer, thanks to the monthly riding lesson from Max's trainer. Maybe he doesn't see any point in discussing his career with me?

Oh, right, *this* is why I never have boyfriends. The constant, nagging insecurity they bring out in me!

After the third person in Stable B alone has tugged Basil aside to ask him what he's expecting in the course this weekend, I finally have to bring it up. I wait until she walks away, evidently satisfied with Basil's vague comments about sweeping turns and fast times on the clock. Then I grab his elbow. "Hey," I hiss. "You didn't tell me you were riding in the next open."

I try not to be accusatory, but a Grand Prix is kind of a big deal, and it's odd he didn't tell me. Right?

Basil only shrugs in reply. He's not even meeting my eyes; he's looking at his phone, waiting for a text from whatever trainer we're supposed to be meeting. When he finally glances up at me, his eyes widen as he realizes I'm actually annoyed.

"Whoa," he says, holding up his free hand in self-defense. "I'm bringing Jock over on Friday and riding him in the class on Saturday night, then bringing him home right afterwards. It's not a big deal. You won't even notice we're gone."

"I think I'll notice," I object. "I usually do a head-count on the horses in the barn, just to make sure none are missing."

"Oh, but you should come," Basil says, brightening. "It'll be fun—I should have said something before. I was just distracted by all this work stuff, and—"

"Basil!" We both turn our heads as a young woman's voice calls out. She's walking into the barn with a long, confident stride, one more slim thing in sleek blue breeches and tastefully scuffed field boots. Her dark hair is tucked under a scarf, with a few smooth curls escaping around her arched eyebrows. She looks like she's stepped out of a movie from the 1960s, ready to find her leading man and ride off with him into the California sunset.

I know I don't contrast with her very well; my face is shiny with sweat and my unruly hair is about two feet tall in this humidity. But hey, no one's looking at me.

Miss Hollywood 1965 says, "Oh, Basil, sorry I'm late!"

She has one of those rough riding coach voices, I note with satisfaction. Permanently hoarse from shouting all day.

"It's no problem," Basil assures her. "I know how hunter rings can be."

She brays with laughter. "Summer hunter circuits are the devil! I don't know how the Legends PR machine convinced us to stay here and show all summer. I had no idea Florida was this brutal."

"The air-conditioned arenas surely help?" Basil suggests.

"It would be fine if we *never* had to go outside! Unfortunately, we still have to walk between the barns and the indoors." She notices me finally and looks me over curiously. Then she holds out a hand. It's refreshingly calloused; like her voice, her hand betrays the distinct lack of glamor in her life. I like that. "Shana," she tells me, with an expectant air. "Shana Goldman?"

Oops, am I supposed to know her name? I don't know any hunter trainers besides the ones who write articles for *Practical Horseman*, and even then I'm mainly looking at the course diagrams and the pictures. Amanda loves the hunter ring, but I'm more of a jumper myself. Like Basil, actually, just on a much lower scale.

"Oh, erm, sorry," I begin, but she's already talking over me, her eyes on Basil.

"Basil, babe, I can't say enough good things about this horse. He's a half-ton teddy-bear, and he has Young Rider mount written all over him. He can take anyone around a course. He's been doing Children's Jumpers when I don't need him for my Equitation students and absolutely cleaning up. Please tell me you have a client in mind."

"Of course I do," Basil says cheerfully. "Motivated and ready to write the check."

"That's my guy!" Shana gives him a conspiratorial smile, then glances at me. Her expression smooths into something more bland, as she remarks, "You know, Basil doesn't buy a lot of horses, but the ones he *does* pick up go straight to new riders. He's so fast. Efficient, that's what you are, Basil. We need more people like you in this business."

They give each other what I can only call knowing looks.

She's definitely in the cult, I think. This is unbelievable. I'm witnessing the horse-buying cult in action. The only thing I need to prove it is some Celestial Being paraphernalia. What did Posey say about Sylvia Britton that tipped her off? Oh, right: anointing the horse with essential oils and facing it towards its cardinal direction. I glance at the tack room nearby, wondering if there is a shelf of New Age supplies in amongst the liniments and hoof dressings.

"I have a potential Young Rider on my scouting list," Basil is saying, following Shana as she slides open a stall door. "She's based in Washington state, poor girl. It's very hard to compete on a national scale from up there, but she's talented and willing to pay for the right horse."

I suppose this kid is in the Church of Celestial Beings, too. Assuming they take teenagers.

Basil and Shana vanish into a stall housing a tall chestnut gelding, still earnestly talking shop, while I lurk in the barn aisle, forgotten. Embarrassed to be standing in this beautiful stable with nothing to do and seemingly no business here, I pull out my phone and start scrolling. But apparently everything interesting on the internet has taken the day off; or maybe it's just that I've been on my phone so much over the past two days that I have read everything on the internet already. At least the horsey parts.

Suddenly, a text appears from Evie.

New Celestial Being data incoming.

Oh, no. This timing can't be a coincidence.

Suddenly, I don't want to see it. I just want to live in my nice, cheerful Fantasyland where Basil is a perfectly normal horse-riding boyfriend who is not involved with a cult. Is that so much to ask? No, I don't think it is.

Please don't, I start to text, but her bubble pops before mine.

Found a Reddit page about them. Looks like it's all money laundering. Some trainers on this list of members. Hang on will paste.

"Let's take him out to the schooling ring right over here," Shana is saying from behind me. She leads the chestnut horse out of the stall, all tacked up and ready to go. Basil emerges behind them, buckling the strap on his helmet. He gives me a hopeful sort of smile.

"Can you do me a favor? Can you go out to the schooling arena behind the next barn, and pop some fences up for us to school? I wouldn't ask, but—"

"My working student is out sick today," Shana puts in smoothly. "I'm so sorry about that."

"No, no, it's fine," I say, wondering if they're trying to get rid of me so they can do their pre-riding ritual. What if there are incantations? I need to see this.

"We'll be right there," Shana says firmly. "Five minutes, tops."

Dammit, I've been dismissed.

The schooling arena is just one barn away, as empty and pristine as an undiscovered beach on a desert island. The footing, some kind of sand and fiber blend, is a brilliant white, gleaming painfully bright beneath the midday sun. I push open the gate, heading for the cluster of jump standards and poles stacked in one corner, and immediately feel the weight of all these windowless, warehouse-like barns surrounding me. It's not necessarily that I feel like I'm being watched, but I definitely don't feel alone, either. There are just too many unseen beings here: a city full of horses and their human attendants, but with no one on the streets.

Overall, I'd say the vibe at Legends Equestrian Center is a little eerie. It's nice that everything is indoors and air-conditioned, but that's not exactly natural, is it? All the hustle and bustle is hidden indoors; the outside paths and arenas had a little activity when we arrived, but since then, that has subsided. It feels like I'm the only person in the world, like everyone else has been magicked right off the surface of the earth and it's just me, setting fences for a horse and rider who will never walk out to this arena.

Or maybe all this Celestial Beings talk has gotten into my head. A bit too much supernatural in my diet right now. Time to cut back.

So I put it out of my head and get to work, putting up the basic sort of schooling fences you'd expect at a horse show: a vertical, a cross-rail, an oxer. It doesn't take very long; still, when I'm finished, I look around expecting to see Basil and Shana, and it's surprising to find I'm still all alone in a grid of faceless white warehouses.

What are they up to? And can I catch them in the act?

I stalk back up the rubber-paved horse path. They shouldn't have taken so long; shouldn't have given me an excuse to come back. I won't be surprised if I see Shana chanting over the chestnut horse or lecturing Basil on his cardinal direction, but I will definitely be annoyed if I see Basil joining in with it.

Annoyed and a little afraid, to be perfectly honest. I think we can make a great couple, but not if he's in a cult.

Everyone has to draw the line somewhere.

I pause next to the barn's open door, considering my next move. If I creep in, the horse might give me away before I get a good look at what they're doing with him—horses hear the tiniest movements. Better just burst right in and get it over with.

I take a breath and enter the barn.

They're still in the aisle with the chestnut horse, just as I suspected. But now they're standing outside the tack room door, and Basil is next to Shana, holding the reins, while Shana has her hands pressed against the horse's head, right between his ears.

She spins around as the horse lifts his head to look at me, and I immediately see the small bottle she grips in one hand.

Next to her, Basil's lips compress into a thin line.

Of course. I don't have to read the bottle's label to know what was going on here.

"I'll take him out to the arena and start warming up," Shana says, slipping back into smooth trainer mode almost instantly. "Let me just—" She darts into her tack room and emerges a moment later with her hands empty; the bottle is gone.

Basil hands her the reins without a word and she walks the horse past me, her eyes straight ahead, her smile plastered across her face like a mask.

I look at Basil, who still looks as though he swallowed a bug. "Really?" I ask, exasperated.

He holds up his hands as if to ward me away. "It's not what you think."

"Should I go get the bottle?" I tilt my head towards the tack room door. "Would you like me to anoint your forehead? Open your third eye before you ride, maybe?"

"Third eye—no, come on, Kayla." Basil has the nerve to look

annoyed. "Obviously, I'm not caught up in any woo-woo nonsense like that. Give me some credit."

"So what, it was just fly lotion or something?"

"Yes," Basil says. "It was fly repellent lotion."

That was nice of me to give him such an easy out, wasn't it? I probably don't have a future as an FBI agent.

But Basil doesn't know about everything Evie and I have already found out about him, so he thinks he's off the hook. His eyes rest on my face for a moment, then he slowly lifts his hand and touches my cheek. His rough fingertips are smooth as silk on my hot skin. Something flares within me, answering his touch, and I reach up and grasp his hand before he can ignite me further.

But I don't push him away.

His dark eyes bore into mine, and that flame of hopeful desire surges higher. This is Basil, I think. Not my enemy, but the person who has shared my life for more than a month, from breakfast to dessert and everything in between. The man who has helped me with my horse and brought me home from the hospital. Who touches my face to make sure I don't have a temperature. And I don't want to fight with him. I just want this to be a normal, real relationship. No spirits, no sacred oils, no secrets.

Could I possibly just muscle this into reality with sheer mental force?

Yeah, and then I can bend a few spoons with my mind.

I sigh and drop my eyes. "Basil, you know one time is funny and two times is no coincidence, right?" I say softly. "Are you going to come clean with me about this? Or do I have to figure it all out on my own?"

"There's nothing to tell," he says. "I'm not involved."

He's lying to me. I should leave. Just wrench my arm free and walk away from him. That would be the smart move.

But there will be no smart decisions made here today, at Legends Equestrian Center. Not by me, not by anyone else. Just the usual equestrian mistake of letting our hearts decide, over and over and over. We are horse-people and we refuse to learn; we touch the stove, act surprised, and touch it again.

I lift my eyes again and let Basil's dark gaze root me to this spot, right next to him.

If he sees my surrender, he doesn't gloat, and I appreciate that.

"I know what you're thinking," he says. "But can you just walk out there with me? Please. Let's just watch this horse go and you can tell me what you think. I really do want your opinion."

I can't deny that's flattering.

"Of course," I say, and I fall into step beside him. We are just two equestrians looking at a horse for sale. This is a role I know how to play.

We emerge from the cool barn into the dazzling white heat of Florida in July, and suddenly the empty grid of horse paths and walkways around the blank warehouses isn't so eerie, after all. It's just the backstage view, I think. Nothing sinister or weird about it.

We reach the arena, and Shana waves at us from horseback. It's my first good view of the horse in question, and I have to say, I'm not impressed. There's nothing really wrong with him. But he doesn't make me clutch my heart and cry, "I must have him!" either, and for the prices Young Riders prospects go for, I would need that kind of charisma.

"He's not going to win any prizes for looks," I murmur to Basil. "You really think he can do Young Riders?"

"He's apparently got a jump like a kangaroo," Basil whispers back. His mouth is very close to my ear, and I resist the urge to tip my head against his. I'm keeping it professional.

But only just.

"He doesn't seem to have a lot of spark," I observe, as Shana nudges the horse into a trot. He covers the ground with a smooth, attractive gait. I understand now why she's been using him in the Equitation ring. "But I admit that's a pretty trot. Don't you have any clients doing Big Eq classes?"

"I don't, actually," Basil says thoughtfully. "You know, we have a very small client list."

I glance at him. "We?" I repeat. "You and who else?"

"Well, the company," he replies, looking surprised I'd ask. "Han Worldwide."

"I don't like that name," I inform him.

He grins. "Neither do I, actually. But hey-ho, it's not forever. It's just me and my uncle, you know. And before you say he's not a person I should be working for, understand that he gave me my start, so I feel like I owe him."

"Did he give you a start before or after he started a church?" I ask, deliberately sidestepping the word *cult*.

Basil glances at me and his cheeks flush. His eyes flick back to the horse in the ring.

"Bas, who started it for real?" I ask. "Is Sylvia Britton the one behind it? Or is she following your uncle's big book of magical horse spells? And how many people do you guys have locked up like poor Shana here? I know that wasn't fly repellent she was rubbing on his head, Basil, but thanks for thinking I'm an idiot!"

"It's not about magic," Basil retorts, stung into answering me. "I mean—the whole thing is really about—"

"What?" I ask, as he clams up. "What is the whole thing about?"

He shakes his head. "I can't talk about it now," he says. "Can we discuss this at home?"

I glare at him. "Do you promise?" I ask after a moment's consideration. "You won't just try to wriggle out of telling me?

Because I'm not going to let it go."

"I promise," Basil says. "I mean it. I should have known this would happen."

"What? That I'd find out you're part of a horse cult?"

"It's not a cult, I promise."

"I think it is."

"And I'm not part of it."

"I think you are," I tell him. "Maybe you're not waving your magic wand before every ride, but if you're holding her horse for her while she dabs him with oil, you're part of it."

He makes a face. "That's unfair."

Shana canters by. "I'm going to jump!" she calls.

"Great!" I say brightly, when it becomes clear Basil isn't going to say anything. "Don't ignore her, Basil. She's going to think something's wrong and it'll mess up her chakras."

He rubs his face. "There's no chakras in Celestial Beings. I don't think. I'm not actually really clear on what all goes on with it."

"Whatever it is, I'm fine with finishing up here and then discussing it in private. Okay? Forget I said anything. Let's get this horse trialed and go get some food, and then we can talk about your horse gods."

Basil sighs and looks at me with something like resignation. "Kayla, I really like you."

My heart skips a beat, like I've just become a teenager who scored the cutest boy in school to walk her home. I'm such an idiot. "I like you, Bas," I say softly. "I think that's obvious. I just don't want to see you getting into trouble. The show circuit isn't the kind of place where you can be...you know, *different*. Or do something that looks and feels like a weird scam."

He holds up a hand. "I'm not actually in the Church of of Celestial Beings, Kayla. It's important to me that you know that part.

This isn't my game, I promise you."

I don't want to tell him that his promises are pretty worthless to me, since he lied about all of this from the start. We're not starting that fight here, amongst all these silent barns, as Shana canters the chestnut around and around the jumps. "Horse now," I tell him. "Talk later. I'm supposed to be helping you with this, so tell me: do you *have* to buy this horse? Is this just a formality? Or does my opinion actually matter?"

Basil gives my hand a quick squeeze. "Your opinion really matters. My uncle wants this horse to work out, but if it isn't right, we won't recommend the sale."

"Okay," I say, pleased at this part, at least. "That settles it. I will be *extra* critical and objective. Good cop, bad cop, that's how you tag-team on horse sales."

Basil turns his full, beautiful smile on me, filling my head with static. "Sounds perfect, Kayla," he says. "I think we make a really good team."

And with that, Basil waves to Shana, who has the chestnut cantering around the arena. "Ready when you are!"

I'm left on the rail in the blazing sun, feeling wrung out as an old mop.

Basil mounts the chestnut, settling into Shana's saddle with admirable ease. I pick up my phone, intending to take some video we can go over later. When I see all the texts on the lock screen, I realize I can't ignore Evie's Reddit intel any longer. There's just too much here to pretend it doesn't exist.

"What is all this, Evie?" I mutter, flicking through the short texts. Names of trainers who are supposedly associated with the Church of Celestial Beings. Okay, she probably could have sent one text with all the info, but that's not Evie's style. Why make my phone buzz once when she can make it buzz a dozen times?

I flick through the texts, trying to make sense of the names. Most of them are new to me. But I see three I know.

Sylvia Britton, obviously.

And here's Max, ugh. I hate to see it.

And, naturally, here is Shana Goldman.

I feel like if I'd seen this information this morning, I'd be more upset. But now it's just confirmation of what I've already figured out: Edward Han, Basil's uncle, is running an elaborate scam to buy and sell horses to a select client list. It seems like a lot of trouble to me, but hey, everyone has their own thing. Maybe he enjoys being a spiritual guru. I don't know the guy.

I text back to Evie: *at the LEC watching one of Shana Goldman's horses now.*

Her reply is instantaneous. *No way!!*

Yes way, I tap. *The horse is fine. Not amazing. But Basil is going to buy it, guaranteed.*

He kinda has to.

Truth.

A horse sales cult is a really good idea, Evie replies. *Maybe we are just jealous we didn't think of it.*

She makes a great point. I start to tell her so, then I stop. Even as a joke, it's not a great idea. Selling horses isn't just about the money—at least, it shouldn't be. It's about creating partnerships, and if Basil sells this Young Riders prospect to a kid who isn't the right match, someone could get hurt. And at the very least, this teenager dreaming of a career in horses could suffer a serious setback, with years of wasted time and effort going into a horse who isn't right for them. Narrowing the field of potential horse partnerships to just this little group of spiritualists isn't good for anyone.

Except for Edward Han, who is guaranteed a quick turnaround on an expensive show horse—a guaranteed profit that is all but impossible in the horse world.

Damn, he really did come up with the one surefire way to make sure he gets a return on his equine investment.

But you know, if the only way to make a living in the horse sales business is to start a cult, it's probably not right for me. I just don't think I have it in me.

Thunder rumbles from one of those fluffy clouds to the west, distracting me from my bizarre thoughts. I turn to watch the cloud, which has a blinding-white, towering stack reaching high into the sky, and a dark underbelly hanging close to the tree-lined hills in the distance. A quick stab of lightning flickers through the air, and suddenly a piercing siren begins wailing from somewhere on the show-grounds. I look back at the schooling ring and see Basil trotting towards the gate, Shana jogging at his side.

"Lightning detection system," she calls. "Alerts us to lightning within ten miles."

"So, we're going in?" I unlatch the gate and swing it open as Basil dismounts, handing the reins off to Shana.

"Have to," Shana says, shrugging. "Property rules."

Basil hangs back alongside me as Shana leads the hot horse towards the stables. "They really put the fear of God into them with their lightning rules," I observe. "Usually, I just ride until something hits a little too close for comfort."

"This is a different world, alright," Basil agrees, and he's not even talking about cults now, just fancy show-grounds versus life at the farm. He takes off his helmet and shakes back his hair. I watch him like a favorite television show. Even sweaty and fresh off a horse, I want Basil.

Even lying to me and engaging in questionable business practices, I want Basil.

I'm so disappointed in myself.

And then, unaware he's making things a thousand times worse, Basil puts an arm around my shoulders and pulls me close, dropping a light kiss on my cheek. "Let's get you inside where it's safe," he suggests. "I don't want my girl out in a thunderstorm."

My girl.

Of course, this has me over the moon. Are you kidding me? Shana might look like the lead in a rom-com, but guess what—I'm the secret star.

I float into the barn and as the rain pounds down on the metal roof, I watch Basil joke his way through some quick negotiations with Shana. In about fifteen minutes, they've come to an agreement, and Han Worldwide is officially purchasing the chestnut gelding. While they're congratulating each other on a job well done, I slip into the tack room next to the horse's stall.

It's not hard to spot what I'm looking for. There's a shelving unit, each shelf stacked with plastic organizer cubes. Most hold bottles of standard tack room concoctions: liniment, therapeutic gels, antibiotic creams. A few are stacked with white saddle pads and polo wraps. One holds an electric candle—I imagine real candles are against show-ground rules—which flickers in front of a tiny horse statuette. The identical mate to the one on Max's bedside table.

With a glance over my shoulder to make sure I'm not observed, I take the little statue in my hands and flip it over.

Celestial Being Level II.

There's a crack of thunder overhead, which is surely a joke from all the gods, but mostly the ones in charge of relationships.

I put the horse back and skedaddle back into the barn aisle, just as Basil and Shana shake hands and wish each other a nice afternoon.

I take it as a blessing that at least there isn't a weird cult farewell.

Not even a secret handshake. At least they can be normal in public.

"That was easy," Basil murmurs as we walk to the truck beneath a cool drizzle, thunder rumbling in the distance as the storm continues its quick sweep east. "And gets Uncle Edward off my back for a few weeks, anyway. Thank God...I don't need to worry about him this weekend while I'm trying to win this Grand Prix class, y'know?"

I do know. I know what it's like to live for a few hours without worrying about your boyfriend—and that's what he must be, right? He called me his girl, so I think it's official—and his family business, the cult.

Basil Han may not be a cult ringleader, but he's definitely involved with something shady. If word gets out—and it will, because the horse business is small and backstabbing is considered perfectly normal—then it could destroy his future in the show-ring.

And if I stand too close to him, it could ruin mine, too.

Well, there's a nice new worry I didn't start the day with.

Chapter Twenty-Three

I CONTEMPLATE MY future all the way home, while Basil drives one-handed, his free hand on the console between us. Toying with my fingers. Trying to keep me sweet. Reminding me that we've moved to a rich new physical place in our relationship.

It's obvious that both physically and emotionally, we've been jumping ahead a few squares, and I suspect he feels more comfortable with me now that I know at least part of his secret. But I'm not here to be Basil's weighted blanket while he tries to justify his job. I'm trying to build my own career, however slow and stilted my progress has been. Feather, as difficult as she is, has been a ray of light, a promise that bigger things are coming.

I can't let Basil drag me down now.

And yet as he drives his little sedan through the farmlands of Marion County, horses scattered on either side of us like gold spilling from a mountainside vein, I can feel my heart pulling me back towards him. I haven't learned a single thing about Basil which makes me care about him any less. That's the frustrating part.

The surly man I fell in front of at Legends that night has become so important to me, I don't know how to tell him we can't go on like this.

As we pull through the front gates of the farm, I know what I have to do. The only thing I can do. Get out of the house before I fall completely in love with this guy.

I mean, I can already feel it happening. Watching Basil ride like poetry, connect with horses like a shaman from some culture I can only daydream about, then cast all that attention on me with his sweet nothings and soft touches...

How is a girl supposed to resist all this?

But I have to, obviously. I have to take a firm stance. When I moved to Florida, it was in hopes of learning to stand on my own two feet and learning to live without constant support from my parents. Obviously, joining Basil in his little horse-cult deception would be the opposite of this goal. And eventually, Basil will try to add me to the roster, right?

I mean, if he doesn't, that's just insulting. But even as I think about what the invitation might look like (I'm imagining a pale pink card, maybe scented with incense, and a hand-inscribed exhortation to discover my inner goddess) I have to admit to myself that I'm probably not a good enough rider or trainer to even gain admittance to the Church of Celestial Beings. How much value could I add? Neither of my horses are for sale, and even if I were actively looking for a new prospect, I don't think my horse-shopping budget of exactly zero dollars would light any fires with old Uncle Edward.

Really, the whole situation is a strange mix of uncomfortable and embarrassing. I excuse myself from Basil the moment we get into the house, ignoring his disappointed look as I slip into my bedroom and close the door. I'm wondering how I'll spend the rest of the day when my phone buzzes with a text from Evie, asking if she can bring her horse over to school in the covered arena.

An actual social engagement? Yes, please. I text her back immediately, and then fall onto my bed, closing my eyes tightly. I figure I'll just nap until she gets here. But knowing Basil is just upstairs keeps me awake, questioning every decision I've made this summer, for the next hour.

Evie's horse, Easy Breezy, is a bay Thoroughbred gelding with a heart of gold. He loves galloping, jumping cross-country, and powering through massive jumper courses. So it was rough on Evie when he started showing signs of anhidrosis, a weird condition where horses stop sweating. She's had to put him on all sorts of supplements, feeds him a bottle of Guinness every day, and tries to ride him while it's storming in the afternoon—not the safest policy, but she figures it's her only way to keep him in shape all summer. It turns out this is why she decided to show him in dressage at Legends Equestrian Center this summer—the air-conditioned indoors are her only shot at competition.

This afternoon, Breezy is enjoying the shade of the covered arena.

"Thanks for letting me bring him over," Evie says, mounting up and bringing the horse alongside Crabby and me. "With the way it's been storming lately, I haven't been able to get him out much. I mean, there can be such a thing as too much lightning, even for me!"

"You should just leave him here for the rest of the summer," I suggest, thinking quickly. "We could ride together every afternoon, and hang out, and—"

And there'd be almost no time for me to be alone with Basil. Everyone wins. Except Basil, but I'm trying not to think about his feelings right now.

Evie grins and shakes her head. "Uh-uh. I'm no third wheel, Kayla. You're enjoying a summer of bliss with Basil Han. Why should I get in the way? He'll probably sweep you away to a mass marriage ceremony by Labor Day. I wouldn't want to mess that up for you."

I frown at her as our horses move off together. "It's not that kind of cult."

"Maybe not." Evie peers at me. "It was a joke, Kayla. Are you okay?

You look a little freaked out. I don't *actually* think he's going to marry you."

"Trust me, marriage is the last thing on my mind," I sigh. "Evie, I think I need to get out of here. I shouldn't be alone with him."

"Why on earth not? Do you think he's dangerous? Might sacrifice you to the horse gods?"

"No, of course not! I'm not trying to be crazy over here. I'm just..." I shrug. I don't know what I'm doing. "I'm trying to avoid getting caught up in something weird," I conclude. "Something that could affect my future career."

"Maybe you're over-reacting," Evie says.

I give her a skeptical look.

"Okay, or not," she amends, still smiling like this is all a joke. "I mean, Celestial Beings *sounds* very sus. But also, should we consider, maybe it isn't?"

"How can it not be sus when it's clearly a money-laundering operation? With magical horse statues and essential oils? It's probably a multi-level marketing scam, too. I'll bet there's a whole pyramid of ponies."

"But it's the horse business," Evie replies. "Shouldn't you expect something weird? Isn't asking for a nice, normal boyfriend who also rides horses just a little unreasonable? Frankly, I would be surprised if such a thing exists. I mean, Adam Salazar seems normal on the outside, but what *isn't* Posey telling us? Maybe if Basil's only working for his uncle's little cult, instead of actually being a high priest in it, then maybe it's worth giving him a second chance?"

I'm silent. She's making really strong points. But there's still the worry that he'll sink everything I've been working towards. "What about when he slips up and everyone finds out? Then Basil Han's part of a scammy cult and I'm the girlfriend who goes down with him? It's noble, but not exactly a strong career plan."

The Sweetheart Horse

"Maybe you'll get the sympathy vote," she suggests. "Everyone will take pity on you for being hoodwinked by a pretty face."

"I don't think I want that, either."

Evie shakes her head, like she can't believe how difficult I'm being. "Think it over," she advises. "Don't rush anything. You're never going to find another spot like this. And anyway, where would you go if you left here?"

"Your house?" I suggest.

Evie laughs. Loudly. Crabby tips his ears back and snorts at the sound. "No chance in hell," she chortles. "I live in a single-wide! One bedroom, one bath! No roommates allowed."

"I could stay on your couch, couldn't I?" I demand, even though Evie's couch is a Salvation Army number which was evidently designed for people with no feeling in their backsides.

"Absolutely not. Now, you can sleep on Amanda's couch," Evie suggests—heartlessly, I think. "Oh wait, if you went to Amanda's house, she'd have you sleeping on down pillows in a guest room made of rainbows and moonlight."

"Those two things don't go together," I complain sulkily. But she's right. I could probably stay with Amanda if push came to shove. I wouldn't even get to the end of my sentence before she'd invite me in with open arms. Amanda is starved for company in that big, stylish house of hers. "I'll think about it," I decide. "Maybe I won't rush out of here after all, like you said. But I will *not* forget that you abandoned me in my hour of need."

Evie shrugs. "Hey, I get it."

After we've finished riding, Evie takes Breezy in for a bath, and we end up giving both horses a full spa treatment: shampoo, conditioner, detangler on their tails, the works. Evie is impressed with a new miracle coat conditioner she discovered in Max's things

—it's impossible to keep her from rooting around in the tack room like it's her personal candy store—and she keeps running her hands over Breezy's coat as we graze them on the lawn behind the barn.

"Look at him," she sighs. "Like a new copper penny. Give him a pet. He's soft as a baby's bottom."

"It's very slippery, though," I observe, rubbing my slick hand on my breeches. "If you buy it for yourself, maybe don't condition his back. It's almost as slick as Show Sheen."

"I can't afford it," she says. "Won't be a problem."

"I just assumed you were going to steal this bottle. Glad that's not the case."

"I wouldn't *steal* from—oh, who is that?" Evie shoves at my arm. "Going into the arena!"

I look up and to my surprise, see Basil leading a horse into the covered arena. I recognize the horse as Classica; the dark bay gelding is an Intermediare-level competitor with a top-line made of pure muscle. Since our work schedules overlap, I haven't seen Basil ride him before, but I suspect Classica is the toughest ride in the barn. He's already mouthing his bits, foam dripping onto his chest and forelegs.

"He must be riding with Max's trainer," I realize. "I think this is their first lesson together."

"Oh, who's the trainer?" Evie leans back on her elbows, ready for a show.

"Karl something," I reply. "Something German, I can't remember. I've heard Max talking about him before. He says he's really mean. But crazy popular. Max paid for a whole bunch of lessons ahead of time, but it took Basil forever to get on his calendar."

Suddenly, I wonder how Basil will do with a mean trainer. Surely that can't be good for his anxiety. But maybe it's not a big deal when he's in the saddle.

The Sweetheart Horse

Karl Something German marches to the center of the arena and stands there like a ringmaster. He begins barking criticisms the moment Basil mounts. I'm accustomed to the occasional tough dressage lesson, but this Karl is taking things to a whole new level. When Evie mutters, "I'm glad this isn't me," I have to agree.

"I think I'd cry and get off my horse," I say. "And I don't usually mind a mean trainer."

"He'd probably take out a gun and shoot you for insubordination."

"Seriously!"

We watch as Karl Something German grabs his hair and throws a temper tantrum, evidently something to do with Basil's—hand? Leg? Height? It's very hard to tell.

"How does Max deal with this guy?" Evie whispers, incredulous.

"Max doesn't really notice criticism," I explain. "He's kind of in a perpetual good mood and everything just rolls off his back."

"Lucky Max," Evie says. "But I don't think Basil is in the same class at all."

She's right. As the lesson progresses, it becomes more and more obvious that this is a match made in hell. Basil's face has gone pale, his features are strained, and his famously soft hands are trembling on the reins. When he catches Classica in the mouth with the curb, the horse throws up his head in anger. Karl roars his displeasure; Basil gets more tense. It's like watching a house of cards fall down, get trampled into some mud, and then torn up for good measure. Thirty minutes pass like a slow-motion panic attack, and then Karl stamps out of the arena.

Basil looks down at Classica's neck and runs one hand across his eyes.

Oh, no, I think. And almost before I realize I'm doing it, I'm scrambling to my feet.

"Where are you going?" Evie demands, but I just throw Crabby's lead-rope into her lap and run for the arena.

I'm slipping through the railings as Basil dismounts and presses his forehead against Classica's sweaty neck. His helmet is dangling from his fingers. When it falls, I'm beside him just in time to catch it.

"Don't let this hit the ground for no reason," I say. "You don't want to have to buy a new one."

He looks at me like I'm a ghost who has just swept in to spirit him away from this plane. And maybe that's exactly what Celestial Beings do, but I'm really here to ground him. I put my hand on his shoulder and squeeze gently, as if to wring out all the stress he's carrying there. "Hey," I whisper. "You're okay, Baz."

He blinks at me, his eyes wide. For one breathless moment, I think he doesn't even see me. Then comprehension surges into his startled expression, and his eyes focus. He takes a short, sharp gasp, and I realize he has been holding his breath.

"Breathe," I tell him. "Deep breaths."

He makes another desperate gasp. "Can't," he chokes.

"Start down here," I say, pressing my free hand to his stomach. His abs clench reflexively at my touch, hard and defensive. I spread my fingers out in response, ignoring the hot sensation that pools in my center. Totally inappropriate right now, body! We are dealing with a panic attack here. "Breathe from right here," I tell him. "Where my hand is."

He struggles to comply, but after a few moments, his breathing eases. The little gasps turn into deeper, calmer inhalations. "Okay," he says eventually. "Okay. I feel better."

His eyes are too dark; his pupils are dilated as if he's been drugged. "Just stay still a moment," I tell him.

"Classica needs to go in," he protests.

Horses first, always.

I look around for Evie and spot her as she rounds the corner from the barn to the covered arena, hands mercifully free of other horses.

"I turned our guys out," she explains, reaching for Classica's reins. "Here, give me this beast." She starts to walk the horse away, then pauses and looks him over. Slowly, she runs her hand down his neck and back to the saddle. "Oh, no."

"What—" I begin, confused.

"Your saddle slipped back a good inch," Evie tells Basil. "Did you use that coat conditioner? When's the last time you gave this horse a bath?"

I want to bury my face in my hands. Beside me, comprehension is dawning on Basil's face. "I did this morning," he admits. "Max told me Karl always wants them ready for the show-ring. He said do everything but braid. I found that coat conditioner and it promised an instant shine."

"Classica looks fantastic," Evie assures him. So it does work. But —"

"But it's slippery." Basil rubs his face. "That's the most rookie mistake of all time."

"The bottle didn't say it was slippery," Evie declares. "I'm going to hit them up on Twitter tonight. Now, I'm taking this horse in for a shower. You're off the clock, Basil."

Basil watches Evie walk the horse towards the gate. "I can't believe that happened," he says. "But honestly, I can't blame everything on Classica. I rode badly."

"You rode fine," I tell him, squeezing his hand. "Karl is just an asshole."

"He's an Olympian."

"That doesn't give him any right to scream at students."

"Max doesn't mind him. Why should I?"

"Because he's not right for you," I insist. "This has nothing to do with your riding and everything to do with how he behaves."

Basil shakes his head. "I can't even explain what happened. I feel like I just lost control."

"You had a panic attack. Anxiety's a bitch, Basil."

He gives me a searching look, and for a moment I think he must have forgotten he told me about his anxiety. But then he just shrugs and smiles sadly. "I guess I better get over it fast, huh? No room for panic attacks in this sport."

"No, that's not right," I tell him. "Baz, there are other trainers out there. You shouldn't even try to ride with a bully."

"This is who Max said to ride with. This is who they're paying for me to ride with. What should I do?" He looks at me with worried eyes, the face of a boy confronted with an impossible conundrum. And for a moment I'm flustered by his confusion. We're a really good pair, I know.

Seriously, though, it shouldn't be hard for Basil to tell Max that his choice of riding coach isn't going to work out, or even to just quietly cancel the lessons and refuse to reschedule them. Basil knows Max wouldn't be upset. That's not Max's style at all.

"Do what you want," I suggest. "Make yourself happy." It's the answer I'd give Evie if she was being wishy-washy about something, and she'd brighten and nod and say, "Good call, Kayla, that's exactly what I'm going to do."

I wait for Basil to smile and say the same thing.

But he just looks at the ground. "I'm supposed to ride with Karl," he mutters.

I stare at his bowed head, his slumped shoulders, and suddenly I realize something hard and true about Basil...and about myself, too, I suppose. Whatever this thing is with his uncle, this ridiculous church, this so-called client list of theirs, the buying and selling of horses he finds for the company—it's not his choice. Basil hasn't been allowed to make his own choices. I'm sure of it. That's why now, confronted with something as simple as firing a riding coach our boss contracted for him, he falls apart.

I could change things for Basil.

I could be the person who helps him stand up to his uncle, and stand up for *himself.*

The conviction lights a fire in my belly. Basil needs me.

For the girl who has always been supported by everyone, this feels like a revelation. Like the call to action I've been waiting for my whole life.

Someone else needs *me?* Irresistible.

Chapter Twenty-Four

EVIE HEADS HOME after she bathes Classica, and I send Basil back to the house with strict instructions to drink some lemonade and sit in the air conditioning and not come back to the barn until he's fully recovered from his lesson. His face is still pale and strained as he walks away, and I send him a quick text: *I am right here if you need me.* When he reads it, he turns around and raises a hand, and I raise mine in response, feeling my heart lift and fill my throat.

The barn aisle is a mess, so I get started on evening chores. After a while a heavy thunderstorm rolls in to keep me company, and then just hangs out overhead, tossing around lightning and tropical downpours like there's an unlimited supply of both—I suppose there is. As the storm leaches into the evening, I feed the horses their dinner under threat of being blown away by a tornado or swept away in floodwaters. At least, that's what my phone keeps telling me. The damn thing chirps wildly with a new threat every five minutes. I switch it off and get back to mucking out around the horses. Even if the alien invasion we joke about were to commence immediately, the horses would still need fed and watered, their stalls would still need cleaned, and chances were at least half of them would tear down their stall doors if I considered canceling turnout on account of a squadron of flying saucers touching down in the pasture.

This is my first full summer in Florida, but by now I'm getting

The Sweetheart Horse

used to the dramatic storms. I can see why so many people don't stay here year round, though. Maybe the wealthiest competitors can enjoy climate-controlled stabling and arenas, but for most of us, Florida is just a sea of sweat, rainwater, and the impending doom of a lightning strike or a twister touchdown. And that's before you take hurricane season into account.

But I find I like the atmospheric meltdowns, despite the discomfort and inconvenience they present. After all, Virginia's no picnic in the summer, either. Humid days with sudden storms billowing from the west; alternating with hazy weeks when we'd give anything for a shower to break the cap of silty air wrapped across the countryside. The Floridian summer has a comforting sort of sameness to it. You don't really have to check the weather in the morning, unless you want to know if there was a *really* high chance of storms, or just a so-so chance of storms. So far this summer, I've at least heard a rumble of thunder every single day. And on most of these days, I've also felt a cool breeze cutting through the afternoon heat, and the scent of impending rain rising from the baking fields.

Often, I find it comforting.

But this everlasting storm we're having tonight is anything but comforting. I want to get back to the house. I'm anxious to see how Basil is recovering from his panic attack. There is complete silence from my text messages. It's all I can do not to send him constant inquiries, solicitous smiley-faces, begging for an update on how he is feeling. The poor thing is probably trying to take a nap; he doesn't need my hovering, my poking, my own anxiety intruding on his.

The roof rattles as another tree branch hits it. Up and down the row of stalls, horses spook, slamming their buckets against the walls and their hooves against the stall doors. My wheelbarrow is full and I can't empty it until the storm lets up. I'm at a standstill.

So, I retreat to the tack room, sink into a hard wooden chair, and put my head down on the table where we eat quick snacks or scrub tack. Downtime is the *last* thing I need.

When I'm working, I'm too busy to think. Too occupied with my chores to dawdle over my life, the strange twists and turns this summer has taken me on.

I almost want things to go back to the way they were; if not the relative simplicity of, let's say January, then I would accept May, which feels like the last normal month of my life. Before Feather, before Basil. When I was frantically searching for a place to live, but at least I wasn't on a constant emotional roller-coaster. Maybe I *thought* I was back then, but May-Kayla had no idea what July-Kayla would be going through. My life went from kiddie ride to pulling serious G-forces in just eight weeks.

"This whole situation looked like such a sweetheart deal," I murmur, my forehead still pressed into the cool table-top. "I thought I was finally getting rewarded for all my loyalty. All my hard work. Everything I've put into horses. I thought things were going so smoothly..."

Rain rattles against the window; lightning flashes, and I just sit there, unsure *what* I thought. I must have been crazy, that's all. To think things would work out the way I wanted, to think there wouldn't be some huge, deal-breaking caveat to my sweetheart horse.

To think I'd fall for a handsome scammer with a heart as soft and tender and apt to aching as my own.

When I hear a *tap-tap-tap* in the aisle, I assume it's just something rolling down the barn aisle in the wind, a loose bucket or a brush. The gusts are really howling outside; I can hear ghostly shrieking in the eaves above the tack room and my phone is alight with dire predictions: it might as well just be all red, shrieking *fire famine flood*, for all I can do anything about it. The horses are inside and dry; I am inside and dry—that's about all I can control these days.

But then the door squeaks a little as it opens—I should probably get some grease on those hinges—and I look up in surprise.

It's Basil, of course. Who else would it be? He's dripping wet, his hair falling nearly over his eyes. How does his hair grow so quickly? How does the summer race by so cruelly? "Why are you here?" I ask, raising my voice to be heard above the rain, the wind, the constant thunder. "I thought you'd stay in the house tonight."

"I was worried about you," he says, taking off his hat and shaking it. Water arcs across the tile floor. He gives the hat a dirty look and throws it into the sink. "I guess the rest of my clothes should go in there, too."

I try not to think about Basil stripping down to nothing but his bare, wet skin, and am unsuccessful. "You shouldn't have gone out in this storm. I got a phone alert, and it says the Mayan end of the world is finally here."

"Mine says that, too." He grins and sits down across from me, leaving a wet pattern on the floor. "But I guess if it's the end of days, neither of us should have to go down alone."

Maybe I would prefer to be alone, I think, but of course it's not true. I'd rather be with him. It's the awful truth. The whole truth. At least one of us can be honest with me.

"It's going to be a mess out there," he says. "I hate to think about the jumps. Probably all flattened."

"Hopefully nothing broken."

He nods.

So that's all he wanted? To sit out here and make idle observations? He could have texted me to make sure I was alive, in that case.

"Storms don't usually last this long," he says eventually. "In my experience, anyway."

"I guess Florida makes its own rules." He's right. It has been getting worse for the past hour instead of letting up. That seems very unusual.

"My mother would be in the corner lighting incense and asking where you keep your flowers," he says. "Making sure the gods know that she's here and worth saving."

"Don't you mean Celestial Beings?" I ask coldly.

He looks at me with those chocolate-drop eyes I can see in my dreams at night. They're so beautiful, those eyes. It's how he gets away with all his lies, I suppose. The beauty.

"How much do you know?" he asks eventually. "I just want to make sure I know where to start."

I nearly snort with angry laughter, but thank goodness I keep it back. Have to maintain *some* feminine mystique, after all. "I know about all your trainer friends. I know about the horses you're selling sight unseen to buyers in your little cult. I know that you *faked* being freaked out by all of it, by Feather's training records, by Max's little horse statue. I know you've been lying to me since you got here. I guess that's enough, right? What else could I possibly need to know?"

A million things, starting with *why*.

Why is he doing this, a man who can ride like he can? Why is he on this self-destructive course? Because the horse world will not forgive him once they know the truth. Maybe I'm too foolish to run away screaming, but not everyone is going to look into those brown eyes, the rich, earthy tones of a dark and dappled horse, and lose track of the time, the day, themselves.

I'm just lucky that way.

Basil closes his eyes, takes a long breath. I wait for him to defend himself.

But he doesn't.

"I'm sorry," he says at last, his voice tight, as if he's holding something back. "I didn't want you to find out this way."

I shake my head in disbelief. That's all he has to offer? "You mean, through Reddit channels and web searches? How *was* I supposed to find out? Were you going to tell me? Or were you just going to wave some of that incense around my head and take my money? I don't have any, by the way. Joke's on you."

Then I remember that from the very beginning, Basil has had his eyes on one thing.

My horse.

"I was never going to do any of that," he begins.

"I know you weren't," I snap, my anger surging like a flood, drowning all the affection I have for this man beneath a King Tide of hurt and outrage. "Let's be real here, Baz. You just want Feather. Don't you? Isn't that why you've been such a *big help* with her? Riding her for me, without even asking my permission? Oh, big, strong man! So helpful! What would I do without you?" And then I stop, because the truth is, he *has* been helpful and I don't know what I'd have done without him. He's more experienced at training young horses than I am. End of story.

At least, it's the end of that story. Our story.

"I wasn't here to take your horse," he insists. "At first—" Basil runs a hand through his wet hair and looks around the room, as if the racks of saddles and hooks of bridles will hold the key to getting out of this mess. Then he says, "At first, I just didn't want to see you get killed, and then later on, I thought..."

He trails off and looks at the table in front of him.

Thunder rumbles through the barn like a freight train barreling down the aisle, shaking everything from the floor to the rafters. A rack of spare bits jingles gently, silver wind chimes shivering in an indoor breeze.

"What did you think?" I whisper.

"I thought I could help you see she was wrong for you," Basil admits, his voice rasping in his throat. "I thought I'd buy her from you and you'd have the money to buy a better horse. For *you*," he adds, looking up through his long eyelashes, freezing my outrage with a look of such honesty and warmth, I can't possibly believe he's lying. "I know you want to move up. I know you need a good prospect. I'm not saying she's bad, but she's so young, so green, so—*reactive*. I just thought I could give you a head-start on a better horse."

"But the Church," I begin, and he interrupts me.

"No, Kayla. This isn't about the Church. This is about you. Don't you know I care what happens to you? *Both* of you, Feather matters, but mostly you." He glances up at me again through his black lashes, as vulnerable as a fawn. "I care what happens to you," he repeats. "Is that so wrong?"

I wish I didn't believe him. I wish I could tell him that *yes,* it's wrong, it's wrong because he has lied to me again and again and I don't trust him any farther than I can throw him, which probably isn't very far because while I have excellent upper-body strength, he is mostly muscle and sinew and probably weighs a lot more than he looks.

But none of that matters, because when he looks at me like that, with his heart in his eyes, I am completely undone. All my resistance topples. Much like the trees outside are probably toppling in this insane, unending storm.

And then he says it: the words I can't choke out.

"It doesn't matter, does it?" He stands up roughly, pushing the chair back with a screech on the tiles. Water from his wet shirt spatters across the table and is sucked up by the thirsty wood. He looks around wildly, as if he wants to run away, but can't find the door. "None of it matters, because I lied to you. Like I lie to everyone. My whole life...the rest of my life, I'll be running from these lies. And there's *nothing* I can do to make it up to you."

I'm frozen in my chair, my heart unraveling, and Basil is nearly at the door before I realize he's leaving. "Baz, wait," I beg him, leaping up from my chair. "Don't go out there in this storm, please."

"I can't stay here with you." Basil's eyes rake over me; his chest is heaving. I've never seen him lose his cool before; I can't deny the effect it has on me. He's the opposite of the man who dismounted so unsteadily after Karl left the arena; he's lost control but in a completely different direction. I want to draw him against me and feel those taut muscles, that staccato heartbeat, and assure him that his passion won't go unanswered. But his hand is on the doorknob; he's dying to get away from me, and the realization holds me back, blushing in embarrassment. "I can't stay here and be your enemy, Kayla," he says hoarsely. "I care about you too much for this, okay? So please, just let me go. I promise I won't bother you about—about anything. Any of it. Feather, too."

"It's fine," I rasp, wondering where my voice has gone. "Really. Please sit back down."

Basil laughs, a rough sound lacking all humor. "But it's not fine. You really have no idea, do you? How far this goes? What I've done to my own chances?"

Of course I know that. Why else does he think I'm still here? As if I had the power to just leave him to the wolves when I know I have to drag him out of this mess, even if he's kicking and screaming the whole time.

"I know enough," I say. "But it's not too late to stop this."

He starts to shake his head. And then an awful electronic squeal fills the tack room.

It's our stupid phones. Another emergency, more terrible timing. Basil grabs at his pocket while I spin around, see my phone on the table, and leap for it—only to slip on the wet floor.

I go crashing to the tile on my side, just managing to stop my head from hitting the ceramic. Because that would be great. All I need this summer is another concussion. As if my thinking isn't erratic and questionable enough as it is.

Basil is beside me instantly, his hands slipping beneath my arms. "Easy there," he murmurs, as if I'm a horse who needs to be calmed. "Hold still a second. Let's make sure nothing's broken."

"I'm *fine*," I snap, equally annoyed and excited by his touch. It's a weird sensation. I suppose it's the whole thin line between love and hate thing. Desire and anger must be two sides of the same kind, because I am absolutely furious at Basil for coming into this tack room, acting like a diva with his whole 'boo-hoo I'm a fraudulent huckster no one understands me' bit, and at the same time I want to rip his clothes off and throw him on the pile of clean saddle blankets and have my way with his wiry body. "I'm fine, and I'm getting up," I say, with less conviction this time; the desire side of the coin landed heads-up.

Basil is crouched beside me. His grip loosens, then softens. He could let go, I know, but he doesn't. "Kayla," he murmurs, then stops.

I realize our phones have stopped shrieking. The wind is still howling in the eaves and moaning around the tack room door; the thunder is still shaking the ground beneath us, and the rain is still battering the window, but all of that becomes little more than a hum in my ears. The only thing which matters is Basil, looking down at me with eyes the color of rich, black cold brew on a hot afternoon. My breath catches in my throat as I realize he's going to kiss me. I should shove him off me, the lying bastard.

But of course, I don't.

If the power hadn't gone out, we might have stayed there all night.

The Sweetheart Horse

If the window hadn't broken, we still might have.

But the smash in the dark, and the rain-chilled wind howling through the newfound gap in the wall, is enough to rouse both of us from our nest of saddle blankets. We fumble for the loose ends of our clothing, disoriented and just a little afraid. Well, maybe a lot afraid, if I'm being perfectly honest here. It's pretty scary when your shelter starts disintegrating.

Luckily, the window breaking seems to have been the last gasp of the seemingly endless storm. By the time we've managed to get a horse blanket over the broken window, holding it in place with some carefully stacked tack trunks on either side, the wind is already dying, and the thunder has become a distant rumble.

We look at each other for a long moment. I can feel my face cracking into a nervous smile, and a giggle slips out before I can stop it. Then Basil is giggling, too, and he sounds so silly that I burst into full-on belly laughter, and we're both laughing like a pair of crazy people for what feels like forever.

When the chuckles dry up, Basil lifts an eyebrow at me. For a moment, I think he's going to say something meaningful, something that's going to send me into paroxysms of undeniable, unconquerable passion.

Instead, he says, "I guess we should turn the horses out, huh?"

Chapter Twenty-Five

AND HONESTLY?

It makes me like him even more.

Basil is a guy who gets it. Horses come first, no matter the weather. Horses are hard work, no matter how much money you can throw at them. Horses are more important than feelings or passion—of any sort, whether it's love or hate. If our eyes are open, we probably have horses on our minds, and that can't be a problem for the other person in the relationship.

Yes, this is a relationship. For better or worse, all that jazz. I'm all in, and so is he. No one says the things he said to me, while looking as intensely as he looked at me, without meaning every word. And if he believes it's too late to get him out of this mess, I wholeheartedly disagree. My entire adult life, I have been rescued, loved, supported.

I am ready to return the favor.

It's two o'clock in the morning when we get into the house, but neither of us can go right to bed. With any luck, half of Ocala will have lost power in this storm (naturally we have not, since we only lose power when the weather is perfect) and Amanda will be included in that half, so I suppose I can delay my return to work by another day. Otherwise, that alarm clock is going to ring awfully early in the morning. I lean uncertainly against the kitchen counter, wondering what Basil wants to do next.

He pushes back his messy hair and looks around the kitchen, eyes wandering around the cupboards. "Do you want eggs?" he asks after a moment.

"What?" I'm startled. "Eggs? At two in the morning?"

"Omelette," he explains. "It's kind of a British thing, I guess."

"Late night eggs. You party harder than I realized over there."

"It's very good," Basil promises, pulling out a pan from the cupboard beside the flashy steel oven. "Some cheese, some chili oil..."

"Hot sauce," I interject. "We use hot sauce here."

"Fine, hot sauce," Basil agrees. He's already got the burner going; he's pulling cooking spray from the cabinet. "Whatever makes it burn on the way down is fine with me."

I pull up a stool and put my elbows on the kitchen bar, watching him cook me a late-night snack. I think lazily that he looks remarkably good despite getting soaked in a storm, then tumbling around with me in a pile of saddle pads, then helping me cover a broken window with a horse blanket and then turning out a herd of horses. I think that I haven't felt so content in a very long time... maybe ever? Or at least not since I was a little child? And I think, with a sensation like tingles running up my spine, that I could live like this forever.

And as he slips a plate in front of me with one gorgeous, golden omelette in the center, I think, with a certainty almost equally thrilling and dismaying: *I'm in way too deep to just walk away.*

We made a pact to let the horses stay out an extra hour in order to steal some sleep, and I sent Amanda a text that I needed another day off to get my head right. She keeps her phone on Do Not Disturb all night, so I knew it was safe to text her at three in the morning. Then we went to bed, me closing my door slowly while Basil smiled at me from the hall, his eyes twinkling in a way which suggested he'd come in and keep me company if I just said the word.

I didn't, though. I really needed some sleep.

And now here I am at five o'clock, wide awake while he is no doubt snoring away one floor above me, sleeping the sleep of the blessed. While I sit here wondering how this happened. I don't know exactly when Basil stopped being rude and domineering, or when I stopped hating him—maybe it all just happens so subtly that it's impossible for a person to tell?—but whatever was happening between us, I didn't expect *this*.

And by this, I mean my current state of affairs: flipping over my pillow in search of a cool spot to lay my hot cheek, tousled and nervous and bothered because the guy upstairs, the one who is running some kind of fraudulent cult for gullible horse-people, is stealthily stealing my heart.

Ugh, I can't even use that phrase! So gross. But it's true.

I flip over the pillow again.

It's true.

And apparently that means I'm just never going to sleep again.

Basil Han, you just keep ruining my life.

I wish we were getting up at the normal time. I'm longing and longing for my alarm to go off so I can slip into the kitchen, find him at the coffeepot, and kiss him.

When my alarm does go off, I sit upright so fast that my head pounds and I have to fall back down to the pillow, hand at my forehead. Against all odds, I drifted back to sleep, and that last hour was a doozy.

"Ow, gosh," I mutter. "I guess I did need another day off." The doctor warned me I'd still feel rotten for a few days after the concussion, but added he knew horse-people never stopped working, so any pain caused by exertion would be my own fault. I guess he had me pegged from the moment he read, "Head-butted by horse" on my chart.

I close my eyes again, but immediately I hear creaking overhead and know he's up. Know he's coming downstairs any minute. He'll make coffee and pour a cup for himself...will he pour one for me? Does he remember I like two sugars and some cream? I think if he does, my heart will burst with emotion.

And I am already stretched at the seams.

I check my phone, trying to keep things as normal as possible. A text from Amanda, sent just seconds before, lights up my screen: *No problem kid, you take it easy! Just take off the next few days. I'm fine.*

Thanks, I write back. *Be back next week, promise.*

She adds a little heart to the message, which means she's too busy to write a reply. That's fine. She's busy. We're all busy. I'm busy losing my mind.

Slowly, I dress, taking care to put on things suitable to do the morning barn chores without looking too much like a foundling in a Victorian melodrama. That means casting aside my favorite pair of old boxers and torn t-shirt, soft clothes perfect for bringing horses and feeding when there's not a man in the barn. I settle on workout shorts with a phone pocket, paired with gray and purple sleeveless top made of some cooling technology that activates when wet. I wonder what would happen if I hosed myself down in the wash-rack while I scrubbed water buckets. Too much? Probably, yes.

But if it's really hot out there, I can't see how I can be blamed for my actions, either.

By the time my hair has been tamed into a taut braid and I'm ready to be seen in public, the coffeepot is gurgling to itself and the scent is wafting beneath the door, sending my *other* appetites, the ones which can't be satisfied by canoodling with my house-mate, with my boyfriend, into blissful overdrive. Even my headache has retreated. All my body actually wants right now is coffee.

Far be it for me to deny my body its desires, right?

I step out of my room just as the coffeemaker chimes that it's finished. I pause for a moment in the hallway. This is his chance to pull down two mugs instead of one, to set up a cup for me...

Clink. Pause.

I catch my breath.

Clink.

He did it! I don't walk into the kitchen, I float.

And there is Basil, holding out a mug. "Good morning, sunshine," he says, with a smile that reaches all the way to his eyes.

"Good morning," I reply softly, suddenly shy.

"There's nothing in that," he says apologetically. "I didn't want to get it wrong."

Oh, well, expecting him to know how I take my coffee would be unreasonable. We don't usually start the day together. "That's no problem," I tell him. "Thank you."

He leans back against the kitchen counter and sighs. His coffee is the color of pale toast.

He seems me looking at it. "Oh, I like it very sweet and milky," he explains. "I know in America, I'm supposed to be manly and take it black. But I'm not that acclimated yet."

"Don't bother acclimating," I tell him, topping my coffee with creamer. "Have you seen the dairy section at the store? Most of the square footage is devoted to different ways to make your coffee taste like candy bars."

"Now, that's something I should try," he laughs.

"Snickers bar or Milky Way? I'll pick some up next time."

"Oh, no Mars Bar?" Basil sighs and shakes his head. "Maybe I *won't* ever fit in here."

We flirt our way through a few slices of toast, and then Basil

The Sweetheart Horse

suggests we head out to feed. From the living room windows, we can see the horses gathered by their gates, waiting for us to come and rescue them from the coming day's heat and flies. Sunrise is shimmering beyond the trees lining the farm's border, a buttercup-yellow sky feathered with fine wisps of candy-pink clouds.

We're pulling our boots on, side by side, when he turns his head and smiles at me. His face is just inches from mine, and the urge to slip my fingers around his neck and tug his lips to my lips is nearly unbearable. He asks me, "What are you doing Saturday night?"

I lift my eyebrows. Surely he knows I almost never have plans more complicated than inviting over Evie and Posey. "It's too soon to know for sure, but I suspect I'll fall asleep on the sofa while watching *Mean Girls*."

"But I'm taking Jock to the Grand Prix," he reminds me., startled I've forgotten already.

"I'm bad with dates," I chuckle. "And it's really early."

And I barely slept.

"Well, will you come with me?" he asks, giving me the most charming puppy-dog eyes I've ever seen. It's like he *is* a beagle for a moment. An enduring, heartwarming, lovable pup.

"I'm not going to groom for you," I warn, but Basil laughs mischievously.

"I already saw what a bad jumper groom you are," he jokes. "Come as my cheering section."

"Oh, I don't know," I tease. "What if you don't win? I'd be so embarrassed to cheer for a big old loser."

Basil's calloused fingers suddenly lift my chin, and he gives me a lingering kiss that alights an early morning fire in my midsection. I suddenly wish we didn't have a dozen horses waiting on us. "Come as my date, then," he says. "And we can be embarrassed together."

I'm too charmed to say no. But I can't deny the fear I feel as we start off to the barn together. Every time I'm seen with Basil in public, I'm putting my future at risk.

And if we both lose our careers to his uncle's business, what will we have to fall back on? There's nothing in this world for either of us but horses. I can be falling head-over-heels for Basil right now and still know, with total certainty, that without our riding careers, we are nothing.

Chapter Twenty-Six

How do horse girls know when a guy really likes them? It's not about the cleavage poking through a quarter-zip riding shirt, ladies. At least, not in Florida, not in summer. It's all about how awful a girl can look, without scaring him away.

The torrential storms seem to be here to stay, long-lasting storms which start mid-afternoon and hang around through late evening. The sky stays gray and heavy, the humidity hangs over us like a sopping-wet blanket, and any idea of being cute goes right out the window. I am muddy, sweaty, and stomping around in knee-high rubber boots most of the time. Basil says I remind him of a Yorkshire farmgirl, which I assume is meant as an endearment, although I've seen pictures of those old trainers of his, and they look like wizened ancient trees which have lived through a few too many storms. I make a joke about them and he looks away, as if he regrets bringing up his time in Yorkshire, leaving me wondering once again what secrets linger in Basil's locked-away brain.

But it's only a slight hiccup, and on Saturday evening I'm excited to watch him defend his title at the July Grand Prix. I make an effort to clean myself up, and for once, as if in answer, the storms stay away. As the sun sinks over Legends Equestrian Center and the huge lights over the Grand Prix ring snap to life, lightning flickers in the south, but no thunder rumbles this far north. Still, a dry day is challenging as well. The day's heat hangs heavy over the broad arena, the intricate jumping course, the pink-faced women holding cocktails in the hospitality section of the grandstand. I'm wearing skinny jeans and paddock boots, a long blue button-down on top with the sleeves rolled up above my elbows, and I look very cute, which almost makes up for feeling like I'm going to melt into a puddle.

"At least you're not riding," Evie says, appearing at my elbow.

I nearly jump out of my boots. "Evie! What are you doing here?"

"Came to watch the man himself jump his big horse," she says. "Don't worry, I won't crowd you two. But I figure while he's in the arena it would be nice for you to have company. Only problem with coming with a competitor is the part where you're on the ground."

She's right about that. I helped Basil tack up back at the stable, but at the arena he's being assisted by a working student of another trainer he knows, someone he worked with in Wellington. This working student is a fresh-faced teenager; she's more than happy to run, fetch, and carry as Basil requests. I'm not bothered by the way she gazes at him worshipfully as he rides. Well, not too bothered, anyway. She's going back to Wellington on Monday. Let her look.

As the girlfriend (an unofficial title I am claiming until further notice), my job is to stand near the warm-up arena rail, looking confident and supportive. And it's not hard to keep that kind of expression on my face when I'm watching Basil ride Jock. This horse was *made* for him. Or maybe it was the other way around. Either way, I know I'm watching the kind of partnership riders wait and hope for, sometimes their whole lives. I think Jock could take Basil all the way to the top, as long as Basil stays patient and kind. Two traits which seem to sum him up in the saddle. Someday, I want a horse like this. When I was a teenager I foolishly thought it would be Crabby; now I barely dare to hope it could be Feather.

"Wow," Evie breathes next to me, as they sail over the schooling fences. "Look at the two of them together!"

"I know. I think focusing on dressage with Max and Stephen has been really good for Basil."

Evie nods. "Makes me wish someone would give *me* the ride on a schoolmaster dressage horse."

"Maybe you can be the next one to come work at the farm," I joke.

"After you and Basil run away together?"

I glance at her, bemused. "What makes you say that?"

"What, you're getting defensive?" She grins and shakes her head. "I see the way you two look at each other. Also, way cute outfit, player. Things have gotten real, huh?"

"Very real," I agree. No point in trying to keep it secret if the truth is written all over my face. And anyway, I suspect Basil will trot over for a good-luck kiss before his round. In which case, all of horsey Ocala will know about us by breakfast. I don't know how I feel about this.

"I knew he was the answer to all your problems," Evie says blithely, somehow ignoring every gut-wrenching conversation we've had about this guy. "I hope you two get married from Max and Stephen's place. I bet Max would arrange an amazing wedding. When are they coming home, again?"

"Let's not plan the wedding yet," I scoff. But I can't help admitting to myself that she's right. Max *would* be an incredible wedding host…

Basil is riding up to us with a stern expression, putting a quick end to my daydreaming. He pulls up Jock by the fence and I step up on the bottom rail, leaning over to get closer to him. "What's up?"

"We're just a few rounds away," he says. "Maybe go and find a seat so you don't miss us?"

"Right, will do." I give him an alluring look—at least, I hope it is. I'm very sweaty.

Basil blows me a kiss.

Fair enough.

I hop down from the fence as he walks Jock away, giving the horse a few moments to catch his breath and steady his body temperature. The groom is standing nearby with a bucket of water and a sponge, ready to give him a drink and dab away the worst of the sweat. For Jock, I mean. The water bottle in her hand is for Basil. I briefly consider taking the bottle from her and performing that duty myself, but decide not to be a jealous psychopath. The choice is, as always, entirely mine.

Evie grins at me as I return to solid ground. "Cute," she says.

"That's us," I tell her. "Absolutely adorable."

"The couple of the year," she suggests. "Love's young dream? What do we call you? Basla sounds like a disease."

"Kaysil isn't much better."

"It sounds like the cure to Basla."

We head for the grandstand, giggling.

Legends Equestrian Center is built for international events that bring the best riders in the world to Ocala for the winter, but summer is a work in progress. So, there's no trouble finding a good seat for a summer Grand Prix. Even though half the riders in the warm-up ring tonight are world-class competitors, the stands are less than half full. The stands are mostly occupied by trainers, riders, and grooms who are stabled at the show-grounds but don't have a horse in tonight. This is just built-in Saturday night entertainment for them, saving them the effort of finding something to watch on Netflix back in their RVs or hotel rooms.

Most of the circuit riders and employees know each other by sight after weeks of showing and suffering together, and it's pretty clear from the constant whispers and frequent beady-eyed glares that the exhausted equestrians have been working on their feuds all summer.

The Sweetheart Horse

Evie, as a sharp-eared lover of gossip, is in seventh heaven.

"The redhead woman in the second row is having an affair with that lady over there wearing the Devon Horse Show hat," she hisses into my ear, her lips nearly touching my skin. Odd, how it's not erotic when she does it. The body knows the difference between friends and lovers, I suppose. Evie keeps going, unaware of my own internal dialogue. "Their husbands don't know, but one groom does. That's their groom—" She gives a tiny gesture, as if waving her hand to a friend, and points out a dark-browed young woman a few seats away, looking across the sparse crowd with a thundery expression. After a moment's searching through the surrounding faces, I realize the woman's gaze is trained on the red-haired woman in the second row. I recognize something in her expression now: something hungry and guilty at the same time.

"And the groom is jealous?" I whisper back, enthralled. "She wants the redhead, too?"

Evie nods, her eyes wide, but she's already tilting her head away, and I realize she's listening in on another sordid tale.

It's almost alarming, though. Outwardly, all these people—Evie included—are here to watch these well-trained horses roll around this challenging jumping course. And they *are* watching, attentively—there's the usual chorus of clicking tongues as the horse on course sucks back before an airy vertical, the typical group hiss as he rubs the top rail but doesn't bring it down—but they're also desperately involved in each other's lives. They all want to eat each other alive. I wonder if there are any real friends in this place at all.

Or maybe it's just the way Evie is portraying them to me, her eyes alight like a cat playing with a mouse as she picks up whispers and hones in on secrets.

It's an eerie realization, and it's hard to shake off the feeling that I'm being watched. But of course I'm not part of this crowd. I'm just a farm-sitter. For now.

Then Jock and Basil enter the arena, and as I sit a little taller, proud of my connection to this dynamic horse and rider duo, I know I'm fair game, after all. Everyone stills and watches them. Jock is that kind of horse, and Basil is that kind of rider, and I'm the girl who will be seen with him after he wins this class.

Jock is a gorgeous horse by day, but somehow even more so at night, galloping under the lights and groomed to perfection. The arena is lit up like a hockey rink, the white footing reflecting back the high-powered lamps, and his dapples glisten across his hindquarters as he halts like a starlet in the spotlight. Basil touches his cap to the judge; she nods back, and Jock springs into an easy canter.

The course is twisty, with a few airy verticals and complicated approaches which have caused some difficulty tonight. Jock is more than up to the challenge, and Basil never has to work hard—at least, not in my eyes—to get the horse around the course clean. There's a sigh and then enthusiastic applause as they clear the last jump and canter through the timers. I release the breath I've been holding for the entire round, thankful that a jumper round isn't as long as a dressage test. Otherwise, I might have passed out.

Evie turns to me, eyes aglow. "That was sensational."

I nod, feeling like I'm going to float right out of my seat. "I know."

"He's your *boyfriend*." She says it as if I powered that clean round with my presence.

Behind her, a head swivels. Inquiring eyes land on my face, drop to my chest—really?—and then back to my eyes. The woman turns away before I can say anything, her ponytail bobbing as she leans over to whisper to her companion.

Well, the cat's definitely out of the bag now. I feel equally dismayed and thrilled, which seems about right, considering how complicated things are with Basil.

The Sweetheart Horse

Another horse is already entering the ring, and I start to rise, ready to go and meet Basil out at the warm-up. I can find my seat again for a jump-off if I have to. But Evie is already making that listening face of hers, and she clutches at my arm. "Wait," she whispers. "Not yet. Listen."

And I realize that until word sweeps around the stands about the face in the crowd which belongs to the girlfriend, people will feel free to talk around me without any fear of being overheard. Evie doesn't have to relay these stories to me; they're being discussed in normal voices, by a group of people who believe the subject has no allies in this grandstand.

"Did you hear about the horse he sent to Ruby Brody? Complete psycho. Ruby's father is considering a lawsuit. Ruby won't let him, though."

"It's that weird religion of his. You know his uncle is some kind of spiritual guru."

"Oh, because they're from China?"

"Hong Kong, and no, it's something else. I think they made it all up!"

"No, really?"

"Suzanna Wilkes, down in Wellington, says it's one hundred percent a money laundering scam."

"Wouldn't surprise me one bit."

The voices aren't raised, but they're like a clamor in my ears. I look at Evie wildly, and she shakes her head slightly. She could mean a hundred things by it, like, "Of course it's not a scam" or, "Don't get up now, or they'll all look at you."

And I know one of those statements is true.

But we have a problem now, and it's huge: Basil's entire career. Somehow, I guess I'd hoped we could work this out, get Basil free of this idiotic scam, before things blow up in his face and he loses everything he's ever wanted. Now, I'm not sure there's time.

The word is already out. And even if the Church of Celestial Beings is a real, religious entity (it's not, obviously, this is just speaking in hypotheticals), the horse world will not forgive Basil for being different. Or for deliberately keeping people out, buying and selling only within one select group. Suddenly, everyone on the show-grounds will have wanted that chestnut equitation horse, the one Basil bought for a client just a few days ago. And the elaborate stories of how they tried to buy the horse, and were turned down for being the wrong religion, will fly faster than the truth could ever hope to spread.

"I have to go talk to him," I mutter.

"Are you kidding?" Evie puts her hand on my arm. "He's getting ready for a jump-off in two more rounds. He could win this. Leave the poor guy alone."

She's right. In about fifteen minutes' time, Basil will be putting Jock over the jump-off course. I can't distract him now.

But this can't wait much longer. He needs to know the truth about what Ocala is saying...and he needs to tell *me* the truth about his family's business.

And the Celestial Beings. I need all of it. I can help him. I can save him.

I have to.

The gossip has shifted away from Basil by the time the initial rounds are over, but their wavering attention is a false flag. Because the moment the announcer informs us, in her bright Aussie sing-song, that the jump-off will between three riders, including Basil Han, everyone jumps happily back on the gossip train. And things are worse now, as if they've been coming up with new stories, nursing new grievances, in the twenty minutes since he was last in the arena.

A jump-off is a quick competition by nature; this course seems insanely short, just forty-five seconds on the clock. My heart leaps every fence with Basil, but Jock seems to know his way around the fences as if he built the course himself, and they win easily, two whole seconds between them and the next rider.

Is it my imagination, or is the applause less enthusiastic now?

Is it my imagination, or are people looking at me now?

"Go," Evie says, and I dart from the seat without having to be told twice, running down the steps towards the exit. And now I can feel eyes on me, see heads turning. The truth is overwhelming, terrifying. They know who I am.

And now, Basil Han has the power to take me down with him.

Chapter Twenty-Seven

THINGS NEED TO be said.

But we're not alone back in the barn; a few dozen people who loosely know Basil want to come back and congratulate him, and hang around in the aisle acting like they're connected with the winning horse and rider. He's a celebrity for one night, and since this is his second win of the summer, there's a greater chance that he'll be a real equestrian celebrity in due time. This gets people hungry for deals down the road to start sticking to him, like sand spurs cling to socks when you're walking through the pasture, hollering for your horses to come in.

So I have to let my fears go for now, and it's terrifying to stand here smiling and playing the adoring date he surely must expect, when I'm so afraid he's about to lose everything he's been working for. If the gossip from the grandstands follows us back here—if someone calls him out on his business practices—well, let's just say that if Basil goes down, it's more than a private heartbreak.

If Basil goes down, I go down.

That's a lot of pressure to put on two people who haven't swapped "I love you's" yet.

Luckily, my hovering and worrying is all for nothing. The crowd is still here for a good time, not a witch-hunt, and they don't last long, anyway. Horse-people tend to fade quickly at parties, and when one person remembers the six a.m. alarm, everyone starts thinking about it. There's a general shuffling for the exits, like the lights have come on at a club, and suddenly it's just Basil and me in the barn aisle. Even the borrowed groom has finished wrapping Jock's legs, topped off his water buckets, and peaced out for the night.

Basil sits down on a padded tack trunk and looks at me, his smile broad and satisfied.

I stand across the aisle, leaning against a stall door, and gaze back at him, wondering what we do now.

In every way that counts, I want to do nothing at all. I want things to just limp along as they have been. Two people stumbling through the opening rituals of a relationship, hooking up and guessing at each other's intentions, surprising one another with unexpected mood swings or changes of heart, until it either all irons out or we never speak again.

And I want to think this *will* all iron out. At this moment, it feels like it might. I can pretend the looming problems don't exist, and without them, I have nothing but hope for the two of us. Just looking at his face, at the way I can read his familiar expressions, is comforting. I've gotten used to Basil Han in intimate ways that have nothing to do with sex or desire. I know the way he looks first thing in the morning, freshly woken and ready for coffee. I can tell when he has slept badly, or not at all. I know the way he looks in the evening, when he's had a full day and he's not satisfied with it, or something has disappointed him, and he's just desperate to throw himself on the sofa and eat his bowl of noodles. I've learned the way his moods sweep across his slim features like clouds through the Ocala sky.

And I can see it when the exuberance in his expression fades to exhaustion, with something else in the details, like a screen across an open window. Exhaustion with a trace of hungry ambition, if that's something that can be written across a human face.

I know what it means.

Basil has tasted success twice in two months, and for him, that is just enough to know he wants it all.

It's not what I want to see right now.

What I *want* to do is convince Basil the timing is all wrong. He needs to lie low, maybe even get off the show circuit for a while. Disengage himself from Han Worldwide and the trouble that his uncle's company means for him, then wait until people have moved onto a new scandal; there is no shortage of fraud in the horse business. Only then can he come back out swinging.

Now is not the time for Basil Han to become a household name. If he does, and scandal breaks, he will never recover from it.

And if I stand beside him, neither will I.

Jock bangs his water buckets together, splashing with his nose, and Basil shifts his gaze to his horse. "You're a good boy," he says. "God, tonight was special. I'm so proud. And lucky." His voice is husky, worn thin with so many congratulations and compliments to respond to.

So many hangers-on who will drop him in a moment if the gossip gets too hot to handle.

"It was a great ride," I allow, guarding my words. "I'm tired now, though."

"Yeah, it's late." Basil looks at his watch, a big silvery show-piece I've never seen before in place of his Apple Watch. "Whoa, almost midnight! Way past our bedtimes. Let's go home. Any chance you can drive us? I want to leave the truck and trailer here, if I can. Jock deserves a rest; he can stay overnight."

"Of course." I pause. "But who will drive you back? To get Jock, I mean. I have to work in the morning."

Basil shrugs lazily, pushing up from the tack trunk. "Oh, I'll check around. Should be someone from the group tonight who can give me a lift." His smile is satisfied.

I can't wait anymore. "Basil, you need to know something."

He's gathering his show clothes, his face turned away from me. "You sound very serious."

"I am serious. I heard things tonight. About—your business."

I watch as his shoulders freeze in place. "What about it?" he asks after a long pause.

"That it's a scam. That you're selling horses based on the Celestial Beings memberships. That you're making promises about horses you can't keep and someone got hurt." I know my words are clipped, but I don't know what else to say. I didn't have a speech written in my head. Just a mountain of hurt and fear I have to push over somehow, without knowing what is on the other side. "People *know*, Basil. And they're going to end your career for you, if you don't get out of it."

He doesn't start talking until we're in the car, and then it's nothing that either of us can work with. A lot of self-defense, a lot of deflection, a lot of *this isn't me.* It turns into *you don't know me* and then I just try to tune it out. Because I do know him. And that's what makes this so hard.

At the house we start out heading in the same direction, towards the kitchen, but then he turns in the hall, just spins on his heel like he's had enough, and tramps up the stairs. I hear the landing treads squeak, I hear the bathroom door close.

I go into the kitchen and pour myself a glass of wine. A small glass. Medicinal.

There are texts from Evie on my phone, asking if I've said anything to him, asking if I've gotten a straight answer. Yes and no, I think, and then I type exactly that and flip my phone face-down on the counter. Not that I expect a reply; it's past midnight. I'm the only one in my group awake. I might as well be the only person in the world, for all the good all those billions of other souls on Earth are doing me tonight.

This should have been such a good night, I think, listening to the faint rush of water in the walls. Basil is in the shower. In another version of tonight, I might have joined him in there. We might have celebrated his win together, another step up the ladder for him.

I want to be in that version, but I guess it's just my luck to have lost the way into Fantasyland. Now I'm stuck in the real world.

The thought makes me consider calling my mother, who might be up, who might have something to say. But the idea of explaining all of this to her is the most tiring thing I could imagine. It's easier to throw myself into bed and flick through my phone, scrolling away the madness, waiting to feel something besides despair. But all I have in my mind are short, painful truths that all the memes in the world can't obscure.

I'm going to lose him.

I never really had him.

It's him or your career.

It was fun while it lasted.

It's past one o'clock when I give up and turn out my light. Upstairs, I can still hear movement, and I wonder if he's going to bed at all.

He doesn't come into the kitchen in the morning. I go out and feed the horses alone, some of yesterday's leftover coffee in my mug because I didn't have the heart to stand there all alone and listen to the coffeemaker grumble through its cycle. We're out of milk, so I sip at its rainbow surface and wince at the bitterness and wonder where he is.

I hope he's sleeping. I hope he's not avoiding me. After I've dumped the feed and the horses are plowing through their breakfasts like wild beasts, I stand in the barn aisle and look back at the house. His bedroom light is on. That probably answers that, then.

It's hard to go back to the house; I'm afraid he'll be in the kitchen and he'll avoid me there, even while we're in the same room. That will be unbearable. But I have to get to work. So I go back and walk through the empty kitchen, feeling like a fool.

Amanda is happy to see me again, her fresh face bright as if she has spent the past five days enjoying spa treatments and a steady diet of self-improvement books. She hugs me and exclaims, "It's been forever without you here! I sold Monkey, and you weren't even here!"

"Monkey? Who bought him?" I feel a fresh squeeze of sadness around my heart. Monkey is a silly boy who makes faces in the crossties and jumps everything he's pointed at without fear or caution; he was definitely one of my favorites in the barn. "He's gone already?"

"It was a same-day thing. They brought a trailer." Amanda gives a little snort; that's a classic horse-buyer mistake. Bring a trailer along and you not only give up all bargaining power, you can't even stop yourself from putting a horse in the empty slot. It's just chaotic equestrian brain. "It's such a good match, too: a fifteen-year-old girl who wants him for the Children's Jumpers. He can take her in Adult Amateur when she's in college, too. They'll probably be together forever."

"I hope so. Monkey deserves a forever home."

This is the way it's supposed to work. Amanda made a good match, putting together a horse and rider who belong together because their skills match up. Not because they belong to the same cobbled-together horse cult.

And I'm happy for Monkey, but still, I avoid looking at his empty stall as I walk to the tack room to fetch the saddle for my first horse. My poor heart can only take so much today.

In the arena, Amanda takes the lead and we swoop through serpentines and changes in direction on our green off-track Thoroughbreds. My horse, a chestnut gelding named Positive Energy (we call him Poz—it's not a great barn name, but it gets the job done), has a definite right-handed bias and bending to the left is like rocket science for him. I'm grateful for the full-body concentration that he requires of me. When all my muscles are engaged and I'm fully aware of where all my body parts are in order to direct Poz's parts, I don't have any room in my head to think about the devastating turn my personal life has taken.

Whereas the walk breaks we take between trotting and cantering our changes of direction? They're a little more open to wallowing. With my horse on a loose rein and my seat at ease in the saddle, the only thing I have to think about is my own private misery.

"You look really low today," Amanda remarks, bringing her horse alongside mine. Jakers is a plain bay Thoroughbred—plain except for a startling splash of white across his dark brown face that gives him either a rakish look (for those who like chrome) or a cow-ish look (for those who do not). Amanda looks me up and down, then asks, "What's the matter? Does your head still hurt? We can ride indoors if the sun is too much."

"No, that's okay." I do like riding in Amanda's covered arena, but it's kind of small and dusty—possibly the only imperfect thing about her beautiful farm. "I promise my head is fine. I guess I'm just tired from staying out late last night."

"Oh, you went to the Grand Prix, didn't you? How was that? I always mean to go but..." Amanda trails off.

I glance at her, curious. "But?"

She shrugs, and for once her beautiful face looks discontent. "A lot of people at Legends know my ex," she says. "He's a polo player. He's really...popular."

The Sweetheart Horse

The way she says *popular* is all I need to know about Amanda's ex.

"Some people never seem to get in trouble," I muse. "And other people, the mob just tears up instantly. Why is that?"

"I don't know." Amanda rubs her hand along Jakers' neck, thinking. Finally she says, with a trace of embarrassment, "To be perfectly honest, for years I would have said I was in the first group. Ending up with a husband who cheated was probably no more than I should have expected."

That feels unanswerable, so I look down at Poz's bristling mane instead.

"Sorry," Amanda says, laughing ruefully. "Anyway, I stopped chasing around committed men and got my own house in order. But I still don't want to see him living it up like I was the one who had to change."

"Maybe it's a looks thing," I suggest. "Looks plus gender bias. The hot guys get away with murder. But if that's the case, well, Basil is—" I stop myself.

But it's already too late.

Amanda shifts in the saddle and Jakers halts. Poz is happy to stand next to him. The horses touch noses and snort. Heads toss. We let them fool around, and as Poz nips at Jakers' reins, Amanda asks, "What's going on with Basil?" in a voice so hushed and caring, it's all I can do not to burst into tears.

"Oh, I don't even know where to start," I say, trying to give it the brush-off. But Amanda gives me a piercing look, and I'm weak, so I capitulate pretty quickly. "There's a lot of gossip about Basil's family business and whether it's legit or not. They buy and sell horses—"

"I know about Han Worldwide," Amanda interrupts.

"Does *everyone*?"

"Not everyone. But, I know people, babe. Not much around here gets past me."

Evie should really hang out with Amanda.

She shifts in the saddle. "Why do you look like you've seen a ghost when you talk about him? What's going on?"

I skip over everything that's happened between Basil and me in the last week, getting straight to the heart of the matter. "The things I heard last night made me think that people are getting upset about his whole...situation. Apparently a girl got hurt with a horse they sold her—"

"But Kayla, that happens." Amanda shrugs. "Listen, people are responsible for buying horses they can handle, not the other way around. Obviously, I don't want anyone to buy the wrong horse, right? But at the same time, I'm not the horse police. If they try the horse and things seem okay, it's their right to take the horse home, and it's my right to move on with my life, you know?" She gestures at the barn behind us. "There's an entire barn full of horses who need to be trained and sold to new riders. Not every match is going to be made in heaven."

In heaven. For some reason, her words make me think of the Celestial Beings, of all that woo-woo nonsense catching up with good people, like *Max,* someone I admittedly don't know that well but who I like, who has changed my life in so many ways. I can't reconcile the way I feel about Basil with his involvement with the crystals and incense his uncle is peddling as a way to move horses, even if Amanda thinks it's a non-story.

In fact, I think she's wrong. I think it's a problem, and here, removed from his presence where I can think clearly, I think I really do have to get away from it all—for my own career's sake. The thoughts that kept me awake last night are still with me: I can't have him *and* a place in the horse business. And there's no other place in the world for me, even if I'm not the star show jumper I'd like to be. I'll never leave horses; if that means I'm a career farm-sitter, like

Posey once suggested, so be it. But I can't even manage that without my reputation intact.

Amanda nudges her horse, and he walks forward, tipping his ears back questioningly as Poz doesn't immediately move alongside him. I cluck, and the chestnut sighs, stepping into a walk. Amanda glances at me as Poz catches up with them. She softly asks me, "Why do you care what Basil's family is doing?"

"I don't care," I say, keeping my eyes on the arena in front of us. "It doesn't matter."

She laughs. "Oh, you care. Stop lying."

I look at her, and I must look as miserable as I feel, because Amanda's eyes widen. She says, "Honey."

There they are. There are the tears. My eyes are hot and burning. I swipe at them with the back of my hand. "I can't help it," I sniffle, hating myself for crying at work. On horseback. So embarrassing.

"Is it mutual?"

"It was," I say. "Until we fought about this last night."

"Well, then, you have to be straight with him."

"I was."

"And he won't listen to you." Amanda sighs. "Of course not. Men never listen. This is why we ride geldings."

I swipe at more tears. They're mixing with the sweat on my cheeks, hot and salty. I'm going to be so dehydrated. "What should I do?" I ask, desperate for someone else to take the reins.

She looks at me with sympathy before a hint of bitterness hardens the smooth curves of her cheeks. "Honey, believe me when I say that I am *not* qualified to *ever* give relationship advice."

"But you helped Posey with Adam," I protest, momentarily distracted. Why am I not good enough to get her dubious advice? I want it!

"I got lucky with Posey," Amanda agrees. "Because, you know, they were never really fighting about each other. They were fighting about Adam's dad, and all of Ocala knew he was a worthless waste of space." She tilts her head, thinking. "Funny. This isn't really about Basil, right? It's about his family. It was the same with Adam."

"Close," I say grimly. "Because Basil is part of all this mess. He's the public face of it."

"Oh, that's true." Amanda looks thoughtful, but I'm done discussing my disaster of a life with her. Another second spent wallowing in it, and I'll throw myself off my horse and have a full on crying fit in the middle of the arena.

And that's not what good horse girls do, is it? No, we sit up straight, shake out our reins, and ride on.

"Let's trot," I say to Poz, and the lazy horse sighs and shuffles into a half-hearted jog.

He's a work in progress, Poz. Just like my life.

Chapter Twenty-Eight

WE LIVE TOGETHER, so it's almost impossible to avoid him completely, but we've got good practice and we're both determined not to see each other, so it works out. As July slides into August and Max sends us blissful emails from the east coast of Africa, Basil and I slip around one other in the palatial house we share and ride our horses when the other person isn't around, and at night I stretch out in bed and stare at the shadows until well past midnight, wondering if he's awake, too.

The lack of sleep shows in my riding and Amanda starts giving me easier horses, taking the tougher ones for herself. When I fall off a potential school horse after one casual buck in a flying lead change, she suggests that I take some time off. But I can't stay home all morning, not with Basil around. I beg her to let me work until she relents, promising I will get more sleep. With some serious application of home yoga practice, meditation, and melatonin, I actually manage it. To tire myself out more, I ride Feather for a full hour every evening, sometimes taking her for a long hack afterwards. She thrives on the extra work and the lengthy baths I give her afterwards, filling out along her top-line, growing a rich, reddish coat in place of her yellowy-gold summer coat. She always smells good, always has a tangle-free mane and tail, always has brilliant white socks and scrubbed, polished hooves. It's possible now to say my no-breed, Celestial Being horse is the best-looking beast in the barn. I take as much pleasure in that as I possibly can, but everything is tinted gray now.

It will pass.

It's just hard because we live together. But it will pass. I murmur this in my meditation; I remind myself of this when we meet in the kitchen, or when I hear his footsteps in the hall, or smell the rich broth of the soups he's gone back to eating now that our shared dinners are a thing of the past.

Basil comes in second in the August open Grand Prix. I don't go. Evie does, and she reports back that the crowd's whispering is even more vicious. "Nothing new," she says, handing me an iced coffee. "It's just that more people know. It's becoming common knowledge."

"Are they blaming him?" I ask. "I mean, are they saying the whole thing is his deal?"

"Of course they are," she replies, blinking at me as if she doesn't know why I'd ask such a ridiculous question. "He's the one in the saddle. He's the one trying and buying horses. The uncle might as well not exist."

"Can he get out of this?" I still hope, somehow, that Basil will decide to abandon the business. Survive on his own terms.

"I don't know," Evie says. She leans against the kitchen counter and looks at the ceiling; we both know Basil is upstairs. Like a ghost who isn't haunting us right now, but could at any moment. "Maybe, if he really wants to."

My coffee isn't sweet enough; I dump in enough sugar to form a sludge at the bottom.

Evie averts her eyes and moves on to other topics. "So, what are you doing about the hurricane?"

It's my turn to blink in consternation. "What hurricane?"

"The one that's like, heading directly for Florida?" Evie snorts at my ignorance. "Mama, you have to keep up with the outside world. It's big-time hurricane season. These storms are no joke."

I feel like I should know about a hurricane barreling towards the farm, but then I reflect back on my recent internet history. Meditation and melatonin are running out of juice, so I've been trying out different ways to bore myself to sleep. Learning to play online poker has been an effective sleeping aid, but it's not the best way to keep up with the news. "How big are we talking here?" I ask, even as my fingers scramble across my phone's screen.

Evie shrugs and finishes taking a long drag on her straw. "I guess it's going to be a lot of wind and rain. Posey is saying not to worry about it and we'll just play work hours by ear. But Adam has the maintenance crew bringing in anything that could blow away, and I think she and her mom are both staying in the main house with Adam. They invited me to stay, too," she adds, ultra-casually. "Since I live in a mobile home and all."

"Uh, yeah, you should definitely be staying with them." I have a local weather page up now, and sure enough, Hurricane Desiree is moving towards the Bahamas and, eventually, according to this prediction, will sweep right through Ocala. "They're predicting more than a foot of rain and maybe hurricane-force winds? This sucks."

"Posey says it'll blow over," Evie says diffidently. "I trust Posey."

"I didn't realize Posey was the local weather girl!" I'm more tense than I expected. I'm not *scared* of a hurricane, I don't think. It's just a lot to process on top of everything else. I have enough to deal with, real world.

Evie shrugs. "She's from Florida, Kayla. I think she knows what she's talking about. Also, I heard her talking to Jules and Alex in the broodmare barn yesterday, and Jules said the same thing. And she's from *south* Florida, so that's even more hurricane street cred. Plus, she lost her entire farm in a hurricane like ten years ago or something. She told Posey about it."

"You hear everything," I grumble, "except for good news."

"I hear the news that's out there," Evie says. "It's not my fault none of it's good."

Great, so now I have to plan for a hurricane. Fortunately, Max has an emergency preparedness binder in the office. Unfortunately, it's on the second floor...some place I haven't ventured in weeks, ever since Basil and I mutually agreed we were done seeing each other.

Well, since I insisted, and he went along with it, because otherwise he'd be a crazy stalker. And Basil, like me, has enough to worry about.

Evie takes off after our coffees are gone and the gossip has run dry, leaving me to gauge the possibilities of locating the emergency prep binder without running into Basil. The afternoon sky is blue with a hint of acrid yellow, a giveaway for the sizzling temperature outside, so I figure there's a decent chance he's in his room, napping away the worst part of the day. I creep up the staircase with my socks on, stealthy as a cat burglar, and pause on the landing, listening. Sure enough, I can hear his white noise machine humming away behind his closed door.

My brain is devious enough to stop thinking about hurricanes so that it can spend some of my valuable time concentrating on the delicious prospect of a nude Basil all wrapped up in his sheets, one foot hanging over the edge of the bed, but fortunately my feet stay on track, taking me right past his door and down the hall, to the office next to Max and Stephen's bedroom.

I glance at their closed door as I pass it, remembering the Celestial Being horse, the way Basil acted shocked when we found it. Just the memory of the lie is enough to make my fists clench. He knew Sylvia sucked him in with her sage and her essential oils and her stupid cardinal directions. But he sat next to me and pretended he had no idea.

It doesn't matter now. There's a hurricane coming. Real world, Kayla. Emergency prep binder. Let's get on with it.

I go into the office and run my finger over the binders, lined up neatly on a shelf against the wall facing the window. Every ritual of farm life is in these binders, from pasture maintenance to veterinary care schedules—procedures first developed by Max before being put into impeccable order by Stephen's tautly organized brain. There's a specific hurricane binder,—next to the wildfire binder, one I really don't ever want to open—and that sucker is a half-inch thick. Not too bad. I pull it out and set it on the desk, settling into the leather chair so I can flip pages in comfort.

Quickly, I realize there are so many checklists that I'm either going to be schlepping this big old book around the farm with me or forgetting half the order of things, so I start taking pictures of it all with my phone. There's a list for prepping the house, for the barn, for the jumps in the outdoor ring, for the well (jeez, Max, I didn't even think about the well) and for the machine shed. There's a checklist for how much feed to have on hand, how much hay, how many buckets, where to stash the hoses, how to check the levels in the water storage tanks, how to fill them, how to use them if the well is out for an extended period of time. There are notes on checking the gasoline and oil stores to be sure I can operate the chainsaw, the hedge trimmers, and several other pieces of equipment I wouldn't ordinarily touch, but which apparently can be necessary after a hurricane. I imagine being stranded in this big house with all the trees between it and the barn collapsed in a heap, and I realize that if this storm really hits us hard, I'll have to sleep in the barn to make sure the horses can be fed and watered with all these emergency rations I'm supposed to be stockpiling.

With a mountain of work in front of me, I sit back and look with dismay at the binder. But then I realize the last page is a list of what to do, in order. It's long, but it's welcome. Stephen left nothing to chance.

Step 1: Check feed, hay, and supplement supply levels. Call feed store and order delivery to match emergency supply requirements.

"Okay," I say. "I can do that."

I stand up and then immediately trip over one of the chair legs, crashing to the floor. The chair comes with me. The sound? Oh, roughly like if all the horses in the barn came galloping up the stairs.

I'm still pushing the chair off me when I hear the white noise machine shut off.

And a door into the hallway opens. I freeze. He won't be able to pinpoint the sound that woke him, I decide. Not with the white noise distorting everything. I'll just wait right here and—

And there is Basil, standing in the doorway with sleep lines on his face and his hair rucked up so adorably that I want to run my hands through it. He looks surprised to see me standing behind Max's desk, or perhaps it's because the desk chair is shoved drunkenly against the wall.

"Hey," he says. "Are you okay?"

I'm on my feet by now. "Fine," I say brusquely, straightening the chair and pushing it into its nook beneath the desk. "I have to go out and do hurricane prep, so—"

"Hurricane prep?"

"Oh, you didn't know? There's only like a category three hurricane heading this way."

Basil gives me a blank look. "You're not serious."

"Dude, read the news for once," I say unfairly, and I push past him, rushing down the hall and away from him before his presence overwhelms me and I give up on this insane plan to keep away from him forever.

We're about to ride out a hurricane together? For that reason alone, I hope all of this prep is a lot of work for nothing.

Chapter Twenty-Nine

IT DOESN'T SEEM to be for nothing, though.

The next morning, all the horses are on edge. Amanda gets tossed off Stuffy McGoo, of all the reliable horses I wouldn't have picked to take a bucking fit for no apparent reason, and I bite the dust when Poz decides that jumping is for suckers and butterflies are birds of prey. The butterflies *do* seem more numerous, though. When I mention this, Amanda agrees, then she comes to a surprising conclusion.

"There aren't any birds out to eat them," she says. "They don't have to hide."

And as I turn my head slowly, looking around the lush landscaping encircling the barns and arenas, I realize Amanda is right. The birds are gone. "Where did they go?" I ask, feeling a little pit of uncertainty in my gut.

"When there's a storm coming, the birds go *in*," Amanda says, shrugging. "Into deep brush, into eaves, into thick trees, and holes..."

"Already? But we're supposed to have two more days." There isn't even a hurricane warning for Ocala yet. Just a watch. *A watch means hurricane conditions are possible in the next thirty-six hours.* I've read the terse explainer again and again as I try to keep up with where Hurricane Desiree is going next. The general consensus is that the storm heads for south Florida, and after that? Anything could happen. The entire forecast has a haphazard feel to it. But birds—birds probably know what's happening, right? They have some metaphysical connection to the planet, magnetic forces and so on. I saw a special on PBS once.

"They must feel the change in the wind," Amanda says. "The horses certainly do." She nods down at Jakers, who is side-stepping anxiously beneath her. He's been doing it for her entire ride and she isn't even reacting to it, just letting him get out all his nervous energy as best he can. "I think we'll take tomorrow off, and I'll help the grooms finish up prep. Are you guys all set at your place?"

I wince when she says *guys*, like Basil and I are working together to prep the farm. The opposite is true; I did everything I could yesterday, working late into the evening and knocking out about half the checklists, while Basil got into his truck and drove off to do who knew what. He came home late, well after I'd eaten a solitary dinner of cold pizza, and went straight upstairs to his bedroom. I assume he's worried about the hurricane hitting where his mother and uncle live in West Palm Beach, but I don't know if he's planning to leave me alone to deal with it. And I can't ask, because that goes against our plan of pretending the other person doesn't exist. I'm not going to be the one to act like I care.

"Almost set," I answer finally. "A few more things to do around the house, and I have to get gas and oil for the tools, and make sure the farm truck is gassed up, but I can do that this afternoon."

"Oof," Amanda sighs. "You're going to be waiting in line, I'm afraid."

Turns out, she's right. Maybe Stephen should have prioritized gas over feed, because it takes me over an hour to get to the pump, sitting in a long line of cars and trucks along the side of Highway 441 with diesel tainting the air and a constant patter of weather doom from the meteorologists on the radio.

But at least, I figure, I'm not at home. Avoiding Basil, thinking about Basil, hating Basil, worrying about Basil.

Although it turns out I can do those things pretty practically on the road, too.

"I can't get him out of my head," I complain.

Posey and Evie look sympathetic. Jules looks impatient.

I drove over to Posey's farm in hopes of someone to talk to in the last free moments before the storm. The hurricane warning has finally been posted and we're expecting rain to start tomorrow afternoon, with the worst of the weather coming in two days' time. It's time to get off the roads and stop using up the gas I just spent an hour getting, but first, I need a little human contact.

Posey and Evie have been in the training barn all afternoon putting up storm shutters along the exposed shed-rows, so I drove there to see them. I didn't expect Jules Thornton-Morrison, the acid-tongued but ultimately satisfying event rider from the next county up, to be there as well.

"I just stopped by on my way home with grain," she explains. "The feed store near me was already sold out of what I use. Always good to have Ocala for back-up."

"It's nice to see you," I say, and I mean it. Jules is kind of a hero to me. She's a self-made woman who came up from suburban working student to top-of-her-game event rider. If I could find her level of focus and dedication, instead of hopping around riding other people's off-track Thoroughbreds and just kind of hacking through life, maybe I'd be a real professional, too. Instead of being a farm-sitter who also rides green horses.

She also managed to marry a top event rider and form some kind of power couple dynamic, which I can't help but think would have been a great look for Basil and me.

The Sweetheart Horse

Now she leans back in her chair and surveys me frankly, like she's checking to see if I've improved any since the last time she saw me. "You look tired," she announces finally. "And worried. Trust me, I get it. Those are my normal looks, too."

"Well, there's a hurricane coming," Evie supplies, laughing lightly. But the sound is fake and Jules knows it. She looks at Evie closely, then back at me.

"What's going on with you?"

There's no subtlety with Jules; she's asking questions because she's curious, not because it's her business, and if I tell her to mind her own business, she'll wrinkle her nose at me but she'll accept it because that's the way she would respond, too.

I tell her anyway. "I'm in love with my house-mate," I say. "But we're not actually speaking to one another, because he lied to me about a cult run by his uncle."

Posey makes a little squeak, and a barn cat who was sleeping on a pile of saddle towels looks up, blinking green eyes.

"Sorry, Posey," I say, laughing ruefully. "I should have told you. Or Evie should've." Evie shakes her head. "We had a little thing going on and then I found out he's involved in some weird stuff and I broke it off. But I'm still completely into him, and it's a huge bummer, to say the least."

Maybe if I'm flippant, the heartbreak won't show.

"With who? Basil Han, right?" Jules is more caught up on my private life than I expected. "Pete was telling me about him. Nice kid, he says."

"Pete? Your husband knows Basil?" I lean forward in my seat and nearly tumble right out. Way to play it cool, Kayla.

"Yeah, Pete does a lot of jumper sales," Jules says, her tone running a little bored. I guess plain old show jumping isn't scary enough for her. I get it. I respect it. "He's looked at some horses with him, given him some pointers on what to look for. He says Basil needs direction, though. Too young to be out on his own."

"He's almost thirty," I point out. As if I, a few years south of thirty myself, have a real direction and focus in life besides *horses yay*.

Jules shrugs. "It's all about your prior training, right? Pete has been in a lot of sales barns in his life. He knows the business. Better than me, if I'm being honest." She grins. "And I'm not always honest about stuff like that."

"What else did he say about Basil?" I ask. "Anything about...um... his business?"

Jules's grin turns into a smirk. "Oh, the scam church? Yeah, Pete says he needs to get clear of that. He says everyone's talking about it."

I sigh so heavily, the cat jumps off the pile of towels and walks over to me, rubbing against my legs as if that will help. "What am I going to do?"

Jules shrugs. "If you're broken up, what can you do?"

Why did I think Jules could give me relationship advice? This must be a sign of how far gone I am.

"Maybe I need to move," I say, although the idea of leaving Basil behind in that echoing, empty house is impossible to bear.

Jules shakes her head. "Whatever you do, running away is never the right answer. Take it from me: if you want something, fight tooth and nail for it."

I look at her admiringly. "Damn, Jules," I say. "That's some good advice."

Jules gives me a knowing look, as if to say, "Obviously."

I decide to mull it over while I'm riding Feather. I usually have good ideas while I'm riding.

Not today. Feather is a bouncing ball of nervous energy, no doubt due to the approaching storm. "What was I thinking?" I moan as she drags us across the covered ring at approximately a hundred miles an hour, her head in the air and her mouth gaping against my hands. "Feather, you are a *disaster!*"

So, all my brain power has to go towards fixing Feather to get a good enough circle around the arena to justify going back to the barn on a good note. My time riding baby racehorses comes back to me in tiny drifts of muscle memory, and by widening my hands, sitting well back in the saddle, and posting trot so slowly it makes my thighs ache, I gradually bring the hot mare down to something resembling a casual jog.

Then I dismount quickly before she can do something else which needs correction.

"Good girl," I tell her expansively, totally over-playing it. "Good *girl!*"

Feather, delighted with this revelation, leans into me and rubs hard, nearly knocking me over.

"You'll want to stop her doing that," says a clipped voice. I recognize it at once; a sinking feeling washes over me. Feather goes in for another good rub and those arrogant tones insist, "Now, don't give her praise when she's treating you like a scratching post, girl. She's overpowering you."

I turn around slowly, hoping that I'm wrong. But of course, there's only one person it could be. Basil's Uncle Edward, standing in the walkway to the covered arena, watching me with a hungry expression.

Or, I should say, watching Feather.

It's unnerving seeing him there. As if by discussing Basil's family with Jules and Posey, I've somehow summoned this force of dark energy straight from West Palm to Ocala. Maybe he's the opposite of a Celestial Being. Maybe he's a…a…Solid Nothing?

No, that can't be right. I'm going down a dumb path here. Real world, Kayla!

Real world, the one with Edward Han of Han Worldwide, the man responsible for Basil's imminent ruin. Dramatic? No, I don't think that's too dramatic.

He's dressed blandly in slacks and a golf shirt, *Han Worldwide* embroidered on the chest like he can't go anywhere without announcing he runs his own business. He has one hand tucked into a pocket; the other is clutching an iPhone. And he's clearly waiting for me.

I'm already on the ground, so I can't use the excuse of working my horse to get away from him. Reins in hand, I walk Feather towards the barn, and he steps to one side to let me pass. "Sir," I say, nodding formally.

He falls in alongside me. "Is that the horse?"

"What horse?" I walk Feather into the wash-rack and hope she stays content in the cross-ties for once. "This is my horse."

His face creases with exasperation. "The Feather horse," he says. "The one from the Britton stable."

"Oh, *that* horse?" I slip off her bridle. "Yeah, it's her."

My horse, I think again.

"A nice horse," he says, sliding his iPhone into his pocket. "You having luck with her?"

"A lot of luck," I reply shortly. Feather tosses her head as I try to get her halter on. So much luck, I think. Just gobs and gobs of good luck. "She's a good horse," I can't help but add. "A lot of potential."

Time to stop talking, Kayla! I don't want to make him mad.

Feather whacks me in the shoulder with her head, and I suppress a grunt.

"High spirits," he comments.

"Yes," I agree, somehow getting the halter over her ears. She's still so full of herself even after a solid ride, flinging her head, pawing at the ground. So full of fuss, all about the changing weather. How do they know? In a season where it storms every day, how do all these animals know about a different kind of storm on the way? I want a sixth sense, I want the kind of intuition that helps me know what the future is bringing. Horses and birds are so lucky; I hope they know what they've got. She digs with one foreleg and I murmur, "Feather, stop pawing."

She ignores me, and I pretend I didn't ask her for anything special.

"Maybe she is a bit too high-spirited," Edward suggests. I wonder if he realizes his smile is more of a smirk. It's a tell; he's trying to manipulate me by being helpful. Well, maybe he only plays online poker, like me. He gives a jerky little laugh, as if he's forgotten how a chuckle should sound, and asks, "Have you ever thought she's a bit too strong for someone of your size? Maybe she's a man's horse."

I give him a disgusted look at this. "A man's horse? That's not a thing. Feather, stop pawing."

He purses his lips, annoyed. "Certainly, it's a thing. Some horses just need a firm hand, a firm personality. They find a woman is a little too soft—"

Whack!

Feather stands at attention and gives me a hurt expression.

"I told you to stop pawing," I inform her, rubbing my hand on my thigh. Smacking a horse's hard neck comes with its own punishment.

She blows hard through her nostrils and curves her neck, trying to reach me with her head. I guess she figures if she can't paw, she might as well rub on me again.

"Difficult," Edward pronounces, with satisfaction.

At least he's no longer saying I'm too soft to handle a tough horse. I resist the urge to tell him to get out of my barn and focus on untacking. She's sweaty beneath the saddle pad. Damn. She needs a shower. Feather still isn't the best at accepting bath-time. Suddenly, I wish Basil would walk into the barn and hold her for me. Ugh, where is he, anyway? I got used to having him around again. After all these weeks of solitude, avoiding him whenever possible, this hurricane upsets all my emotional balance and I just want him back in my life.

I turn on the hose, and Feather's hooves scrape on the wash-rack floor as she turns to look at me. Her eyes widen, showing the whites. Today, it would seem, her brain has decided she's never been hosed off in her life. She's going to make a fool of me in front of this pompous idiot, isn't she?

"Feather, stand still," I say, in what I hope is a masculine and commanding voice.

Feather tugs back on the cross-ties but thankfully doesn't rear or do anything embarrassing like that.

"Yes, she's a difficult one," Edward says happily. "Basil wanted her, but I told him she had a bad background and wasn't right for him. I knew what she needed. Someone who understood these kinds of horses."

"What?" I can't help it. This is the story I've wanted for weeks, coming straight from the old horse's mouth. I turn off the water and ask, "*What* kind of horses?"

He looks pleased with my newfound interest. "Horses with high vibrations, you know. She's not a horse who can be tamed easily. She needs a perfect match for her vibrations. I found a woman in—well, never mind where she's from. I have the right match for her, let's just say that. And as soon as your friend Max is available for a quick phone call, I'm going to get it sorted out."

"Sort *what* out?" He can't mean what I think he does.

"I'm going to buy her and send her to her correct match," Edward declares. "It's for the best."

Feather is pawing again, but I'm not bothering to discipline her, not when this is all coming out. I stare at him. One thing out of all this nonsense really strikes me. "You believe it all, don't you?" I tilt my head, as if I can get a better view of the personality inside the man. "Vibrations and energy and reiki and the spirits...it's not a game to you, is it?"

His brows came together. "Of course it's not a game! The universe is not a joke, madam."

That's interesting. Maybe he made up the Church of Celestial Beings to make money...but he believes in everything he invented.

Oh, well. Still a crook.

"But you were wrong," I say, turning the water back on. "Basil *is* good with this mare. You read her vibrations wrong."

"She was meant for someone else," he insists. "She shouldn't be with Basil."

"That's fine," I say cheerfully, aiming the nozzle at Feather's legs. She side-steps, looking back at me, but she doesn't rear or kick. I call it a win. "Because she *isn't* with Basil. She's with me. She's mine. And that's not changing."

Chapter Thirty

BASIL ACCOSTS ME the moment I walk into the house. He looks so frantic, I almost forget we aren't a couple anymore and move to give him a hug. But luckily, I remember our boundaries. Also, I'm wet and soapy from Feather's bath. No one needs that pressed against their tidy riding clothes.

But he doesn't notice anything off about me. He's too busy being freaked out. "What did you say to him?" he hisses. "He's *furious*. Why would you make him so angry?"

"Excuse me, why is he even here?" I counter. "Why was he in the barn watching me ride like some kind of crazy stalker? I don't appreciate that at all, Basil. You should have told me he was coming."

"He drove up here to make sure I'm not thinking about quitting," Basil says. "Apparently word has made it down to Wellington that I'm involved with a weird church, along with Sylvia. So it's becoming a whole thing. Trust me, I didn't know he was coming."

"It's a cult, not a church," I mutter, more to myself than anything. I set my boots in their place beneath the bench with almost fanatic neatness, lining them up just so. Anything to keep me from going back outside, facing Edward Han myself, and telling him to get the hell out of Ocala before he upsets Basil more than he already has. I'm almost frantic with my need to protect him.

But Basil doesn't need my protection. He needs my support. I just don't know how to make him accept it.

"Fine, cult," Basil agrees, through his teeth. "I work for my uncle's cult. Is that what you want me to say?"

"No, Basil," I reply wearily. "I want you to say you're *quitting* your uncle's cult."

He shakes his head. "I can't say that."

"Why *not*?" I stand up so quickly the blood rushes to my head. Fighting through a wave of dizziness, I clench my fists at my side and fix him with my most commanding, dangerous lunatic-look. The one I try on Feather all the time. "What does he have on you? Is this about Yorkshire?"

Basil's brows come together in confusion. "Yorkshire—no—Kayla, what have you heard?"

"I haven't heard anything," I admit, trying to hang on to my burst of rage, the strongest emotion I've got right now. "But you always trail off when you're talking about your time there, and I think something bad happened. And I think that's why you won't go against your uncle now. Am I wrong?"

He looks away, and I realize I've got him.

Incredibly, the only feeling it gives me is disappointment. "Oh, Bas," I sigh, feeling my fingers unclench. "Tell me what happened."

He looks around, as if to be sure no one can be listening. Then he shrugs, giving up his secret for good. "Uncle Edward wanted me to funnel him information about the Hullworths," he mutters, his gaze dropping to the floor. "Horses prepping for sales, prospects they were interested in buying. He decided it would be interesting to buy and sell horses. So I had to tell him about any horse the Hullworths thought was worth buying."

"And then..."

"And then, he'd swoop in and buy it. Then knock the price up. Tell anyone who came asking that the mighty Hullworths of Yorkshire thought this horse was a cinch for international competition."

"And they found out you were spying on them," I say.

"Ian went to look at a horse he'd bought, one they really, really wanted. And Uncle didn't know it was Ian Hullworth." Basil's face splits in an unwilling smile, and he raises his eyes to meet mine. He shakes his head. "He told Ian Hullworth that those pompous Hullworth brothers were after this horse!"

"Oh my God." I can't help but laugh. "What an idiot."

"Yeah." Basil's smile fades. "And then they fired me. And told me if they saw me at a show in England again, they'd tell everyone what a lying cheat I was."

Silence stretches between us as I take in those words. This is why he's in America at all. Edward Han got his nephew banned from the horse business in the U.K.—or as good as banned. Because who would do business with someone who had cheated the mighty Hullworths of Yorkshire?

"Kayla," Basil whispers, "I don't have anything but Jock, and even he belongs to my uncle. It all belongs to him. He takes care of my mother, he pays for my show fees, he covers everything. My job is to run the horse sales for him. In exchange, I'm allowed to have Jock as my personal horse and compete him. I could give up my uncle, go somewhere and start over, but what about Jock?"

What about Jock, indeed? Who would give up a horse like that? Basil has put his horse before everything else...including me.

And I get it.

I'd do the same.

Not about Feather, bless her. I really like Feather, don't get me wrong. And someday I might love her. But it's Crabby Appleton who has my heart. My big, grumpy, unmotivated Dutch Warmblood from the wrong side of the fence. I'd do anything for him. Cheat, lie, steal, betray—who cares? Crabby comes first.

So I open my arms and draw Basil against me, feeling his thin shoulders tremble against my clavicle, his muscled arms tightening around my back. Our flushed cheeks rest together, and for the moment, it's not that white-hot lust racing through me at our touch. Just love, understanding, empathy. Even if we can't be together, even if our ambition and our horses force us apart, I think I will always love him.

"I want to help you," I whisper as our embrace slowly ends. "I'm sorry about all the fighting. Just let me help you."

"There's nothing—" he begins, and then he lifts his head and looks past me.

"Kayla," he says, "there's a horse trailer leaving the barn."

I race out the back door, bare feet drumming over the sharp green knives that passes for grass in Florida. The farm truck and trailer, which are kept down by the machine shed, are cruising up the driveway at a lively pace. For a moment, I think, *at least they didn't steal the Peter-Bilt,* and then I realize this isn't a truck and trailer theft. I mean, it is, but the vehicles are not the point.

The payload is.

I hear Feather's whinny, plaintive and lonesome, on the hot, gusting breeze. And then I see him in the cab. It's Uncle Edward, leaving Bent Oak Farm with my boss's truck and trailer...and my horse.

I can't believe what I'm seeing. As Edward realizes he's spotted, he accelerates and the truck roars, plunging forward. Feather bangs and kicks in the trailer, not happy about the way she's being driven. For some reason, that animal communicator report in her file comes into my head: "Feather expects to be respected." Well, she knows her chauffeur doesn't respect her now, and she's letting him know she doesn't appreciate it.

I just hope he listens to her and drives more carefully, so she doesn't get hurt.

Wait a minute. What am I doing, hoping he drives safely? I need to do something. He just stole my horse. Not Crabby, but my foolish, talented, piss-and-vinegar sweetheart of a Feather. He really *stole* her.

I know I should be doing more than standing here. But I'm rooted to the ground, lost in confusion. This can't be real. You can't just *steal a horse* in the twenty-first century. There are rules. We live in a society.

A voice in my ear brings me back to reality. Basil is next to me, holding my boots and, surprisingly, my purse. "Get these on," he says, gesturing at my bare feet. "The idiot left his truck here. We're taking it and we're going after him."

In evacuation traffic, with long lines at the gas stations and the on-ramps to the interstate, we drive south.

It's insanity, of course. There are dark clouds gathering, the sky above cast in a yellow-gray hue that grows progressively more steely from north to south. The highest clouds arc in a broad, sweeping curve over the peninsula, giving away the buzz-saw shape of the approaching hurricane. Even without radar loops and satellite imagery, no one could mistake this sky for an ordinary gray day.

I'm as yet uninitiated to the wonderful world of tropical cyclones, but even I can see the shift in the weather patterns. The way rain blows through in short, staccato blasts, sometimes lasting no longer than thirty seconds before we've passed through the squall. It's so fast the windshield of Edward's truck fills up with water before Basil can even find the wiper control, and so fleeting that by the time he's fumbled with the switch and cleared the glass, the way ahead is dry.

People are going every which way. North, south, west. Tampa isn't expected to get more than a few thunderstorms; in southwest

Florida, the forecast is sunny and hot. The one thing everyone can agree on is that staying on the stretch of peninsula from West Palm Beach to Ocala to Jacksonville is out of the question. There's no way around the traffic jams. I hate thinking of Feather being buffeted against the walls of the trailer in stop-and-go traffic.

And I feel bad for thinking that I didn't love her as much as I love Crabby. I do love her; I just couldn't admit it to myself. Who would fall in love with a half-broke mare with wild eyes and a short fuse who has been nothing but trouble since the day she arrived? Jumping out of paddocks and making up her own mind about where she wants to live, who she wants to associate with, what she wants to do in the ring or in the barn aisle? Who sent me to the hospital over an obsession with alfalfa treats and an inability to recognize the word *no*?

I mean, seriously, who wouldn't love a chestnut mare with absolutely no sense? Of course I do.

And beside me, Basil Han. The other misfit I can't seem to get enough of. He's navigating the punch-drunk traffic with narrow eyes and a set jaw, but every now and then, he manages to glance over at me, meet my eyes with his, and give me a taut smile. Encouragement? Support? An acknowledgment that we're finally in something together?

It's all good. I put my hand on his shoulder and give him a little squeeze, and I swear some of the stiffness in his jaw slips away.

I think Basil is going to be fine. Eventually. If we can just figure out this mess with Feather, maybe we can use it as leverage to win Jock's ownership as well. Then Basil can be free.

And then I can convince him there's still a chance for us.

But that's all a long way away, and, I think, it's pretty far-fetched, too. Still, a girl can dream. And she can also threaten to file a police report which might send a man to jail for theft if he's not careful.

Once we're through the tangled maze of Orlando expressways, the evacuation direction becomes more pronounced. Everyone is heading north.

Except for us.

"We're lucky they haven't turned the southbound lanes around," Basil remarks as we fly down a nearly empty turnpike. On the other side of the median, cars inch along, bumper to bumper. Their passengers have to wonder where we're going, why we're heading south into the eye of a hurricane. "I think a lot of times they do, to speed up the evacuation from the coast. Then we'd have to find our way around on back roads, and I don't know this part of Florida at all."

"Neither do I," I admit. "I've barely left Ocala since I got here. But what are they doing over there?" I point to a road crew setting up pylons. They're blocking an on-ramp to the turnpike.

"Uh-oh," Basil says, and he hits the accelerator. The big truck growls to life with impressive energy and we rocket through the pine forests and prairies in this vast empty section of central Florida, somehow staying one jump ahead of the impending southbound shutdown.

"Well, we've got one thing going for us," I say as we pass another crew setting out cones across an on-ramp. "At least when we head back north, we'll have all these extra lanes to use."

Basil grins wryly. "Way to look on the bright side, Kayla. Also, I was thinking, when we get back..."

"Yes," I ask, my heart leaping with excitement. *Yes, we can get back together,* I think. *Just ask!*

"Maybe we should stop leaving the keys to the farm truck in the ignition," Basil says.

"Oh," I say. "Yeah. Good call."

* * *

The Sweetheart Horse

The gas lines and grocery store backups in the outskirts of West Palm Beach are severe, and we limp along two-lane roads as rain begins to patter on the windshield with dismaying regularity. The squalls come with wind gusts that send the palm trees lining the roads into frenzies, their loose fronds flying loose and scattering across the pavement. Cars swerve to avoid them as if they're living things, displaced creatures shivering in the roadway.

I'm starting to feel the tiniest bit afraid of what might happen next. The outer edges of the hurricane are already here. We've driven straight into their curving embrace. Should we have waited until this whole thing was over? Or called the police?

"Maybe we should have let the cops handle this," I say as we slam to a halt outside another shopping center, cars piled up like dominos ready to topple forward, their drivers desperate to get back to their houses with supplies of bottled water, bread, canned food they'd never eat ordinarily. "South Florida is a war zone."

"The cops?" Basil chuckles. "Do you have anything saying that you're Feather's legal owner?"

I turn in my seat, staring at him. "I don't. Oh my God, Basil. I don't! Why didn't I think of that?"

Everything is in the farm's name. Feather's mine because Max and Stephen said so...but they didn't make it legal. So few horse sales *are* legal. They're just under-the-table transactions, made with checks or Venmo transfers or even regular old cash. Horses get traded for boats, cattle, four-wheelers, occasionally houses. But they aren't deeded; there's no county registration office where a certificate of ownership rests in a filing cabinet, ready to be taken out if there's a dispute.

There's a saying in the horse business, trotted out regularly when someone stops paying their board bill or a horse is abandoned and a farm owner is stuck with it. "Possession is nine-tenths of ownership,"

I say slowly.

"So, let's go take possession," Basil replies.

The police in this town, even if they weren't busy with a thousand traffic jams and fender-benders as a hurricane bears down, aren't going to show up and make Uncle Edward hand Feather back.

Although they might have something to say about the truck and trailer.

"Almost there," Basil says as he navigates the last shopping center on a straight, two-lane road which seems to disappear over the horizon. We're driving west now, away from the turnpike and civilization. There are deep canals on either side of the pavement, and thick hedges of mangroves and shrubby trees. Occasional driveways reveal pastures, tree farms, and vast green fields of reeds which must be sugar cane.

I feel nervous out here in the south Florida sticks. This the land of Florida Man, of disappearing bodies, of human arms found in the stomachs of alligators. It's not exactly the ideal location for a final showdown with an unethical businessman running his own cult for fun and profit.

Scratch that. It's the *perfect* location for this kind of drama.

I'm just not really excited about being one of the players.

Chapter Thirty-One

SYLVIA'S BARN LOOKS normal on the outside. Center-aisle barn on a slight rise, surrounded by paddocks. A few cars on a crushed-shell parking lot out front. A doublewide mobile home nearby, with bright fuchsia flowers blooming along the skirting. An arena at the far end of the barn, with white sand footing and a collection of jumps. They've been tugged to the side of the arena and wrapped up tight with nylon rope to keep them from blowing over or breaking in the storm.

And behind the barn, the Bent Oak Farm truck and trailer.

Rain patters gently on our heads as we get out and look at each other from either side of the truck's hood. I don't know what we're going to do. "Should we have a plan?" I whisper.

Basil shakes his head, his jaw jutting with determination. "This is a bridge too far," he says. "Let me handle this."

But as he starts for the barn, resolution in every firm step, I decide to stay right next to him. He glances at me, a ghost of a smile passing over his lips, and I know he's glad I didn't drop to his heels. Basil doesn't need a shadow. He needs a partner.

And when he stops dead in the barn aisle, his hand grips at my elbow. Part shock, part the need to protect me.

Feather is in the cross-ties, and as usual, she doesn't like it.

* * *

Edward is at my mare's head, his hands on her halter as he tries to steady her. He's doing a really poor job of it, which isn't surprising, since he's no horseman. And when he sees us in the barn aisle, his hands tighten on Feather's halter. She flings her head in annoyance, nearly smacking him in the face. He steps back, grunting with surprise, and a woman comes out of the tack room next to the crossties.

She's nothing like I pictured. If this is Sylvia Britton, and I assume it must be, she's no Stevie Nicks-style witch. Forget the flowing sleeves of a silken blouse and the long locks of an uncut mane; Sylvia is one of those particularly tanned and wrinkled Floridian horsewomen who have spent their lives in the sun without worrying what SPF is in their moisturizer. Her brown hair, streaked liberally with gray, is pulled back in a stringy ponytail, and she's wearing cut-off shorts and a pink tank top.

I feel a strange blend of disappointment (she's not an interesting sorceress at all!) and relief (same reason!). I know women like Sylvia. If I don't keep up with the latest and greatest in UV-blocking technology, then one day I might *be* a Sylvia. Minus the theft, and the horse-cult, and the smoking bundle of sage in one arthritic hand.

She brings faded eyebrows together and glares at us. "Can I *help* you?" she sneers, as if we are seriously inconveniencing her on her perfectly normal, law-abiding day at the barn.

Basil hesitates, and as I press closer to his side, I feel his heartbeat fluttering like a frightened animal's. He's not afraid, though. This is just his old friend, anxiety.

How many times has Basil stood down from a row with his uncle because his brain tricks him into believing things are much, much more dangerous than they really are? It's not fair, the way our own senses deceive us. But lucky for Basil, he has me here. And I might have the usual amount of social anxiety, but no one has ever taught

The Sweetheart Horse

me to be afraid of a fight.

Because in my happy little life, I've never had to get into one.

And so, as Feather paws the concrete aisle and Sylvia waves her sage threateningly at me and Edward stands off to one side, looking uncomfortably at me, it feels perfectly natural to step forward and demand that they step aside so I can load up my horse again.

Sylvia stares at me. "And you are?"

Edward makes a small sound, like a mouse in a trap.

"I'll need the truck keys," I tell him. "I hope you left me enough gas to get home."

One hand goes to his pocket, as if to reassure himself the keys are there. And I see the moment when he realizes he's left them in the stolen truck.

I turn to Basil. "Go get the keys."

He nods and turns, running out of the barn before anyone can react. Then Edward gives a shout and goes after him, a good twenty feet behind.

Feather rears in the cross-ties, her head perilously close to the cross-beams above the aisle. "Get down, stupid," Sylvia hisses, clutching at the cross-tie. "You're going to crack your skull open. Here, let me—" and as Feather comes down to earth, Sylvia digs into a pocket and comes out with a tiny spray bottle. She starts flicking a mist at Feather's nose.

What the hell is *that?*

No one poisons my horse with her nasty potions! I leap forward and run at Sylvia, intent on slapping that spray bottle out of her hand. Feather sees me coming and shies backwards, snapping one of the cross-ties. It hits the wall, and she keeps running backwards, her hooves skidding on the concrete.

I hate this barn! Concrete and low beams, it's so old-fashioned! Can't the cult pay for a remodel and some safe equine-friendly pavers, for goodness' sake?

"Give me that," I snarl, snatching at the bottle, and Sylvia tries to jump out of my way. She still has a hand on the last cross-tie standing, but Feather is rapidly reaching the literal end of her tether and Sylvia realizes she has to make a choice. She drops the bottle and lunges after my mare. I stumble in my hurry to pick it up, but when I read the label, I realize what I took for a potion is nothing but Bach's Rescue Remedy.

"You're using damn floral essences?" I shout. "I thought you were some kind of powerful Celestial Being Master! This has a literal Wal-Mart price tag on it!"

Sylvia is still wrestling with a struggling Feather, but her head swivels and she stares at me for a moment. "You're mad at me because I use Rescue Remedy?" she asks, incredulous. "And how do you know about Celestial Beings?"

"I know everything," I inform her. "I'm on to the whole game you've been playing with Edward Han."

Rain rattles on the roof as a squall blows over the farm, but Sylvia's watching me closely now and doesn't notice the worsening weather. She drags Feather forward, clipping a lead-rope to her halter, never taking her eyes off my face. I have the uncomfortable feeling she's memorizing my features.

Hopefully, this woman never shows in Ocala. The last thing I need is a warm-up arena nemesis.

"You can hand me that lead-rope," I tell her. "That's my horse."

"No," she says. "No, this is Edward's horse. He just brought her. I don't know who you are or what you want, but I think you should leave my barn."

"I'm Max and Stephen Slidell's farm manager," I tell her grandly, giving myself a slight promotion. "And this mare belongs to my farm."

It's a wrench, not calling Feather my own. But I figure I'd better keep this as legally defensible as possible.

And it does the job: Sylvia's eyes widen, and she looks at Feather, still pawing and carrying on beside her. "I think you're mistaken," she says, but her voice lacks conviction. "Edward says he bought her back. We were going to do a cleansing ritual just now, to make sure her aura is clear. And then I have a buyer coming to try her, right after this storm is gone."

"He stole her," I inform her. "Edward is a horse thief."

Sylvia shakes her head. "I don't want any part of that. Here, hold her a second," she says, and to my surprise, she shoves the lead-rope at me. She scurries into the tack room before I can say anything.

Feather looks at me and takes a long breath. Her nostrils flutter as she lets it out. That silent little whinny I love so much. I run my hand up her head, slowly, speculatively, and she leans into my touch.

It's not a miracle; I'm just the first familiar thing she's encountered since Edward drove off with her this morning. I doubt she's hung onto any fond memories of this barn, and the storm is stirring up everything anyway, making it harder for her to understand her surroundings. But for a moment, Feather lets me be her rock, and I feel deeply grateful.

I'm sure once she's back at our farm, she'll be a maniac again.

That's fine, too.

As long as she comes back, I'll take the troublesome Feather over no Feather at all.

Sylvia comes back out of the tack room with more bottles in one hand, that sage bundle burning away in the other. She tries to pass it to me. "You hold this and we'll just finish up the aura cleanse," she suggests. "Then we'll have the boys come back in here and explain themselves."

"The boys?" I retort, refusing to take the smudge of sage. "Edward

Han is a thief. Basil is just here to help me bring my—the—horse back to the farm safely. He doesn't owe you any explanations."

Sylvia cocks her head. Her dark little eyes seem to glitter at me in the dim barn aisle. "How do you figure?" she asks. "That Basil is the black sheep of the family. Stands there and lets his uncle shoulder all the burden of caring for his mama, paying for his showing and that horse, while all he does is complain and bring bad luck with him wherever he goes. I swear every time he stands in the aisle making his little faces, something else breaks around here. His vibrations are bad news, believe me."

"Thanks," I tell Sylvia, and I mean it. "Thanks for telling me that, seriously." I cluck to Feather and she follows me down the aisle, her hooves ringing on the pavement.

Sylvia dashes after me, still waving her smudge. "Where you going? Right back out into a hurricane? I don't think so. You better just stop—"

I hear a truck roar over the rain thundering down on the roof, and everything Sylvia says is drowned out by the hopeful, fearful pounding of my heart. Please be Basil, I beg. Please, please, please, please—

The truck appears in front of the barn, and behind the wheel, Basil smiles at me, waving for me to hurry up. As he puts the truck into park, the squall passes, and I walk Feather into the soggy world outside. Basil runs around and puts down the ramp.

"Where's your uncle?" I gasp, as we team up to coax my disbelieving mare back into the trailer she just escaped a little while ago. "Did you tie him up or something?"

Basil laughs. "Not necessary, although *thank* you for thinking I could be such a dashing hero in all this. He's actually in Sylvia's house thinking about his sins. I reminded him about how poorly Celestial Beings are treated in this nation's prison system. Evidently, he believes they are a very downtrodden religion."

"Prison, because he stole the truck and trailer?" I ask, already wondering how we could go about proving that when we're about to drive it back to north Florida. There's no way we're waiting around here to file a police report. The sky is already darkening again.

Feather lurches into the trailer at last and Basil springs into action, pushing her into a stall and hoisting the chest bar into place so she can't change her mind. Once she's secure, he replies, "The truck and trailer are the least of his worries, Kayla. But I'm out of it now."

"You told him it's done? But what about Jock?"

He smiles at me. "Something you said on the way down here stuck with me. That old line about possession?"

"Yeah, but isn't Jock in your uncle's name? I mean, I just assumed—"

"He's in the business's name," Basil says, hopping out of the trailer and waving merrily at the dumbfounded Sylvia, standing in the aisle and staring at us. "And the business, I'm *pretty* sure, belongs to my mother as much as it does to my uncle."

I'm excited and nervous about meeting Basil's mother. I also wish we weren't going right now. Another squall is ripping through. There has been a report of a waterspout moving onshore out at the beach, and the weather service is warning of more tornadoes to come as Hurricane Desiree nears the coast.

But Basil swears she's on the way back to Ocala, and it helps that the roads are beginning to clear. The grocery stores are closed; a lot of the gas stations have bags over the pumps and pylons in front of their entrances. The "hunker-down" period has begun.

We should be hunkering down, too. But at least if the turnpike traffic has eased, we'll be able to drive north faster than the storm is traveling. Last report, Desiree was moving at twelve miles an hour.

We ought to be able to beat that, I think.

Basil keeps us on main roads and off the turnpike for almost an hour, expertly navigating the strange grid of rural and suburban roads here on the far western side of south Florida civilization. The only worrisome moments come when strong squalls roll through, with wind gusts that buffet the truck and trailer. I stare at the dark water in the deep canals lining the roads and wonder what happens if Basil loses control. Are we just torn limb-from-limb by alligators immediately, or is there a period of time where we flail around, hopelessly aware of our own impending doom?

"You can stop looking at the water like it's going to eat you," Basil teases. "I know these roads."

"It's the wind," I protest, but my words are choked off by a blistering gust that scatters rain across the windshield like an overturned water bucket. When the wipers clear the view, Basil has mere seconds to steer around an oak tree which has half-toppled over the road. The leaves slap my window and scrape against the side of the truck and trailer. "This is getting dangerous," I say, unnecessarily. "How far?"

"Not far," Basil says, his voice taut and flat. His knuckles are white on the steering wheel.

I sit back and bite my fist to keep quiet. He doesn't need my anguished looks and panicked questions now.

And sure enough, after another mile he pulls the trailer up to a fancy residential neighborhood, guarded by a peach-colored security kiosk. He has to park alongside it, but before he can get out of the truck, the gate opens. I notice a handwritten sign in the window of the security kiosk: *Gate on automatic.*

"Even security has clocked out," I joke nervously.

"They don't need it, anyway," Basil says.

The neighborhood is expensive, but bland: the same Spanish-colonial facade repeated over and over, the same orange-red barrel tiles on the roofs, the same traveler palms in the front gardens. The same impregnable hurricane shutters installed over the windows. Basil pulls up in front of an anonymous house and turns off the truck. He looks at me. "You coming in?"

I glance at the house. With its gleaming metal shutters, it looks like a house commandeered by an invading army. I'd rather not. But Basil has come all this way to save my horse for me. I can walk up to that front door with him and help him save his horse.

"Let's go," I say.

His knock echoes on the door, and for a moment, I think no one is coming. Then the door opens, and there she is.

Basil's mother is small, but imposing. Her jaw juts as she looks us over. Then she smooths her gray hair, tucked into a tidy bun, and shakes her head. "Basil, my son, what on *earth* are you doing here now?"

In a pretty breakfast nook—which is probably even nicer when the windows aren't boarded up—we drink tea while Basil sketches out the events of the day. Mrs. Han looks tired and annoyed. "Your uncle is a fool," she says when he gets to our escape from Sylvia's barn. "Jail is too good for him."

"I can still try to put him into prison," Basil offers.

"I'll help," I chime in.

She gives me an approving look, then shakes her head. "No, I told your poor father I'd look after his idiot little brother. And I think I have. But maybe it's time I take more care with the business. I knew he was getting too wrapped up in his little church."

This time, I don't correct her by saying 'cult'—I would probably never dare correct Basil's mother on anything, ever. She might be short of stature, but she has dignity and a commanding presence which would make her a terrifying enemy.

And maybe I don't know if Basil and I have a future, but if we do, I need this woman to like me. That much, I'm certain of.

Basil is *not* going against his mama.

Indeed, I doubt any of us are brave enough to try.

"Well," she says, as our phones bleat anxiously with fresh weather warnings. "If you aren't staying here, you'd better get back on the road. Of course, you can always put that horse in the garage. This house is hurricane-proof. Not in a flood zone, and the power is underground."

Tempting as the offer is, I have to shake my head. "She's a very bad horse," I tell her.

Mrs. Han chuckles. "You don't have to tell me about bad horses. Basil here has had a pony or two that I'm sure came directly from Hell itself."

"Oh, really?" Despite everything, I lean forward, ready for a good bucked-off-Basil story.

"Oh, yes. There was one, in England—"

"Mother," he interrupts. "We really better go."

"Right, of course you should." She looks around. "You want Jock in your name, then? That's fine. Let me go into the office. I have his paperwork in there."

I look at Basil as his mother leaves the room. "Your mom is cool," I say.

He laughs. "Yeah," he says. "Yeah, she is. That's probably why Edward has gotten away with so much, honestly. She doesn't want to bother anyone. She thinks everyone should be free to live their own lives."

"But—" I look around and lower my voice. "But Edward has been running your life. Isn't that different? Why didn't she stop him?"

Basil rubs his face and sighs. "Honestly? I've always had a choice. I just didn't want to rock the boat. And he really did hold Jock over my head, always saying he thought we should sell him..."

"You stayed to avoid making him mad," I say.

"Yeah," Basil agrees. "Kind of a dumb reason, right?"

Not for someone who has a panic attack over raised voices, I think. And I lean across the table, taking his hand before I even realize what I'm doing. "I get it," I whisper. "You've done everything the only way you can."

Chapter Thirty-Two

WE ALTERNATE BETWEEN local news and music on the way back to Ocala. It's not a bad trip, despite the squalls which race up from behind us, shaking the truck and blinding us with tropical downpours. We wait at the turnpike service station in Fort Drum for an hour, my fingernails digging into my palm as police-escorted gasoline tankers arrive to replenish the pumps. When we finally inch up to the service island and a rain-jacketed attendant tells us to stay in the truck while he fills the tank, I let out a sigh of relief, which makes Basil smile.

"Did you think we were going to run out of gas?" he asks.

"No," I say. "I *knew* we were."

Then we're back on the road, racing north on wide-open roadways. The contraflow on the turnpike is still in effect, and police cars sit at every on-ramp, lights flashing, making sure we're safe as we drive the wrong way at seventy miles an hour.

And though things snarl again in Orlando, and we go back to regular turnpike traffic on the road north to Ocala, we stay ahead of the storm. That's the most important thing, I remind myself as we slow for another mass of red brake-lights. We're ahead of the storm.

While the truck growls impatiently in creeping traffic, Basil's hand rests protectively on the file resting on the console. It has been there between us since we left his mother back at her hurricane-proof fortress, waving affectionately from the porch before she disappeared back inside the steel front door. Jock's registration papers, with Basil's name written in the transfer section. She promised to send a notarized bill of sale from Han Worldwide to Basil Han once her attorney was back at work.

"And you owe me a dollar, young man," she told Basil. "You can't just get horses for free around here!"

Then she patted his cheek and laughed. "I can't wait until your uncle gets back," she said. "He and I are going to spend this hurricane having a *serious* chat."

Despite her assurances that Edward's horse business is about to be shut down, I want a similar sheet of paper for Feather. Sadly, I know I have to wait. Once Max and Stephen are home, though, it's the first thing I'm asking for.

"What are you going to do now that you own Jock?" I ask him.

"Go to Disney World," Basil jokes.

"Oh, it's the other way," I say. "Also, I think they close for hurricanes."

"Typical." He sighs, then glances at me, grinning. "I guess now I go into business for myself! You hated the name Han Worldwide, so I'm sure you're full of suggestions for a new business name."

I stare at him. "You want me to name your business?"

Basil's grin slips. "I mean—if you want to help me—it doesn't have to mean anything, you know, significant—"

"Basil," I say, determined to get it out. "We should start dating again. Or—whatever we were doing. Being—in a relationship. I'm sorry we broke up."

He starts to say something, and then traffic takes that exact opportunity to screech to a full halt. Basil focuses on the road, and I'm afraid the moment is lost.

But it turns out, this is too big a moment to get swamped by a little thing like a hurricane evacuation. As the sea of cars around us sit in exasperated silence, Basil puts one hand over mine. "I'm sorry, too. Yes, please. Let's do whatever we were doing again, okay?"

I have to laugh at that, even though my heart is so full, I feel like it could burst from my chest. I squeeze his fingers. "Basil Han, be my boyfriend?"

And at that, Basil puts the truck in park, leans over, and kisses me.

"I'm feeling really good about that high-impact window we had installed," I say, looking over the replaced window in the tack room. "Now Stephen can't say it cost too much."

Basil looks up from the pile of bedding he's trying to resolve into a comfortable place for us to ride out the hurricane. The storm is still determinedly making its way up the peninsula, and rain is tapping steadily against the window glass, occasionally splattering in a sudden gust of wind. He eyes the window noncommittally and says, "I could still put a piece of plywood over it."

"I don't think so. Have you ever boarded up windows on a concrete block building before? There's no anchors out there to put a screw into."

His face screws up in a grimace. "I have to admit, I don't know what any of that means. So I guess you're right?"

"Afraid so." I tap the glass again. "My dad likes to build things in the backyard. And he builds them to last. So I know a little about how buildings work."

"More than me." Basil arranges a duvet to his satisfaction. "But I figure I can always hire someone to do that sort of thing for me."

"Not so fast," I remind him. "You said you're going to run your own business, right? You can't just send the invoices to your uncle anymore."

"God, you're right." Basil plunks down on a pillow and holds out

The Sweetheart Horse

his hand. I take it, laughing, as he tugs me down beside him. "I better go back to the cult and get my job back before my bank account runs dry."

"Liar," I chuckle, then sigh, as his lips touch my neck, sending delicious shivers up and down my spine. "You don't have anything in your bank account *now*."

"That's unlikely to change," he assures me in a seductive whisper. "Because I am very bad at anything that isn't riding horses."

"I wouldn't say you're bad at *everything*..."

Deciding to ride out the storm in the barn wasn't a light decision. I was very hopeful we'd stay in the house, with electricity, for the entire storm—after all, the power only goes out here when the weather is beautiful. But after we'd gotten home, given poor Feather a liniment bath to help with her sore muscles after all that trailering, and finished up with the other horses for the evening, we switched on the local weather and found that the hurricane had slowed down.

"Barely moving," is how the meteorologist put it. "Looks like we're going to be in for a full day of heavy rain, wind, and power outages, folks."

Basil and I shared a look. The initial plan had been to feed them up ahead of the heaviest squalls, then stay put in the house until they let up. But if we were talking more than twelve hours in the red zone for high winds, it wouldn't be safe to try to run back and forth between the barn. The live oaks around the horse area could come down, stranding the horses without food or fresh water.

So, we moved our hurricane party to the barn.

It was fine at first. The horses were loaded up with hay, and Basil and I went to sleep around midnight. The worst noise was the rain pounding on the window.

But now! It's three a.m. and I've just been woken up by a

symphony of sounds.

The barn is creaking, in the throes of some horrible hurricane band that is a violent crimson on the radar app (I still have phone service, but how long will it survive?), with howling winds and a deafening roar of rain against the metal roof and the windows. The rain is pouring down the high-impact glass like we've been set down in the middle of a car wash.

I look up sharply as something outside hits the driveway with a crashing sound. Next to me, Basil is pushing himself upright, his expression taut. "What do you think it was?" I ask, hating how quavery my voice is.

"I'm guessing it's part of that live oak that leans over the parking lot," he says. "Thank God we don't have anything parked out there."

"Oh, no," I whimper. That tree is two hundred years old, according to Max, who is very proud of it. "Surely it's lived through worse storms than this, though."

"Has it?" Basil is consulting his phone. "The weather service says the Ocala Airport just had a hundred mile an hour wind gust."

That's strong. Even I know that, and I'm no Floridian. The middle of the peninsula doesn't get winds like that very often. Jules said it wasn't even hurricane winds that took out her farm back in the last big storm; it was a tornado.

I remember something else about that story. Jules was in the tack room when it happened.

I look up at the ceiling, listening to the unseen rafters squeak, and feel a distinct sense of unease.

Maybe unease isn't enough word. Maybe *panic* is closer to the truth.

There's another crash, this one on the other side of the barn, and a sound of bending metal. My head whips around, as if I can see it through the walls.

"The machine shed," Basil says. "That tree on the south side."

Now I'm running through a mental checklist of every tree on the property, specifically the ones right next to the barn. There are two. But neither are towering live oaks like the ones we've presumably just heard come down. I don't know what they are...I'm no tree expert. They're about twenty feet tall, they've got limbs and leaves and—

A branch flattens itself against the window for a moment, hangs suspended there like a ghoul in a horror movie, then flies away.

Fewer limbs and leaves than they used to have, anyway.

"This is going to pass," Basil says. "We just have to get through this band and we'll be okay."

"You don't know that," I choke, half-laughing. Hysteria, super. "I think there's a decent chance we won't be okay."

Suddenly Basil is beside me on the couch, his arms encircling me, tugging me close to him. His lips are against my hair; I feel them move as he murmurs, "I haven't gotten this far to let go of you now."

A thrill runs through my entire body. And something more than that: confidence. We can do this. We just have to get through this band. I take a deep breath and turn my face against him, pushing against his broad chest. I feel safe.

And that's when the high-impact window shatters.

Out in the barn aisle, the blast of the storm as it batters the building is too much for us to talk without shouting. The rain roars like stones on the roof; the wind is rattling the metal barn doors and whistling in the open rafters above us. I know we can't stay out here, so I wrench open the feed room door and we hustle inside. It's not air-conditioned, but as the electricity fails and our lights flicker out, I realize nothing is going to be air-conditioned. Possibly for a while.

We sit in the dark and consult our phones, our thighs pressed together in a desperate need to feel safe through numbers, until the wind slowly dies down and the rain drops from a deafening roar to a dull racket.

Basil looks around. "I think we made it?"

"Through that," I agree dubiously, although looking at my phone, it really seems like that might be the worst of the storm for us. The hurricane has been downgraded to a tropical storm and is falling apart fast as the eye approaches land, dry air showing up as clear patches on the radar that grow and grow. It's still moving slowly, but it looks like this won't be the storm of the century, after all.

Well, except for what has already gone down out there. I know there's damage. And I'm afraid to find out what we might have lost in that heavy band of wind and rain.

"Do you want to go out and look around?" Basil asks. "I think it's done blowing like that, at least for a while."

"There might be power lines down," I remind him. "We better wait for daylight."

"That's in two hours," he muses, checking the time. "You want to make for the house?"

"No," I say. "Can't we just wait out here?"

Basil runs a hand over my hair. "What will we do? Just sit on these feed bags?"

"We can talk," I suggest.

"About what?" He moves closer to me, clearly ready to do something besides talk.

"About what you're going to do next," I tell him.

"Right now?"

"Can you think of a better time? We just lived through a very scary hurricane. Maybe this is the best moment to know exactly what we want to do with our lives. Mortality and all that."

"Fine," Basil agrees. "I want to ride Jock, keep a few prospects in training, and sell horses along the way to pay expenses. There.

Nothing too surprising, right?"

"But how are you going to do it?" I persist. "That's the question. Let's work that out."

While we're pondering this problem, our phones go to sleep quietly, one after another, leaving us in darkness.

Through the walls, I hear the horses pacing.

"We have until November to figure this out," Basil says finally.

"Not enough time to put it off," I reply. "Trust me, I know."

The rain picks up, hammering on the roof, and then there's a sudden flash. For a split second, the feed room is lit an electric blue-white. Then a crash of thunder shakes the building down to the foundation.

Basil grips my arm. "Good *lord!*" he gasps. "Where did that come from? There's been no thunder all night!"

I take a breath to steady my own nerves. "Rain causes lightning," I say eventually.

"What?" I feel him shift to look at me, even in the darkness. "How does that work?"

"Friction. Electrons. I'm not sure, actually." I laugh. "It's something my dad says."

Lightning flashes, far away this time, and the answering rumble is more restrained. More normal.

"Intense," Basil murmurs.

"Like Yorkshire," I reply, and he chuckles bravely against my shoulder.

"Yes," he says. "This is *just* like Yorkshire."

Chapter Thirty-Three

By morning, the wind has dropped enough to let us go out and clear up the broken branches and tree limbs scattered around the barn. The rain falls in fits and starts, and the air is unnervingly cool for mid-August, but otherwise this could be a normal wet day. We decide to get the paddocks clear and then turn out the horses. They snort and trot along the fence lines, spooking at puddles. I find a wad of wet insulation in one of the water troughs, which must mean someone else had a much rougher night than we did. But there's no telling how far the storm blew it before it landed in this trough.

We stand in the barn doorway and watch the horses dance and play in the rain.

"I need a job," Basil says after a while. "I've been thinking…I don't know how to sell horses to people who don't *have* to buy them from me."

I choke back a surprised laugh. "I guess that does make a difference! Any idea who you'd like to work for?"

"Not really," he says. "But there's time. I can find something by November."

"I envy your confidence," I say drily. "But I guess I can go back to riding babies for the winter. Posey'll give me a job."

But the idea doesn't sound very exciting. Basil's right—he needs to work on his one weakness, which is the business side of selling horses. He doesn't need another riding job.

What is my weakness?

Hah, I think. Where do I begin?

"Basil," I ask, "what do you think my weakness is?"

He grins. "Me?"

That earns him a punch in the arm. "I'm serious, here! What should I be looking for in a job?"

"I think you're doing fine at Amanda's," he says, surprised. "But...if you were to change anything, I guess I would say you need to ride older horses. Your problem, if you don't mind my saying so, is that you only ride horses at a very specific point in their lives. After they're fully started, but before they do anything advanced."

"That's true." He's right. Even at Amanda's, I'm focused on the same skill-set I've been honing since high school: riding off-track racehorses until they're jumping and doing basic dressage, then selling them and starting on the next horse. Not starting green horses, like Feather, and not continuing the training of well-started horses, like Jock or the dressage horses here. "I'm stuck at the novice levels, aren't I?"

"That's it," he agrees. "Maybe Amanda will keep a horse a little longer if you can convince her it's got a lot of potential? A project horse that could make her some money if she keeps it around a year or two?"

A year or two. Gosh, horses take a long time. We really have to put our roots into the ground and grow in one place, don't we? I imagine spending another year or two riding with Amanda, mornings at her pretty farm, and I find I don't hate the idea. If I can save up enough money before Max and Stephen come home, I won't even need a second job to afford to rent something small and shabby on the wrong side of Ocala.

At the moment, nothing could sound better.

Except maybe renting it with Basil.

But all that's down the road, I think. Right here, right now, watching the horses splash in puddles and kick up their heels in the light rainfall, my hand snug in Basil's grip—well, this is good enough.

I don't need anything else.

One month later

"No one ever told me September would be so hot," Basil moans. He hops off Jock and presses his hand against the horse's sweaty neck. "Look at my poor horse! I know we have to prep for the Grand Prix, but this weather has to give us a break."

"Oh, stop your whining and give your poor horse a bath," I tell him, looking down from Feather's back. The mare sidesteps and tosses her head, but I don't pick at her about it. Standing still at the halt is for big, grown-up girls, and no one would mistake my silly mare for a grown-up. But she's getting better.

Slowly, the way a young horse should.

Basil walks Jock in a circle around us. "Are you going to bring Feather to the show-grounds with us? Decided yet?"

"Yes," I say, although I'm nervous about it. "Giving her some time to look at a new place will be a nice step towards showing her in a couple of months."

"That's good." Basil looks up. "Hey, here come Posey and Evie. I wonder what they want."

"Oh, I asked Posey about starting the yearlings this month," I say, kicking my feet free of the stirrups. "Maybe they came over to offer me a job." And I hop down from Feather's back, eager to see what Posey has to say.

It's not a job offer. Posey looks embarrassed as she explains they're not doing as many yearlings at the farm this year, and she doesn't need another rider. "Not yet," she amends. "Someone could still quit. Probably will. If you can just wait—"

"It's fine," I say. "Honestly, I don't need another job. I'm just trying to save as much as I can. Rentals are already going up in price because of the winter circuit." I'd been hoping that if I squeezed in some early morning rides at Posey and Adam's farm, I could afford more than a shack with a weedy paddock for Crabby and Feather. When the time comes to get my own place. I still don't know if that will be November or next spring. I don't even know what I'll say if Max asks me to stay on through the winter.

Something in me is ready to move on. I love it here, but as Basil and I have tried to nail down what stands between us and our career goals, it's become increasingly clear that Max and Stephen are just stand-ins for my parents. Two wonderful, darling people who love me and want the best for me and give me way, *way* too much.

I've been so lucky, but I know I have to start making my own luck, or I'll never learn to stand on my own.

And as for Basil, he's not planning on staying through the winter, either. Even though he'll be giving up the ride on Twistie Treat, which is part of his compensation for working here, he says it's not the right move for his career.

"I need to stick to my discipline," he realized one night, as we sat over tamales at El Bronco and struggled through another conversation about our futures. "What I really need is a job with another jumper trainer. Someone who has too much work for one person. Any ideas who that might be?"

I had to grin and shrug.

Evie is playing with Feather's forelock as the mare stands (politely!) in the wash-rack. "Hey, did you guys hear about Pete Morrison?"

"No," I say, hanging up Feather's bridle. "What happened with him? Is he okay?"

"He's fine," Evie says. "But he's closing up his partnership with Gomez Peña. Gomez is moving to California. I heard it over at the OBS feed store."

"No kidding," I say absently, turning on the water. "Wonder what he'll do next."

"I'm guessing start looking for a new partner," Evie says. "He always has more horses than he can train alone, and his wife is too focused on eventing to want to mess around with straight jumpers."

I look over my shoulder. In the next wash-rack bay, Basil has turned his head. Our eyes meet.

He doesn't have to say anything. I know he's going to call Pete Morrison. And when I glance back at Evie and see her smile, I know *she* knows it, too.

"You're clever," I tell her.

"Who, me?" Evie sits down on the chair outside the tack room. "Maybe I'm just better at figuring out everyone else's life than my own."

"Your life seems pretty figured out!"

She shrugs. "You guys seem to be pulling ahead now," she says ruefully. "Posey's all happy with Adam, you're settling into old married life with Basil—"

"Hardly," I snort.

But Evie continues as if I didn't interrupt her. "It's just me and Breezy out at the farm, and honestly, if his sweating doesn't get better, I'm not going to be eventing him anymore."

"Oh." I hardly know what to say. "Oh, Evie, I didn't know."

She rubs a hand over her face. "It's okay," she says finally, squaring her thin shoulders. "I love him no matter what, and we've been getting into the sandbox life. I guess I can just do dressage with him.

It's not what I hoped for, that's all."

I waver between offering words of comfort and words of advice, and while I'm still trying to figure out what to do, Feather begins pawing and I'm forced to run over to the wash-rack and chastise her. When I turn around again, Evie is up and getting ready to leave.

"Don't go," I call. "Let's talk about this."

"It's fine," she says, waving. "I promise I'll be fine."

And I know she will be. Changing disciplines with Breezy is disappointing, but hardly a fatal blow. In fact, I think, turning back to Feather, maybe dressage is just what Crabby needs in his golden years. "After all," I tell my naughty mare. "I have you to jump over sticks. But I'll bet Evie could use my company in the warm-up ring with all those real-life dressage queens riding around."

Posey walks by as I turn on the hose, surprising me. "I forgot you were here!" I say.

She grins. "I get that a lot. Have you seen Evie?"

"Already out of the barn."

"I better go. She's my ride." Posey starts off, then hesitates and looks back at me. "Hey, I know you're not going to be riding with us, and I'm sorry. But I'll probably have some flunked-out trainees coming back in late winter."

"Oh, yeah?" I'm intrigued. "What are you thinking?"

Posey shrugs. "Just—they're yours if you want them. You can take your pick. Whatever I've got that won't go back to the track...you have first dibs."

I'm speechless. Free off-track Thoroughbreds are still a thing that exists for savvy trainers looking for prospects, but they're not as common as they used to be. I'm sure Adam and Posey have sold unsuccessful racehorses to trainers this summer. "You don't have to do this," I say, trying to be selfless, but Posey waves away my protest.

"Come on, who better to take on my racetrack rejects than one of my best friends in the world? Just get some space to keep them, and I'll let you know when I have something for you to look at."

Posey walks away, leaving me feeling dazed. Beside me, Feather dips her head and tries to bite my elbow. Her teeth graze my skin, and it's enough to shake me out of my stupor. "Knock that off, missy," I tell her firmly. "Looks like you won't be my only project for long."

In the neighboring wash-rack bay, Basil looks over and I realize he's heard everything. He lifts his slender eyebrows and asks, "So, should I expect a move this winter? Somewhere of your own where you can keep all these new horses?"

"Maybe," I tell him, smiling smugly. "And if you're really nice, maybe I'll let you come, too."

Basil nods. "One thing at a time," he says. "Let's see if I can find a job. I'd hate for you to have to pay all my bills."

And before I can start planning to make Basil a kept man, he really does make the call.

It takes a few days for him to work out what he wants to say, and a few hours after that to work up the courage to actually call Pete Morrison. They've met briefly at Legends, and even competed against one another in some August jumper classes when Basil took Jock over for some tune-ups over the big jumps.

Pete won. He's a gorgeous rider, to say the least. And multi-talented. Posey said he's got a book coming out about dressage for eventers. That part of him, at least, reminds me of Basil and his skill at both the jumpers and the dressage.

But the one thing I really noted that day, watching Pete Morrison walk around the Legends grounds, was how much people liked him. People waved, called out, stopped to show him pictures on their phones. And I think that makes a trainer stand out; it could definitely make or break a sale if there are two good horses in the running.

It's just a call, I think.

A simple phone call. How long could it take?

But this could be the one that changes things for Basil. And, hey, maybe for me, too. In the long run.

I mean, I like the idea of my boyfriend being a wildly successful trainer and horse broker. Who wouldn't?

That's why I'm riding Feather right now, just letting her trail around the arena with the longest reins I can manage for my silly mare. I'm waiting for Basil to finish that call, come out here, and tell me what's going to happen next.

And here he comes!

I pull up Feather by the gate as Basil walks out, his face not giving a thing away. This guy could play real poker, in person, not just the online kind.

"So?" I ask.

"So, we're doing this," he says, looking up at me with a smile. "I'm going to work with Pete three days a week, and he's going to give me everything he's got on assessing sales horses and matching them with riders."

Feather sidesteps and tosses her head, and I give up trying to maintain normalcy. I'm too happy. I kick my feet free of the stirrups and hop down to the ground. Gripping the reins in one hand, I reach for Basil with the other and tug him close. It's a hug, nothing more, I swear. But my lips are very close to his ear when I say, "I'm really proud of you," and his skin is warm and smells of hay and leather and when he turns his head and kisses me, I'm not mad.

I kiss him back.

Next to us, my silly Celestial Being kicks and stomps, then stands still, waiting her turn. I guess Feather finally figured out that sometimes she just has to be patient.

She's a tough horse, alright. But if I've learned anything this summer, it's that the toughest things are worth the trouble.

Epilogue

As Basil turns the car off the highway and heads west, the trees seem to grow thicker around us. I glance around, a little nervous, at the rich green foliage wrapping around the old two-lane road. Spanish moss drapes from thick, grasping branches hanging over the road. It feels like we're in a movie. I'm just not sure what genre.

"It's like we're in a film," Basil says, craning his neck to look at the trees overhead.

Exactly.

The tree tunnel ends after about a mile and fields open up on either side of us, rolling grassy country with a few live oaks along their boundaries. There are run-in sheds, and horses, and round hay bales which haven't been brought in to cover yet.

"Now *this* is like Virginia," I say.

"No, really?" Basil lifts his eyebrows. "Maybe we should be moving to Virginia."

"Ice and snow," I remind him. "Let's see how this place turns out, first."

He misses the driveway at first; we go too far and end up at a crossroads that isn't listed in the directions. A country store advertises ice-cold beer, alligator jerky, and bait; on the opposite corner, a Depression-era gas station sinks slowly into the clutches of the jungle. Basil turns around, but not without a slightly nervous glance at the country store.

"I'm sure they're very nice," I say chidingly. "Don't get all English about it."

He gives me a dry smile. "I'm not English," he reminds me.

"No," I laugh. "You're Floridian. These are your people now."

A man with a long, yellowed beard pulls into the country store. A spotted dog stands on the metal toolbox in his pickup truck's bed, wagging his tail and grinning into the wind. The stickers on the truck declare the driver's allegiance to the Florida Gators, the Fair Tax, and something called Guppy's Fish Bait.

"The trucks in Ocala all have horse stickers on them," Basil reminds me, turning back onto the road.

"It's not far away," I say airily. "You just get more variety out here, that's all."

And cheaper rent. The property we're going to see is ten acres on a hundred-acre ranch, with a barn, an apartment, paddocks, and even an arena. For less than half of what we'd pay in Ocala. The only catch? We're an hour away from the horse capital of the world.

But Pete found the place for us, and Basil liked the idea of living close to his business partner. Pete and Jules' Briar Hill Farm is near here, and they say that living up the road from Ocala is just fine. Since Jules doesn't appreciate anything coming between her and her eventing career, I trust that she wouldn't lie about something like this. And anyway, an hour isn't that far.

"It's practically still Ocala," I mutter, and Basil grins.

This time I spot the driveway, two tracks of white sand with grass growing right up the middle. We drive along it, surrounded by wide open fields and shaded by live oaks, for what feels like forever. It's probably five minutes. Ahead of us on a rise, more massive oaks surround a low white barn with green shutters and stall doors.

"How many stalls?" Basil asks, peering through the windshield.

"Sixteen," I say. "And the feed and tack rooms, and the apartment at one end."

"Sixteen stalls," he mutters, and I know what he's thinking.

So much potential.

He parks at one end of the barn, where a concrete-block wash-rack juts out. There's an old manure pile, and some forgotten bags of shavings from the last tenant. The grass is thick and unmown, the seed-heads almost waist-high in places, and I see a few telltale low patches around trees in the paddocks that are probably stinging nettle beds. A great egret looks at us from a shallow pond in the nearest paddock, then goes back to her hunting.

Something about that tall white bird gives me a good feeling.

We poke around the barn for a few minutes, then Basil finds the combination for the lock on the info sheet we've been working off and lets us into the apartment. It's a bland, damp, two-room flat with linoleum on the floors. The kitchen cabinets are painted in the same bold kelly green as the shutters and stall doors. There is a dead mouse in the bathroom.

"At least it's dead," Basil says.

"We can get a cat." I peer through the bedroom window. "Nice view of the driveway here," I say. "No one can ever surprise us."

"I think we should get a big dog, too," Basil says, joining me at the window. He takes in the view, and I know he's feeling the incredible isolation of this place. "One that barks and shows its teeth."

I wrap an arm around him, laughing. "See? Already a Floridian, like I said."

Back outside, we walk the shed-row again and consider what we could do with this place. The barn is in good shape, the stalls are ready to hold horses. The apartment is a little sad, but it just needs furniture and some paint to cheer it up.

"The owner will be here in about ten minutes," Basil says. We stand at the end of the barn and look across the property. The sun is hanging near the horizon, and golden light floods the pastures, catching the Spanish moss hanging from the ancient trees. "So we have exactly that long to make up our minds."

Ten minutes. I take a deep breath and try to soak it all in. This place couldn't be much more different from Bent Oak Farm. A two-room barn apartment in place of a gleaming mansion of a house. A dusty shed-row with rust showing through the paint on those garish green stall doors, instead of a center-aisle barn with the latest in stylish touches and accents. A riding ring of native local sand in place of two full-size arenas with specialized footing—and definitely no covered ring. It has to be acknowledged that riding here will be hotter.

But the trees will provide some shade, even over the arena. We can build some jumps and buy some others. We can have a load of better footing delivered to mix into the sand. We can hang flowerpots along the shed-row overhang. We'll mow the knee-deep grass and ask the landlord to take a weedtorch to the stinging nettle patches. We can make this place into our home, and more than that, a headquarters for our business.

Because that's happening.

The past few months have been amazing. Under Pete's tutelage, Basil has learned how to truly match up horses and riders, not just draw connecting lines on a client list. And at Amanda's, I have a more advanced ride now—she decided to keep Stuffy McGoo and is letting me work with him on big courses, with an eye to showing him when the winter circuit gets going in January. Feather will be starting her show career in January, too, and Crabby has a new interest in dressage, thanks to those riding lessons Max paid for with Karl German Something—I decided to take the lessons earmarked for Basil, and when Karl yells at me I just imagine his head exploding, and it's fine. The important thing is that Crabby is happy and now I can show with Evie, which I think eases some of her disappointment over giving up eventing with Breezy.

We've reached the point where we feel ready to pick up some prospects of our own, and that's when Basil started talking about renting a place.

And after some thought, I decided I was ready to move on from Max and Stephen, too.

Don't get me wrong, I *love* them. They're basically my absentee surrogate parents, if such a thing can exist. But I don't need surrogate parents. I already have really great parents who give me all the support (and then some) I could ever need.

I guess it was easy to let Max and Stephen's cushy life suck me in when I came to Ocala in search of a new challenge. But in the end, I know I can't grow at their farm. And I've loved being a farm-sitter, but it's not my life's work.

As I look around this cobwebby barn, shining golden in the slanting light of a fall evening, I think my life's work might be waiting for me here. Or at least, the very foundation of it.

"Let's do it," I tell Basil, clutching his hand. "Let's start our own farm here."

His smile lights up his face, and those earthy brown eyes twinkle at me with joy he can't hide. "I would love to start a farm here with you," he says, and tugs me close, his arms wrapped around me and hands clenched at my heart. I tip my head back against his shoulder and look into the endless cerulean of the Florida sky, letting the cool autumn breeze tug at my hair. And I know that things are only just starting for Basil and me.

The Regift Horse

EVIE BALLENGER HAS loved watching her friends fall in love...but she knows romance isn't really for her. She's devoted to horses, and her equestrian career is her priority. Even if her promising event horse, Easy Breezy, is now permanently sidelined from the demanding sport. At least Evie is making a killing galloping racehorses, right?

In Ocala, the next horse is never far away. So, even though Evie has put eventing on the back-burner, it's not through with her. And when an unwanted gift horse appears on the scene, she realizes her eventing days might not be behind her...if another trainer doesn't get in her way.

And if she doesn't fall for him, completely by accident.

The Regift Horse is filled with fast horses, big hearts, and friendship. Coming in April 2023 — order it from your favorite store!

Visit nataliekreinert.shop or books2read.com/theregifthorse

Acknowledgments

I LOVE WRITING these books, and I'm so grateful to my dedicated readers for continuing to buy, read, and review my books—and for sending me messages, chatting with me online, coming to my author events, and basically making me feel like a million bucks. You guys are simply the best.

As always, a special thanks to the Patreon members who read my first drafts, often one or two chapters a day for several weeks on end. Your comments, concerns, and cheers keep me going like nothing else ever could! I love you all so much, even when you tell me something didn't work and I'm mad at you for like, a day. My books are so much better thanks to your feedback.

You can join us at patreon.com/nataliekreinert.

My Patrons include: Sally Testa, April Lutz, Julia Koeger, sklamb, Heidi Schmid, Cathy Luo, Elena Rabinow, Laura, Dörte Voigt, Empathy, Tayla Travella, Gretchen Fieser, JoAnn Flejszar, Nancy Neid, Elizabeth Espinosa, Renee Knowles, Libby Henderson, Maureen VanDerStad, Genevieve Dempre, Jean Miller, Susan Cover, Sherron Meinert, Leslie Yazurlo, Nicola Beisel, Mel Policicchio, Kylie Standish, Harry Burgh, Alyssa, Kathlynn Angie-Buss, Katy

McFarland, Peggy Dvorsky, Christine Komis, Annika Kostrabula, Thoma Jolette Parker, Karen Carrubba, Emma Gooden, Katie Lewis, Silvana Ricapito, Risa Ryland, Sarine Laurin, Di Hannel, Jennifer, Claus Giloi, Heather Walker, Cyndy Searfoss, Kaylee Amons, Mary Vargas, Kathie Lacasse, Rachael Rosenthal, Orpu, Diana Aitch, Liz Greene, Zoe Bills, Cheryl Bavister, Sarah Seavey, Megan Devine, Tricia Jordan, Brinn Dimmler, Lindsay Moore, Emily Nolan, Caitlin Harrison, Rhonda Lane, C. Sperry, Heather Voltz, and Kim Keller.

That list just keeps getting longer. I'm so grateful to you all. Being a writer is a hard, solitary job. You make it a little easier.

About the Author

A FULL-TIME writer, I work from my farm in North Florida, where I live with my family and two horses. In the past, I've worked professionally in many aspects of the equestrian world, including grooming for top event riders, training off-track Thoroughbreds, galloping racehorses, patrolling Central Park on horseback, working on breeding farms, and more! I use all of this experience to inform the equestrian scenes in my novels. They say that truth is stranger than fiction, and those of us in the horse business will certainly agree!

Visit my website at nataliekreinert.com to keep up with the latest news and read occasional blog posts and book reviews. For previews, installments of upcoming fiction, and exclusive stories, visit my Patreon page at patreon.com/nataliekreinert and learn how you can become one of my team members.

For more, find me on social media:
Facebook: facebook.com/nataliekellerreinert
Group: facebook.com/groups/societyofweirdhorsegirls
Bookbub: bookbub.com/profile/natalie-keller-reinert
Twitter: twitter.com/nataliegallops

Instagram: instagram.com/nataliekreinert

Join my email list for exclusive offers and news at nataliekreinert.com

Email: natalie@nataliekreinert.com